Beaut

BROKEN PIECES

THE
SUTTER LAKE
SERIES

CATHERINE
COWLES

BEAUTIFULLY BROKEN PIECES

Editor: Susan Barnes
Copy Editor: Chelle Olson
Proofreading: Grahame Claire
Paperback Formatting: Stacey Blake, Champagne Book Design
Cover Design: Hang Le

Dedication

This book is for anyone who has lost someone. Just remember, the cracks in your heart will let others' light shine in if you let it.

And, as always, for my Dad. I carry you with me always. Eternally grateful to be your daughter.

Prologue

Taylor

Did you know that when you choose to take someone off life support, they mute the heart monitor? That continual beeping you hadn't realized had become your constant companion is suddenly gone. So, the room is completely silent when your whole reason for being slips from this Earth.

Completely silent and deafening, all at the same time.

CHAPTER
One

Taylor

THERE WAS SOMETHING ABOUT THE AIR HERE. IT WAS clean. Pure. And it had a fragrance to it I hadn't encountered before. It was something the trees released into the atmosphere around them. I pulled a long breath into my lungs, holding it there as I stared out at the scene below.

Craggy mountaintops still topped with snow shifted into heavily forested slopes which met up with a pristine lake. I sucked in another breath. It was beautiful. Peaceful. Largely untouched by humans in all the ways we could fuck things up.

An arm came around my shoulders. "It's beautiful, right?" Carter asked.

I glanced at my best friend. Her strawberry-blonde hair was piled on top of her head in a haphazard attempt to keep it out of her face while we hiked to the top of this lookout. "It is."

"I'm so glad my mom recommended it—" Her words were cut off as color leached from her face, and she dropped her arms from my shoulder. "I'm sorry, I shouldn't have—"

This time, it was me cutting her off. "You can talk about your mom, Carter."

"Okay..." Her words trailed off, and an awkward silence descended on us.

It had been ninety-seven days, twelve hours, and fifty-two minutes since my mother's heart had stopped beating. I couldn't help but mark that time. Always aware of every minute the world kept spinning without her. That seemed crazy sometimes. Absolutely insane that the universe could still exist without her. That *I* could exist without her.

There were moments when it still didn't seem real. Times when I could convince myself that this had all been a terrible nightmare. That I hadn't really watched her body slowly start to fail her. Hadn't seen her struggle to even lift her hand to hold mine. That her skin hadn't turned so papery, I could see right through to her veins.

But it had happened. No begging, pleading, bargaining, or praying had kept her with me. My rock, my safe place, my best friend was gone.

I shook my head, attempting to clear it. Forcing cheeriness into my voice, I asked, "How did your mom find out about this place again?" Carter was from Georgia, and we were currently in the middle of nowhere Oregon.

Carter twisted her fingers into a series of complicated knots at her side. "She has a sorority sister who grew up here. Told her it was pure magic. It is, right?"

Pure magic was a perfect description. "It is." I snuck a peek at Carter again. Lines of worry creased her brow. I hated that I was the cause of it. "Thank you for bringing me here."

A genuine smile tipped her lips. "I'm so glad you finally agreed."

After months filled with arranging a funeral, handling the never-ending minutia that came with someone dying, and packing up my mom's house in Houston, I was spent. Carter had begged me to let her plan a trip for us that would be full of nothing but rest, relaxation, good food, and nature. I had been too exhausted to put up more than a half-hearted fight, even though what I wanted more than anything was to be alone.

The constant assessing stares and carefully couched questions about how I was doing were almost more than I could bear. My fists clenched, nails biting into my palms. All Carter wanted to do was take care of me. She was the best friend a girl could hope for, and I couldn't even give her that.

Cracking branches and rustling underbrush sounding from behind us had Carter and I turning around.

"Jesus, I'm pretty sure I just got poison ivy on my ass," our good friend, Liam, bellowed.

Carter tried to hide her giggle by covering her mouth. I did nothing to disguise my snort of laughter.

Carter's husband, Austin, trailed after Liam, a disgusted grimace on his face. "I really don't need to hear about that."

"Hey, you might have some, too. Nothing could be worse than poison ivy on your junk."

Carter slipped her backpack off her shoulders. "I have some hand wipes. Why don't you both use them."

Liam grinned at Carter, taking a wipe from her outstretched hand. "Thank you, ma'am." After tossing the used towelette into his pack, Liam made his way towards me. He pulled me to his side. "How are you holding up?" His tone had gone from teasing to gently serious, and I freaking hated it.

"I'm good." I elbowed him in the gut. "Now get your possibly contagious, dirty fingers away from me."

Liam chuckled, but there was concern in his eyes as he studied me. I felt like a bug under a microscope.

I tightened the straps of my pack. "What do you say? Race you back to the car?"

I didn't wait for an answer, just took off down the trail at a fast clip. Voices drifted on the air behind me.

"Since when is she the athlete?" Liam asked.

"She started running the first time her mom got sick…" Carter began.

I pushed myself faster until I could no longer hear my friends.

Our rented SUV hugged the curves of the mountain road as we headed away from the peaks towards town. An old-timey sign declared *Welcome To Sutter Lake* in white lettering. My eyes traveled down Main Street, taking in the storefronts that looked like they had been frozen in Old West times, complete with hitching posts in front of most of them. Baskets of bright blooms hung from each street sign, and benches sat in shady spots below trees with vibrant green leaves.

Austin pulled into a parking spot in front of an old-fashioned saloon. No parking meter. That was different from the two cities I'd most recently called home. I released my seat belt and pushed open my door. We'd been told by the woman who rented us the vacation home that the saloon had the best burgers in a hundred-mile radius. I doubted anything could beat In-N-Out, but I was willing to do some research to find out.

Carter stepped up next to me, squeezing my shoulder. "This place is so cute, right?"

I fought the urge to shake off her hand. The overabundance of comforting gestures lately had begun to make my skin crawl. "The cutest."

Austin pulled his wife to his side, brushing his lips against her brow. "What I care about is how good the burgers are."

"And the beer. Don't forget the beer," Liam called.

We pushed through the pair of swinging doors and made our way to the hostess station. A young girl, probably high-school aged, stood behind a podium. "How many—?" Her words cut off as her eyes bugged out. "Y-y-you're Liam Fairchild."

It was funny, I so often forgot that Liam was a celebrity. It wasn't until we were in situations like these that I remembered he was a world-famous musician.

Liam put his charming-bugger smile in place. "That I am, darling. But what do you say we keep that little secret between us? Wouldn't want my vacation hideout to get discovered." The girl nodded vigorously. "I'd be happy to sign something for you if you'd like."

"That would be awesome," she whispered and then fumbled for a paper and pen.

While Liam made the young girl's year, I studied the space. The Old West theme continued with wagon wheels and wood signs decorating the walls. The combination restaurant and bar was about half full, most inhabitants opting for one of the cozy booths that hugged the outskirts of the room.

My eyes continued on towards the bar area and stuttered on two men eating lunch and watching some sports thing on the TV in the corner. They were both well-built. One blond. One with hair so dark brown, it was almost black. The second man threw his head back, letting out a bellow of laughter that was so rich and carefree, it hit me right in the chest. *Would I ever laugh like that again? Like I had no worries in the world?*

Someone bumped into my shoulder. "Enjoying a little eye candy?"

I grimaced at Liam. "No. Are you done fulfilling every teenage fangirl's dream?"

He wrapped an arm around my shoulders to lead me towards the table that Carter and Austin were already seated at. "It's a heavy burden being America's sweetheart."

"America's sweetheart is Julia Roberts, you jackass," Austin called from the table.

I let my friends' voices fade into background noise as I twisted to get one more peek at the man with the captivating laugh—but he was already gone.

CHAPTER
Two

Taylor

THE SMELL OF ANTISEPTIC STUNG MY NOSTRILS AS THAT *damned beep, beep, beep sounded in my ears. "I love you to the moon and back, my sweet girl." My mother's voice was haggard and rough. Then, there was silence. That dreaded silence that meant she was gone.*

My eyes shot open. The covers seemed to suffocate me as I struggled to get free. Finally, I was able to extricate myself from the tangled mess. I swung my legs over the side of the bed, trying to slow my breathing and steady my heart rate. I needed air.

I stood on shaky legs, making my way through the darkened cabin towards the back deck. My t-shirt, damp with sweat, clung to my back. If I were alone, I would have torn the damned thing off.

Sliding the door open and moving forward, my feet touched chilly planks. I gripped the railing, bending to press my forehead against it. The cool mountain air rushed over me, calming my overheated skin, and the sweet smell on the breeze seemed to ease my panicked breaths. Slowly, my heart rate began to return to normal.

I straightened and tipped my face up to the sky. The stars were so bright here. I'd never seen anything like it. No ambient city lights to dull their shine. "Mom, are you up there?" I mouthed the words to the silent breeze as tears pricked the backs of my eyes. What I wanted more than anything was a promise that I would be reunited with her one day. In Heaven, in the stars, anywhere I could feel her presence.

The pastor at my mom's memorial service had promised that she was in a better place. But how did he know for sure? I prayed to God and the Universe for a sign constantly. Anything that would let me know she was at peace. That I would see her again. I never got a damn thing, and I was looking.

I blew out a long breath and settled myself in one of the rocking chairs on the porch. The sounds of a bubbling creek nearby, crickets chirping, and the blades of the rocker hitting the boards of the deck were my only companions. It was kind of perfect. It was quiet, without the deafening silence of my nightmares.

Sleep wouldn't find me anytime soon, though. No matter how hard I tried, rest always refused to come after one of those dreams. It was a nightly battle I won, only if I had exhausted my body the day before. I needed to be so tired that I fell into sleep so deep, the nightmares couldn't find me. It was so very ironic. I used to hate working out with the passion of a thousand fiery suns, but now, it was my salvation.

Soft footfalls sounded against the wood-planked floor. I fought the frustration that rose at my solitude being interrupted. I wiped my face to erase any stray tears and attempted to blank my expression. I wanted no pitying looks or careful tones.

The problem was, I didn't know *what* I wanted. Or needed. All I knew was that I wanted to crawl out of my skin when people looked at me like I was going to crumble at any moment. Maybe because I was afraid I *would* crumble. That I would break apart into a million pieces and never be able to put myself back together again.

Carter appeared at my side. She looked a mess. Rumpled PJs, blurry eyes, and the hair piled on top of her head resembled a rat's nest. I was fairly certain it had gotten into that state thanks to her husband's ravaging. Austin loved my best friend with a ferocity that made my heart ache.

Carter slid into the chair next to mine. "Couldn't sleep?"

I let a single shoulder rise and fall. "Sleeping's not really my strong suit these days. Did I wake you?"

Carter gave me a sympathetic smile. The same one she'd been giving me for months. An expression that made me want to throttle her. And I loved this girl to the depths of my soul. "You didn't really wake me. Since having Ethan, I feel like I never fully descend into sleep. I'm always half listening for sounds of baby distress."

I inwardly cringed at my earlier frustration. My best friend had left her child at home for the first time since having him because she was worried about me. Because she wanted to take me away from any place that held memories of my mom. Needed to do something to help ease my pain.

"How is the little monster?" I asked.

A happier smile came to her face. "He's great. I talked to my mom before bed, and it sounded like he's enjoying being spoiled rotten by his grandparents."

A small grin spread across my lips. "Ethan's lucky to have them."

Carter froze. "I didn't mean to bring up—"

I cut her off, waving a hand in front of my face. "I didn't mean it like that. I just meant that he has amazing grandparents." Would every conversation from now on be a careful traverse of a minefield?

I took another deep breath, letting the smell of the surrounding pine trees calm me. "I really love it here."

Carter's eyes scanned the fields that turned into vast forest. "I'm so glad. I do, too. There's something really special about it."

I smiled to myself. "There's a peacefulness I've never experienced before. Something about the sound of the water and the smell of the air. I feel like I can breathe here."

Carter chuckled. "Well, compared to home, the air is just a little fresher."

Carter and I had met in Los Angeles as teachers working in the Teach For Our Youth program. We had bonded quickly, and soon became roommates. But when my mom got sick, I'd had to return to Texas to take care of her. And I never made it back to LA. It just wasn't home anymore.

An idea flickered in my mind. It was crazy, but maybe that was exactly what I needed.

The smells of bacon frying and freshly baking biscuits tickled my nose as I took in Carter at the stove. "Can I do anything?" I asked.

Carter bit the corner of her lip. "Ummm, why don't you help Liam set the table."

"Sure thing."

I headed into the dining room to find Liam with a stack of dishes and cutlery. "Here, let me help," I said, reaching for the pile of forks and knives.

"She wouldn't let you touch anything that was cooking, would she?" Liam said with a chuckle.

"Oh, shut up. So, cooking isn't my strong suit." That was the world's biggest understatement. My mom used to swear I could burn water. No matter how often she tried to school me in her culinary ways, I was a hopeless student. A pang hit my sternum. She would never have the chance to remedy that, to see me finally master her famous mashed potatoes or decadent lemon meringue pie.

These types of twinges came often, brought on by something different each time and taking me by surprise more often than not. It always felt like my heart was being squeezed by an unrelenting fist. The constriction would tug on all the surrounding strands of connective tissue, sending zaps of pain throughout my body until I finally pushed the memory from my mind.

Liam threw an arm around my shoulders. "Good thing you can order takeout with the best of them."

I shook off the phantom spasm and forced a smirk to my lips. "Like you're any better? You eat half your dinners at Carter and Austin's, *and* you have a personal chef. Spoiled rotten, I swear."

"What are you two bickering about now?" Austin's voice called from the other room.

I turned to see his large fighter's frame filling the doorway. "I'm just trying to keep Liam honest."

Austin let out a snort. "Good luck with that. At least you've got his over-indulged rock star-self setting the table."

"Hey!" Liam said, his face the picture of affront. "I'll have you know, I washed dishes last night."

Placing a hand over my heart, I gasped. "No. Dishes? Did you break a nail?"

Liam set his stack of plates down with a rattle and darted for me. "These hands could be insured for millions." It was probably true. Over the past few years, Liam had become a Billboard Top 100 sensation. He'd created some sort of hybrid between Southern rock and country, dominating both markets, and raking in the cash.

I laughed, spinning in place and extending a butter knife in Liam's direction to stop his attempted assault. "Okay, okay, you are the most famous, talented, handsome boy in all the land. Happy now?"

"That's a little bit better..." He sniffed.

I rolled my eyes at Austin, who only grinned.

We finished setting the table, and then it was time to inhale whatever Carter had cooked up in the kitchen. All talking ceased, and the only sounds were those of forks and knives against plates.

I took a sip of my OJ, steeling my nerves. I cleared my throat, and three sets of eyes turned my way. "So…I think I'm going to stay in Sutter Lake."

Carter's brows furrowed. "What do you mean? Like, extend your trip?"

I twirled the ring on my right ring finger. It had been my mother's. I liked to think that it had the magical ability to give me strength. "I mean, I'm going to move here." Carter's jaw slackened. "Not necessarily forever. Just for a while," I hurried to say. "I need some time away."

Tears filled Carter's eyes, and Austin immediately reached out to grab her hand. "I was hoping you'd move back to LA. I know you needed time to handle all your mother's affairs, but now that you've done that, you need to be around people who love you. You don't know anyone here."

She was right. I didn't know a single soul in Sutter Lake. That was a large part of its appeal. I sent Carter what I hoped was a reassuring smile. "I think I need some time on my own, to get my head straight. Then, I promise I'll think about moving back to LA."

Liam studied me intently, his face solemn. "Are you sure this is a good idea?"

I gritted my teeth but forced a lightness into my voice when I said, "I am. I just need to find a place to live. And maybe a job so I don't die of boredom."

Technically, I didn't *need* a job. My father—or sperm donor, as I liked to call him—had set up a trust fund for me that had more money in it than I knew what to do with. His attempt to assuage his absentee-father guilt. He'd also given my mother a large sum. His attempt to quell his guilt over being a cheating, abandoning asshole. My mother had never touched the money, other than to pay for my schooling. I had no qualms about using mine to buy myself a little break from reality, but I knew I would go stir-crazy if I wasn't doing something productive.

A fresh start where no one knew me as the girl who had just lost her only family. Solitude away from well-meaning, prying eyes. Peace. It was all I wanted. And if I had to move to the middle of nowhere Oregon to get it, then that's just what I'd do.

CHAPTER
Three

Taylor

I STUDIED THE DIFFERENT STOREFRONTS AS MY FRIENDS AND I walked down the sidewalk of my new home. Moving here was impulsive, I knew it, but excitement fluttered in my belly at the prospect. No memories that held me hostage lurking around every corner like they did in Houston or even LA. I could be free here. Able to explore and discover what the next phase of my life might look like. Free to feel whatever emotions came on, without the need to hold it all in so I didn't worry my friends. Able to simply *be*.

An older gentleman passed by with a tip of his hat and the greeting of, "Ma'am." I smiled in return.

An imposing form appeared next to me. "You know," Austin began, "people in small towns are nosy. As soon as they figure out you're not a tourist passing through, they are going to want to know all about you. Where you're from. Who your family is. What your *story* is."

I gritted my teeth. Apparently, Austin had been nominated by the group to try and convince me that this was a horrible idea and that I needed to go back to LA where they could watch over me and scrutinize my every move. "Maybe so, but when they realize I'm boring, they'll move on fast enough." They would. And I didn't have to tell anyone shit. I was just a girl from Texas, ready for a change of scenery.

Austin attempted a different tack. "It's not safe."

I snorted at that. "What? You think that kind, old man was getting ready to mug me? Or maybe the woman who rented us the house and told us not to worry about locking our doors because no one in town does, was thinking of robbing us blind? Give me a break, A. This is probably the safest place on the planet."

Austin's jaw worked. "There can be bad seeds anywhere. And you'll be here all alone, without knowing anyone. That's a recipe for disaster."

I gentled my tone. I knew Austin only meddled because he cared. "I appreciate the big-brother, protective streak, but I'll be fine. I promise. I'll get a job and meet some people that way. Then you won't have to worry."

"Where? At the local hardware store because you have such a way with power tools?" he asked, gesturing towards an adorable mom-and-pop shop that advertised: "We have a little bit of everything. Come on in and have yourself a look." Austin pressed on. "Or, maybe you'll get a job as a line cook because you haven't almost burned down your own kitchen more than once."

Spikes of frustration and annoyance pricked at my skin. "I'm perfectly capable of taking care of myself."

"That may be true, but it doesn't mean you shouldn't let your friends step in when you've had a tough go of it. Carter and I were talking…there's plenty of extra room at our place, why don't you move in with us for a while."

My muscles tensed. It was an incredibly kind offer. And it came from the most generous and caring of places. But it sounded absolutely miserable. Me, Carter, Austin, and their nine-month-old son. Controlled chaos is what that would be. Bedlam that would result in me biting my best friend's head off and making her cry.

No. Just no. "That's really kind of you—"

Austin raised a hand to cut me off. "Just think about it."

"I'm sorry, Austin. No."

His jaw got even tighter. "This is going to be a disaster."

I'd had enough of this anti-pep-talk. "Your opinion is duly noted," I snapped and picked up my pace. I passed a café, a Western art gallery, and an old-fashioned movie theater. I'd be visiting the theater for sure.

"Taylor, wait." My shoulders stiffened at the sound of my best friend's voice. "I'm sorry. He means well, he just doesn't always have the most gentle way of communicating."

My shoulders slumped. "I know y'all think this is a *terrible* idea, but maybe you could just keep that opinion to yourselves. I like it here. I think it's the right place for me to be." Just because it was a spur-of-the-moment decision didn't make it wrong.

"I'm sorry. We're just worried about you and want you close."

I was going to scream. Yell so loudly, shop owners would probably call the cops because they thought someone was getting murdered. How did telling someone that you were worried about them ever help the situation?

Carter must have seen the exasperation in my expression because she hurried on. "But I support you. Whatever you need. I'm team Taylor. Even if that means being a long-distance team member."

I let out a long breath. I couldn't stay mad at this girl. She was too sweet. I bumped her shoulder with mine. Well, I bumped her arm, since she had a good six inches on me. "Thank you."

Carter rolled her shoulders back. "All right. What's the first order of business in making Sutter Lake your home?"

I grinned at my bestie. "House and job."

Her eyes widened, but they were focused on something

behind me. "I think we've got one of those taken care of."

I turned to see what she was looking at. The store at the end of the block that we had stopped in front of was in its own free-standing building. It was set back from the street just a bit, giving it enough space for a wraparound porch filled with a scattering of rocking chairs and assorted tables. Huge windows boasting flower boxes looked out onto Main Street, making it the perfect place to people watch. A sign hanging from the porch's awning read *The Tea Kettle*.

Warmth filled my chest. A tea shop. My mom and I had shared tea from the time I was four years old, and my mom had to fill my cup with half tea and half honey. That familiar pang hit again, but this time, it was mixed with hope. Hope that this was a sign that Sutter Lake was where I was supposed to be.

I glanced at Carter. "Do you think they're hiring?"

Her smile answered my own as she pointed to the window. A sign in what looked like calligraphy read: *Help Wanted – Waitress/Cashier*. "Want to go in?" I nodded as Carter motioned to the boys to let them know where we were headed.

Liam grimaced. "I think I'll pass on the tea shop. Why don't you meet us back at the brewpub when you're done."

I couldn't help the chuckle that escaped me. Men…no appreciation for the finer things in life. "All right, we'll see you in a bit."

Carter and I headed down the brick pathway and up the porch steps. As we opened the door, the familiar scent of tea leaves drifted over me, along with something that meant there were also baked goods on the premises. I hoped cooking wasn't a job requirement.

"Welcome to The Tea Kettle. What can I get for you today?" a woman greeted from behind the counter. She was breathtakingly beautiful with a flawless olive complexion and dark brown hair. She looked vaguely familiar somehow, but I knew I'd never met her before.

I shook the random thought from my mind and walked the handful of steps to the counter. "Hi. I'm Taylor. I'm new to town and looking for a job. I saw the sign in your window, and thought I'd come pick up an application."

The woman's brows rose slightly. "Well, welcome to Sutter Lake. I'm Jensen, and this is my place. We're not really the application type, but if you have a few minutes, we can chat and see if you're a good fit."

I liked the woman's comfortable ease. It was as if she were completely secure in who she was. "That would be great." I gestured behind me. "This is my friend, Carter."

"Nice to meet you both. Why don't I grab us some tea, and we can sip and chat."

"That would be great."

Within a few minutes, we were settled at a back table with delicious cold-brew teas and a plate of cookies. "These are delicious," I said after swallowing a mouthful of cookie.

"Family recipe. I'd share it with you, but state secrets..." Jensen said with a wink.

I twisted the straw in my cup. "It wouldn't do me any good even if you did share it." Jensen's forehead wrinkled. "I'm a horrible cook. I'm more likely to burn my kitchen down than successfully make cookies. So, I'm really hoping that's not part of the job." Carter attempted to cover her giggle with a cough.

Jensen did nothing to disguise her laugh. "It's not. I've got a gal. Tessa,"—she gestured to someone I could just make out through the open kitchen door—"who's a gem with all the baked goods and drinks. I'm just looking for someone to man the front of the shop a few days a week. I can only offer you part-time right now."

"Part-time is perfect. Exactly what I'm looking for."

Jensen eyed me carefully. "Do you have any waitressing experience? Know how to run a cash register and credit card machine?"

"I do. I waitressed for two years of high school and all through college. It's been a minute since I've run a register, but I'm sure it'll come back."

"That's great." Her eyes seemed to search deeper, and I wondered what she was looking for. "So, what brought you to Oregon?"

I did my best to keep my face a neutral mask. "I was just ready for a change of scenery. I was sick of all the pollution and traffic in Houston."

Jensen seemed to take that in, but I wasn't quite sure she bought it. "Is that where you lived before?"

"Yup. Houston and Los Angeles."

"This is a big change of pace. Small town. Not a lot going on."

"That's exactly what I'm looking for, a little peace and quiet."

A grin pulled at Jensen's mouth. "Well, you'll definitely get that here. Where are you staying?"

I hoped Jensen's expression meant that this weirdly informal interview was going well. "We're at one of the rental houses out on Spruce Valley Road, but I'm looking for a place to rent longer-term."

Jensen rubbed a thumb across her lower lip, seeming to consider something. "My parents have a place they might be willing to rent to you. We have a ranch about ten miles outside of town, and there's a little guest cabin that barely gets used. It's not close to the main house, so it's pretty isolated. You'd obviously need a car."

I straightened in my chair. Isolated was just what I was looking for. I could practically feel my body relax at the idea of some true alone time for the first time in forever. "That sounds perfect."

Jensen's grin widened. "I'll give my mom a call right now and get you a new employee form to fill out."

"I'm hired?"

"You're hired."

This time, I was the one grinning. "Thank you so much!"

"You're welcome. I'll be right back after I talk to my mom."

As Jensen walked away from the table, I turned to face Carter. "That was amazing, right? Like this is all meant to be."

Carter had a very forced smile on her face. "It's great, Tay."

"See, everything's going to be just fine." I just hoped I wouldn't be made a liar.

CHAPTER
Four

Walker

THE SUN SHONE DOWN ON THE ROLLING FIELDS AROUND me, a truly perfect spring morning. My boots kicked up just a bit of dust as I walked up to my parents' ranch house. My stomach growled. While I had my own place on our ten-thousand-acre spread and could technically feed myself, I never passed up the chance to sit down at one of my mother's epic breakfast spreads.

I pushed open the front door without knocking. The sounds of dishes clattering and voices chattering came from the kitchen, so I headed in that direction. My nephew, Noah, raced around the island with his toy airplane, making what sounded like a cross between a "vroooooooom" and a "whooooooosh."

"Hi, Uncle Walker," he called as he whizzed past me.

I bent, kissing my mom's cheek as she stood at the stove. "Morning, Ma."

"Good morning, my handsome baby," she answered, just as she flipped a pancake on the griddle. The perfect shade of golden brown.

"You're the reason the boy has such an ego, Sarah. It's no

wonder he hasn't settled down," my grandmother said with a good-natured harrumph.

My mother giggled. She was in her late sixties, and she still laughed like a schoolgirl. I think a large part of that was due to the fact that my father still made her feel as if she were in high school with her first real crush. "How's my girl?" my dad asked, dipping to brush his lips against my mom's.

"Get a room, you two," my sister, Jensen, called from the dining table.

My mom shuffled the last of the pancakes onto a platter. "Everyone grab a seat."

We all hurried to our chairs, my dad plucking the platter from my mom's hands. He never let her do any heavy-lifting if he was around. "Thank you, Andrew," my mom said as she kissed his cheek.

Conversation flowed, each of us discussing our plans for the day and the latest town news. As we finished up, my mom inclined her head towards me. "Walker, would you mind running something out to the Harris's rental place on Spruce Valley?"

"Sure. What is it you're wanting me to take?"

"Well, there's a young woman staying there who's going to be renting our little guest cabin for a year. So, I need you to run a lease over to her, along with a clicker for the garage."

My forehead creased. "You're renting out the cabin? Why?" My parents' two-bedroom guest cottage on the edge of our property was usually reserved for out-of-town friends, and my mom and dad liked to keep it open. They'd never rented it out before.

My mom took a sip of her OJ before answering. "Your sister hired this woman to work at the Kettle, and she needs a place to live. You know there aren't many decent places to rent around here. So, why not help?"

I fought a sigh. My mom and sister were forever taking

in strays. My dad thought it was adorable. I thought it was dangerous.

My mom's lips pursed. "Oh, don't give me that look, Walker Cole. Jensen says she's lovely, and she offered to pay first, last, and a security deposit." I eyed my sister skeptically. Her judge of character wasn't always the best. My mom kept talking. "She's staying at the Harris place with a famous musician and…what do you call those boys in the fights you're always watching?"

My eyebrows raised. This was getting more interesting by the second. "An MMA fighter?"

"Yes, that's it. One of them is a mixed martial arts fighter. At least that's what Helen told me."

"What's his name?" I asked.

My mom tapped a finger on her pursed lips. "Hmm. What was it? Adam? No, Austin. Austin Lyons."

My jaw practically came unhinged. "Austin Lyons?"

"The Bulldog is here?!" my seven-year-old nephew shrieked.

Jensen's head snapped around so fast, she looked like the creepy little kid from *The Exorcist.* "You've been letting him watch that violent garbage again? I told you, he's too young."

That was the wrong thing to say. Noah's face turned the shade of a ripening tomato. "I am not. I'm a big boy. You say so all the time. And the boys gotta hang. Right, Uncle Walker?"

I cringed, trying to paste on my most charming smile. Which, of course, got me nowhere with my sister.

"Walker Cole, you are on my you-know-what list."

Noah's face scrunched in confusion. "No, Mama, what?"

My grandmother cackled. "My Noah's a smarty-pants, nothing gets by him."

I shoved my chair back from the table, eager to escape my sister's wrath. "Well, I better get going. Ma, just give me whatever you'd like me to take over, and I'll go right now."

Jensen snorted. "You better run."

Noah bounded up from his seat, hopping around like he'd just mainlined ten candy bars and twelve sodas. "Can I go with him, Mama? Pleeeeeeeeeease? I gotta meet the Bulldog. I just gotta!"

I bit the inside of my cheek to keep from laughing. My sister threw her hands up in the air. "I give up. He's already been inundated with violence, it's probably too late for him. Walker, when you're arresting him in ten years, you'll only have yourself to blame."

Noah cocked his head to the side. "Does that mean yes?"

This time, I couldn't hold in the laugh. Jensen's eyes narrowed on me.

My dad let out his own chuckle. "I believe it does, Noah. Why don't you grab a piece of paper and pen from my office. You can ask for Mr. Bulldog's autograph."

Noah's face lit with the epitome of child-like glee. Then he took off for the other side of the house.

My mom got to her feet, retrieving what looked like a basket of muffins from the counter. "These for me?" I asked, sniffing the bundle. Marionberry, my favorite.

She smacked my hand away before I could lift the towel covering them. "No, you greedy little troublemaker. These are for Taylor, the young woman renting our cabin. I want you to bring them with the lease and keys. And invite her to dinner next weekend, would you? We need to give her a proper welcome."

Taking the basket from her hands, I kissed her cheek. "Yes, ma'am."

"Suck-up," Grandma said with a cough.

"You got that one right," Jensen joined in. "He always had Mom fooled. Guess nothing's changed."

I circled the table, giving Jensen a thorough noogie. "Just for that, I'm going to take Noah to an MMA fight live and in person."

Jensen whirled, trying to grab hold of my forearm so she

could pull out my arm hair, a move she'd been perfecting since I'd hit puberty. But I was too quick for her this time, narrowly escaping her grasp.

"Now, kids…" my mom began.

"Gotta run," I called. "I'll drop Noah back on my way home."

"Watch your back, Cole," my sister growled.

I ran into Noah in the entryway and headed out the door.

CHAPTER
Five

Walker

MY TRUCK BUMPED FROM A DIP IN THE DIRT ROAD AS Noah and I drove towards the Harris's vacation rental and this mysterious new tenant who had famous friends. I took in the sight of Willow Creek, cutting through the rolling meadows as we rounded a bend in the road. The view never got old. I'd grown up with so many kids who couldn't wait to get out of Sutter Lake. When I left for college in Portland, I couldn't wait to get back.

Noah bounced in the back seat of the truck cab, a constant stream of barely recognizable words escaping his mouth. "Uncle Walker, remember when Bulldog knocked that guy out in two seconds?"

"Yeah, buddy. It was pretty cool, huh?" It was fourteen seconds, but still a ridiculously impressive feat that had netted Austin "Bulldog" Lyons his second heavyweight Ultimate Fighting League championship. I had to admit, I might get a little star-struck myself meeting the guy. My friend, Tuck, and I had salivated over Bulldog's career. Tuck would be pissed that he missed out on this.

"So. Freaking. Cool." Noah punctuated each word by punching the air with his fist. My nephew was cute as fuck.

I swung my rig into the gravel drive at the front of the house. I'd barely thrown the vehicle into park when Noah unbuckled his seatbelt, jumped out of his booster seat, pushed open the truck door, and took off running towards the house.

"Shit." I switched off the engine and threw open my own door. "Noah!" I hollered.

But it was too late. Noah was already pounding on the front door with those tiny but determined fists, calling for "Mister Bulldog." Double shit.

Before I reached the porch steps, the front door opened, and one of the most stunning women I'd ever seen appeared. She was so beautiful, I felt like I'd been sucker-punched by Bulldog himself. Her golden-blonde hair swirled in the breeze of the open door, framing a heart-shaped face with bewitching, gray-blue eyes. She was petite, almost tiny, and an image of me curling around her as we slept immediately popped into my mind.

What in the actual fuck?

I had a girlfriend. It wasn't serious, but I was committed. And I was certainly not *that* guy. And since I wasn't *that* guy, these were not the images I needed floating around in my head.

Shaking myself from my inner mental meltdown, I realized that the porch was now full of people. "I'm so sorry—" I started.

I was interrupted by my nephew, whose head was tipped back, gaze full of pure awe as he stared up at Austin Lyons. "Bulldog..." he whispered reverently.

Austin grinned down at Noah, and I breathed a sigh of relief. "Hey there, little man. What's your name?"

"Noah," my nephew breathed, the word barely audible.

"Hi, Noah. Is this your dad here?"

Noah glanced over his shoulder. "Nope, that's my Uncle Walker. I don't got a dad."

The redheaded woman standing next to Austin paled, and I stepped in before the awkwardness could get worse. "Hi. Sorry about that. I'm Walker Cole, and this troublemaker is my nephew, Noah." Noah sent a toothy grin up at me in response to my description of him. "My mom sent me over with a few things for Taylor?" It came out as a question as my gaze searched out the elfin beauty who'd stolen all my brain cells a moment ago.

The blonde stepped forward. "That's me." She extended a delicate hand, her guarded eyes studying me. "Taylor Lawson."

I took her hand in mine, immediately feeling a zap of electricity. "Walker Cole. It's nice to meet you."

Taylor quickly pulled her hand from mine. "You, too."

Another familiar face stepped forward then. Liam Fairchild, the rock-country crooner who'd been all over the radio and TV lately. "Hey, man," he said. "Liam."

I briefly wondered if Liam was Taylor's boyfriend as I took his hand in a manly shake. "Hey."

Introductions continued. Austin motioned to his wife, Carter, who had a kind smile for Noah and a warm one for me. Then, Austin officially introduced himself to a still wide-eyed Noah. "It's nice to meet you, Noah. I'm Austin."

"I know," Noah breathed. "You're my very favorite fighter. My Uncle Walker and Tuck let me watch the fights when we have *guy time*, even though my mom says I'm too young."

I pulled Noah back against my legs, quelling his runaway speech. "We're big UFL fans, and when Noah learned that Bulldog was staying here, he just had to come along."

Austin sent a genuine smile Noah's way. "Well, I'm so glad you did. Why don't you guys come inside. I think I might have a UFL hat with your name on it, Noah."

"Really? That is freaking awesome!"

I chuckled. "Let me just grab a few things from the truck."

I jogged over, snagging the basket of muffins and the lease.

Heading back to the porch and up the steps, I could hear Noah yammering away to Austin from inside. I grinned. As I stepped inside the rental, my eyes traveled over to Taylor, who was set just apart from the group, arms wrapped around herself protectively.

Moving forward, I offered the basket to her. "These are muffins, fresh out of the oven, along with a copy of the lease for you to sign."

Taylor straightened, extending her arms to take the basket and lifting it to her nose to get a sniff. A genuine smile tipped her lips as her gaze met mine. "Thank you. These smell amazing. Are they Marionberry?"

A grin tugged at my mouth. "They are. You're not from here, so how'd you know?"

Her light laugh tinkled the air. "The bakery was one of our first stops in town, and I've found I have a weakness for pretty much anything Marionberry."

"You'll love these, then. My mom is an amazing cook. In fact, she wanted me to invite you over for dinner next weekend so you can have an official Sutter Lake welcome."

A shadow passed over Taylor's eyes, and her expression became shuttered. It was a look that reminded me a lot of grief, something I recognized all too well. "That's very kind of you, but I think I'll be too busy getting settled. My stuff should arrive from Texas by then, and I'll need to unpack."

I moved us away from the topic that clearly caused her pain, even though I had the urge to dig deeper to find out why dinner was such a touchy subject for her. "Texas? I thought you guys were from LA."

Liam appeared at Taylor's side. "We are, but Taylor moved back to Texas a couple years ago to—"

"To be with my family," Taylor interrupted, clearly not wanting Liam to finish whatever he'd been about to say.

Interesting. "So, you're exploring your options for where you want to go next?"

Taylor's eyes narrowed ever so slightly. "Something like that." The girl did not like questions about herself.

I raised my hands in a gesture of apology. "Sorry. Curious nature. I'm a town cop."

Carter joined us, slipping an arm around Taylor's waist. "She'll be here for a year, but we're hoping she'll move back to LA when that time is up. Although, it does make me feel better that there's a police officer nearby."

"My house is just over the ridge from where Taylor will be staying. And I'll leave her my phone number in case she needs anything."

Taylor scowled, but Carter beamed. "Oh, that would be great. Why don't you come have a seat. We can eat some of whatever smells so good in this basket, and I'll fix us some coffee."

"That sounds great. I can never resist one of those muffins."

Everyone migrated to the cluster of couches. I wrangled Noah onto one of the sofas, but his energy could not be contained, and he seemed to hover more than sit. Austin's large frame took up much of the loveseat, while Liam seemed to sprawl on the largest couch, and Taylor sat in an armchair that was about as far removed from the group as possible.

Carter reemerged, carrying a tray laden with a coffee pot, mugs, plates, and napkins. Austin jumped to his feet, taking the serving platter from her hands and setting it on the coffee table. "Firecracker, you should have asked me to help you."

Carter shook her head, a smile on her face. "I can carry a tray."

Austin's answer was to dip his head down and brush his lips against hers. They had an ease with each other, a love that reminded me of something I'd once had. A long-past phantom pain gripped my chest for a brief moment before I shook it off.

"Did you hear that Walker is a police officer?" Carter asked

Austin, now curved into her husband's side on the loveseat.

Austin's gaze met mine. "Really? How long?"

"Almost eight years now."

Austin grabbed a muffin from the basket. "That's great. And you're from here?"

"Born and raised. My family and another actually founded Sutter Lake."

"It must be so special to have that kind of connection with a place," Carter said, reaching forward to pour herself a cup of coffee.

"It's pretty great. My whole family resides somewhere on our ranch property. It can be a little chaotic at times, but I wouldn't have it any other way."

Noah bounced up and down on the couch cushion. "We have horses and chickens and cattle and goats. You guys could come see."

Austin chuckled. "We might just have to do that. As long as you don't make me get up on one of those horses."

Noah's face scrunched up. "You don't like horses?"

"I like to look at them just fine, but I don't think I'd be a big fan of riding one of them."

Noah studied his idol. "You're not scared, are you? You're the Bulldog."

The rest of the room fell into a chorus of laughs and chuckles, but I could pick Taylor's out of the array. Light and airy. Delicate. Just like her.

Austin grinned at Noah. "Everyone's scared of something."

Noah nodded, considering the statement as his eyes traveled around the room. They stopped on Taylor. "What about you, Tay Tay?"

I tried to hide my laughter with a cough. Only Noah would give someone he'd met fifteen minutes prior a nickname and ask her such a deeply personal question.

She had a soft smile for Noah. "Well, I'm not much of a fan of getting up on horses either, but…" She tapped her lips with a finger as if really considering what her greatest fear might be. "What I'm *really* afraid of is moths."

Noah dissolved into giggles. "Moths? Moths aren't scary."

Taylor grinned. "But they are! With their freaky wings, and when they fly in your face. Yuck!" She gave an exaggerated shiver. "Will you protect me from all the moths while I'm here, Noah?"

Noah puffed up his chest as if he'd just been asked to guard the President. "I'll protect you from all the moths, Tay Tay."

We polished off the muffins, and I told them all about my favorite Sutter Lake haunts, a hike they should take, and items on the secret menu at the bakery.

Austin's face grew serious. "Are there any bad neighborhoods or people Taylor should avoid?"

Taylor rolled her eyes. "Austin, would you quit it?"

I waved a hand. "No, it's a smart thing to ask." Austin wore a triumphant grin, while Taylor scowled at us both. "On the whole, Sutter Lake is an incredibly safe town. Most people don't even lock their doors. Though I wouldn't recommend that. There's a small drug culture, but as long as you don't mess with that stuff, you'll be fine."

I placed one of my business cards on the coffee table. "My cell's on the back of that card. Call me anytime. I'm happy to help if you have any questions or concerns."

Taylor's shoulders straightened. "I'm sure I'll be fine."

It appeared that Taylor had an independent streak. I fought a grin as I stood. "Well, we should get going. It was great to meet you all."

"Aw, do we have to?" Noah moaned, still clutching the hat Austin that had signed for him.

I pulled Noah to his feet. "We do. I need to get you home, and then I have to get some work done."

Austin stood. "I'll walk you out."

Taylor didn't rise from her chair but gave Austin a searching, slightly suspicious look. He ignored her and headed for the door. Noah followed as Carter and Liam called their farewells.

Something told me that Austin wanted to discuss something, so I bent to whisper in Noah's ear. "Why don't you go wait in the truck, I need to talk to Bulldog for a minute."

Noah's face took on a pout. "Aw, man. I always miss out on the good stuff." But like the good kid he was, he headed to my rig.

Austin chuckled. "He's a great kid."

"The best." I studied Austin's face, but his expression was unreadable. I guessed that was a skill he would've had to master as a cage fighter. "What's up? Are you having trouble in town?"

"Oh, no. Nothing like that. I have a favor to ask."

"You've made my nephew's year, so if it's within my power to give, it's yours."

"I was hoping you'd say something like that." He paused, seeming to search for the words he wanted to voice. "I want you to look out for Taylor."

My brows furrowed. "Are you just worried about her being here alone? Or is something else going on?"

"Taylor's been through a lot the past few years. She took care of her mom through two battles with cancer. Lost her a couple months ago." My chest tightened. It *was* grief I had seen in those pretty eyes.

Austin pushed on. "She's shutting us out, and I'm worried that by moving up here, she's only going to isolate herself more."

"That's a heavy load."

Austin ran a hand over his buzzed head. "It is. And she doesn't have any other family. Her dad's a deadbeat. A rich one, but still. She's alone in the world except for us. She's family, and I hate the idea of leaving her up here while we head back to LA. You seem like a stand-up guy. You're a cop. You take good care of your nephew. You're the best option I've got, other than moving my entire family to middle-of-nowhere Oregon. No offense."

I chuckled. "None taken. The peace and quiet isn't for everyone." Austin grunted an agreement. "I'm happy to keep an eye on her. And if she's working at The Kettle, my sister will look after her, too. I've got a big family who'd love to bring Taylor into the fold. But that means she's gotta say yes to things."

Austin pursed his lips. "You might have to get creative on that front."

"I sensed that. All I can do is give you my word I'll try."

Austin grasped my hand in a firm shake. "Thanks, man. And I'll send you some tickets to the next UFL fight in Portland."

"Not necessary, but certainly appreciated."

"Happy to do it. Glad to meet you, man."

I squeezed his hand back. "You, too."

As I descended the porch steps, Taylor's haunted blue-gray eyes flashed in my mind.

CHAPTER
Six

Taylor

I COLLAPSED IN THE ROCKER ON THE BACK DECK OF MY NEW home and took in the scene. Fields rolled out before me for what looked like miles until forests of pine trees sprang up. A creek cut through the pasture directly in front of me, snaking through the grass and providing the handful of lazily grazing horses water to drink.

My friends had left late that morning, but not before Carter had stocked my fridge and freezer with groceries and dishes she'd prepared over the last couple of days. I was pretty sure they all thought I was going to starve to death, and that Walker would be calling to tell them that he had found my malnourished body.

Don't get me wrong, I loved my friends. So much so, that it freaked me out. Because the depth with which you loved someone determined the amount of pain you felt when they were gone.

I let out a long breath. This would be good. Quiet, but not overly so—solitude, peace. The cabin itself was perfect. Two bedrooms, including a master suite that had an amazing soaking tub, an open-concept living area that transitioned into a kitchen with all the appliances I was determined to learn how to use, and a back deck that I could sit on for hours.

Except I was already getting twitchy. Already eager to get back to my workout routine. I craved the feeling of my muscles crying out for mercy and passing out into a dreamless sleep each night. It was the only high I needed.

I checked the time on my phone. Two p.m.. Plenty of time to run the ten miles into town and back before dark. Maybe I'd pop by The Tea Kettle to see if my shift schedule was ready. I hopped up and headed off to change into my running gear. The afternoon sun shone brightly, so I opted for a tank top and shorts and then slipped into my favorite sneakers.

Grabbing my phone, a twenty-dollar bill, and my house key, I headed out the front door. I felt rusty for the first mile, and when I paused to stretch, my muscles protested the action. I picked up the jog again, and it wasn't long before I found my zone and lost myself in the pounding of my feet against the road.

Gravel crunched beneath my shoes with the rhythmic beat of my stride. I had missed these workouts, the quiet times when I could take out my rage on the pavement or in the pool. No machines—the payoff just wasn't as good.

I relished the burn in my lungs and the fatigue in my muscles as gravel turned to asphalt and, soon, storefronts started to appear. Slowing my run to a jog, I returned the friendly waves or nods from passersby. The town was pleasantly busy but not too crowded. I'd heard that it was a bit of a tourist destination for families from Portland on weekends. I'd just avoid coming into town on those days, but right now, it was perfect.

When I reached The Tea Kettle, I took a moment to stretch and wipe sweat from my brow. Grimacing, I wondered if showing up a sweaty mess was the best way to make a good impression at my new job. I gave a mental shrug. I wasn't actually on the clock, and this seemed like a pretty active and low-key town.

I was sure it would be fine.

I made my way up the walk and pushed open the door. Cool air caressed my skin, and the wonderful, familiar aroma I'd smelled the first time I entered the shop filled my nose.

"Well, hello there." A voice sounded from behind the counter, and I looked up to see a woman who appeared to be in her sixties. She sent me a warm smile that socked me right in the stomach. The expression was wide and open, just like my mother's had been. The damnedest things could sneak up and punch you right in the gut.

I pushed the memories of my mom down and cleared my throat. "Hi. I'm Taylor. I'm going to be working here starting next week. I was on a run, and figured I'd stop by to see if my schedule was ready."

The woman came around the counter now. "Oh, Taylor, it's so lovely to meet you. I'm Sarah, Jensen's mom and sometimes helper here at the shop." Her smile faltered as she took in my appearance. "You ran here?"

"Yup. It's such a beautiful route. Thank you for renting me the cabin, by the way. It's just perfect."

"You're welcome," Sarah said distractedly, a look of stunned concern filling her face. "But it's ten miles into town."

I had to fight a smile. "I like to run."

"Well, you'd have to love it to run that far."

"Not a runner, I take it?" I asked.

"Not a fan of it, no. I like a good walk or going for a horseback ride with Jensen, but running is not at the top of my list of hobbies."

The bell on the door sounded, and five girls who looked to be in middle school poured in. "I'll let you help them. I can get my schedule later or just text Jensen."

Sarah waved a hand in front of her face. "Just go on back. The schedule is hanging on a clipboard next to the fridge."

"Thank you." I ducked around the counter and moved into the kitchen. A brunette woman stood with her back to me while she prepared drinks. "Hey," I greeted.

The woman whirled, upending the tea she was making and sending it everywhere.

"I'm so sorry." I started to move forward to help, but she skittered back. Stilling my movements, I spoke softly. "I'm Taylor, I'm going to be working here and was just coming back to check out the schedule."

Her eyes were still wide. Though a bit fearful, they were the most gorgeous eyes I'd ever seen—a shade of blue that almost seemed purple in the afternoon light. "S-sorry," she stammered. "I was just startled. I'm Tessa." When she extended her hand to grasp mine, it shook.

I gave her a reassuring smile. "It's my fault. I shouldn't have snuck up on you like that."

Tessa ducked her head. "The schedule's right over there."

"Thank you. Can I help you wipe up the mess since I'm the one that caused it?"

She shook her head. "It's all right. I've got it."

As I snapped a photo of next week's schedule with my phone, and Tessa cleaned up the spilled tea, I noticed that she never turned her back to me, as if afraid I might startle her again. "Okay. I'm all set. I'm so sorry I caused a mess, but hopefully, I won't cause any more when we work together."

Tessa gave me a small smile. "It's no problem. It was nice to meet you."

"You, too." I headed back out to the shop's main room. As I did, the bell sounded again, and the door opened. Noah rushed in, trailed by a frazzled Jensen. I was struck by how much she looked like her brother.

I wanted to smack myself. Walker Cole had popped into my mind more times than I was comfortable with over the past few days. All charming smiles and too many questions. He was trouble.

Noah skidded to a stop in front of me. "Tay Tay! Is Bulldog with you?"

I grinned. Noah seemed unable to call Austin anything but *Bulldog*, no matter how many times he was told he could call Austin by his given name. It was adorable. "Hey there, little man. He left this morning, I'm sorry."

Noah's face fell. No more one-on-one time with his hero. "Will he come back?"

"He just might. He liked Sutter Lake."

"I'm glad he did, and that you do too," Noah's mother's voice cut in. "Hey, Taylor. Thank you so much for being so sweet to my little fight fan here."

"I'm not little!" Noah said with a stamp of his foot.

"Sorry. My big-boy fight fan here," Jensen corrected with a grin.

"Not a problem. Austin loves to meet his younger fans."

"I can't say I'm crazy about Noah watching those fights, but at least this Bulldog is a stand-up character."

I let out a light laugh. "The fights are definitely not for the faint of heart."

Jensen grimaced. "So, are you settling in okay? Need help finding anything?"

"I am, but now that you mention it, is there a pool in town where I can swim laps?"

"Unfortunately, there's no public pool since the lake is so popular, but we have one at the main house you can use."

I pressed my lips together before answering. "That's really kind of you, but I don't want to disturb your family."

"You wouldn't be—"

Jensen was cut off by her mother putting an arm around her shoulders. My heart clenched. "Hey there, baby girl. I finally met

Miss Taylor here."

Jensen slipped an arm around her mother's waist. It was an effortless gesture that spoke of years of comfort and love. Tears stung the backs of my eyes. "Good. I was just telling her that she could use our pool to swim laps."

Sarah's face brightened. "Oh, yes, please do. We put that thing in a few years ago for Noah, but it hardly gets any use. Come over anytime. It'd do my heart good to see someone enjoying it."

I twisted the ring on my right hand. I really didn't want to give anyone the chance to initiate curious conversation, but I worried I'd go crazy if I couldn't swim. I could try the lake, but I wasn't exactly keen on communing with the fishies while I tired myself out. I gave in. "Thank you. I think I'll take you up on that. Do you want me to call you before I come over?"

Sarah waved a hand in front of her face. "Oh, no, that's not necessary. People are constantly in and out and around the ranch house. Just come on over whenever you like. And we'd love to have you to dinner once you're settled."

I gave a noncommittal, "Thank you." I didn't want to answer the inevitable questions that were always asked. I didn't want to see the looks of pity. I didn't want to talk about any of it. Working here, the shop was busy enough that I doubted there would be time for any in-depth conversations, but a family dinner was a whole different ballgame.

I made a show of glancing at the clock on the wall. "Well, I better get going, finish my run."

"She ran all the way here from the cabin," Sarah told Jensen.

Jensen's brows rose. "Whoa. You aren't messing around."

I gave another shrug. "I like to run."

Sarah shook her head as if perplexed. "Just be careful on your way back. You have Jensen's number if you need anything, right?"

"I do. Thanks for everything."

"You're very welcome. Hope to see you for dinner soon."

Noah saved me by shouting from behind the bakery case. "Bye, Tay Tay!"

Jensen whirled. "Noah Nolan Cole, you better not be stealing treats out of there."

With that, I made my escape.

CHAPTER
Seven

Walker

COOL AIR RUSHED OVER ME AS I PULLED OPEN THE DOOR to the station, the smell of freshly brewed coffee wafting out.

"Good morning, Walker," a soft voice called from behind the reception desk. Ashlee Elkins was as sweet as apple pie and as shy as a groundhog during a particularly long winter.

"Morning, Ashlee."

"I have your cup of coffee," she said, a blush staining her cheeks.

She also had what I was pretty sure was a massive crush on me. I gave her a kind smile. I didn't want to encourage it, but I also didn't want to be an asshole. It wasn't that she wasn't pretty, she was. In a sundress-wearing, church-every-Sunday kind of way. But she'd forever been like a little sister to me. It was just a no-go. I would never see her that way. Plus, her brother had recently started dating my sister, and that felt incestuous. "I told you, you don't have to make my coffee."

Her blush deepened. "I don't mind."

I dipped my chin. "Well, thank you."

"You're welcome. Also, the chief wanted a word when you got in."

I nodded, taking the mug from her hand and heading towards Clark's office. I rapped twice on the door. "Come in."

I entered the room. "You wanted to see me, Chief?"

"Morning, Walker." Clark Adams was a great Chief of Police for Sutter Lake, but as he got closer to retirement, he'd begun grooming me to take over the role. "Grab a seat."

I sank into a chair opposite him and took a sip of my coffee. Just as I liked it. Black, one sugar.

Clark placed a stack of papers on his desk and gave me a careful look that put me on edge. "We've got a missing hiker out there." He gestured at a map, indicating the miles of national forest that surrounded our town. "A girl from Seattle."

Straightening, I placed my mug on the desk. A lead weight settled in my gut, reminding me of another missing girl all those years ago. I told myself that this was different, just a hiker lost in the woods. We'd find this girl. And she'd be alive. "Search and rescue been called?"

"They've been put on alert, but the search area is large. The young woman's parents don't know exactly where she was going hiking. Just some trail near Sutter Lake."

"Hiking alone?"

"Yup."

I groaned. When would these people learn? You never hiked alone, and you *always* told someone where you were going and when to expect you back.

Clark rubbed a hand over his jaw. "There's not a lot we can do at the moment, but I wanted to make you aware of the situation."

"I appreciate that."

"Of course." Clark continued to hold my gaze. Searching. Sending the same silent apology he always did whenever there was a case that hit too close to home.

Almost a decade had passed since the spring I'd lost Julie. Since she was *taken* from me. I still held out hope that a clue would appear or a witness would come forward. I went through the case file every year on the anniversary of her death, hoping that something would jump out at me that I hadn't noticed before. It never did.

And it wasn't for Clark's lack of trying either. He'd done everything he could to find answers. To get justice for Julie. He hadn't been able to. What Clark had done was light a fire in me to become a cop. He'd encouraged me every step of the way. "Take that anger and turn it into something productive," he'd said. So, I had.

I shook myself from the memories pressing down on me and pushed from the chair. "I have some paperwork to wrap up, but let me know if there's anything I can do."

Clark jerked up his chin as I headed out. "Will do."

Pushing open the door to my office, I blew out a long breath. The ghosts were going to be running rampant today. I rounded my desk and sank into the chair. I punched a few keys on my keyboard to bring my computer to life, then just stared at the home screen, unable to force myself to descend into the dull world of police reports.

My phone buzzed on the desk, sending vibrations through the wood. I snatched it up.

Caitlin: *Hey you. Want to get dinner tonight?*

Guilt flared in my gut, but I tamped it down. Thinking about Julie didn't mean I cared any less for Caitlin. Didn't mean that I wouldn't be able to *love* Caitlin one day. I just wasn't there yet.

I typed out a reply.

Me: *I'd love to. Pick you up at 6?*

Moments later, my phone buzzed again.

Caitlin: *I'll be waiting. ;-)*

I turned back to the boring-as-hell police reports. At least those didn't make me feel like an asshole.

I took a pull on my beer as Caitlin gazed at me from across the table, her light brown hair curled to frame her heart-shaped face, her makeup perfect. I strained to feel something deeper for her, just a faint flicker of what I'd felt for Julie. It wouldn't come.

Caitlin took a sip of her wine. "So, how was work?"

"It was good." I glanced around the bustling restaurant. Folks from town and tourists I didn't recognize filled the tables. "Mostly just catching up on never-ending paperwork."

Caitlin's mouth turned down. "That doesn't sound like too much fun."

I chuckled. "A lot of police work is boring. Still needs to get done."

"So—" Caitlin's words were cut off by the appearance of someone at our table.

Arthur Grigg was a staple in town. Seventy-eight years old and nosy as all get-out. "Walker, Caitlin," he greeted, then turned to face me. "I heard there's a missing hiker."

"There is." I eyed Caitlin from across the table. Her lips pressed together in a way that said she wasn't too happy I had neglected to share this news with her.

Arthur huffed. "Well, what are you doing about it?"

"There's not a lot we can do at the moment. Search and rescue is on standby, and we have an APB out on her vehicle. Other than that, our hands are tied."

Arthur's eyes narrowed. "You're telling me there's not one thing you could be doing for that girl? I'd think you of all people would want to be looking for her."

My jaw tightened, and Caitlin sucked in a breath. "I'd love to be looking for her, but there are thousands of miles of forest around here. Where would I start, if I have no clue where *she* started?" My chest burned, and I fought against the urge to put the old guy in his place. I knew Arthur didn't mean any harm, but his words cut deep.

"Well, you could at least put up some missing-person flyers."

I wanted to ask what posters would do if the hiker was in the middle of the woods, but I resisted. "Tell you what, Arthur. Why don't you come by the station tomorrow. I'll print up some flyers, and you and the rest of the bridge club can help me put them up around town."

Arthur's chest puffed up as though I'd nominated him for knighthood. "I could get the boys together, and we could help you out."

"Thank you. That'd be a big help."

He patted me on the shoulder. "That's what good communities do, help each other when the chips are down. Now, I'll let you two youngins enjoy your supper."

"Thank you, Arthur," Caitlin said with a strained smile.

I took a long drink of my beer as Arthur walked away. *What a day.*

My careful gaze swept over Caitlin. She toyed with her fork, staring intently at it. "Why didn't you tell me about the hiker?"

Shit. It wasn't that I was trying to keep things from Cait, it was just that I didn't want to dwell on it. I cleared my throat. "I just didn't want to darken our night together."

Her gaze moved to mine. "I want to be there for you. Support you when this kind of thing happens. But I feel like you never let me in."

A muscle in my cheek ticked. Caitlin couldn't pick and choose which of life's hardships she wanted me to share. I'd tried to talk about Julie with her once, but she'd just gotten defensive, as if she were competing with a dead girl. I got it, I did, but she couldn't have it both ways. "I'm sorry, Cait. I'll try to share this kind of stuff with you more, but to be honest, sometimes I just want to leave it at the office."

Caitlin reached across the table and squeezed my hand. "Thank you." Her gentle smile turned sultry. "I just feel like we should be closer, spend more time together. Which reminds me, I've been wanting to talk to you about something."

"Okay…" Conversations that began like that usually didn't make me happy.

"I think we should move in together."

I nearly spit out the sip of beer I'd just taken. Instead, it went down the wrong pipe, and I started coughing. "Cait. I thought we talked about taking things slow?"

Her eyes took on a pleading quality. "I know, but I just love it when you spend the night at my apartment, and you have that big ol' house up at the ranch that's practically sitting empty. Don't you think it makes sense?"

I took a sip of my water, trying to buy time. How I answered this, had the potential to send Caitlin into hysterics. But, honesty was the only option. "I'm not ready for that. And, honestly, I'm nowhere near there. I might never be."

Caitlin's face fell, and her lower lip wobbled. "Is this because of Julie?"

My hand tightened around my water glass. "It's because I'm not there. If you're looking for someone who wants to settle down quick, that's not me. I'm sorry."

Caitlin's eyes widened. "No! I want you. I don't care how long it takes."

A weight settled in my chest. I was a total schmuck, leading Cait down this path when I had no idea if it would end in me committing to her. I needed a drink stronger than beer.

CHAPTER
Eight

Taylor

MY BODY CUT THROUGH THE WATER, THE LIQUID caressing my skin in a way that brought soothing comfort. Nothing gave me peace like the water. Looking at it. Listening to it. But, best of all, was immersing myself in it.

Sometimes, my laps were angry. Vicious strokes of rage, taken out on the calm surface. Other times, like now, they were peaceful, my body barely creating a splash or waves as my limbs propelled me forward. Either way, the water welcomed me. Soothed my soul, put me back together to fight another day.

My fingertips touched tile, and I stood, reaching for my water bottle. "It looked like you were running low," a familiar voice said in a deep and husky tone that sent a shiver down my spine.

I pulled my goggles off to see Walker extending a water bottle to me. He was casually dressed, wearing dark jeans that hugged his hips and a worn tee that did nothing to disguise the muscles underneath. I swallowed hard, taking the bottle from his outstretched hand. "Thanks. I'm done if you want to use the pool."

Walker took a seat on the edge of one of the lounge chairs

on the pool deck. "Lap swimming isn't my preferred method of workout."

I shrugged, peeling back my swim cap and quickly dunking my head under the water to smooth out my hair. Placing my palms on the lip of the pool, I propelled myself up and out. Water sluiced down my body as I wrung out my hair. When I looked up, Walker's eyes were traveling up and down the length of me. My skin suddenly turned hot despite the cool night air.

I held out a hand. "Do you mind?"

"Oh, sorry." Walker stood, shaking his head and grabbing the towel he had been partially sitting on. He extended it towards me, but when I went to take it, he held firm. "Where's your car?"

I blinked. "My car?"

"Yes, you know, the four-wheeled vehicle that gets you from point A to point B."

"I know what a car is, smartass."

"Well then, where is yours? I didn't see one at the main house."

I gave a firm tug on the towel, and Walker finally released his hold. I quickly wrapped the terrycloth around my body, wanting protection from the stare that seemed to light my blood on fire. "It's not here yet. It should arrive tomorrow."

Walker frowned. "So how did you get here? Jensen pick you up?"

"I walked," I said, side-stepping him to gather my belongings.

"You walked?"

"Yes."

"Are you crazy? It's over a mile, and it's dark out now."

I straightened, my hands fisting around the towel. "No, I am not crazy. We're in Oregon, not South Central. It's perfectly safe."

Walker let out an exasperated sigh. "From gangbangers maybe, but not from wild animals. Come on, I'll drive you home."

The thought of being in a small, confined space with Walker had my body stiffening. Something about him just set me on edge. It was as if he saw too much. "That's not necessary. I'm sure the wild animal kingdom won't bother me if I don't bother them."

Walker scrubbed a hand over his stubbled jaw and then let his arm fall to his side. "We have regular sightings of cougars and bears around the property and in the surrounding woods. It's not safe for you to walk home alone. If you try to, I'll just have to follow you. At least I carry a gun."

My teeth clenched. "Fine. You can drive me."

"Thank you, Short-stack."

"Short-stack? What am I, a plate of pancakes?" I snarked, attempting to cover up the sense of unease I felt. Nicknames meant familiarity. Familiarity meant prying eyes and questions. I wanted neither. Quiet. Solitude. Peace. That was all I wanted. Teasing nicknames had no place in my safe zone.

"Well, you are kind of tiny. It's pretty adorable actually," Walker said with a grin that made his eyes dance in the twilight.

I fought the urge to laugh. I didn't want to find this man charming on top of handsome. Nope. Didn't want to go there. Couldn't go there. I bent forward, slipping on my shorts over my bathing suit before I stuffed my towel into my bag. "Ready when you are."

Walker bit the inside of his cheek. "You could've gone inside and changed if you wanted to."

"Not necessary."

"Well, all right then." He grabbed the bag I was holding from my hand before I had a chance to stop him and headed towards the front of the house.

I had no choice but to trail behind. Walker stopped at a large, fancy-looking truck and opened the passenger door. His eyes scanned me from head to toe, and that same heat I'd felt earlier flared back to life in my blood. "You need a lift up?"

My jaw fell open. "I'm not *that* short."

Walker simply chuckled.

"I don't need your help getting in the truck," I gritted out.

He kept right on laughing, motioning me on with a wave of his arm. "Then, go right ahead."

He didn't move from beside the door. I huffed and hoisted myself up onto the running board and then into the truck. It might have taken some extra effort to do so, but I didn't need the help of some overprotective behemoth of a man.

I reached out an arm. "Bag? Or are you unsure if little ol' me can lift it without some help?"

"Spunky. I like it."

My teeth clacked together, but I said nothing. The man was infuriating. Thinking he knew what was best for me, just like everyone else in my life.

Walker gave me my bag, and I watched as he rounded the truck, strides a bizarre mixture of relaxed and purposeful. He exuded a casual authority. It made sense that he was a cop. I didn't think many people would give him grief—just me, apparently.

The driver's side door swung open, and Walker effortlessly took his seat. Tall jerk. The engine roared to life. "So, why don't you come to dinner tomorrow night."

I rubbed my thumb against the metal of my ring. "I don't think so, I'm still not settled."

"So you can't come to dinner, but you can use our pool?" There was a devilish tone to his words.

I grimaced. "Look, I'm going to be honest with you—"

"I'd appreciate that."

"I'm probably not going to spend a ton of time with your family. You're all unbelievably kind, but—"

"But you're committed to this aloof loner vibe you've got going?"

My hands gripped the leather seat tightly. "Would you stop interrupting me."

"Of course, please go on explaining why having dinner with my family would be a fate worse than death."

I blanched at the word *death* but forced my vocal cords to work. "I moved to Sutter Lake for the peace and quiet. I need some alone time right now, and I'd really appreciate it if you would respect that."

Walker ran a thumb across his full lower lip. "It sounds like you've been going through a tough time. If that's the case, you need to be around good people. Everyone needs people, Taylor."

My shoulders stiffened. "Not me." I blew out a breath. "Don't get me wrong, it's nice to have people in your life. I love my friends, they're wonderful. But I don't *need* them. I don't need anyone."

Silence filled the cab, and I worried I might have just come off like a raving bitch. That wasn't what I wanted. Polite distance I could handle. Someone poking around and trying to figure out what made me tick, I could not. I glanced at Walker's profile.

"You might not need anyone, Taylor, but maybe someone out there needs you. Just think about that."

The silence returned, and I just stared out at the dark fields surrounding us, Walker's words playing over and over again in my head.

CHAPTER
Nine

Walker

ICY-COLD WATER RAN OVER MY HEAD AND ONTO THE DIRT as I bent over. A hard slap on my back had me straightening. "Gettin' a little slow there, old man."

I sent an elbow into Tuck's gut that had him grunting. "I'm six months older than you. If I'm old, you're old."

Tuck and I had known each other since birth. Both of our families had shared in the founding of Sutter Lake. They still owned much of the property the town sat on and kept ranches that butted up against each other to this day. We'd both gone to school for criminology, but Tuck served as part of a Forest Service law enforcement team, and I joined the Sutter Lake police force. We worked cases together semi-frequently and harassed each other monthly at these SWAT team trainings.

Central Oregon had several small communities like Sutter Lake. None of us would be able to have our own dedicated SWAT teams, but when we all came together, we were able to have an emergency response team that served the tri-county area. We responded to all sorts of calls and had special tactical and search and rescue training. Specialty instruction and risky call-outs meant monthly refreshers to make sure our team stayed sharp. These guys were the best of the best, and I was grateful to have them at my back.

Tuck snatched the water bottle from my hand, taking a long swallow. He offered it back to me, but I shook my head. "Keep it. I don't need your nasty-ass germs and STDs." He was a total manwhore.

Tuck chucked the bottle directly at my head, but I was too quick for him and plucked it out of the air. "Hey, you know I always wrap it up."

"No, I don't know, but I'm glad to hear you're playing by health-class standards."

"Don't be jealous of my love life just because you're stuck in the land of monogamy." Tuck pulled down the tailgate of my truck and hopped up. "Speaking of, what's the latest on Miss Caitlin?"

I gripped the edge of the tailgate a little tighter than was necessary as I hopped up beside him. "Things aren't great."

"What do you mean? I thought you were feeling that situation."

"I was. I mean, I am." I blew out a frustrated breath.

"Come on, you know you can talk to Papa Tuck about your feelings."

Chuckling, I shook my head. "She wants things to be more serious than they are. Then I want them to be. Maybe ever."

Tuck grabbed another water from the cooler in my truck bed. "I never could figure out why you were so set on these relationships. Just go out and have fun. No muss, no fuss, no chicks angling for a ring."

I groaned. Tuck was a dog. Don't get me wrong, he was always honest with the girls he took to bed, but he had zero plans of settling down anytime soon. "I'm just not built like that. I like the company as much as everything else. Don't you miss having an actual conversation with a woman?"

Tuck shrugged. "I have plenty of conversations. They're just with a lot of different women. Variety is the spice of life, my friend."

An image of Taylor pushing out of the pool flashed in my mind—water running down her curvy body, turning her golden skin slick. God, that made me the biggest kind of ass. Couldn't even stay focused on my girlfriend when I was thinking of breaking up with her. Maybe I was more like Tuck than I thought.

"You dog, you. You've got your eye on someone else, don't you? Who is it?"

I grimaced. "I don't. I mean, there's this girl, but it's not like that." I wouldn't have been surprised if the skies had opened up and lightning struck me right there.

Tuck clucked his tongue. "Uh-uh. We are blood brothers, cradle to grave. Spill."

I toyed with the water bottle in my hands. "Did you hear that someone moved into our guest cabin?"

Tuck straightened. "Permanently?"

"For a year. A girl from LA."

"That sounds promising. If she's from LA, she's probably smoking."

"She's pretty." World's biggest understatement. "She's also this weird, walking contradiction. One-part cold aloofness, the other sarcastic spunk." Taylor Lawson was fire and ice. And the combination had intrigued me from the moment I met her.

A sly smile crept over Tuck's face. "You like her."

I lifted a single shoulder. "She's nice."

Tuck's smile grew. "You *really* like her."

"What are you, five? I told you, it's not like that. I have a girlfriend," I griped.

Tuck's face grew serious. "Walk, you've had one foot out of every relationship you've been in since Julie." I tightened my grip on the water bottle and tried to keep my expression passive. "I get it, I do. Her death marked us all. Hell, it's why we're both in law enforcement now. But just because she's gone, doesn't mean you can't have that great love again."

The water bottle in my hand began to crumple as I tightened my grip. "Julie was my one."

"She was one of your ones. God would never be so cruel as to only give us one shot at happiness."

I wasn't so sure. It had seemed like a miracle to find it in the first place. A second time was surely an impossibility. I smacked Tuck's gut with the back of my hand. "What is this? Lessons in love from Sutter Lake's own Casanova?"

Tuck grinned. "You never know, maybe I'm hiding my true nature as a romantic. Maybe I need to meet this new neighbor of yours."

My jaw locked, and I hated myself a little for the jealousy that flared to life within me. "You can't. I don't want your smarmy ass around her."

"Afraid she'll fall for me, huh? It's to be expected, I am the better-looking and richer of the two of us."

"Yes, I'm terrified she'll fall in love with your ego and fart jokes."

"I'll just call up Mama Sarah or Jensen and get them to introduce us. I bet they'd be thrilled to play matchmaker."

"Don't." The word came out harsher than I'd intended, surprising even me. The brief sparks I'd felt with Taylor were more than I'd ever felt with Caitlin. In that moment, I knew I needed to end things with Caitlin. It wasn't fair to her. She wanted something I'd never be able to give her.

Tuck sobered. "All right. I'll stay clear." I let out a breath I hadn't realized I'd been holding. "So, what's new with the Cole family? Jensen still dating that douchebag, Bryce?"

I was grateful for the subject change. "Bryce isn't a douchebag."

Tuck scoffed, straightening his baseball cap.

"He's been good to Jensen. She hasn't introduced him to Noah as a boyfriend or anything yet. They're taking things slow."

"At least there's that."

I studied Tuck. "What's your problem with him? This is the first guy she's dated since that ass in college. Bryce has a good job, he's not a player. We should be relieved there's someone decent in her life."

Tuck peeled back the label on his water bottle. "I don't know, just something about him, I guess."

"Well, get over it. She really likes him, I can tell."

"I'll do my best," Tuck said, the words tight, his cheek muscle popping.

I slapped his shoulder. "Good. Now, let's get out of here and grab a beer."

Tuck hopped down from the tailgate. "You're buying. You still owe me for not calling me when you knew you were going to meet Austin Lyons."

The man had a point.

CHAPTER
Ten

Taylor

THE MUTED SOUNDS OF VARIOUS CONVERSATIONS filtered through the air as I wiped down the counter at The Tea Kettle.

"You're doing a great job. One more day with me here, and then I'm letting you loose on the public," Jensen said as she refilled the bakery case with things that smelled like Heaven. Tessa really had a gift in the kitchen.

My first day had been a success so far. It had only taken me a few bumbling attempts to figure out the register, and I soon fell into a rhythm of busy bursts and lulls. Everyone who came in was super-friendly. Austin had been right. They all wanted to know my story, but I was able to maneuver the quick conversations with vague answers and half-truths.

My favorite customers so far were a group of four gentlemen in their seventies or eighties who were playing a spirited game of bridge at a corner table. Jensen said they came in every week. They were all shameless flirts, and I loved every second of it.

Turning back to Jensen, I tossed the rag under the counter. "Thanks. This is pretty fun. You've got some characters coming through, that's for sure."

Jensen let out a snort of laughter just as the bell over the door jingled. I looked up to see a handsome man with sandy brown hair and sparkling eyes enter. "Hey there, Jensen."

Jensen's cheeks heated. "Hey, Bryce. What are you doing here during the middle of the day?"

He grinned at her. I might as well have been invisible. "I thought I'd earned a little break. Wanted to come and see how your day was going."

The red in Jensen's cheeks deepened. There had to be a love story brewing here. "Things are going great. Bryce, this is Taylor. She just moved here from Texas and is the Kettle's newest waitress."

Bryce's gaze finally came to mine, and a genuine smile tipped his lips. "Nice to meet you, Taylor. Welcome to town. You're in good hands here with Jensen."

"Thank you, I know I am." I tilted my head towards Jensen. "I'm fine here if you want to take a little break."

She rolled her lips together as if thinking it through. "All right. Bryce, you want a snack?"

"I wouldn't say no to one of those ham and cheddar scones."

Jensen nodded. "Coming right up."

While Bryce and Jensen settled themselves at a back table, I straightened things that didn't need straightening and tried not to look like I was snooping. I totally was. Those two had at least a high school-style crush going for each other.

I grinned at the floor. The sound of a chair scraping harshly against the wood had my head snapping up.

One of the older gentlemen who had been flirting with me earlier stood from his chair and threw his cards down on the table. "You're a dirty cheat, Arthur, and you always were."

I hustled around the counter as another man—Arthur I assumed—stood, as well. "I am not, Clint. Just because I'm better at cards than you doesn't make me a cheat."

I made it to the table just as it seemed the two might come to blows. "Now, fellas, what's going on?"

Clint's gaze jumped to me. "That-that no-good Art is a dirty cheat."

"Am not!" Arthur huffed.

"Well, I've never played bridge, so I'm not sure I'd really be a good person to judge if someone was cheating."

Both Clint and Arthur looked at me with shocked stares. "You've never played bridge?" Clint asked, all of his earlier anger suddenly gone from his voice.

I shrugged a shoulder. "Nope."

Arthur shook his head. "Well, that's just a travesty."

Clint leaned in closer to me. "We could teach ya, you know."

"You'd do that?"

Clint's chest puffed up. "Of course."

"I'd love it. I'm not working this time next week. Can I come to your game?"

"We'd love to have a pretty lady like you at our table," Arthur offered.

"I'll be there. But right now, I have to get back to work." I breathed a sigh of relief as I headed back to the counter.

Jensen was back behind the register and wore a shit-eating grin. "You handled them better than I could have. Sometimes, they get so bad, I have no choice but to kick them out."

I let out a little laugh. "They're definitely passionate."

"Understatement of the century. I'd say you've earned a break. Why don't you take your fifteen."

I glanced at my watch. "Sure. Do you mind if I head out back for some fresh air?"

"Of course, not."

I waved to Tessa on my way through the kitchen to the back steps. I'd been careful since our first encounter not to make any sudden movements around her or come up from behind. "I'm just taking a quick break."

She gave me a small smile. "Want some tea to take with you?"

"I'd love an iced lemongrass."

Tessa made quick work of pouring me a glass. "Here you go."

"You're an angel sent from Heaven for overheated waitresses."

She ducked her head. "No problem."

I stepped out into the afternoon sun, the breeze lifting my hair off my neck, and took a sip of my tea nirvana. I slipped my cell out of my back pocket. I had to tell my mom about my date with two vicious bridge players next week. She would get such a kick out of that whole scene.

My thumb froze over the first contact in my favorites. My breath locked in my lungs. I couldn't call my mom and tell her about Art and Clint and all the ridiculous shenanigans at my new job because she wouldn't answer. I started breathing again, but it came in quick pants. She would never answer again. I'd never be able to tell her about something that made me laugh or cry or rage.

My hands started to feel all tingly, and I lost my hold on the glass of tea. It shattered on the asphalt at my feet, liquid splashing my jeans. My mom was dead.

"Taylor?" The soft voice seemed to come from far away. "Taylor, are you okay?"

Tessa appeared in my wobbly vision, but I couldn't seem to form words. *Why couldn't I catch my breath?*

"Taylor, I think you're having a panic attack." I could feel the gentle pressure of what I assumed was a hand on my back. "I want you to focus on that bench over there. Look at that bench, and you're going to breathe in for three and out for three."

My eyes zeroed in on the seat, but I couldn't seem to get my lungs to obey.

"In for three, okay? One, two, three." Tessa's hand rubbed up and down my back. "That's good. Now, out for three. One, two, three."

Tessa kept counting, not stopping until my hands no longer shook, and I slowly came back to myself.

"Here, sit on the step for a minute."

I gazed at Tessa. Her brow was creased with worry, but her eyes held understanding. "How did you know what was happening?"

Tessa sat down on the step next to me. "I heard the glass shatter and wanted to make sure you were all right. When I came out, you didn't answer me, and you were hyperventilating. I put two and two together." My cheeks flamed with embarrassment. Tessa let out a soft huff of air. "I get them sometimes. Panic attacks. So, I know the signs."

I glanced over at her. I wondered what her story was, but I knew I couldn't ask without inviting questions about my own. We sat there quietly for a minute, forming a silent pact not to ask each other the questions neither of us wanted to answer.

I gripped Tessa's hand and squeezed. "Thank you."

"I didn't do anything."

"You did. You kept me from passing out in a pile of glass shards." I winced. "I'll pay for that by the way."

Tessa waved a hand. "Jensen doesn't care about stuff like that. Says it's the price of doing business."

My stomach churned at the thought of Jensen hearing about my incident. "Please don't tell her what happened."

Tessa's head jerked. "I won't if you don't want me to, but don't you want to go home and have a lie-down?"

A small smile tugged at my lips. "Would you?"

Tessa let out a little laugh. "Probably not."

I drew in a steadying breath and rose. "Want to show me

where the broom is? I need to clean up this mess."

"Come on, I'll help."

We swept up the pieces of glass strewn across the pavement, and my hands only shook a little bit. My heart, though... My heart trembled in my chest for the rest of the day.

CHAPTER
Eleven

Walker

MY PHONE BUZZED ON MY DESK FOR WHAT FELT LIKE the twentieth time today.

Caitlin: *Are you sure you don't want to come over tonight?*

It was like she could sense that I was thinking about ending things. She could feel it and was pulling out all the stops. I'd been the recipient of two-dozen homemade cookies and at least three different picture messages that made my eyes bug out of my head.

I typed out a reply.

Me: *I told you, I have plans with my family tonight.*

Not so much premeditated plans, more just me mooching a home-cooked meal off my mom. I was making excuses, I knew it. Normally, I would've told Caitlin that I'd meet up with her after dinner, but I needed some space. Space and a good night's sleep if I was going to have the energy for the epic meltdown that was sure to happen when I ended things tomorrow.

Because I was ending things tomorrow. I couldn't drag this out.

Caitlin: *I could come over to your parents' for dinner.*

I cringed. This breakup was going to be bad. Caitlin was a lot of wonderful things: funny, caring, great in bed. But she didn't always take not getting her way well.

Me: *Sorry, just family tonight. But why don't I come by after work tomorrow.*

Caitlin: *That would be great! I'll wear that red number you like.*

I dropped my head into my palm.

A knock sounded on my door. "Come in."

Clark pushed open the door, stepped in, then closed it behind him.

"Hey, Chief. What's up?"

Clark took a seat in one of the chairs opposite mine across the desk. "We've got another missing girl."

My earlier worries seemed insignificant now. I straightened in my chair. "Another hiker?"

Clark rubbed a hand along his jaw. "No. This is a gal in her twenties from Willow Creek. Her boyfriend reported her missing when she didn't come home from her shift at the diner in town. Her car was still in the lot. No signs of a struggle. Just vanished."

"Is it possible she ran off? Another guy?"

"Don't know. The chief down there didn't know her well, but they have an even smaller department than we do, and way more citizens to cover. He just called to give us a heads-up and asked us to keep an eye out."

"You got a picture?"

Clark reached into his pocket and fished out his phone. After tapping a few things on the screen, he handed it to me.

The photo had me sucking in a breath that felt like it was made of glass shards. The woman on the screen looked eerily like Julie. Straight, dark brown hair, deep brown eyes, and rounded cheeks. My heart spasmed. I swallowed against my dry-as-a-desert throat and looked up to meet Clark's gaze. "I don't have a lot going on here today. Why don't I head down there and see what's what. There might be something else we can do, but at the very least, I can get the full story."

Clark studied me for a moment, surely weighing his options. "Sure, Walk. That sounds like a good idea."

I shoved to my feet, my chair rolling back to softly collide with the wall. "You'll be my first stop when I'm back."

Clark jerked his chin in affirmation and headed out the door.

Ashlee startled behind the reception desk as I strode through. "Everything okay, Walker?"

I was sure I didn't have the happiest of looks on my face. But I did my best to soften my expression. "Yeah. I'm heading out. Will you forward all calls to my cell?"

Ashlee's eyes took on a look of concern, but she nodded. "Of course. Let me know if I can help with anything."

"Thanks. Will do." With that, I was gone.

I clenched my fists so hard, it was a wonder I didn't dislocate a knuckle as I paced the floor in Clark's office. I'd spent the past three hours doing recon that the Willow Creek Police Department was either stretched too thin or too lazy to do. I leaned towards lazy.

"The boyfriend is a total waste of space. A drunk. Word around town is that she supports him, and he thanks her with his fists." Rage was coursing through my veins. This guy had a beautiful, kind woman who only wanted his love, and what did he do? Abused her trust and broke her body.

I didn't know that for sure, but all the pieces led there. "That fucking joke of a PD down there hasn't done shit. Too stupid or too lazy, sitting around with their thumbs up their asses."

"Walker, take a breath."

I scowled at Clark. I didn't want to take a fucking breath. I wanted to plant my fist in that jackass of a boyfriend's face. It was a miracle I hadn't. I clenched and unclenched my fists, trying to slow my breathing.

Clark leaned back in his chair. "Did you fill the WCPD chief in on what you found out?"

I ground my back molars together. "Yes. Of course. But I'm not all that optimistic they're going to do their fucking jobs."

"I'll make sure they do. I'll get county or state involved if I have to, but I'll make sure they follow through."

I let out a slow breath. "I need to get out of here, clear my head. You mind if I take off an hour early? I'll make it up tomorrow."

"I know you're good for it. Get out of here and come back tomorrow with your head on straight."

"I will. Thank you."

Clark nodded and I took off. Thankfully, Ashlee wasn't sitting at her desk when I passed through reception. I wasn't sure I could've made polite conversation this go-around. I jogged down the steps of the building and towards my truck. In less than a minute, I was pulling out of the lot.

I drove in circles for a while, aimlessly crisscrossing town streets, going out into the country and then coming back to town again. But I knew there was only one place I really wanted to go. Somewhere that would bring me peace. It had been the same when Julie was alive. She was always my port in the storm.

I pulled over next to the cemetery and shut off my truck. Climbing down, I let the fresh air soothe my frayed temper. I could only hear the rustling of the branches in the wind, my footsteps silenced by the cushion of lush grass.

I navigated the familiar path to her grave and touched the curved stone's surface, worn rough by weather over the years. "Hey, Angel." It was fitting that the nickname I'd bestowed on her was what she'd become. In my darkest days after her death, I'd convinced myself that I'd caused her demise by giving her the name. I didn't think that anymore, but I was still more cautious with my monikers these days.

"It's been a hell of a day. Just needed to unwind with my best girl for a bit." I crouched in front of the headstone, letting my fingers trace the letters of her name. I always stuttered when I got to her last name. I had been so sure it would become Cole. There was never a doubt in my mind, but life threw you some nasty curveballs.

I sat down on the grass and, for the next hour, I filled Julie in on life. I told her that I was breaking up with Caitlin. "I wish these conversations weren't so one-sided. I could really use some pointers on that one." People would have probably thought it totally weird if they heard me, but Julie and I had always told each other everything. I didn't want to lose that, even if she were no longer here.

The first time I'd slept with someone after she'd passed, I came to the cemetery afterward and bawled like a fucking baby. From that moment on, I just kept spilling my guts to the silent headstone.

Today, I also filled Julie in on my grandma's attempt to learn hatchet throwing, Noah's encounter with his hero MMA fighter, and the new neighbor who kept popping up in my mind. I told her everything I could think of until I ran out things to say. But I felt better.

I pushed to my feet. Bending at the waist, I pressed my lips to the rough stone. "Thanks, Angel. Love you forever and always."

CHAPTER
Twelve

Taylor

I OPTED FOR A WALK TO CLEAR MY HEAD BEFORE I GOT behind the wheel to drive home. Thank goodness my SUV had arrived this morning. I don't think I could have taken a ride home with Jensen. My nerves were too frayed.

I'd made it through the rest of my shift, but barely. It took almost an hour for my hands to stop their faint tremor. I'd dropped someone's change on the floor when attempting to hand it to them. Tessa, sensing I was still a little unsteady on my feet, took to handing the customers their teas directly so there were no more broken-glass disasters.

I let the early evening air, still warm from the sun, ease my frayed nerves. I inhaled deeply, that sweet pine scent so prevalent here easing me even further. It wasn't long before I reached the edge of the downtown area. The sidewalks shifted to grass, and the asphalt of the road turned to dirt and gravel.

A bird call caught my attention, and I looked toward the sound. My stomach dropped. A cemetery. Because what I needed after my afternoon was more reminders of the dead and the forgotten. I was about to turn around when my gaze caught on a figure.

He was sitting on the grass, legs sprawled out in front of him and his back resting against the headstone behind him while he faced another. He seemed to be talking to someone. But there was no one there. Walker. His just-shy-of-black hair gleamed in the sun. His tanned skin picked up the fiery hues of the waning day as the sun sank lower in the sky. He was beautiful.

I stood there, watching him. I couldn't help it. It was as if I were frozen to the spot. *Who was he visiting? Who had he lost?* Both of his parents were alive, and he had a grandmother. Jensen had mentioned all three in the present tense while we worked. Maybe he was visiting his grandfather's grave.

Walker pushed to his feet then bent over and did something that stole the breath from my lungs. He kissed the headstone. The gesture was tender and heartbreaking all at once. A sob clogged the back of my throat, and tears pricked at my eyes. I shouldn't be here. I was trespassing on what was clearly a very private moment.

I turned on my heel to leave but only made it three steps before a voice called out to me. "Taylor?"

I halted my steps and turned to face Walker. I expected his eyes to be sad, his face ravaged by grief and pain, but there was none of that. What I saw was a look of peace and maybe a little curiosity regarding what the hell I was doing at a cemetery on the outskirts of town.

"I'm so sorry." My cheeks heated. "I didn't mean to intrude."

A small grin tipped his full lips. "You didn't. Plus, I'm pretty sure this is public land."

I twisted the ring on my right finger in circles. "I know. I just… You were having a moment, and it was private."

Walker's face softened. "It's okay, Taylor. I was just visiting with someone."

My gaze jumped around, not quite sure where to settle.

"That's nice. That's good that you visit whoever it is." To my absolute horror, my eyes began to fill with tears.

"Hey, hey now. It's all right." Walker strode two steps forward and pulled me into him. His muscled arms held me tightly in what could only be called a bear hug. His embrace didn't make my skin crawl like so many of the other comforting gestures directed my way had begun to do. Maybe because it was firm and strong when so many of my friends' affections seemed unsure. Maybe it was because this man clearly knew what it meant to lose someone he loved.

I let myself relax into Walker's embrace. Just for a few moments. Just so I could pull myself together. I bit the inside of my cheek until I tasted blood. The flare of pain helped the tears to recede, and I pushed away from Walker's hard chest.

"I'm sorry," I mumbled, wiping at my tears while I stared at the ground. "I've just had a long day. I didn't mean to get weepy on you. I'll just get back to my car."

Walker's hand caught my elbow as I turned to go. "Slow down." He turned me back to him, but I refused to meet his eyes. He placed two fingers under my chin and lifted. The pads of his fingertips were rough against my soft skin. I swallowed hard.

His eyes searched mine, looking for something, peering into my soul. "There's nothing to be ashamed about when it comes to feeling deeply."

I pressed my lips together and nodded. His hand fell away.

"I'll walk you back to your car."

He was too close. He saw too much. "That's not necessary. I'm fine now. Promise." I forced a smile that felt wonky.

"I could use an excuse to stretch my legs. Honestly, you'd be doing me a favor."

My nails dug into my palms. He didn't play fair. "Fine."

Walker let out a chuckle that seemed to rumble through my body. "Thank you."

We were quiet for the first few minutes of our walk, only the wind and the beginnings of the crickets' evening song keeping us company. Then, Walker had to go and ruin it. "What gave you the tough day?"

My muscles tensed, and I fought to keep my face neutral. "I didn't say tough, I said long. I'm just tired. I get emotional when I'm tired."

"Mmm-hmm." He might as well have said, "bullshit."

I clenched my fists and picked up my pace. Unfortunately, my short strides, no matter how quick, were no match for Walker's long ones.

As we approached The Tea Kettle, my buddies from earlier appeared. Arthur and Clint wore mischievous grins, but it was Art who spoke. "Now, Mr. Cole, what are you doing with our Taylor this evening?"

Walker's brows rose. "Your Taylor?"

"Yes, our Taylor. We've taken her under our wing and are going to show her the ropes."

Walker's gaze turned to me. "I think that sounds like a great plan."

My skin began to itch as Art's and Clint's gazes traveled from me to Walker and back again. I needed to get out of here. Too many eyes. Too much attention. "It was nice to see you gentlemen again. Great running into you, Walker. I need to get home now. See you later."

I didn't wait for an answer, just took off for the parking lot behind the Kettle. I didn't breathe a sigh of relief until there were at least ten blocks between the man who saw too much and me.

CHAPTER
Thirteen

Walker

D AWN WAS JUST BEGINNING TO SHOW ITS FIRST glimmers of light as rocks crunched beneath my sneakers. I loved running in the early light. The air was cool, few cars were on the road, and I often spotted animals that usually liked to avoid human interaction.

Three miles outside the ranch's main gate, I spotted a small form up ahead. Her strides were strong and purposeful but no match for my own. Before long, she glanced over her shoulder at the sound of my approaching steps, her golden ponytail swinging. Her head swiveled right back around, and she just kept running.

I quickened my pace until I was right beside her. "I thought you promised that you wouldn't go walking or running while it was dark out."

Taylor's jaw tightened. "It was getting light when I left."

"Bullshit."

She blew out a harsh breath. "I have reflectors on my shoes and shorts. I even got a mini bear spray at the hardware store. I'll be fine."

I fell back a step and let my gaze fall to her delectable, heart-shaped ass. There was indeed a reflector there.

"Happy?" she bit out.

Thoughts of the missing hiker we still had no signs of filled my head. "No, I'm not happy. You shouldn't be running alone, it's too risky."

Taylor stopped in the middle of the road and whirled on me. "Oh, but it's okay for *you* to run alone? Why? Does you having a dick, magically stop bears from attacking you?"

My frustration bubbled to the surface. "No. *This* stops bears from attacking me." I pulled my 9mm out of the specialty athletic shorts I wore that allowed me to carry while running.

Color leached from Taylor's face, and I immediately regretted my decision. Shit. I slowly slid the gun back into the holster. "Why are you running with a Glock?"

Surprise flared at her correct identification of my weapon. She wasn't scared of that, but something had her freaked. I crept closer. "Because I'm a cop, and there are wild animals around here that don't always react kindly when startled."

Her head bobbed up and down slowly. I slipped a hand around the juncture of her neck and jaw. Fuck, her skin, damp with a sheen of sweat, was one of the softest things I'd ever felt. "Look at me, Taylor." Her gaze came back to focus on mine. "Everything's fine, I just don't want you running alone."

She made no agreement. I squeezed her neck. "Please. I'll run with you before or after work, anytime you want. But you could get seriously hurt while you are by yourself, and no one would know because you don't tell anyone where you're going."

Stubbornness came into her eyes. I liked that a hell of a lot more than the fear that had been there earlier. Taylor's chin raised in defiance. "I'd run with you, but I'm pretty sure you can't keep up with me."

"All right, Short-stack, let's try it out. I'll take you on my typical morning route." She'd be begging me to turn back before we reached the halfway point, I just knew it.

"Lead on, Bigfoot."

I chuckled and took off towards my favorite spot in all of Sutter Lake. Somehow, her quick, short strides matched up perfectly with my slightly slower long ones. There was a peaceful rhythm to our run. Side by side in silence.

I led her through winding dirt roads around the outskirts of my family's ranch. She was a trooper when we had to scale over a fence to get back onto Cole land, and even as we climbed a hillside. She never tired, never slowed. She was amazing. We went higher and higher until we reached the top of the ridge.

Taylor gasped when she saw the view. All of Sutter Lake—the town and the lake itself—was bathed in the pink light of early morning. I'd never come here with anyone who wasn't my family. Never even brought Julie here. It had been instinct to bring Taylor here. I hadn't even really thought about it.

"It's beautiful," she breathed.

"It's my favorite place in the whole world."

"Thank you for sharing it with me."

"You're welcome."

We stood shoulder-to-shoulder, staring out at the view, neither of us saying anything for a moment. Taylor cleared her throat. I tilted my head to take her in. She was still looking forward, but she rubbed the ring on her right hand with her thumb. She seemed to do that when she was nervous. "I can't sleep."

My brows pulled together. "What?"

"I have a hard time sleeping. That's why I work out so much. It's the only thing that seems to help."

My chest felt tight. It was the first thing she had freely told me about herself. It was worth its weight in gold. I was honored that she'd given it to me, but I knew if I made a big deal out of it, she'd shut down. "Makes sense."

She turned her head so that her gaze met mine. "I'll text you the next time I want to go running."

My lips tipped up. "I'd appreciate it. It'd be bad for business if a tenant got mauled by a mountain lion."

Taylor shoved her shoulder into me, and I wrapped an arm around her. She fit perfectly.

I paused outside Caitlin's door, my hand hovering just in front of her apartment number. Fuck. I did not want to do this. I knocked three times.

Hurried footsteps sounded, and the door swung open. "Baby. I'm so glad you're here." Caitlin's hair was piled on top of her head in artful curls. Her face was done up to the nines, including her lips with that red stuff I hated because I always came away from kissing her looking like the Joker. She wore a low-cut tank top and shorts so short, they looked more like underwear.

I shuffled my feet. "Hey, Cait."

She leaned in to kiss me, but I brushed my lips against her cheek instead, then hurried inside. I headed for the couch, patting the seat next to mine. "Come here."

Caitlin's lips pressed together in a thin, hard line. "Is something wrong, honey?"

What was with all the pet names all of a sudden? She'd only ever called me Walker before. I steeled my spine. "I think we should stop seeing each other." I'd thought of at least a dozen different ways to say it. But, at the end of the day, I needed to shut the door, and she needed to know I wasn't leaving it cracked open for later. Some people might consider me a bastard for just coming right out with it and not tempering the blow, but I've always thought honesty is the kindest route you could take.

Caitlin's mouth opened and closed like a fish on a line. Her lower lip began to tremble as tears filled her eyes. "Why?"

"I'm not the one for you, Cait. You'll find someone who can't wait to settle down with you. Get married, have lots of babies. But that just isn't me."

She reached out and gripped my hand, hard. "Walker, I'm sorry I pushed about moving in together."

I fought the grimace that wanted to surface. "It's not just that—"

Caitlin jumped in before I could continue. "I can wait as long as you need." Tears spilled over her bottom lids, causing my gut to clench. "Please, Walker. I love you."

"I'm sorry, Cait. My mind's made up. I care about you, and you're a wonderful woman. You're just not the woman for me."

Her jaw got hard, and her tears seemed to evaporate into thin air. "It's not you, it's me."

I cringed. It was cliched, but true. There was nothing wrong with Caitlin, we just weren't right for each other. "We're just not the right match."

"And who are you the right match with? That new bitch renting your parents' cabin?" My eyes widened. Where had that come from? "Oh, didn't think I knew about her, did you? Bridgette saw you walking with her in town last night when you were supposed to be with your family." Caitlin stood, throwing her hands wide. "How long have you been cheating on me?"

I pushed to my feet, my gaze going hard. "Hey, now. I have never been unfaithful to you. That's not the kind of man I am, and you know it. I ran into Taylor and was walking her to her car. We're friends." Friends seemed like a bit of a stretch, but she'd told me something about herself that morning. Something it was clear she didn't tell many people.

"Oh, well thank you, Mr. High And Mighty Walker Cole, for breaking up with me *before* you went out and screwed the new girl."

"I'm not going out and screwing anyone right now. I'm just

saying we aren't the right match. I don't know that I'll *ever* find that." An image flashed in my mind of Taylor's compact curves as she ran through the morning air. So, I was attracted to her. That didn't mean I was going to act on it. She was fragile right now. She needed a friend, not some guy trying to get his rocks off with no ability to love her the way she deserved.

"Everyone thinks you're such a *great guy*. Let's see what happens when they find out what a heartless bastard you really are."

Great, just what I needed. Caitlin was going to spread her lies, and in a town the size of Sutter Lake, they'd spread like wildfire. I couldn't believe I'd never seen this side of her before. Jensen had warned me that Cait had a vicious streak, but I'd thought she was exaggerating. Apparently, not. "Caitlin. We were friends before we started dating, can't we just go back to that?"

She picked up an empty wine glass that had been sitting on the coffee table waiting to be filled and threw it at the wall. Glass flew in every direction. "I don't want to be your fucking friend, Walker! I was to be your *wife*!"

My eyes bugged out just a bit. My wife? We'd been seeing each other exclusively for three months. How did three months of seeing each other a couple of times a week equate to getting married? I swallowed. "I'm sorry, but I can't give you that."

"Get out!" she shrieked.

I didn't have to be told twice. I headed for the door.

"And you are going to have to fucking grovel when you come crawling back to me. Because you will come crawling back, Walker Cole."

Dear God, I hoped not.

CHAPTER
Fourteen

Taylor

I HOISTED A BAG OF GROCERIES FROM MY CART INTO THE back of my SUV. It was lucky my wheels had arrived when they did, I'd been running out of food.

"Taylor! Did your car arrive?" I turned to see Sarah and an elderly woman walking towards me. "Walker said you were waiting on it, and I've been meaning to stop by to see if I could take you anywhere."

"It came the other morning, just in time for me to start work."

"Oh, good. Now you won't have to run into town."

I chuckled. "Well, I still might do that."

Sarah shook her head and smiled. "Taylor, this is my mother-in-law, Irma Cole. Mom, this is Taylor Lawson."

Irma gave me a toothy grin. "Ah, the infamous Taylor. Young Noah has been talking about you and your friends nonstop."

"That's sweet."

"I've also been hearing lots about you from Jensen and Walker. It's nice to officially meet you." There was a mischievous glint in the woman's eyes that put me on alert.

It would make sense for Jensen to mention me since we

worked together now, but what reason did Walker have to talk about me? I toyed with the ring on my finger. "It's nice to meet you, too."

The smile deepened on Irma's lined face. "I think you and Walker would be just the right fit. I can tell you're someone who won't let him steamroll you. You'll stand your ground. I know these kinds of things because I'm a little psychic."

A flash of panic seared through me. "I'm not sure what you're talking about. I barely know Walker."

"You will," Irma said with a cackling laugh.

"Mom, quit it, you're scaring the girl." Sarah turned towards me. "She's an instigator, this one. Just giving you a hard time because Walker came home fit to be tied that you were planning on walking back to the guest cabin alone. You shouldn't do that, by the way. He's right about the cougars."

I breathed a sigh of relief. "I won't. Now that I have my car, I won't walk or run anywhere when it's dark out." Walker's frustration and concern from the morning before flashed in my mind.

"I'm relieved to hear it," Sarah said, reaching out to pat my hand. The gesture was so familiar, something my mom used to do constantly when we talked. A pang of loneliness hit me in that spot right between the breasts. "Listen, why don't you come to dinner tonight. We're making a pot roast and all the fixings, with marionberry pie for dessert."

It was on the tip of my tongue to say no. To make up an excuse. I'd planned to microwave some mac and cheese. But Sarah's phantom familiarity made it difficult to refuse. That trickle of loneliness flowing through my veins pushed me into agreeing to something I'd sworn to avoid.

I cleared my throat. "I'd love to."

Sarah clasped her hands in front of her chest. "Wonderful."

"Can I bring a couple bottles of wine? I'd offer to cook something, but I'm afraid I'm pretty hopeless in that department."

One of my goals for this year was to learn to cook. I'd done a search for beginner recipes and printed a few things out but hadn't moved past the planning stage.

"That's so sweet of you. The boys aren't big wine drinkers, but why don't you bring a bottle for us girls."

"I'd be happy to."

"Great. Why don't you come over around six. We eat on the earlier side since Noah has an 8:30 bedtime."

"That sounds perfect. See you then." I turned to Walker's grandmother, who was studying me with an attention to detail that had my palms sweating. "It was lovely to meet you, Irma."

"You too, honey pie," she said with that twinkle in her eye. "I look forward to seeing what tonight has in store."

"Oh, stop it, Mom," Sarah said. Rolling her eyes at me, she continued. "If we let Irma have more than one glass of wine tonight, we're likely in store for some off-key show tunes." A soft laugh escaped my lips.

"You lie, Sarah," Irma huffed. "My pitch is perfect."

I threw my car in park and rubbed a damp palm down my jeans-clad leg. I hoped that jeans were the right choice. Sutter Lake seemed like a casual environment, so as I'd strewn clothing all over my bedroom, I'd decided against the maroon cocktail dress and gone with dark skinny jeans and a pale blue top that brought out the color of my eyes.

I fidgeted with my keys. I could do this. I'd repeated that over and over as I got ready. Over and over as I drove. But one more time couldn't hurt. I could do this. I could spend time with the Cole family and not let them into my heart.

All I had to do was keep an emotional distance. I'd become an expert at dodging personal questions over the past few months. This dinner would be no different. I could enjoy the family's company without their closeness breaking my heart. I just needed to keep that distance.

I pushed open my door and slid out, grabbing my purse and the two bottles of wine from the passenger seat as I went. I studied the house as I walked up. It must have been designed by the same person who built the cabin because the styles were perfect complements to each other. The ranch house had the same dark wood-beamed façade and lots of windows. A wraparound porch hugged the outside and was home to eight rocking chairs and a porch swing. It was the perfect family home.

As I climbed the porch steps, the front door swung open, and Noah rushed out. "Tay Tay! You're here! Come and see my airplanes!"

I let out a light laugh. "I'd love to see your planes."

Jensen appeared in the doorway. "After dinner, okay, Noah?"

"Okay. I know all there is to know about planes. You might not know a lot about them, but don't worry, I can teach you." He had taken hold of my hand and was pulling me up the stairs and inside the house. I grinned at Jensen.

"He's not kidding. If he doesn't end up a pilot or a mechanic, I'll be shocked."

"Fighter pilot, Mom. You know that," Noah said as he dropped my hand and went racing away.

Jensen winced, turning her gaze back to me. "I'm hoping he'll change his mind and shift to a career path that has a slightly lower mortality rate."

"He's got time."

"Thank goodness for that. Ooooh, did you bring wine?"

I raised the two bottles, one in each hand. "You know it."

Jensen clasped her hands under her chin. "My hero."

I let out a laugh. "Girl after my own heart."

Jensen took one of the bottles from my hand, studying the label. "And you've got good taste, too. I knew I liked you." She began leading me back to what looked like an open kitchen and dining space. "We should go out next weekend. The saloon is having a live band, and Mom said she'd watch Noah for me if I wanted to go."

I hesitated for a moment and then reminded myself that spending time with these people didn't mean I had to bare my soul to them. "Sure. That sounds like fun."

"Woohoo, girls' night!" Jensen called, raising the bottle of wine triumphantly in the air.

"What's going on?" The familiar, rough voice that sent a shiver down my spine sounded from my left.

Jensen threw an arm around my shoulders. "Well, big brother, lock up your friends, because Taylor and I are going out on the town on Saturday."

Walker scrubbed a hand over his face. "Shit."

Jensen released me and smacked her brother on the shoulder. "Language." Turning back to me, she continued, "I'll go open this and pour us each a glass."

"Thanks." It came out as a mumble because I was suddenly aware of every cell of my being and my proximity to Walker Cole.

His gaze traveled over my face and down my body, each movement feeling like a physical caress. "You look beautiful, Short-stack."

I cleared my throat. "Thank you. You don't look so bad yourself."

He moved closer until I could feel the heat of his body brushing up against mine. "I'm glad you came." The words were low, only for us to hear.

"It was nice of your mother to invite me."

Walker smirked. "So, it's just my invites you turn down?"

"I—" I started, but was cut off by a cackle behind us.

Irma emerged from what looked like a study. "I love it! You two are going to make gorgeous babies, you know. And lots of them. Your whole house will be full."

Heat filled my cheeks as I instinctively stepped back from Walker, creating space between us. I immediately felt cold.

Walker groaned. "Grandma, quit it with your crazy talk. You're freaking Taylor out."

Irma clucked her tongue at her grandson. "You know I'm a little bit psychic."

Walker shook his head. "You are not. Predicting that our town's little league team would win the state championship doesn't make you psychic."

Irma harrumphed. "I knew Sarah was the one for your father. Without my meddling, they never would have ended up together."

"Whatever you say, Grandma." Walker extended an arm. "Come on, Taylor, let's go get you a drink."

Once I had wine to sip, I was introduced to Walker's father, Andrew, who seemed like a kind man. He had a quiet strength about him, similar to Walker's own. Dinner passed in joyful chaos, and I was surprised to find that it wasn't difficult to be there.

I had never experienced this kind of large family gathering before, one where people talked over and around one another, with three different conversations happening all at once. For as long as I could remember, it had only been my mom and me. My dad had left when I was two, and my mom's parents had passed before I was born.

I wondered what it would have been like to have a sibling to share the burden of the last couple of years with. Or a father who gave a shit. I'd never know.

My life had never lacked in love, though. My mom worked herself to the bone to make sure I had everything a kid with two parents had. She was both mother and father. She was my everything.

I felt tears burn the backs of my eyes as I stared at my coffee cup. A hand brushed my shoulder, and I was suddenly jolted back to the present moment. We had finished dinner and were sitting in the living room, chatting. I turned to see the hand's owner. Walker. He studied me with an intensity that made me want to squirm in my seat. I knew he saw more than I wanted him to. Time to go.

I forced a smile to my lips. "It's getting late. I'd better get home. Thank you so much for dinner, it was delicious."

Sarah beamed. "Thank you for coming. You're welcome anytime."

I rose from my seat, Walker doing the same.

Irma cleared her throat. She was studying me in the same way her grandson did—like she recognized something in me that I didn't want identified. "Walker, why don't you follow Taylor home. Make sure she gets there all right."

My shoulders stiffened. "That isn't necessary."

Sarah stood from her chair, crossing the space to take my coffee cup. "Actually, that's a great idea. The roads on our property are so dark. It would make me feel a lot better if I knew you got home safely."

I was powerless against Sarah and her pleading eyes. I pressed my lips together and nodded.

I said my goodbyes to the rest of the family and headed for the door. A hand pressed against my lower back, and heat flared to life, my body tightening in response. How was it that my brain knew Walker was nothing but trouble and heartache for me, but my body yearned for his touch? There was a magnetic pull between us that had me fighting against leaning into his hand, curling into his side, and nuzzling his neck.

I dug my nails into my palms, hoping the pain would break the spell Walker wove around me. "Let's go." His voice was a low rumble, sending vibrations through my ear, and weaving his hold tighter around me.

I sucked in a breath and moved forward. I tried to rush without looking like I was doing so. I wanted to create some distance between us. I didn't want the heat of his palm kissing my skin. The problem was, I was about a foot shorter than Walker. No matter how fast my little legs moved, they couldn't seem to escape Walker's long, forceful strides.

The walk to my car felt like an expedition up Everest, but we finally made it. I beeped my locks, and Walker opened my door. "Thank you." It came out as a whisper.

His gaze was intense on my face. "You're welcome. Do you want me to lead or follow?"

"Lead." I was worried I'd drive off the road if I knew he was behind me, evaluating my driving, analyzing my face in the rearview mirror, seeing into my soul.

"All right." He gently shut the door.

I tried to force myself not to hold the steering wheel too tightly. The night was almost over. As I followed Walker's truck through the winding gravel road, I imagined the long, hot bath I'd take when I got home. How I'd let the steaming water relax the muscles that had wound tight from Walker's stare and his touch.

I clenched my thighs together in an attempt to relieve some pressure. This was ridiculous. I probably just needed to get laid. Maybe I'd find some tourist to heat up the sheets with when Jensen and I went out on Saturday. A tourist wouldn't stick around, so there was no risk of anyone getting too close. Now that sounded like a good plan.

Walker pulled into an open spot at the front of the cabin, and I hit the remote on my visor. The garage door opened. I prayed that Walker would stay in his car. But, of course, he didn't. By the time I'd shut off my engine, he was opening my car door. I jumped in my seat.

"Geez, give a girl a heart attack, why don't you."

Walker let out a chuckle. "Just trying to be a gentleman."

I narrowed my eyes at him. "Sure, you are." He was trying to rile me. That's what he was doing. He seemed to get some perverse pleasure out of pushing my buttons. I tightened my hold on my keys, the metal digging into my palm. "Can you please move so I can get out of my car?"

He stepped back, but barely. And when I had to squeeze by him to get to the door, our entire bodies brushed. My eyes shot to his. There was heat blazing in his green depths. My heart quickened, and my breaths turned shallow. "I need to get inside."

He blinked a few times as if coming back to himself and then shook his head. "Sorry." The one word had a bite to it, and his jaw tensed. He stepped back even farther, his fists opening and closing.

His change in demeanor had my brows furrowing. I managed to nod but didn't say anything, just ducked my chin and rushed inside, wondering what I'd done to piss Walker Cole off.

CHAPTER
Fifteen

Walker

I SLAMMED MY TRUCK'S DOOR WITH ENOUGH FORCE TO SEND the entire vehicle rocking. I adjusted my jeans, attempting to relieve some of the pressure. My dick was hard enough to split wood. Fuck.

I started the engine and hit the extra clicker to shut Taylor's garage door. The attraction I felt for her was only growing, and I had no idea what to do about it. When her tight little body had brushed up against mine in the garage, I'd felt flames lick my skin.

Honestly, it was freaking me out. What Julie and I had shared was a pure, innocent love. We were each other's first everything. Bumbling and fumbling hands and bodies. Learning what each other liked and didn't. It was perfect. But it wasn't this fiery, living, breathing energy I felt coming to life with Taylor.

It pissed me off. It was ridiculous for me to be angry at someone for turning me on in a way my dead girlfriend never had, but I was. I rolled down my window and let the chilly night air ease my temper and cool my overheated skin.

I inhaled deeply. None of this mattered. What Taylor needed

right now was a friend. And I wasn't even sure she'd let me be that, let alone have more than friendship.

Pulling up my gravel drive, I saw the darkened windows of an empty home. *Was this how it would always be? Empty and dark?*

I switched off the engine and hopped down from the cab to make my way up my front porch steps. "Pull up a rocker, would ya?" The voice had me going for my gun on instinct. But I relaxed when my brain processed that it was my grandmother.

"What in the world are you doing sitting here alone in the dark? And how in the hell did you get here?"

"Oh, relax. I'm just enjoying looking at the night sky. And I took one of the golf carts."

I let out an exasperated sigh. "Grandma, you know you're not supposed to be driving anymore. Do Mom and Dad even know you're gone?"

"Golf carts don't count," Grandma huffed.

I took that to mean that my parents had no idea she wasn't asleep in her bed at that moment. I sank into the rocker next to her. "So, what was so important you had to drag your ass out of bed and come all the way over here?"

She shook her head. "I won't have you sassing me, young man."

"Sorry, Grandma. Please, tell me what's wrong."

"That's better." My grandmother was quiet for a few beats with only the noise of the rocker against the wood-planked porch and the night insects breaking the silence. "I'm worried about Taylor."

I stiffened, pausing the motion of my rocker. "Why?"

"She's grieving," my grandmother said, pain in her voice.

"How do you know that?" I hadn't shared a word of what Austin had told me with anyone, not even my family.

"I've been around the block a time or two. I know what grief looks like."

I reached out, taking my grandmother's papery hand in my own. She would know. She'd lost a child at a young age, and a husband in her prime. She knew grief better than most. "I'm sorry, Gran."

"Thank you, hon. But this isn't about me. I just hurt for her."

I tipped my rocker back and forth, staring out at the dark fields in front of me. "Her mom died a few months ago."

My grandma's face crumpled. "Poor thing."

"And her dad is a fucking loser who abandoned her." I sucked in a harsh breath, the cool night air burning my lungs. "She has almost no one."

"I was worried about that." Gran paused again. "Someone needs to be there for that girl." She eyed me meaningfully. "Knock down some of those walls. If she doesn't let someone in, and soon, those barriers will petrify, and nothing and no one will get through."

My stomach tightened. "I don't know if I'm the right—"

"Of course, you are," my grandmother said, the words forceful and resolute. Her tone softened. "I know you have your own weight to carry, but that's exactly why you are the perfect person to get through those walls Taylor's put up."

I listened to the blades of the rocker as they made contact with the wood planks below. "She's most likely leaving in a year. Her friends want her to move back to LA. It's taken me weeks to get her to share even one thing with me. I'm not sure there's enough time."

Gran squeezed my hand. "No one knows what the future will hold, Walker. Just be her friend. Don't let her push you away. Be there when the breakdown happens so you can help turn it into a breakthrough."

Be her friend. I could do that. I just needed to dull this simmering attraction. As we were around each other longer, it would surely begin to fade. I just had to ignore it until then. "All right,

Gran. I'll do my best."

"I know you will." She smiled, her white teeth shining in the moonlight.

My phone buzzed in my pocket. Pulling it out, I grimaced at the screen.

Caitlin: *I'm sorry I overreacted. Please answer my calls. We can work this out. We are so good together.*

I typed out a reply.

Me: *I don't think there's anything left to talk about. You'll find the right guy. It just isn't me.*

I silenced my phone and shoved it back into my pocket. I couldn't deal with Caitlin tonight on top of everything else.

Grandma eyed me curiously. "Everything okay?"

"Yup. Come on. I'll drive you home."

"I wish you'd just let me take the golf cart."

"I'm a cop. I'd have to arrest you for driving without a license."

"Who knew I'd raise a grandson that would turn out to be a narc."

All I could do was chuckle.

CHAPTER
Sixteen

Taylor

A HORN SOUNDED FROM MY DRIVEWAY, AND I SLID MY LIP gloss into my clutch. Ready to go. I grabbed my keys off the hook by the door and headed out.

Jensen let out a wolf whistle through her rolled-down window. "Girl, you look *hot*! Ready to meet some of the local talent?"

I grinned as I opened the SUV's door and hopped inside. "You know it."

Jensen executed a flawless three-point turn, saying, "I'm driving us there but leaving my car. Bryce said he'd drive us home."

"Bryce, huh?" I knew there was love brewing there.

Jensen's cheeks pinked. "We're dating. God, it still feels weird to say that. It's pretty new. I haven't introduced him to Noah as a boyfriend or anything."

"He's definitely sweet on you." Warmth filled my chest. I was happy that Jensen had someone who made her blush at the mention of his name. "This also means I get my pick of all the guys tonight. You really are the perfect wing-woman."

She chuckled. "You're so lucky to have me in your corner. And since I've lived here my whole life, I know everyone's dirty little secrets. I'll pick you out some winners."

"You're an angel sent to Earth just for me."

"You know it. I may not be looking to hook up, but I am looking to have a couple cocktails. I even wrangled Walker into feeding my horses in the morning so I don't have to get up early."

"Your horses?" I'd seen various horses in the fields as I drove between my cabin and the ranch house but hadn't thought much about them. They were pretty to look at, but as a vertically-challenged person, climbing on top of large creatures and galloping at top speeds didn't really appeal to me.

Jensen's eyes lit with a passion and love I'd rarely seen. "Haven't I told you? I have rescue horses."

"Rescue horses?"

"Yup. There is a herd of wild horses not far from here, but sometimes, horses need to be brought out of the wild for health or injury reasons. I take them in. I help rehab them if I can, and I've even trained a few to be ridden."

"Wow. That's amazing. How many do you have?"

"Right now, twenty. But I may be getting another in a few weeks."

"Twenty horses? Who helps you take care of them?"

"Dad lets me mooch some of the ranch hands for the real labor-intensive work, but I do most of the daily stuff myself." She drummed her fingers against the steering wheel to the beat of the country tune on the radio. "Well, with Tessa's help."

"She helps you take care of the horses?"

Jensen grinned. "She's a wisp of a thing, but she's a hard worker."

"She's really kind." I flashed back to Tessa's gentle comfort during my panic attack.

"The kindest." Jensen's face grew serious. "I don't know her story, but someone hurt that girl. She came to Sutter Lake about a year ago and applied for a job at the Kettle. Barely said two words in the interview, but I couldn't say no. She lives above the shop and helps me with the horses as her rent payment."

My stomach pitched at the idea of someone hurting Tessa, but the pieces seemed to fit. "I'm glad you gave her a place to stay."

"Me, too. She has a special way with the horses, especially one that was hurt real bad. They bonded when no one else could reach the mare. Tessa nursed her back to health."

"That's incredible." What would it feel like to have that kind of connection with another creature?

Jensen swung her SUV into the saloon parking lot. It was already almost full, but she found a spot towards the back. "Let's do this."

We made our way through the swinging double doors. Music poured out into the night, and a frisson of excitement teased my belly.

Jensen grabbed my hand and led me through a packed crowd towards an equally busy bar. She waved at one of the bartenders, a stocky but handsome man, who gestured back and pointed to the end of the bar. "Hey, Little J, what'll it be?"

Jensen's face scrunched in distaste at the nickname. "When will you stop calling me that?"

The bartender chuckled. "Oh, about a quarter till never."

Jensen shook her head. "Yeah, yeah. How about four tequila shots to start us off?"

Both my and the bartender's eyes bulged. "Jensen—" I started.

"Not messing around tonight, huh, Little J? Your brother know you're here?" the bartender asked.

Jensen's hands went to her hips. "John. I am over twenty-one years of age, I do not need your or my brother's permission to drink tequila."

John's lips pressed together in what seemed to be an attempt not to laugh. "Yes, ma'am. I'll get on those shots right away."

I tugged on Jensen's arm. "I don't know if shots are such a good idea for me. I don't have the highest alcohol tolerance."

She sent me a reassuring grin. "Don't worry. We'll just shoot these and then get water bottles to take on the dance floor with us."

I caved to the peer pressure. "Oh, all right."

John re-emerged with four shots, lime wedges, and salt. "Here you ladies go." His eyes traveled down the length of my body. "I don't think I've met you before. I'm John."

I took his outstretched hand, shaking it. "Taylor."

Jensen grabbed two shot glasses, handing me one. "Taylor just moved into the guest cabin a few weeks ago."

"Well, it's nice to meet you. I gotta get back to work, but maybe I can buy you a drink when my shift's over?"

"We'll see," I teased. He grinned and headed for the opposite end of the bar.

"Come on," Jensen said. "Down the hatch."

"Down the hatch" were Jensen's and my famous last words. The country tunes blared from the bar's speakers as Jensen and I twirled around the dance floor in fits of hysterical giggles. This was a blast. Why didn't I go out more?

On my last twirl, I ran smack into a wall of muscle. "Hey there, Short-stack," a deep voice said as hands grasped my arms in an attempt to steady me.

I tipped my head back and found vibrant green eyes staring down at me. "Whoa. You're pretty."

His lips quirked. "Pretty, huh?"

I nodded. Jensen tugged my hand. "Let her go, Walker. We have more dancing to do."

Walker chuckled. "I think you two are done for the night. Bryce is right behind me."

Jensen perked up at that, and I spotted Bryce's sandy brown head making his way towards Jensen. She launched herself at him and, luckily, he caught her. She then proceeded to plant a long, hot kiss on the man's lips.

"Shit. I do not need to see that, guys," Walker grumbled.

I giggled as Bryce slowly set Jensen down on her feet. "Sorry about that, Walk," he said. Bryce's eyes then turned to me, a warm smile in place. "Nice to see you again, Taylor."

"You, too." My body wavered, and Walker slipped an arm around my waist to keep me upright. Shit. Shots were such a bad idea. Walker's arm felt warm and comforting around me. I burrowed into his side, suddenly feeling very sleepy.

"I'm going to take her home. Can you handle J?" Walker's voice rumbled against the cheek I had pressed to his chest.

"Yeah. No problem, man. I'll see you later," Bryce's voice came as if from far away.

"Drive safe," Walker instructed.

My eyes opened as Bryce said, "I will. Precious cargo."

"You got that right."

Walker ushered me towards the exit, and I called over my shoulder, "Bye, J! So. Much. Fun." I punctuated each of the last words with a fist in the air. I could hear Jensen's laughter even over the crowd.

Walker propelled me forward. "Come on, let's go."

The cool night air was a jolt to my system, sending any desire for sleep fleeing. I shivered. Walker must have felt the movement because he slipped off his jacket and wrapped it around my shoulders.

I inhaled deeply. The scent of the coat was a mixture of his woodsy cologne and something uniquely Walker. "Thank you."

"You're welcome."

Walker opened the door to his truck and helped me into the seat in silence, but each brush of his hand sent tingles shooting across my skin. When he leaned across to buckle my seatbelt, my entire body trembled.

"Still cold?" he asked.

I shook my head, not trusting my voice.

He studied my face but said nothing, just shut the door and rounded the truck.

The ride home was silent. I spun my ring in circles on my finger and nibbled at the corner of my lip.

Walker pulled into the cabin's drive, then shut off the truck and came around to open my door. "Come on, let's get you inside so you can catch some shuteye."

He helped me down, and we made our way to the front porch. Two steps up, I turned, leaving me face-to-face with Walker and his gorgeous eyes. "Thanks for taking me home."

"Anytime. I'm glad you let your guard down enough to have a little fun."

"I don't have my guard up."

Walker's head fell back and he let loose that same laugh I'd heard that day at the saloon, back when I didn't even know his name. "Oh, honey, your guard is up so high, you can't even see over it." His face grew serious. "But, maybe one of these days, you'll lower it enough to see that letting people really know you isn't the worst thing."

My breaths came in shallow bursts. Heat flared in Walker's eyes as his gaze dropped to my mouth. Fuck it. I closed the distance between us.

My lips met his in a hesitant caress that soon turned hungry. His tongue parted my lips, and I tasted a hint of bitterness left behind by a beer. My lower belly clenched as his hand drifted to my neck, tangling in my hair. I pushed my body flush against his, needing more contact, more of his body, more of anything to do with *him*.

Suddenly, the hand on my neck was gone, and there were two

on my shoulders, pushing me back. "I can't. This is a bad idea."

I blinked rapidly, still a little dazed from the mixture of booze and lust. "Why not?"

Walker roughly ran a hand through his thick, dark hair. "For one, you're drunk." *I'm not that drunk*, I thought petulantly. "And two…" His voice trailed off as if he were searching for the right words. "The timing isn't right." My spine stiffened. "Don't get me wrong, you're gorgeous."

I bit the inside of my cheek, tasting blood. "I get it." I turned on my heel and headed up the stairs.

"Taylor…"

"Thanks for the ride," I called without turning around. I quickly fumbled for my key, unlocking the door with a speed and dexterity I should not have possessed given how much tequila I had consumed that evening. I was through the door before Walker could say another word.

I knew an excuse when I heard it. I knew when I wasn't wanted.

I flipped the lock and then sank to the floor, my back against the door. The cool wood was a balm to my overheated, traitorous skin. I hugged my knees to my chest.

I was alone. Just like I was meant to be. Everyone left, whether it was by choice or not. It was better to be alone from start to finish. Tears tracked down my cheeks. "I miss you, Mom." The words were the faintest whisper. "I miss you so fucking much."

Pound, pound, pound. The noise at my door mirrored the beating in my skull. "Hold your freaking horses, I'll be right there," I bellowed in the direction of the front door.

I rolled to a seated position on the couch where I had fallen asleep the night before. Apparently, my bedroom twenty feet away was simply too far. I was still wearing my outfit from my night out, and I was sure my mascara had run down my face. Shit. I got to my feet, steadying myself on the back of the couch when the world turned on its axis a bit.

When the living room had righted itself, I headed towards the front door. "Who is it?" I called when I was two feet away.

"It's your partner in crime," Jensen yelled through the door.

A grin stretched across my face, and I pulled open the door. Jensen stood there, holding two cups of coffee balanced on top of what looked like a box of donuts. "Thought you might need a pick-me-up," she said as she brushed past me, making a beeline for the kitchen.

I followed her and the scent of caffeine. "You really are an angel sent from Heaven."

Jensen waved a hand in front of her face as she opened the box of goodies with the other. "I know, I know." She took a bite of a glazed donut as she studied me. "You look like shit," she said while chewing. "What happened to you?"

The color drained from my face as it all came flooding back. Tequila shots. Dance floor. Walker. Walker's lips. Oh, shit.

"Taylor. Taylor! What the hell? Are you okay?" I blinked as Jensen came into focus. She was standing right in front of me now, hand on my elbow.

"I think I might have fucked up last night." Complete understatement. More like I made a total fool of myself.

Jensen's brows raised. "What are you talking about?"

I twisted my ring, my stomach roiling. "I *might* have made a pass at your brother." I covered my face with my hands, unable to watch Jensen's reaction.

"That is awesome!"

I peeked at her through my fingers. "How in the world is that awesome?"

Jensen looked confused. "I love the idea of you two together. Did you think I'd be mad or something?"

I dropped my hands to my sides. "He rejected me. Nothing happened." Nothing but a soul-searing kiss I'd never forget.

Her face fell. "Dang it. He is such a freaking idiot sometimes."

Now it was my turn to look perplexed. "What are you talking about?"

She took a sip of her coffee. "He likes you. I can tell."

"I wouldn't be so sure about that." Jensen hadn't seen how Walker had shoved me away.

Jensen's gaze dropped to her coffee cup as she nibbled on her lower lip. "Listen, Walker was almost engaged once."

I sucked in a breath, a weird stab of jealousy hitting my chest.

"Growing up, Walker was always about Julie. He was head over heels for her from the time he was ten years old and she was nine. He gave her everything from that age on, too. See, she had a crappy home life—single mom who cared more about getting drunk and laid. Jules spent most of her time at our house, and Walker looked out for her like she was spun gold."

I swallowed against my dry-as-a-desert throat. "What happened?"

Jensen's jaw got tight. "They dated all through high school and the first year he was off at college. They were planning a life together. Walker even had a ring, but he wanted to wait until after graduation to give it to her."

Jensen gripped the counter, her knuckles going white. "The week before graduation, she went missing. Her mom didn't even report it. It was Walker who called the school to see if she was there when she didn't answer his calls."

My heart thudded against my ribs. I kept seeing Walker's lips pressed against the headstone in my mind.

"Walker left Portland and came down to help search. He was out of his mind with worry. Two weeks later, they found her body. They never caught the guy who did it." Tears filled Jensen's eyes. "It's why Walker's a cop. He blamed himself for a long time, for not being here to protect her. He decided he would be there to protect others, make sure there weren't other crimes that went unsolved like this one did."

I reached out and squeezed Jensen's hand. "I'm so sorry, J." She'd lost Julie, too. My heart ached for her, but it cracked for Walker. He'd lost the love of his life.

Jensen shook her head. "He's drawn to you, Taylor, but he's never gotten serious with anyone since Julie. He thinks he had his one shot at love and now has to settle for companionship at best. It's so dumb."

My chest tightened. "I don't know about him being drawn to me. I'm not going to lie, there's an attraction there, but I think it was more a case of mixed signals than anything else." She looked doubtful. "Honestly, I'm just embarrassed. I was drunk, and I made a fool of myself." That much was true.

"Whatever you want to believe." She paused for a moment, studying my face. "I think you two would be good for each other. Even if it isn't a forever thing."

The idea of letting Walker into my life in that way, only to watch him go, had panic licking through my veins with such ferocity that I had to grip the counter to steady myself. "I don't think that's a good idea."

Jensen held up both hands. "Okay. I won't meddle. Promise."

I forced a small smile. "Thank you."

She went back to the donuts. "Let's get to work on curing that hangover. What's your poison?"

I studied the box. "Got any Boston Cream in there?"

"Girl after my own heart. I've got two."

She handed me the vanilla custard-filled concoction, and I took a large bite. It tasted like ambrosia. But as the donut settled in my stomach, a shudder swept through me. It could have been the remnants of the tequila, but something told me it had more to do with Walker Cole.

CHAPTER
Seventeen

Walker

S HE HAD BEEN SWIMMING FOR AT LEAST TWO HOURS. Her strokes were vicious as if she were attacking the water. I'd been watching her since I arrived at my parents' house, just sitting in one of the worn leather reading chairs that sat in front of the large window that looked out over the backyard and the surrounding fields.

While her swim was aggressive tonight, Taylor's body still seemed sleek and smooth. Her long legs propelled her forward with surprising speed. I traced her body with my gaze the way I wanted to with my tongue. A flash of her taste filled my mouth, and I bit back a groan.

I had slept like shit last night, tossing and turning. When I finally fell asleep, my dreams were filled with blonde hair and blue-gray eyes.

I stood, the chair legs scraping against the wooden floor. I wasn't going to let her swim until she passed out. I grabbed a bottle of water and headed out the back door.

I stepped to the edge of the pool so she'd catch sight of me. My lumbering frame did the trick, and her head popped up as she reached the wall. She lifted the goggles from her red face. "Hey."

"You're done," I barked.

Her hands went to her hips as she stood in the shallow water. Liquid ran down her face to her neck, kissing her collarbone and then dipping between her breasts. My pants got tighter. Shit.

"Excuse me?" she asked.

"You've been swimming for over two hours, it's time for you to call it quits."

Taylor's face hardened. "Have you been watching me?"

I fisted my hands. "I've been enjoying a beer at *my* parents' house and couldn't help but notice that you've been racing up and down the length of the pool like you're running from Satan himself."

She scowled. "It takes you two hours to drink a beer?"

"Not all of us are lushes." I regretted the words as soon as they left my mouth. Taylor's face reddened even further. "Sorry. I didn't mean it like that. I've just had a shitty day." And I had. Between thoughts of Taylor distracting me, relentless texts from Caitlin, and still being unable to find the missing hiker or the woman from Willow Creek, I was about ready to snap.

Taylor ran her tongue across her bottom lip. My teeth clenched. "Can we just forget that last night happened? I was wasted, I had no idea what I was doing."

Those molars of mine ground even harder together. It was for the best to play along. To let Taylor believe I bought the I-was-just-drunk act. "Of course. Come on, hop out of the pool, and I'll feed you dinner." She blinked up at me. "I know you didn't eat before a swim like that one."

When I went for a run to clear my head that morning, I'd had a little come-to-Jesus talk with myself. I wasn't going to hold myself back from Taylor. That sultry mix of fire and ice that flowed through her just called to me. Ignoring it was stupid. I wanted to be her friend. I wanted to soothe some of those hurts and show her that a full life had plenty of risks, but those gambles were what made the journey worth taking.

But I knew if I wanted her in a way that wasn't just a quick tumble in the sheets that ended with her kicking me to the curb, I would have to move at a snail's pace. I could go as slow as I needed to.

Taylor said nothing, just continued to study me. I cleared my throat. "Look, I'd really like it if we could try to be friends." I felt like a five-year-old asking someone to play with me at recess—a jumble of nerves and anxiety.

She turned her head to look out at the darkening fields, and I held my breath, hoping she'd stay. Moments passed before Taylor returned her gaze to me. "Okay."

"To friendship or food?"

A small smile tipped her lips. "Both?"

The tightness between my shoulder blades eased, relief coursing through me. I reached a hand down to help her out of the pool. Water splashed, and then she was standing in front of me. I grabbed her towel from the lounge chair and wrapped it around her shoulders. A shiver coursed through her, and I rubbed her arms. "Let's get you inside."

She nodded, saying nothing as we walked up the stone path to the back door. I cleared my throat as we stood in the kitchen. "I'll show you to the guest room, and you can shower and change while I fix you something to eat."

Taylor's eyebrow quirked. "You cook?"

I smirked. "I do. But in this case, I'll just be heating up leftovers." My parents had taken my grandma, Jensen, and Noah out to dinner, but I hadn't been up for a crowded restaurant after my crappy day.

"You're full of surprises, Cole." She was still uncertain around me after last night's events, but we were slowly finding our way back to normal.

I led her towards one of the downstairs guest rooms. "Here you go," I said, opening the door. "There are towels and soap in the bathroom. Do you need anything else?"

"Nope. Thank you."

"You're welcome." I shut the door on her towel-clad form, fighting the desire to follow her into the shower. I shook my head and turned towards the kitchen.

I busied myself heating up last night's lasagna and reciting baseball stats in my head. Before long, I heard soft footfalls on the hardwood floor. Turning around, I took in Taylor, pink-faced and freshly showered. Her wet hair was piled on top of her head, and she was wearing short-shorts and a t-shirt that clung to her petite yet curvy frame.

It was apparent that she wasn't wearing a bra. My gaze zeroed in on a pair of perky little nips, and I ground my teeth together so hard, pain shot through my jaw. "Do you want to borrow a sweatshirt? It's pretty chilly."

She flushed. "Yeah, that'd be great."

I jerked my head in a nod and went in search of one of my high school football hoodies in my old room. Finding a worn, gray one, I returned to the kitchen to see Taylor nibbling on her thumbnail. "Here you go." My voice was rough, even to my own ears.

"Thanks, not just for this, but for dinner too." She slipped the sweatshirt over her head. It almost came to her knees, meaning it looked like she could be naked underneath.

I imagined sliding a hand up one of her tanned legs to find her bare beneath. Fuck. I had to stop. "You're welcome." It came out half choked. Grabbing an oven mitt, I pulled the two plates out of the oven. "Hope you like lasagna."

"Love it." Taylor's eyes sparkled when she said it, in a way that told me she did indeed love food. "Can I get us drinks?"

"Sure," I called as I made my way to the dining table. "Help yourself to anything in the fridge and grab me a beer."

"Got it." I placed our plates across from each other just as she returned with a beer and a bottle of water. "Thanks."

"This looks amazing," Taylor said as she sat.

"Tastes even better."

She took her first bite and moaned. Fucking moaned. I choked on my drink. Her eyes looked panicked for a moment. "Are you okay?"

I coughed, then got out, "Yeah, fine. Just a little beer down the wrong pipe."

"This is delicious. Even better than my favorite Italian restaurant in LA."

"Gran will be happy to hear that. It's her recipe."

"Impressive."

I took a pull on my beer. "I have a favor to ask."

Taylor sent a quizzical look my way. "What?"

"You used to be a teacher, right?"

She tensed but answered. "Yes."

"I was wondering if you could help Noah with his reading. His teacher thinks he's a little behind. We've been trying to read with him more, get him to sound out words and stuff, but he's still struggling." Noah did need a little help, but I might have been exaggerating things as an excuse to have Taylor around more.

Taylor twisted the bottle of water by her plate. "What grade is he in this year?"

"First."

"I don't know. I taught fifth grade, it's pretty different."

I could see the apprehension in her eyes, the desire to run, to isolate. She didn't want the Cole family any closer than we already were. I pushed. I had to. "But you learned the basics of how to teach reading, right?"

"Yes…" She let the word trail off.

"It would be a huge help. And I know it would mean a lot to Jensen." I went for the death blow that I knew would mean her agreement. "Being a single mom, she needs all the help we can give her. It's a lot to have on a single pair of shoulders."

Taylor stared me down. "You don't fight fair."

I popped a crispy corner of lasagna into my mouth. "Nope. I fight to win."

CHAPTER
Eighteen

Taylor

BALANCING A PILE OF BOOKS AT LEAST A FOOT HIGH, I reached out and knocked on the Cole family's front door. I had spent the past week brushing up on reading techniques and going in search of books that might entice Noah. I had to admit, this project had reminded me why I had decided to go into teaching in the first place. Maybe it was time to think about going back to work.

The door swung open, and Sarah appeared. "Oh, my goodness. Let me help you with those." She slid the top half of my book pile into her own grasp. "Well, you've certainly come prepared. I'm afraid your student is sulking in the study. He's not too excited about this."

I followed her inside. "Hopefully, these books will help." Sarah sent me a quizzical look. "Part of getting a child excited about reading is giving them a wide variety of material about subjects they're interested in. I asked Jensen to fill me in on the things he loves. So, lots of books on airplanes, fighter pilots, animals, and even a children's biography about Muhammed Ali."

Sarah beamed. "This is wonderful. I can't thank you enough

for doing this."

I returned her smile. "I'm happy to help. We'll start off with shorter sessions. Maybe thirty minutes, a break, and then another thirty?"

"That sounds perfect. I'll be in the kitchen, working on some cookies. They should be just about ready in time for your break."

"That's great. A little reward for hard work is always good. Also, it would help to have everyone in the family read to him as much as possible. Instilling the habit now and seeing his family enjoy the activity will go a long way."

Sarah nodded. "We can do that. Jensen always reads to him before bed, but we can start doing some reading during the day, too."

"That should help. Reading before bed is wonderful, but it's also when Noah is most tired. Picking up a book when he has more energy to focus will help him to retain more of what he learns."

"That makes a lot of sense. Come on, I'll show you to the study."

Sarah led the way to a pair of glass French doors and swung them open as she revealed not a study but a gorgeous library. The room was large and housed floor-to-ceiling bookshelves on every wall except one—the one dominated by a large bay window. There were worn and cozy-looking chairs and a couch that just begged you to curl up on it with a good book. "This is incredible," I whispered.

Sarah patted my shoulder gently. "You're welcome to come over and read anytime you'd like."

I chuckled. "Careful what you offer, with a room like this, you might never get rid of me."

She smiled in return and then turned to Noah, who was sitting in one of the chairs facing the window, clearly sulking. "Noah, Taylor is here." He said nothing. Sarah sat the books she was holding down on a side table. "Noah Nolan Cole, you know that isn't how we treat guests. You get your cute little butt over here before the count of three, or no TV tonight."

Noah slowly rose, dragging his feet as he walked over to us. "Hi, Tay Tay."

I had to hold my cheeks taut to fight the grin that wanted to appear. He was so freaking adorable. "Hey there, Noah." Turning my head to Sarah, I said, "You can go. I've got this."

Sarah looked skeptical but headed out, and towards the kitchen. I placed my stack of books on the side table and got down to eye level with Noah. "This stinks, huh?"

Noah's eyes flared in surprise, then uncertainty filled his gaze. "Yeah…"

"Here's the thing, I'm always going to be straight with you, okay?"

"Okay…" He fidgeted with the toy plane in his hands, unsure of where I was going with the conversation.

"I *love* reading." Noah's face closed down. "But not everyone does."

"I like TV and playing outside."

"Those are both super awesome things, and I like them, too." Noah's face brightened. "But, sometimes, we have to do things we don't want to do." Noah's lip jutted out in a pout. "I will do everything I can to make reading as fun as possible for you, but at the end of the day, we just gotta get through it, okay?"

Silence.

"I'm also a firm believer in rewarding myself after I do something I don't want to do. So, how about after our first exercise, we get some of the cookies your grandma is making? And after the second one, we play outside?"

Noah's eyes traveled from me to the piles of books and back again. "Oh, all right."

I patted my knees and rose. "Great. First things first, I want you to pick out a book you think you might like to read."

Noah studied the titles without actually touching the books. Then, he hesitantly reached out, slowly flipping through his options. My heart warmed as I saw his interest pique. He stopped on a yellow one. He looked up, his eyes wide. "Is this one about a fighter?"

A grin pulled at my lips. "It is. Have you ever heard of Muhammad Ali?"

"No. Who is he?"

I took a seat on the couch and patted the cushion next to me. Noah joined me. "He is one of the greatest boxers to ever live. Think you might want to know a little more about him?"

"Yes," Noah breathed reverently.

"Awesome. Let's do this."

The next thirty minutes flew by. There were a fair number of bumps in the road, but all in all, things went well. Noah was motivated enough by wanting to learn about the boxer that he pushed through the frustration of not knowing certain words. I taught him how he could use the surrounding words in a sentence that he did know to figure out the ones he didn't.

He would be flying through books in no time. "You did great, Noah."

He gave me a shy smile. "I guess it wasn't *so* bad."

"I'm glad. Now, how about some cookies? I think I can smell them from here."

"Yes!" Noah cheered, sending one little fist into the air.

"Let's go." I followed behind Noah as he charged from the study towards the kitchen, laughing softly as I went.

Sarah was standing at the counter, working on her next batch of dough while the first batch of cookies sat on the cooling rack. "How'd it go?" she asked Noah.

"Great," he called, skidding to a stop next to her.

"Hop on up here, and you can lick the beater." A grin spread over Noah's face, and Sarah bent to lift him up onto the counter. Handing him a beater from the mixer, she tapped his nose, leaving a dusting of flour there. "There you go."

A memory slammed into me so hard it stole all the air from my lungs. My chest burned as I saw my own mother standing in front of me while I sat on the counter, swinging my legs back and forth.

"One for my girl, and one for me," my mother said with a smile.

"And maybe a spoonful of batter for me?" I asked, eyes wide with hope.

My mom let out a laugh. "At this rate, you'll never go to sleep."

I smiled widely, showing my missing front tooth. "But it'll be worth it."

"It just might," she said, tapping my nose and leaving a trail of flour in her wake that tickled my sinuses.

Sarah's voice dragged me back into the present moment. "Taylor, are you all right?"

I could feel the lack of blood in my head and knew I needed air. "Yeah," I croaked. "I just need some fresh air for a minute." Sarah initially looked like she might go with me, but I held up a hand. "I'll be right back."

She nodded hesitantly, and I rushed out the back door. I made a beeline for the pool, toeing off my sandals and submerging my feet in the cool water as I sat. My heart clenched in a rhythm of quick spasms that wouldn't let up, and tears leaked from my eyes. I didn't lift a hand to brush them away.

The pain was so real, dug in so deeply, I knew I would never be able to get it out. I battled with the thought of whether I ever wanted it to. Because digging out that pain would mean forgetting my mom. I would deal with this soul-crushing, panic-inducing pain every day for the rest of my life if it meant keeping her fresh in my mind.

I gripped the edge of the pool harder, trying to get my

heartbeat under control. Willing it to relax. I jolted as someone sat down next to me. It took me a moment to recognize Walker through my blurry vision.

I quickly wiped at my face to rid it of tears. It was useless because they just kept coming. It wasn't the kind of crying where you sobbed and heaved. It was the silent kind. The kind where you just had so many emotions inside of you, they had to leak out somewhere.

Walker wrapped an arm around me. I tried to escape it, but he only held me more firmly to him. "Don't. You're going to let me be here for you right now."

The tears and heart pangs kept right on coming. Walker squeezed my arm. "Let it out. You have to stop holding it all in."

I let the tears flow heavier then, allowed my heart to beat unchecked. Walker kept his arm around me through it all. Finally, the tears waned, my breaths slowed, and I came back to myself. "I'm so sorry—" I started to say, cheeks flushing.

"Don't you dare apologize." His voice cracked like a whip. I slammed my lips together. "You don't have to apologize for feeling deeply. You lost someone who meant the world to you."

I blinked up at him. "You know?"

"It wouldn't have taken a genius to figure it out, but Austin told me."

I gritted my teeth. "He shouldn't have. That wasn't his information to share."

"Taylor. I spent all of two hours with your friends, but it only took fifteen minutes for me to see how much they love you." I let out a slow breath, knowing he was right. "And they're worried about you."

"I know they are." I stared at the rippling water, watching it shimmer in the sunlight. "Does your family know?"

Walker gave my arm another squeeze. "Just my grandma. But I can tell the others if you want…so you don't have to."

"Might be a good idea. So your mom doesn't think I'm a crazy person."

Another squeeze. "She doesn't. She's worried about you, too."

I grimaced. "I'll have to apologize for freaking out on her."

"I told you, you don't have to apologize. What happened?"

I let out a shuddered breath. "I–I just–Sarah was baking… and something reminded me of my mom."

He pulled me tighter against him, and a rush of warmth filled me. I felt safe. For the first time in a long time, I felt protected from all the overwhelming feelings. And that terrified me. "Do you want to tell me about it?" he asked.

I stiffened beside him. "I don't like to talk about her."

He tipped my face up so our eyes met. "Remember her. Sharing her with others might help you heal. Tell me a memory you have that makes you ridiculously happy."

I put up a mental wall to the onslaught of images that wanted to fill my mind. I shook my head. "Even the happy memories… they break my heart."

"Still gotta let yourself experience them. Then, maybe one day, you won't cry because of what you've lost, you'll smile because of what you had."

His words landed with a thud in my gut. "That might be true, but I don't know if I'm ready to talk about her yet."

"Well, whenever you are, I'll be here to listen."

"Thank you." It was another of those moments. But this time, alcohol wasn't skewing my perceptions. There was definitely heat in those green depths staring down at me. His eyes dipped to my lips. My breath caught. His arm tightened around me.

A vibration sent us jumping apart. "Shit." Walker reached into his pocket. "My phone."

It was then that I realized that Walker had sat down next to me, submerging his shoes and pant legs in the water. He hadn't taken the time to even slip off his shoes and roll up his jeans.

He'd seen me hurting and didn't delay to bring me comfort. My stomach dipped with a mixture of joy and fear.

"Cole," he clipped into the phone, rising to his feet. "Shit. Really? Okay, I'll be there in about thirty. Did you let Tuck and Forest Service know?" Silence. "Okay, thanks."

I got to my feet, studying the hard set of Walker's jaw. "Everything okay?"

"Not really. A couple of hikers found a body in the woods. I gotta get out there, head up the investigation."

My entire body went ramrod straight. How could I have let myself forget? Walker was a cop. His job was dangerous. Potentially lethal. I fought down the panic. "Be careful." My voice sounded stilted.

Walker's eyes roamed my face. "Always am."

"Good," I replied.

I headed back to the house, and Walker headed towards danger.

CHAPTER
Nineteen

Walker

T HE SUN SHONE DOWN, CASTING SHADOWS IN LEAFY patterns across the ground as I made my way up the hiking trail. It was a haul from the trailhead, and I was thankful that I'd stopped at home to change out of my wet jeans and to pick up my hiking boots. Several officers appeared as I rounded a bend in the path.

"Hey, Walker," Greg called.

I flipped my ballcap around so the brim wasn't obstructing my vision. "Hey. Fill me in."

"It's a gnarly one. Husband and wife were out here from Portland. Thought they'd take in a little nature during their weekend of R&R." I bit back a sigh. Greg, still green, was known for his long-windedness. "The wife needed to take a leak and headed about thirty feet off the trail. Nearly popped a squat right on the body. She and the husband called it in."

"Crime techs here?"

"Arrived just before you. First glance, looks like it might be our missing hiker."

"Shit." I had been hoping for a much better outcome than this one. "Animal attack?"

Greg swiped sweat from his brow. "They can't say for sure yet. The animals have definitely been at her, but no idea if that's cause of death."

I jerked my chin in a nod. "Take me to her."

Greg stepped off the trail and led me south. Voices sounded from up ahead. My stomach roiled at my first glimpse of the body. There wasn't much left of the poor girl to use for identification. Just a crumpled mass of flesh and bone, torn apart by scavengers. I took a breath through my mouth to avoid the stench in the air.

I flashed back to another body found in the woods a decade ago. Julie's sweet smile burst to life in my mind. Her life stolen from her. From me. My fists clenched as I pushed the memories back.

I forced myself to study the crime scene. Guess the path the hiker might have taken. Search for any signs of a bear or cougar. My eyes caught on strands of blonde hair. They were matted in patches, stained a red-brown from blood. This time, it wasn't Julie I saw but Taylor's golden-blonde tresses.

Shaking my head to clear it, I asked the crime techs, "What do we know?"

Bryant straightened from his crouched position and handed me a small, clear evidence bag. "It's the hiker."

I pressed my lips together, studying the ID. Lucy Gaines. Age twenty-two. From Seattle, Washington. Gone way too fucking soon. I turned to Greg. "Call the station, let them know we have a preliminary ID, but I don't want the family notified until the medical examiner confirms. All right?"

"You got it, Deputy Chief." Greg turned on his heel and headed back towards the trail.

I met Bryant's gaze. "I know it's not your job, but any thoughts on cause of death before the M.E. gets here?"

Bryant glanced back towards the body. "I'm not sure, but I

don't think it was an animal."

I raised my brows, studying the carnage. "You sure about that?"

"I can't be sure of anything until the M.E. says so, but I think there would be more blood if an animal had made the kill. The corpse has been destroyed by scavengers, but there's a lack of blood in most of the tissue."

I nodded, wondering if the woman could have been injured while hiking or if something more sinister was at play. A rustling sounded behind me, and I turned to see Tuck heading towards me in his Forest Service uniform. "Greg said it's the hiker."

"Unfortunately. What took you so long to get here?" I asked.

Tuck worked his jaw. "I was tracking a poacher when the call came in, so I couldn't exactly hop in my car." Tuck was an expert tracker, a skill that had been passed down through his family for generations. "You just got here, didn't you?"

"I wasn't trying to give you shit, I was just curious."

Tuck shook his head. "Sorry, I'm in a crap mood. A hunter's been trapping in areas of the forest he shouldn't, but every time I feel like I'm getting close, he slips away."

"Sorry, man, that sucks. You'll find him. Give yourself a little time."

I filled Tuck in on the little I knew while we waited for the M.E. "She was so young," Tuck said.

"I know," I echoed as I saw the medical examiner making her way off the trail. Tuck and I made a beeline to help her with her gear.

"I love working around Sutter Lake, the men here are always such gentlemen."

Both Tuck and I chuckled, but it was Tuck who spoke. "We try our best, ma'am."

"Maybe draw the line at *ma'am*. Call me Carly."

"All right, Carly."

As soon as Carly spotted the body, she switched into professional mode, throwing questions at the techs and Greg, who had been the first officer on the scene. Then, she got to work, doing all sorts of things I knew nothing about. It became a waiting game.

Tuck and I did our best to survey the area, but between the hikers who had discovered the body tromping around, and law enforcement trekking through, there was little to be gained.

"Fellas," Carly called. "You might want to come take a look at this." We rushed back over. "I believe I've found cause of death." She held up a relatively small-caliber rifle bullet between the tongs of a pair of tweezers.

Tuck cursed under his breath as I studied the bullet. "Definitely not an animal attack."

I pulled my gaze away from the bullet. "Hunter hunting illegally? Maybe your poacher?"

Tuck's jaw looked hard as granite. "Could be," he gritted out. "I've been wondering if I should pay a visit to Frank Pardue."

"It might not be a bad idea. I can go with you if you want." Frank was a coot of an older guy who lived in a cabin with no running water or electricity. While technically on the edge of national forest land, it had been grandfathered in because it was passed down from generation to generation in the guy's family.

"I can handle Frank," Tuck said through gritted teeth.

"He's always pissing and moaning about not being able to hunt when and where he wants to."

Tuck looked from the body to the bullet and back to me. "So, what do you think? He accidentally shoots the girl, and when he realizes it, he leaves her here to die?"

"People panic. Killing an animal is one thing. A person is a whole other ball of wax."

Tuck ran a hand through his hair. "I guess you're right."

Carly broke in then. "I won't know for sure if it was the bullet that killed her until I do an autopsy, but I don't think it was animals. I need to get her back to the lab so I can do a full examination."

"All right. Let us know as soon as you have more information," I said.

"Will do." Carly placed the bullet in an evidence bag and got to work putting what remained of the corpse in a body bag.

I pulled out my phone to check the time. "I'm going to head back into town to update the chief. Will you give me a call once you've made a go at Frank?"

"You got it," Tuck said, his jaw still carrying some residual tightness.

I picked my way through the brush and moved back to the trail. I gave some instructions to Greg and then trekked back to my truck. I clenched and unclenched my fists as I walked. Someone had ripped this woman's life away from her, from those who loved her. The pain they would feel when they learned what happened would seem insurmountable.

Longing filled my chest. A desire to share my day with someone who really understood loss. Someone whose simple presence was a balm. Taylor. I fought the urge. Unloading all the shit in my mind wouldn't exactly be taking it slow. Instead, I opted for a cold beer and the solitude of my front porch.

CHAPTER
Twenty

Taylor

A KNOCK SOUNDED AT MY DOOR, JUST AFTER I'D THROWN the rest of my ruined dinner in the trash. Learning to cook was not a task I was taking to well. I wiped my hand on a kitchen towel and yelled, "Coming," in the direction of the door.

My socked feet shuffled against the hardwood. My heart did a little stutter at the thought that it might be Walker. I hadn't heard from him since the day he'd sat with me by the pool and then was called out to deal with the dead body.

Almost a week had passed since then, and if I hadn't seen Jensen at the Kettle, I wouldn't know if Walker were dead or alive. I had his cell phone number and could have called him if I was really worried, but that just seemed too forward somehow, inviting an intimacy I wasn't sure I was ready for. Especially after sobbing on his shoulder.

I took a deep breath and pulled open the door. Standing on my porch were Jensen and a hopping up and down Noah. "Tay Tay!" he exclaimed. "You're coming to the movie with us!"

My brows pulled together as I looked at Jensen. "What?" We

didn't have any plans.

Jensen grinned. "Grab a sweatshirt, you're coming with us to the Cole family outdoor movie night." When I didn't move, she continued. "We're not taking no for an answer, so hurry your booty up."

"Yeah, Tay Tay. Hurry your booty, this is *so* fun! We get popcorn and candy and watch the movie outside on blankets, and I get to stay up way past my bedtime."

My face stretched into a smile. "I can see how that would be a blast, but I'm pretty tired."

Jensen held up a hand. "Uh-uh. Sweatshirt, keys, on our way."

I let out a laugh, helpless against Jensen's determination. "Oh, all right. Give me a second." A movie meant no talking, so it wasn't like Walker could attempt another heart-to-heart. I grabbed a hoodie, bypassing the one Walker had given me a couple of weeks ago. I wasn't quite ready to give that one back, and I didn't want to study my reasons for that too closely.

I nabbed my keys and phone from the kitchen counter and headed for the door. "So, Noah, what are we watching tonight?"

"*The Sandlot!*" he cried, jumping down the last few stairs and nearly giving me a heart attack.

"An oldie but a goodie," Jensen said, twirling her keys around her finger.

"I've never seen it," I admitted.

"Really?"

"Nope."

"You're going to love it. It's hilariously adorable. This is Noah's first viewing, but he's excited because it was his uncle Walker's pick."

My cheeks heated at just the mention of Walker's name. Shit. I needed to get this under control. I cleared my throat. "Well, this all sounds like fun."

Noah chattered the entire ride back to the ranch house, barely letting Jensen or I get a word in edgewise. When Jensen parked, Noah bounded out of the car and rushed towards the backyard where I had seen a glimpse of a large projection screen.

Jensen opened her door but then paused, her fingers drumming on the armrest. "Bryce and his sister, Ashlee, are coming, too. Noah knows them, but he doesn't know that Bryce and I are dating. This is my way to feel it out to see if they get along."

"Are you nervous?"

She bit her bottom lip. "A little."

"I'm sure it'll go great. But if it helps, I think you're smart to take it slow."

Jensen reached over and squeezed my hand. "Thanks."

I gave her a reassuring smile and slipped from the SUV. Rounding the side of the house, I saw that the Cole clan had gone all out. Not only was there a massive screen up against one of the pasture fences, there were also blankets spread everywhere, each housing a few pillows. There was a table laden with snacks of all kinds, including old-fashioned boxes of popcorn. "J, this is incredible."

She grinned. "I know, right? We do this at least a couple times each summer and invite friends and neighbors. It's always a blast."

"Lead me to the snacks. I haven't had dinner." Because the food I had made, or attempted to make, was very much inedible.

"We'll get you fixed right up. I can make you a sandwich too if you want some real food."

I shook my head. "A few pounds of popcorn and candy should do the trick."

"Yet again, a girl after my own heart."

I bumped her shoulder with mine, well I nudged her arm since she was so much taller than I was. We perused the snack table offerings with the rapt attention of true junk food connoisseurs. Popcorn, check. M&Ms to dump into the popcorn, check.

Red Vines, check. Bottle of water, check. And Diet Coke, check.

Jensen snickered. "I'm not sure you can carry all that."

"Oh, hush you."

"I'll help her," a warm and weathered voice piped in.

I turned to see Irma walking up to the table with a stride of a much younger woman. "Thank you, Irma."

"I like a girl who likes her food," she said with a grin.

"Then you and I will get along great."

She patted my shoulder and then relieved me of my popcorn, Red Vines, and water. "I'll show you to a blanket." A mischievous glint shone in her eyes, but I followed anyway. She led me towards a blanket on the outskirts of the grouping with two large pillows. "Here you go. Best seat in the house."

I cocked my head, studying her expression. This didn't seem like the best seat in the house, but who was I to argue with Irma. "Thanks for your help."

"No problem, honey pie. Now, I gotta go grab me some Junior Mints before my son steals them all."

I chuckled. "Good luck."

"I don't need luck, I'll duel to the death for some Junior Mints."

I shook my head as I watched Irma make a beeline for the snack table. I took in my snack bounty and set to work getting ready for the movie. I lined up my water and Diet Coke to the side of the blanket, Red Vines next to them, and then tore open my bag of M&Ms.

"You're in my spot." The rough voice sent a thrill through me.

I blinked up to see a large form against the white of the projection screen. Broad shoulders encased in a navy Henley cut to a narrow waist. The shirt showcased the dips and curves of well-developed muscles. I swallowed hard. "Hey, Walker. You know, there are about twenty other open blankets."

He frowned down at me. "I always sit here."

I started to giggle, couldn't help it.

"What's so funny?" Walker put his hands in his jeans' pockets.

"Your grandmother sat me here." The sneaky little minx.

Walker shook his head and looked heavenward as if asking for guidance. "It's all right, there's enough room for us both."

My body tensed. Hours lying on the same blanket as Walker, the human embodiment of temptation? Not a good idea. "I can move. It's no big deal."

"Stay." His voice was rough, sending a shiver through me.

I pressed my lips together. I would look like a fool if I made a big deal out of this. It was just a movie. A movie surrounded by more than a dozen other people. "Okay."

Walker eased onto the blanket with the perfect balance of power and grace, only some popcorn and a beer in his hands. I squirmed in my seat and turned my eyes back to my M&Ms. Carefully, I dumped the contents of the bag into my box of popcorn.

"What in the world are you doing?" he asked, grimacing. "Are you pouring your M&Ms into your popcorn?" Disgust filled his voice.

My eyes narrowed at him. "Don't use that tone. Have you ever even tried it?"

"Why would I?" he scoffed.

"Because it's the perfect balance of salty and sweet. Don't judge unless you've tried it."

Walker reclined against one of the pillows. "I don't need to try anchovy pizza to know that it's disgusting. I think I'll pass on the chocolate and popcorn."

I shrugged a shoulder. "You don't know what you're missing." A combination of crickets chirping and people chatting filled my ears. Walker and I said nothing. A nervous energy began to course through me, and I became aware of every miniscule movement my body wanted to make. Setting my popcorn down,

I got to my feet. "I'm going to run to the restroom. Do you need anything?"

Walker's gaze trailed over my face. "Nope."

"'Kay. Don't eat any of my delicious M&M popcorn."

Walker gave an exaggerated shudder. I turned on my heel and strode to the house. In my distraction, I almost ran smack into another woman. "Ohmigosh. I'm so sorry," I said, reaching out to steady her and her popcorn.

She gave me a soft smile. "It's okay. I wasn't paying attention."

"No, it was all me. I'm distracted. I'm Taylor by the way."

"Nice to meet you, I'm Ashlee." Ashlee was pretty in an understated way. She wore no makeup, and her hair was pulled back in a tight braid.

"Oh, Bryce's sister, right?" She nodded. "I've only met him twice, and I'm afraid the second time I'd had a few too many cocktails, so it's a little hazy."

Ashlee giggled softly. "It happens." Her eyes traveled to the blanket I had been sitting on and then back to me. "Are you and Walker dating?" she asked, her voice hesitant.

I let out an uncomfortable chuckle. "Oh, no. I'm just the neighbor. I moved into the guest cabin a couple months ago, and the Cole family has kind of taken me under their wing. Like a sister they knew nothing about until recently." It was a lie. A bald-faced lie, and I knew it. But I didn't know what else to say to this semi-stranger.

Ashlee's face brightened, and then it all became clear. She had a crush on Walker. My stomach churned because she would be perfect for him. A pretty girl who clearly had deep roots in Sutter Lake. And from the look in her eyes, she'd do anything to make Walker happy. I hated her a little bit then. But I swallowed my pride and forced a kind smile.

"They really are a wonderful family," she said wistfully.

"They are. If you'll excuse me, I need to run to the ladies' before they start the show."

"Of course. It was nice to meet you."

"You, too," I called over my shoulder as I hustled inside. I rushed to the bathroom, closing the door behind me and flipping the lock. I ran the water as cold as it would go and splashed it on my face. Patting my skin dry, my reflection stared back at me like an angry taunt.

I needed to get it together. So I was attracted to Walker. That didn't mean I had to act on it. All I had to do was avoid copious amounts of tequila and stay strong in the we-are-no-good-for-each-other mentality. *Get over it and enjoy the movie, Taylor.* I willed those words to be true and opened the door.

Blades of grass tickled my sandal-clad feet as I walked. More people had arrived since my bathroom meltdown. I spotted Bryce talking with Jensen and Noah. Noah was pressed against his mom's side, but I heard his little-boy laugh from across the yard. I grinned. It was going well.

Steeling my nerves, I steered myself towards a Walker-filled blanket. As I approached, my jaw dropped. "You little jerk, you're eating my M&M popcorn!"

Walker raised a single shoulder in a shrug. "You were right, it is good."

I snatched my popcorn out of his hands. "Get your own."

"But maybe yours tastes better," he said with a devilish smile.

Trouble. Nothing but trouble.

"Can I get your attention?" Walker's father, Andrew's voice rang out over the crowd. "Thank you for all coming tonight. We love sharing this tradition with you. We're about to get started, so grab your snacks, snag a blanket, and enjoy *The Sandlot.*"

I pulled my sweatshirt over my head, the twilight air already a bit chilly, and leaned back on the pillow.

Walker tugged on a strand of my hair. "Glad you came."

I sucked in a breath. "Me, too."

I turned my gaze to the screen as the opening credits started to roll. As one minute melted into the next, my eyes grew heavy. The heat from Walker's body only added to fatigue's call. It wasn't long before sleep claimed me.

I awoke to gentle ministrations on my scalp and my cheek pressed against a hard surface. "Time to wake up."

That had my eyes popping open with a start. I bolted upright. "Wha—?" It was a partially formed word, but my brain wasn't quite awake yet. Looking around, I saw that almost the entire movie crowd had cleared out. I had slept through the whole show...on Walker's chest. I was pretty sure there was a spot of drool on his shirt.

"I'm so sorry—" I started.

Walker shook his head. "What did I tell you about apologizing?"

I grimaced. "You shouldn't have let me sleep on you. You should have shoved me off or something."

He chuckled, and the low, throaty sound hit me right in the belly. "It's fine, Taylor. Really. I never mind a pretty woman cuddled up next to me." *Unless that woman is me, and she tries to kiss you*, I wanted to say. "Still not sleeping well?" he asked.

"Not really." To be honest, I couldn't believe I had fallen asleep so easily next to Walker. Taking inventory of my body, I realized that I felt incredibly rested. God, it was wonderful. I didn't even feel this rested after an entire night's worth of pseudo-sleep.

I cleared my throat. "I should get going. Do you know where Jensen is?"

"She's in the guest house, putting Noah down. I told her I'd take you home."

Great. Let's just extend the mortification. "Thanks," I mumbled.

"All right, let's get on then."

I followed Walker to his truck and half jumped, half slid into the passenger seat. He let out a low laugh. "Oh, shut up," I sniped.

He rounded the hood of the truck and, in seconds, we were on our way back to my house. "So," he began, "we're going to the lake tomorrow."

"That'll be fun," I replied, the picture of polite distance.

"You're coming with us."

My head snapped in his direction. "No, I'm not."

"Come on, what are you going to do? Stay home alone and work out all day?"

I had planned to attempt another cooking project and swim laps, but I didn't say that. "My plans are none of your business."

"Your plans are coming to the lake with the entire Cole family. I'm not taking no for an answer."

I huffed, crossing my arms at this familiar refrain. "Does pushiness run in your family gene pool or something?"

Walker let out a bark of laughter. "Why, yes, ma'am, it does. So, you might as well give in now." He swung his truck to a stop in front of my stairs. "I'll be here at nine a.m. to pick you up."

"Fine," I gritted out.

"Goodnight, Short-stack," he called as I jumped down from the truck.

"Goodnight, Bigfoot," I called. But to myself, I huffed, "Stubborn, ornery, no-good, troublemaking men." Apparently, I was going to the lake.

CHAPTER
Twenty-One

Walker

MY TRUCK BUMPED ALONG THE GRAVEL DRIVE AS I pulled up to the guest cabin to pick up Taylor. I grinned as I remembered her reaction to me telling her that she was going to the lake with us today. She had been a hissing, spitting little kitten.

I loved getting her riled. It had become a favorite pastime of mine. Over the past few weeks, we'd gone running together almost a dozen times, and I always got a perverse joy out of heckling her along the way. She needed to know that she couldn't push me or any other members of the Cole family away with her prickliness.

I shut my door with a soft push and climbed the stairs, rapping on Taylor's front door. "Coming," I heard through the wood, followed by the thundering of footsteps. Geez, the girl was all of one hundred ten pounds soaking wet, but it sounded like a herd of elephants were headed my way.

The door swung open, and the sight that greeted me was enough to have my shorts tightening and my jaw hardening. Taylor stood before me, sunglasses perched on the top of her head, long, golden hair tumbling down over her shoulders. She wore ridiculously short denim cutoffs with frayed edges and a tank that dipped low enough to give a peek of the white bikini underneath.

I was fucked.

"Hey," she said, tossing her beach bag over one shoulder. "I'm ready."

"Great." My voice sounded hoarse.

Taylor quirked a brow at me. "Are you okay? Not getting sick, are you?"

I cleared my throat. "Nope. Probably allergies," I lied through my teeth. I led the way down her steps to my truck. Opening the passenger door, I said, "We have to make a pit stop at the bakery on our way to get donuts for everyone."

Taylor clicked her seatbelt into place. "The bakery? You'll get zero arguments from me."

I grinned at the ground and rounded the truck. Less than ten minutes later, we had snagged a prime parking spot in front of the bakery. "Have you had donuts from Sutter Lake Bakery yet?"

A faint blush stained Taylor's cheeks. What in the world was that about? She coughed. "Uh, yeah. Your sister brought them by one morning. They're amazing."

Huh. I'd have to get the rundown from Jensen about why Taylor blushed over donuts. "They're the best. I called ahead, so they should have our order all ready to go."

"Perks of being a town cop?"

"Perks of any lifelong town resident."

She nodded, and I pushed open the bakery door. The place was packed. The to-go line was at least fifteen people deep, and another crowd of twenty waited to be seated. I loved checking out who was out and about on a Saturday morning. I spotted Tuck in a back corner with his latest bed buddy. Bryce and Ashlee were being shown to a table. And, unfortunately, Caitlin was there with her bitchy friend, Bridgette. I turned my gaze away as Caitlin's eyes narrowed on me.

I ushered Taylor ahead of me with a palm on her lower back. I swear my skin tingled. What was this, the fifth grade? Hard-ons and butterflies without so much as a kiss?

Shaking the thoughts from my head, I scanned the bakery staff. Nina raised a hand in a one-minute gesture, and I jerked my head in a nod.

"It always smells amazing in here." I had to lean my head down so that I could hear Taylor's words, and her minty breath tickled my ear.

"Best donuts in the county."

"I believe it."

I soaked in the delicious smells and the feel of Taylor pressed up against me. But my happy buzz was soon ruined by a shrill voice. "You have *got* to be kidding me." I turned to see Caitlin's face a mottled red. "You drop me like a piece of trash, saying you're not ready to commit, and I find you here weeks later with this skank."

My spine went ramrod straight, but Taylor let out a chuckle. "Friend of yours?" she asked. "She's charming. It's hard to see why you'd ever want to get rid of her."

The comment had me biting back a grin. "Caitlin, this isn't the time or the place."

Caitlin's hands went to her hips, and her eyes narrowed to slits. "Since you refuse to return any of my phone calls, this is exactly the time and place."

Taylor peeked around my frame. "Honey, never admit that to a crowded room."

I swung my gaze down to Taylor. "You aren't helping."

Caitlin's face grew even redder. "You bitch!" She lunged.

Thankfully, Tuck had spotted the start of a scene and made his way over just in time to catch Caitlin around the waist. "Now,

now," he said. "That's not behavior befitting a lady."

"Let me go!"

"Not until you calm down." Tuck turned to me. "She's probably just hangry."

I raised a brow. "Hangry?"

Taylor piped up again. "You know, when you're so hungry, it makes you angry."

Tuck extended a finger, pointing at Taylor. "This one, I like. Are you the infamous Taylor perchance?"

Taylor beamed. "I am. I'd shake your hand, but I don't want to get kicked."

Caitlin was indeed throwing a righteous fit, kicking her legs and slapping at Tuck's arm secured around her middle. I looked heavenward. "Jesus."

Tuck turned a shit-eating grin on Taylor. "I'm Tucker, but everyone calls me Tuck, Walker's partner in crime since childhood."

"Nice to meet you."

"You too, dollface." Tuck turned his attention back to the hissing creature in his arms. "You gonna calm down?"

"No, you asshole. Let me down."

Just then, Nina appeared with three boxes of donuts. "Here you go, Walker. Tuck, you can set her down outside, because after going after a paying customer like that, she's banned."

"Nina," Caitlin whined. "You can't do that."

"You bet your ass, I can. Now get."

Tuck took Cait right out the front door. The restaurant clapped.

Bridgette stomped up to me, drilling a finger into my chest. "That was cruel, Walker Cole. You know she's in love with you."

I cringed, removing Bridgette's finger. "Bridgette, I didn't mean to hurt her. Sometimes, relationships just don't work out."

Bridgette eyed Taylor up and down, her lip curling. "You're going to regret leaving Caitlin for that cheap trash." My jaw tightened, but before I could say a word, she turned on her heel and stomped out the door.

"You certainly know how to keep things interesting, Cole," Taylor said, and then promptly dissolved into a fit of laughter so strong she was doubled over.

"Get it together so we can get out of here before Caitlin plots her return."

Taylor rested a hand on my shoulder to right herself and tried to take deep breaths to slow her laughter. "I'm sorry. It's just… You dated that crazy?"

I ground my teeth together. "It wasn't that serious." She quirked a brow, and I felt the need to defend myself overtake me. "I was clear about wanting to take things slow. She seemed to be down with that."

"Until she wasn't, right?"

"Right. I missed the signs that she was ready to get married next week."

Taylor glanced out the front door. "I shouldn't be laughing. Every girl has that guy they want but know they'll never have."

My gut burned. Taylor seemed to be talking from experience. An image of some guy showing up on Taylor's doorstep with flowers and apologies, begging her to take him back, filled my mind. It made me want to punch something. I hated the idea of her with anyone else. Anyone but me.

Shit. Slow. I needed to take things slow. *Snail's pace*, I re-minded myself. I shook my head in an attempt to rid my brain of the thoughts that would get me nowhere.

Tuck swept back in the front door. "You're good to go. They took off."

"Thanks, man."

"No problem. Enjoy the lake." He turned his gaze to Taylor, eyes twinkling. "It was lovely to meet you."

"You, too. Thanks for saving me from the bitch attack."

Tuck chuckled. "Anytime."

Taylor held open the door for me and my stack of donuts, but over her shoulder said, "Let's hope it's only necessary once."

With that, we headed out. The drive to the lake was short, and by the time we got there, my dad had the boat ready to go. There were a handful of private docks scattered around the shore, and we were lucky enough to have one.

"The donuts have arrived," I called as Taylor followed me down the dock.

Noah jumped, shooting a fist in the air. "Yes! Donuts! I want a chocolate one with sprinkles!"

I grinned at my nephew. "I got extra sprinkle ones just for you."

"You're the best, Uncle Walker!"

Jensen strode up, taking one of the boxes of donuts. "Just for that, you can put him to bed tonight when he's bouncing off the walls on a sugar high."

I ruffled her hair, and she elbowed me in the side. "Do you see what I have to put up with?" she called to Taylor.

"It's a travesty," Taylor answered.

Jensen pulled her into a hug. "Glad you came." I saw Taylor stiffen slightly but then relax. I felt a swell of pride. My family was good for Taylor.

"He didn't really give me a choice."

Jensen threw her head back in a laugh. "Us Coles are stubborn you-know-whats, aren't we?"

"Understatement of the century."

Jensen linked arms with Taylor. "Don't worry, we grow on you. Now, let's eat some donuts and catch some rays."

"Sounds good to me."

I watched Taylor's pert little ass stroll down the dock, Daisy Duke shorts mocking me with every sway of her hips. It was going to be a long day.

CHAPTER
Twenty-Two

Taylor

THE LAKE GLIMMERED IN THE LATE SUMMER SUNLIGHT, sending sunbursts across the surface. This place really was magic: serene water surrounded by forests, and mountains that seemed to spring up from the lake's edge. I was determined to enjoy this day. I wasn't going to let my mind obsess over this attraction I had to Walker anymore.

I nearly choked on my water as the subject of my inner vow peeled off his t-shirt. A feast of bronzed skin greeted me. He was ripped. Not in a bodybuilder kind of way. In a *real* way. In a way that said he earned the muscles from hard work, not hours on end spent at the gym. He had a dusting of chest hair that perfectly completed the picture.

I wanted to trace the ridges with my fingertips. Feel that dusting of hair tickle my skin. I gulped, forcing myself to avert my eyes. I needed a distraction. I stood, pulled off my tank, and quickly shucked my shorts. "Who wants to go swimming?"

Noah bounded up immediately. "Me! Grandpa, can you take me and Tay Tay out on the tube?"

"Tube?" I asked.

Jensen grinned. "It's Noah's favorite thing in the whole world. We have a double tube that my dad tows behind the boat. It's pretty fun."

Cold water and an adrenaline rush. This was just the ticket to distraction. "I'm in."

"Yes!" Noah cheered. "Can we, Grandpa? Can we?"

Andrew smiled indulgently at his grandson. "You got it. Let's get this show on the road."

Andrew guided the boat away from the dock and far enough from shore that we could set the tubes in the water. Noah was already in a life vest, but before I could jump into the deep blue depths of Sutter Lake, a voice sounded from right next to my ear.

"Let me put this on you."

I turned to see Walker standing all too close and looking way too tempting. I took a half step back to gain some distance. "I don't need one. You know I'm a strong swimmer."

His jaw hardened. "Being a strong swimmer won't help you if you get knocked unconscious."

I rolled my eyes. Always such an alarmist. First, I was going to get mauled by a cougar while on a run. Now, I was about to sink to the bottom of the lake because I didn't have a life jacket on. Geez. "All right. Gimme." I reached out a hand. He didn't pass it off to me.

"I'll do it. Make sure it's secure."

"Because I can't tell if a life jacket's fastened?" I sniped but turned around so that he could slip it over my arms.

The combination of the rough material and the graze of Walker's fingertips had chill bumps peppering my skin, and a shiver running down my spine. Walker grasped my shoulders firmly, spinning me around, and I wondered what it would feel like to have those fingers digging into my hips as he took me.

His eyes met mine, and I saw a flare of heat in them that

surely matched my own. His gaze didn't waver even as he snapped the buckles into place. He gave a quick, harsh tug on the life vest, bringing me flush against him. "Just making sure it's secure."

All I could do was bob my head up and down in agreement. Walker Cole had me wrapped up in a spell so strong, so intricate, that I knew it would take me years to unravel it.

I felt a tug on my hand. "Come on, Tay Tay, let's go!"

Walker released his hold, backing away but never letting his eyes leave mine. Shit.

Another pull on my fingers. "Taaaaaaylor!"

I shook off the remnants of Walker's grip. "Okay. Let's go."

Noah and I got situated on the contraption, and both of us held tightly to the handles as the tube drifted away from the boat. The farther away we got, the more my nerves kicked up. I snuck a glance at Noah, who was alight with joy and anticipation. Zero fear shone on his face.

"You've done this before, right?" I asked.

"Only all the time. It's my favorite thing to do in the summer. I wish we lived at the lake, then I could go all day, every day."

My lips tipped. If a seven-year-old could handle this, then so could I. Jensen lifted her hand in an alert that we were about to take off. My stomach dipped.

The jolt of the tube still took me by surprise, even with the warning. Water sprayed up, misting my face, and the wind sent my hair flying. We bumped over the waves left by the boat's wake, and both Noah and I shrieked with glee. Noah was right, this was the absolute best.

Andrew made at least three loops around the lake before slowing to a stop. Walker and Jensen pulled us back towards the boat. My cheeks hurt from smiling so widely.

Walker offered me a hand to help me into the boat. "Have fun?"

"That was amazing. I want to do this every single day."

His rumbling chuckle sent chills down my water-kissed skin as warmth filled my chest. I loved the carefree joy I heard. How could the simple sound of laughter have such an effect on me? And every single time. "Here, I'll get your life jacket for you."

I batted his hands away. "I think I can unbuckle myself."

His teasing grin had me wanting to smack him or kiss him. I settled for rolling my eyes and hunkering down next to Jensen, who eyed me with a knowing look. I slapped the bill of her ball-cap. "Shut up."

Her mouth stretched wide. "I didn't say a single word."

"Your eyes say it all." I groaned. Her smile only grew.

The rest of the day passed with more tubing adventures, a race across the skinny width of the lake, a picnic lunch, and lots of laughter. A sense of belonging filled my heart, something that I hadn't felt in a long time. I just hoped it lasted.

I shot up in bed, sweat pouring down my face. I lifted a hand to swipe the hair out of my eyes and realized I was shaking. Just a nightmare. Just a stupid fucking night terror that felt all too real.

Images from the dream flashed in my mind. The boat capsizing. Me trying to dive below the water's surface to reach Noah, Jensen, Sarah, Andrew, and Walker. But the stupid life jacket kept me from being able to dive, and each time I tried to unfasten the buckles, my fingers turned to mush. The minutes passed, and then bodies rose to the surface of the water.

I threw off the covers. My skin felt as if hundreds of insects were crawling beneath the surface. I needed to move. I needed to run and experience the pounding of my feet against the road. I needed to push my body to its breaking point and feel anything but this terror that had seized my heart.

Growing to care about this family so deeply had been stupid. Idiotic. Especially for someone who knew how badly it hurt to lose someone. I fisted my hand and pounded it against my thigh. "Stupid, stupid, stupid."

I glanced at the clock and then studied the early morning sky. Five a.m.. It would be light soon. I needed that run, and I needed it alone. If I ran into a bear, I'd just spray it with my bear spray and keep right on going.

Dashing into the bathroom, I quickly splashed water on my face, rinsing away the sweat that lingered there. I grabbed shorts, a sports bra, and a long-sleeved shirt. Changing robotically, I went in search of my sneakers.

Within minutes, I was on the road, the gravel crunching beneath my feet. A few minutes in, I paused to stretch, even though I didn't really want to. But a pulled muscle would only keep me away from my drug of choice. I limbered up as fast as possible and hit the road again.

This time, I pushed my muscles, lungs, and heart to their limits. I craved the burn. Relished it. Ate up every moment of its delicious torture. It reminded me that I was still alive and distracted me from every other pain.

As I reached the top of Walker's hillside, my legs buckled, sending me sprawling. I let myself lay there. Head turned to the side, soaking in the view. Pink hues kissed the clouds as the sun began to rise. It embraced the treetops of a still-dark forest and shone on the lake. I shuddered as I took in the lake's inky depths, flashing back to the images of my dream.

I turned my gaze to the sky. "I need you, Mom," I whispered, a sob clogging my throat. "I'm a mess without you." Like always, nothing and no one gave me a reply. I would have given anything to hear her voice in that moment. To feel the gentle reassurance of her presence. But I was alone.

I pushed to my feet, brushing the gravel from my tumble off

my legs. I gave my hamstrings and calves a quick stretch before beginning a gentler jog home. I let the pounding of my feet lull me into a numbed state, so I didn't notice the figure ahead of me until he was almost upon me.

Walker. And he was *pissed.*

"What in the hell are you doing?" he barked.

I ignored him and kept right on going. I didn't have it in me to deal with his overprotective ass this morning.

"Taylor. Jesus, what the fuck?"

I still kept going. Or I did until a hand clamped around my arm, spinning me in place. Fury blazed in Walker's eyes. "I. Asked. What. The. Hell. You're. Doing."

"Well, I'm not doing the cha cha."

"Don't be fucking cute."

"I'm running, Walker. And this morning, I needed to do it alone. I have my phone and bear spray. I'm fine."

His jaw tightened, and I swear I could hear his teeth grind together. "You gave me your word that you wouldn't go running alone."

I felt my blood begin to heat. "If you'll remember, I told you I'd text you the next time I went running. Which I did. I didn't promise to let you know every time I left the house. You're not my brother, you're not my dad, you're not my fucking keeper."

"No, I'm the idiot trying to keep you from getting killed."

I jerked my arm from his grip. "Well, congratulations, you're off duty. Now leave me the hell alone."

And with that, I took off down the road at a brisk run. Wind stung the tracks that my tears had left in their wake. I was so tired of feeling. Of caring. Why couldn't I just be left alone? That's what I had wanted from the beginning. But no one would listen. Well, from now on, it was polite distance.

My chest burned at the idea of stepping away from the Cole family, but I knew it was what I had to do. I'd keep tutoring

Noah and working at the Kettle, but that was it. No more family gatherings or tearful heart-to-hearts. I was alone, and that's the way it was meant to be.

"That's the way I like it," I huffed. I kept running and ignored the bitter taste of the lie on my lips.

CHAPTER
Twenty-Three

Walker

"**W**HAT?" I BARKED IN ANSWER TO THE KNOCK ON my door.

Ashlee hesitantly poked her head in. "S-s-sorry, Walker, but someone is here to see you."

I grimaced and pinched the bridge of my nose. I was an asshole. And a grumpy one at that. It had been three days since Taylor had nearly bitten my head off and stormed away. I had been sleeping for shit since then. I hadn't once seen her around town or at my parents' house. My mom said that she didn't think she'd even been by to go swimming, and Jensen said she'd been polite but mostly silent while at work.

I was worried about her. And I was fucking pissed. And then I'd swing back to worried again. Something was wrong. The more I thought about that scene on the road, the more I realized that Taylor hadn't even been close to okay that day. There were dark circles under her eyes, and her hands had been shaking the way a victim's did when they were in shock.

Once I'd realized that something was off, I went by the guest cabin. No answer. I called, left messages, texted. Not a word.

When I finally threatened to let myself in with the extra key I had, I got a single text back: *I'm fine. Just need some alone time. Please respect that. If you can't, I'll find someplace else to live.*

That had pissed me right the hell off. She knew she had the trump card and had no qualms about using it. So, I'd left her alone. And much to everyone around me's chagrin, I'd become a prickly curmudgeon in the process.

Ashlee uneasily cleared her throat, and I was brought back to the present moment.

"I'm sorry. I've been a dick lately. Been frustrated about a few things, but that doesn't give me the right to take it out on my co-workers."

Ashlee's entire frame relaxed. "It's all right. We all have bad days." She eased into my office, clasping her hands in front of her. "Is there anything you want to talk about? I mean, just as friends," she said, blushing.

I thought about confessing to Ashlee that I had a tenant who I was insanely attracted to, possibly falling for, who was driving me up the wall, but I decided against it. "No, that's all right, nothing you need to worry about."

She pushed her hair behind an ear. "Okay, but if you ever need to talk, I'm here."

"Thank you, Ashlee. That means a lot." I straightened a pile of papers on my desk. "Now, who's here to see me?"

"Right." Ashlee jolted slightly as if just remembering why she had come to my office. "Barry Stevens is here." She bit her bottom lip. "Do you think Caitlin sent him?"

I groaned. God, I hoped not. If Caitlin had told her father that I had used and then dumped her, this would be one uncomfortable conversation. "Go ahead and show him in. And ask him if he'd like anything to drink."

"Will do," she said, scurrying to the door.

"Thanks, Ashlee. You're a big help."

She turned, and an even deeper blush stained her cheeks. "You're welcome. I'm glad you think so."

I took the next few moments to steel my spine for the possible onslaught to come and straightened the cluttered nightmare of my desk. A quick rap sounded at the door. "Come in."

"Deputy Chief, Mr. Stevens for you," Ashlee said in a more professional tone.

"Thank you." I turned my gaze to Barry, who looked exhausted. "Mr. Stevens, please have a seat. Can Ashlee get you anything to drink?"

He took a seat opposite me. "No, no. She was already kind enough to ask. And please, call me Barry."

I nodded at Ashlee, and she turned to leave. "All right, Barry. What can I do for you?"

The man, somewhere in his sixties, wrung his hands. "Caitlin's missing."

My shoulders straightened, and I leaned forward in my seat. "How long has it been since you saw her?"

"About four days now. She's usually real good about calling her mama and checking in, even if she doesn't come out to the farm as much anymore, but we haven't heard from her in over three days."

I grabbed a notepad and pen and began to scribble notes as I nodded at Barry to continue. "I thought she might've taken off for a few days to lick her wounds. See, I heard what she did at the bakery, going off on you and your lady friend." His cheeks pinked slightly. "I'm real sorry about that, by the way."

"No apology necessary. When emotions are involved, we can all say and do things we don't mean."

"That's kind of you to say." He rubbed a palm over a stubbled cheek. "Well, at first I thought she'd taken off because she was embarrassed-like, but my wife finally got ahold of Bridgette, and Bridgette hasn't heard from her in days neither. Now, Caitlin might not call her mama and me, but you know her and Bridge. Attached at the hip, those two. Something's wrong, Walker. I can feel it my bones."

I didn't have a good feeling either. Caitlin was more likely to cause trouble than go quietly into the night. "Barry, we're going to get right on this. I'll get the word out to all patrol units in the county to be on the lookout for her and her vehicle. Do you have a key to her apartment?"

"Yessir. I brought it with me." Barry's hand shook as he handed me the brass key, and I felt a tightness in my chest as I took it. Caitlin and I might've had a rocky ending, but she was a good daughter.

I stood. "I'll send some officers over to her apartment now to take a look around. We'll do everything in our power to find her as quickly as possible."

Barry rose, as well, reaching out a hand to shake. "Thank you. I appreciate you taking this seriously."

"Of course. I'll keep you updated." I shook his hand and handed him a business card. "Here's my card. It has my cell number on the back. Call me if you hear anything."

He nodded and made his way to the door. As soon as it was closed, I sank back into my seat. This was not good. I quickly put out an APB on Caitlin and her car and then sent Greg and another officer over to her apartment in hopes they'd find something that would point us in the right direction.

My cell buzzed, and I glanced at the screen. "Hey, Little J."

"Walker." Jensen's voice sounded worried.

"What's up?"

"I think Taylor's missing—"

CHAPTER
Twenty-Four

Taylor

I GLANCED AT MY PHONE FOR ABOUT THE MILLIONTH TIME, still no service. I shoved it back into my pocket. I was officially lost. So freaking lost, it wasn't even funny. And all I could hear in my head was Walker telling me not to go running or hiking on my own. It was on repeat, and I was about ready to bash my own head in to get rid of the refrain.

Everything had started out fine and dandy. I had looked up intermediate hikes in a book that the Coles had left at the cabin for guests. I found one that promised some gorgeous views but wasn't too far outside of town.

When I got to the trailhead, I'd studied the map on the Forest Service sign. It seemed simple enough. I had veered slightly off the trail to try and catch a view of the lake from above and, apparently, hadn't been paying close enough attention to the path I charted because when I turned back, I couldn't find the trail again.

A tree branch smacked me across the face. Shit. I glanced at my watch. I was supposed to be at Jensen's to tutor Noah two hours ago. Guilt churned my stomach. She was going to worry.

On the upside, maybe she'd send someone to find my ass.

I picked my way through the underbrush, thorny bushes tearing up my shorts-clad legs. I was going to take the longest bath known to man when I finally made it home. The foliage began to thin, just a bit, and before long, I'd reached the edge of a ravine that allowed me to see down to Sutter Lake.

At last, a landmark. I just had no way of judging how many miles there were between me and the lake, and my water supply wasn't the greatest. I studied the sun and my watch. It was still staying light until somewhat late into the evening, so I had at least five hours of daylight left. Could I make it to the lake or some other form of help in five hours with half a bottle of water?

Better yet, how would I get to the lake? The ravine was far too steep for me to traipse down, and the chances of me spraining an ankle or worse going that way were way too high. I nibbled on my bottom lip and spun my ring in place on my finger. Maybe if I just followed the edge of the ravine, I'd make it to a place that would be easier to cross.

At least following the gorge would take me downhill, which meant towards civilization. I rolled back my shoulders in an attempt to alleviate some of the tension that had made a home there, and set off again.

A rustling noise sounded to my right, and my head snapped up. I tightened my hold on the mini-canister of bear repellent. *Please, God, don't let this be a cougar or a bear. Please.* I slowly turned my head towards the noise, eyes boring into the underbrush.

I couldn't see a freaking thing. Probably just a rabbit or some other small, harmless creature. As carefully and noiselessly as possible, I continued on.

There were no sounds for several minutes other than my own muted footsteps on the pine needle-riddled forest floor and the faint sound of water at the bottom of the ravine. I let out a sigh.

I had let Walker's paranoid ramblings infiltrate my mind. All his talk of bears, cougars, and falling down with no one finding me until I was a pile of bones had gone right to my head.

My blood began to heat. The nerve of Walker, wielding his authority as an officer of the law just to freak me out. I was going to give him a piece of my mind when I made it back to civilization. He'd probably just said all those things so that I would run with him. So that he could have the time to delve into my psyche. Maybe he was one of those do-gooders who got off on putting damaged girls back together.

I inwardly cringed. That was a little harsh. Even for me. I rubbed at my temples. Being freaked out apparently brought out my inner-bitch. I sighed as a vision of Walker's green eyes looking at me with concern filled my mind. I melted at the mental image alone. What was wrong with me? How could this man have such control over my body and brain when we'd barely touched?

I took another step, and a crunch sounded. *That was me, right? Dry leaves beneath my sneakers?* I glanced down, seeing nothing but dirt and pine needles. My heart rate picked up its pace. I slowed, searching the woods all around me for any signs of life.

Another rustle sounded to my right. Shit, shit, shit. I tried to remember if the hiking book said anything about possible encounters with wild animals. Did cougars stalk their prey? Was I supposed to freeze, play dead, or run if I came across one? My palms were slick with sweat. I frantically tried to adjust my grip on the bear spray. Would bear repellent work on cougars? My heart began to rattle against my ribs, and blood pounded in my eardrums.

A twig snapped even closer, and I froze. My breathing and the wind were the only things I could hear before a crack filled the air. Bark spit back from the tree mere inches from my face. *What the hell?* On instinct, I reared back. Something went whizzing by.

Holy crap. Someone was shooting at me. Bullets. Real, life-ending bullets headed straight for me. I didn't think, I just ran. Skirting the edge of the ravine, I kept my hands out in front of me in an attempt to protect my face from the onslaught of branches.

The sounds of someone crashing through the underbrush came from behind me, and I pushed myself harder, not looking back. I begged my legs to not give up on me now. My harsh breaths cut through the mountain air.

I turned my head just slightly, trying to catch a glimpse of how close my invisible attacker was when my foot caught on a tree branch and I began to fall.

CHAPTER
Twenty-five

Walker

I GRIPPED MY PHONE SO TIGHTLY, I WORRIED IT MIGHT break. "What do you mean you think Taylor might be missing?"

The sound of Jensen clearing her throat drifted across the line. An old, anxious habit. "Well...she called early this morning. Said she wanted to get in a hike before she tutored Noah and asked if she could push back our meeting time. I said that was fine, but she was supposed to be here over two hours ago."

My stomach churned. This was not fucking good. Jensen kept talking, a nervous vomit of words. "I've called, and it goes straight to voicemail. I even put Noah in the car and drove over to the guest cabin. Her car's gone. And I, uh, let myself in. I know it was invading her privacy, but I was worried. She wasn't there, but all her stuff is, other than her keys, phone, and the basics."

I squeezed the foam back of my office chair. It wasn't fulfilling the need I had to break something, though. I hissed a breath through my clenched teeth, and the forced air made a whistling sound. "You knew she was going hiking *alone*?" The words were low, a guttural threat.

"I-I wasn't sure. You know she's been pulling away from us, so I didn't want to push. And it isn't like she's not a grown adult."

I shot my chair across the room. "But she didn't grow up here, J. She grew up in a fucking city. She's only lived in fucking cities. *You* grew up here. *You* know the kinds of trouble someone can get into while hiking alone."

"I'm sorry, Walk." Jensen's voice was ragged and resigned. "I fucked up. And if we don't find her without a hair on her head harmed, I'll never forgive myself."

The guilt in Jensen's words took all the bluster out of my sails. "It'll be okay, J. We'll find her. Did she mention an area specifically?"

"No. And I'm kicking myself for not asking."

"All right," I grabbed my desk phone off the receiver. "I'm going to put out an APB on Taylor and her car, see if we can find out what trail she's on. I'm also going to call Tuck and have him put the word out with the Forest Service guys."

"Okay. I'm going to trailer two horses so that you and I can search on horseback whenever we find her car." There was steel in her voice now.

"Thanks. But, J?"

"Yeah?"

I swallowed roughly. "Be fucking careful. Taylor isn't the only girl missing. Caitlin's parents and friends haven't seen her in over three days."

"What the hell is going on, Walker?"

"I don't know. But I'm sure as hell going to find out." My mind began compiling all the things I needed to do. "I gotta go, but careful, yeah?"

"I'll be careful. Promise."

"'Kay. I'll keep you in the loop."

"Thanks."

I punched *end* on my screen and immediately dialed dispatch from my landline. After getting the word out for yet another APB in a thirty-minute period, I called Tuck. He didn't answer. "Call me whenever you get this. It's important. I'll have my cell."

I slammed the phone down in its receiver. "Why do you have to be so fucking stubborn, Taylor?" My office gave me no answers. I ground my teeth and tried to think through where Taylor would have gone. The possibilities were practically endless.

She needed to be back in time to tutor Noah, so she wouldn't have driven more than thirty minutes away, an hour tops. I drummed my fingers against my desk and pulled out a map. I drew a large circle over the area she'd most likely stick to and then studied my options.

Taylor loved the water. Gravitated towards it as if she'd been a mermaid in a past life. That narrowed the possibilities down to three options. I picked up my desk phone again and hit the extension for dispatch. "Send officers to check the trailheads at the lake, the falls, and the Creek Line trail for Taylor Lawson's car. It's a navy Mercedes SUV with California plates. Thanks."

I studied the map more closely. Was there something else I was missing? My cell buzzed in my hand. I answered without looking at the screen. "Cole."

"Walk, it's Tuck. What's up?" He sounded slightly winded.

"I need your help. Taylor's missing."

"What?"

"She went for a hike this morning and didn't come back when she was supposed to. I've narrowed it down to three likely areas. The lake, the falls, and Creek Line. Probably not the lake because there's a lot of people there, and it'd be easy to get help if something went sideways."

Tuck muttered a curse. "Didn't you tell her not to go out on her own?"

I began to pace back and forth behind my desk. "What do you think?"

"Right. You definitely told her. She's a stubborn wildcat, that one."

I shook my head and stared up at the ceiling. "That she is. Now, we need to *find* her."

"On it. I'll put the word out with my guys, and I'm not far from Creek Line now. I'll start searching for any signs of her."

The tight grip on my chest loosened a bit. Tuck was the best tracker in the county. If anyone could find Taylor, it would be Tuck. I just prayed she was in the Creek Line area and not somewhere else I hadn't even thought of. "Thanks, man. I really appreciate it."

"Of course. Keep me in the loop."

"Will do." I ended the call just as my landline rang. "Cole," I answered.

"It's dispatch. They've found the vehicle belonging to Taylor Lawson at the trailhead for Creek Line trail."

My chest loosened even further, but my gut still churned. Anything could have happened to her. "Thanks. Call in search and rescue. Let them know that Tucker is searching the area on foot and that Jensen and I will be on horseback."

"You got it, boss."

I hung up and shot off a text to Tuck, letting him know that Taylor was in the area. Then I dialed Jensen. She picked up on the second ring. "Find her?"

"Not her, but we did find her car. Can you meet me at Creek Line with the horses?"

"I'm on my way."

"See you soon." I ended the call. I just hoped we got there in time.

CHAPTER
Twenty Six

Taylor

A QUICK LOOK BACK COULD COST ME EVERYTHING. I knew if I went down, whoever was hot on my heels would be right on top of me. I tried frantically to right myself, wind-milling my arms, attempting to find purchase on anything. I caught only air.

The overcompensation sent me careening to the left. *Shit, shit, shit.* I landed with a thud, and then I was sliding—over the side of the fucking ravine, I realized. Downed branches and tree roots gouged at my body as I continued in a half slide, half roll. I did my best to shield my face with one arm and grapple to slow myself with the other.

What I assumed was a rock jabbed me in the tailbone, right before I was sent into what felt like an overgrown Brillo pad. I lay frozen. I strained to hear the sounds of anyone following me down the incline. I heard only the gurgling of the creek, and a bird call overhead. At least at the bottom of the valley, I had gained some distance from the psycho hot on my trail.

Ever so slowly, I pulled my hand away from my face. Dry, thorny branches scraped against my arm, and my skin burned like a million fire ants had bitten me all over. It took a few moments for my eyes to adjust to the brightness. Apparently, I'd lost my sunglasses on the way down. And my water. *Shit.*

Taking in my surroundings, I realized that I had landed in the middle of a patch of some sort of briar bush. I peered through the brambles at the ridgeline above. There was no one. I ran my gaze along the rim of the ravine as far as I could see. Nothing.

My breath came in quick pants. What should I do? Stay where I was, or get out of here as fast as humanly possible? The crazy had a gun. What if he were lying in wait for me to leave my cover so he could shoot me dead?

I forced myself to slow my breathing. I counted as I inhaled for three, then when I exhaled for three until my heart began to slow, as well. "Think, Taylor," I said quietly to myself. "Use your brain to figure a way out of this."

I took a moment to get the best look I could through the bush's branches. Maybe I could army-crawl towards the creek and then let it carry me downstream? That way, at least I wouldn't be a standing target. I shivered at the thought of how cold I would be once the sun went down. Maybe that wasn't such a good idea.

The sound of a snapping branch had my spine going ramrod straight, and my heartbeat seeming to trip over itself. Tears of fear and frustration leaked from the corners of my eyes. This was it. I was going to die. I would've thought I'd almost welcome death, feel relieved that maybe, just maybe, I'd be reunited with my mom.

My breathing picked up its pace again as I realized that I really didn't want my life to end, even if dying meant seeing my mom again. I wanted to keep learning how to play bridge with Arthur and Clint. Help Noah fall in love with reading. Have too many tequila shots with Jensen. Be subjected to another of Irma's schemes. Hear Walker call me "Short-stack" with a smile in his voice.

I wanted more of this life I was building.

Attempting to stay as still as possible, I tried to silently count my breaths again. It didn't work this time. I was too freaked.

I tried to see who or what was coming, but I didn't have a good angle. Footsteps grew closer, and I held my breath, my lungs burning.

"Taylor? What are you doing in the bushes?" It was a voice I recognized. Tuck.

I shot from the brambles and launched myself at him so fast, you would have thought I was an Olympic sprinter. Tuck caught me with a grunt, stumbling back a few steps. I then proceeded to burst into tears.

Tuck patted my back awkwardly. "There, there now. Everything's okay. You're not lost anymore."

I started hyperventilating at the reminder that I hadn't only been lost, I'd been shot at. I pushed away from Tuck. "We have to go. Someone's after me." Tuck's brows pulled together in a look that was part concern, part disbelief. I tugged on his arm. "I mean it. Someone was shooting at me!"

That had his shoulders straightening and his gaze moving to the ridgeline. Mine followed. Just as I was about to beg him to get us out of there, I heard a gruff shout. "Tuck!" Two people on horseback appeared a ways down the creek, and as they got closer, I saw that it was Walker and Jensen.

I let out a sigh of relief that turned my muscles into mush. Just as Walker slid off his horse, I started to crumple to the ground. He reached me just as my knees were about to hit the dirt. "Fuck," he barked, pulling me into his arms. Turning to Tuck, he asked, "What the hell happened?"

"I don't know. I just got here about sixty seconds before you did. She says someone shot at her." The last statement had the two of them eying one another, having some sort of silent conversation.

Walker carried me over to a smooth boulder. Gently setting me down, he turned to Jensen, who was in the process of dismounting. "J, grab me some water, a granola bar, and the first-aid kit." Walker's gaze came back to me, roaming over my face in a way that was full of warmth and comfort. "Are you okay?"

"I-I think so."

Jensen was by Walker's side in a matter of seconds, carrying all the items he'd asked for. She studied my face while opening a water bottle. "Here you go," she said, handing me the container.

As I reached out to take it, my hand shook. I willed it to stop, to steady, but it wouldn't obey. "Thank you." It came out as a whisper. I took a small sip and then a larger swallow, it tasted like heaven.

"Go slow," Walker warned. "You don't want to get sick."

I nodded and paused my chugging. Walker broke off a small piece of the granola bar and handed it to me. "Eat this. You're in mild shock. The sugar will help."

I said nothing, just took the offered bite and chewed. It tasted marvelous. Walker then began to open the first-aid kit, examining its contents. "Tuck, will you radio in that we've found her and tell them to call off search and rescue?"

"No problem." Tuck walked off, speaking into a radio in muted tones.

Walker gently grasped my chin in his fingers, turning my head first one way and then the other so he could examine both sides of my face. "What hurts?"

I swallowed another sip of water. "Um, everything?" Everything did hurt. Not in a way that made me think I had any life-threatening injuries, but like I would be one giant bruise by tomorrow.

That got me a small grin. "Anything feel broken?"

"Maybe my ass." He raised a single eyebrow, and I went on to explain. "I fell down the side of the ravine when the guy was chasing me. A rock jabbed me in the ass on the way down."

Walker's entire demeanor changed in a flash. His eyes turned hard, glinting in the afternoon light. His shoulders straightened, and his jaw tensed. "What do you mean when the guy was chasing you?"

I glanced down at my hands, not wanting to meet Walker's gaze. "I was stupid. I went off the trail to try and catch a view of the lake from above, but I didn't pay close enough attention to where I was going and then couldn't find my way back. I had finally found the edge of the ravine when a bullet hit the tree right in front of me. Whoever it was shot at least once more, and I took off running. I could hear them behind me, but when I tried to look back, I tripped and went over the side. I landed in those bushes." I pointed towards the briar patch.

Forcing myself to suck in air before I continued, I counted the seconds of my inhale and exhale. "I tried to see if the psycho was still up there, but I couldn't spot anyone. I wasn't sure what to do. Didn't know if I should stay hidden or try to run. I just didn't know. But then Tuck found me." I brought my gaze to Tuck's. "Thanks for that, by the way."

Tuck forced a smile when he said, "Always happy to help a damsel in distress."

Walker whirled on Tuck. "This isn't something to joke about. She could have been killed!"

Tuck clamped a hand on Walker's shoulder. "I know, Walk. I was just trying to ease a little of the tension. Bad move."

There was some sort of stare-down slash silent conversation again. After a few moments, they both jerked their heads in a nod, ending the standoff. I let out a breath I hadn't realized I'd been holding.

Tuck's gaze continued to roam the area as if looking at a map that no one else could see. "If you can get Taylor home on your own, I'm going to see if I can find any signs of our shooter.

Maybe I can track him back to wherever he came from."

"I've got Taylor, but you need to be careful. This guy could be lying in wait somewhere."

Tuck slapped Walker on the back. "You know I'm always careful. I'll call you if I find anything."

"Call me when you're back either way. We can debrief."

"Will do." Tuck took off towards the wall of the gorge and began climbing it like a spider monkey.

I glanced up at Jensen, who was watching him with apprehension as she nibbled on a thumbnail. I reached up and squeezed her free hand. She jolted slightly, turning her gaze to me. "He shouldn't be going off by himself when there's a crazy person out there."

Walker shook his head. "You know he likes to track alone. He says bringing anyone else with him just confuses the trail and distracts him."

Jensen let out an exasperated sigh. "It's stupid."

"It's Tuck," Walker replied. Jensen had nothing to say to that. Walker turned back to me. "I'm going to clean the scrapes on your face, but everything else will have to wait until we get back."

"That's fine." I looked at the two horses waiting patiently at the creek's edge and then back to Walker and Jensen. "How am I getting back?"

"You'll ride with me," Walker answered.

I swallowed hard. "I'm not the fondest of horses. Maybe I could just walk?"

Walker shook his head. "It's too far for you to walk, and you're exhausted. You'll ride to the trailhead with me, and you're not driving home either." Before I could get in a word of protest, he continued. "You could have a concussion. I'll send someone back to pick up your car and bring it to the cabin."

I bit back any arguments and nodded. "Okay."

Walker ripped open an alcohol wipe. "This might sting a little."

"That's all right. Better than dying of gangrene, right?"

Walker did not laugh. He gently swiped at my face with the wipe. I hissed out a breath. "Sorry," he grumbled, then blew lightly on the scrapes, easing the sting.

"Thanks." I stared into his eyes that were mere inches from mine, seeing the ring of blue around his green irises for the first time. His eyes were magic, captivating in a way that had me fighting the urge to lean in just a little bit closer.

I blinked rapidly, attempting to clear the fog his spellbinding eyes had me in. Jensen cleared her throat. "Ready?"

Walker straightened. "Yeah. Let's go."

He extended a hand to me, and I took it. His fingertips were rough but warm. Sandpaper kisses to my palm. A shiver raced through me. As we got closer to the massive beasts enjoying a drink, my nerves began to rise. "A-are you sure about this? I've never ridden a horse before."

Walker took my shoulders gently, bending down so that his eyes were level with mine. "You're going to be fine. These guys are gentle as newborn babes, and Jensen trained them herself, specifically for trail riding in rough terrain. It's almost impossible to spook them."

He led me over to a horse so dark brown, his coat almost looked black. He had a blaze of white down his face and astute eyes. "This is Lightning."

I jerked back slightly. "Lightning? Like fast as lightning?"

Walker let out a soft chuckle. "He can be fast when you want him to be, but he's also happy just plodding along, which is all we'll be doing."

My throat was suddenly dry as dust. "Okay," I croaked.

Walker lifted my hand for Lightning to sniff. His whiskers tickled my palm. "He wants to see if you have a treat for him."

"I'll give him all the treats in the world if he gets me home in one piece."

"He will. Don't you worry. Now, let's get you in the saddle." I tensed. "Jensen will hold the reins while I help you up. Then I'll get on behind you."

My muscles screamed in protest as Walker lifted me up, but I bit my lip to keep from crying out. I settled into the saddle, holding onto it for dear life. It took Walker mere seconds to swing up behind me. His arms came around me, and I instantly felt safer. "Relax," Walker whispered in my ear. "You can lean back against me. I've got you."

I slowly let myself melt into him, inhaling the comforting mix of his cologne, sweat, and something that was uniquely Walker. Jensen flipped the reins over Lightning's head and handed them to her brother before mounting her own pale blond horse and leading us away.

The rhythmic swaying of Lightning's stride and the warmth of Walker's arms soon had me fighting sleep. "Stay awake for me if you can, Taylor. As soon as you're in the truck, you can take a little nap."

"Okay," I mumbled, but soon, my eyes were falling closed.

CHAPTER
Twenty-seven

Walker

SILENT CURSES LEFT MY MOUTH AS I FELT TAYLOR slump against me. She was in full adrenaline crash-mode.

"She asleep?" Jensen called from up ahead.

"Dead to the world."

"Can you balance her and Lightning, or should I call for some help?"

I tightened my hold around Taylor. "I've got her. We're not far now."

Silence filled the air as we continued our journey. My mind drifted to what the hell was going on in my town. Two girls missing. One found, but only after nearly being shot. My teeth ground together. Taylor's recounting of events didn't sound like a hunter mistaking a person for game. I hoped she was wrong. Maybe she just thought someone was chasing her. Dealing with a misguided hunter was a hell of a lot better than dealing with a murderer.

I breathed a sigh of relief as I caught sight of the truck and horse trailer. Leaning forward, I whispered into Taylor's ear, "It's time to wake up." Nothing. A little louder and with a slight shake of her shoulders I said, "Taylor, we're here."

She gave a small lurch, eyes blinking rapidly. I gave her a gentle squeeze. "You're all right. We're just back at the cars. It's time to get down." She nodded silently. "Hold onto the saddle horn while I dismount." She nodded again. I slid off Lightning, grabbing the reins and tying him to the trailer after I did.

"Put one foot in the stirrup, and swing the other around," I instructed.

Taylor hesitantly obeyed. As her leg rounded Lightning's rump, I grasped her waist. "I've got you." I eased her to the ground. She wavered on her feet a little, so I kept hold. "Let's get you in the truck."

She tucked a stray strand of hair behind her ear. "Thanks. Do you think I could have some more water?"

"Of course." I grabbed a bottle from my saddle bag. Guiding Taylor towards the rear of the truck's cab, I opened the door. She eased herself in with a little help from me, and I handed her the water. "You can lay down if you want. It'll just take a few minutes for Jensen and me to get the horses loaded up."

Taylor gulped down half of the bottle of water. "Okay. Thank you." She grabbed my forearm, sending a jolt of electricity up my limb. "For everything."

"You're welcome." She released me, and I headed to help J with the horses. By the time we had them unsaddled, loaded, and ready to go, Taylor was passed out in the back seat.

Jensen peeked in at Taylor's sleeping form. "She's exhausted."

I opened the passenger door of the rig. "No kidding. I think it's an adrenaline crash. A few hours' sleep and some food, and she'll be good as new."

Jensen hopped into the driver's seat, turning the key to start the engine. "It could have been so much worse. She could've been killed."

I fisted my hands, trying to release some of the rage inside me. "I know."

Jensen pressed her lips together. "You're going to figure out who's doing this, right?"

I reached over and squeezed her hand. "I will. I promise." She nodded and began navigating the trailer down the mountain.

Staring out at the passing landscape, I went through all of the possible suspects I could think of. Tuck and I needed to pay a visit to Frank Pardue tomorrow. But as crazy as the man was, I couldn't see him going after a woman like this. I wondered if we could have some survivalist who'd lost it holed up in the mountains. I hated the idea of it being someone I knew. Someone who got their coffee at the bakery just like I did, who sat next to me at the saloon bar, who lived life in *my* town. I hoped it was a random stranger.

Before long, Jensen pulled up to the guest cabin. Officer Greg was waiting for us. I slipped out of the truck as quietly as possible and handed him the keys to my and Taylor's vehicles. "She okay?" he asked, motioning with his head towards Taylor.

"She will be. I'll brief everyone tomorrow. Has there been any sign of Caitlin or her car?" Guilt flashed through me at the fact that I'd been so focused on Taylor, I'd barely thought of Caitlin.

Greg shook his head. "Nothing. I'll give you a call if we hear anything, and I'll have the guys drop your vehicles back here."

"Thanks, Greg. Just have them leave the keys under the floor mats. I don't want anyone knocking and waking Taylor up if she's resting."

"Sure thing." Greg pocketed the keys and took off.

I headed back to the truck and opened the door to the cab. Taylor let out whistling exhales of air. It was fucking adorable.

I brushed her golden-blonde tresses away from her face. Her skin, even scratched raw, still felt smooth as silk. "Time to wake up. You're home."

Taylor's eyes fluttered open. Watery gray-blue depths stared

back at me. I wanted to sink into them and disappear forever.
"Hi."

I grinned down at her. "Hi. You feel ready to sit up?"

She nodded, and I slowly helped her. "Ow."

My brow furrowed in concern. "You hurting?"

"A bit."

"Okay, let's get you inside. We'll get you something to eat and some pain meds. Then you can shower, and we'll doctor your cuts."

She nodded. I knew she wasn't back to herself because she was agreeing with everything I said. My Taylor would have been arguing just for the sake of it. *My Taylor.* She wasn't mine yet, but I was determined to change that soon enough. I shook my head as I helped her around the truck.

"I'll keep you updated," I yelled to Jensen.

"Thanks," she called back. "Feel better, honey."

"Thank you," Taylor said in a voice that barely reached Jensen.

Taking her arm, I led Taylor up the steps, then unlocked the front door to usher her inside. "Why don't you sit on the couch, and I'll make you a sandwich."

"Okay. Thanks."

I settled her on the overstuffed sofa in the living room where I could still see her from the kitchen. "You don't have to keep thanking me."

"Yes, I do. You came for me." Her eyes bore into mine, a blazing fire within them.

"I'll always come for you." My voice came out ragged, as though ripped from my throat.

"I'm glad," she whispered.

I forced myself to step back, to put some distance between us. "I'll get to work on that sandwich." Spinning around, I headed for the kitchen.

In a matter of minutes, I had a turkey sandwich, a glass of

orange juice, a bottle of water, and a couple of painkillers sitting on the coffee table in front of Taylor. She looked from the food to me and back to the plate again. Then she inhaled it all with a speed I would have thought impossible. When nothing was left but crumbs, she eased herself back against the pillows.

"Feel better?" I asked.

"Much. Now, I just need a shower."

I stood, taking her plate to head back to the kitchen. "Do you want me to sit outside the bathroom in case you feel faint?"

Taylor's head snapped in my direction. "Um, no I don't want you to stand outside my bathroom while I shower. That's just creepy."

I chuckled, but inside, I felt something loosen. Taylor was back to her old self. "All right. I swear I'll stay out here." My tone grew serious. "But promise me you'll sit down in the shower if you feel lightheaded. If you do, call, and I'll come in. I swear I won't look."

Taylor snickered. "Sure, you won't. Perv."

I shook my head. At least she was giving me shit again.

As Taylor headed for her bedroom, my cell buzzed in my pocket. I fished it out and saw Tuck's name flashing across the screen. "What'd you find?" I answered.

"Well, your girl was definitely shot at."

I ignored the ripple of pleasure I felt at the *your girl* comment. "Bring me up to speed."

"At first, I tracked Taylor's movements, which brought me to a tree that, low and behold, had a bullet in it. Looks like a .223."

"Same caliber as the one found in the hiker."

"One and the same."

Letting out a litany of curses, I began to pace. "What else?"

"I tried to follow the bullet's trajectory and was able to find the unsub's trail. I tracked it for a few miles before I came to what I think were ATV tracks. Unfortunately, I lost that trail in the rocky shoreline of the creek. I have no idea where the shooter went."

A muscle in my cheek ticked. "So, we have a probable bullet match but not much else."

"That about sums it up."

"Okay, let's reconvene tomorrow morning at my office. Let's say, ten? I want to bring Frank Pardue in for questioning."

"Sounds like a plan, but good luck finding Frank. I've been by his place three different times. He's never there."

I popped my jaw. "I'll sit an officer at his place until he returns if I have to."

Tuck's voice grew serious. "We'll get this guy, Walk, I promise you."

"I know we will."

"I'll see you tomorrow. Call me if anything changes."

Rinsing Taylor's plate, I bent to stick it in the dishwasher. "Will do. Stay safe."

"Always. You do the same."

"Always." With that, I hit the end button on my screen.

Leaning back against the kitchen counter, I set my phone aside and scrubbed both hands down my face. What a fucking day. Images flashed through my mind, memories of how worried I had been for Taylor. Things could have ended so differently.

I could have been studying a crime scene of her dead body right now. I saw the mangled remains of the hiker in my mind's eye. Remembered the glimmer of blonde hair in the afternoon light that had reminded me of Taylor. I rubbed at my eyes, trying to clear away the picture filling my brain. Taylor's stubborn streak was going to get her fucking killed.

The squeak of a door sounded. Taylor shuffled out with her damp hair piled atop her head. She wore a flimsy tank and sleep shorts that cupped her pert, heart-shaped ass. My jaw tightened. "We need to talk."

She padded towards the couch and dropped down onto it, pulling her knees to her chest. "Okay." Her eyes trailed over my face as if searching each micro-expression for signs of what would come out of my mouth next.

I took a seat on the opposite end of the couch and tried desperately not to stare at her ass and legs, or worse, the juncture between her thighs. I gave myself a mental slap. This was not what I needed to be thinking about. I refocused on the subject at hand. "Do you realize today could've ended very differently?"

Taylor straightened in her seat. "I'm not stupid, I know I screwed up."

"So you'll agree to never go hiking or running without a buddy again? And you'll always tell someone else where you're going?"

Taylor let out an exasperated sigh. "I won't be going hiking in that area again anytime soon. I have zero desire for a bullet in the brain. But I am going to run on my own." I started to interject, but she held up a hand. "I promise that I will text Jensen and let her know when I leave, the route I'm taking, and when I expect to be back by. I'll bring my phone, and text her if anything changes. But I need to do my long runs alone."

I fisted my hands and tried to keep my tone even. "You were almost *shot* today."

Taylor rose to her feet. "I know that! I know that better than anyone. But I'm not going to let some psycho hunter who thought I was Bambi keep me from doing something I love. Something I need to stay sane."

I got to my feet, frustration rippling through every muscle of my body. "I told you I would go running with you. Morning or night. All you have to do is text me. What is so hard about that?"

She threw her arms wide. "Because it's something I like to do *alone* most of the time. I don't need to explain myself to you. I don't owe you anything. I'm a grown woman, I make my own choices. I take care of myself. I don't need you swooping in and trying to control every damn little thing!"

Breaths came through my nose in quick bursts as I pressed my lips together to keep from saying something I might regret. "I'm not trying to control anything. I'm trying to keep you safe."

Taylor snorted. "I don't need you to keep me safe. I can keep myself safe."

"Oh, so was today a shining example of how well you can take care of yourself?"

"Today was a mistake. I told you that. I fucked up. It won't happen again. Just drop it!"

I glanced at the ceiling, holding tight to my temper. I needed to try a different tack. "What is so bad about leaning on someone? About letting someone help you?"

Taylor's jaw had a hard set, and her delicate hands were balled into fists. "There's nothing bad about it."

I studied her face, searching her eyes for some hint of what she was hiding. What she held onto with a vise-like grip. "You don't mean that. Tell me why you don't want people to be there for you. To help you with *anything*. It took my mom and sister double-teaming you with their persistence to even get you to use our fucking pool."

"God! You push and push and *push*! Why won't you just leave me alone? I don't want to need anyone, okay? Just let it go! I'm fine on my own!"

"Why? Just tell me why, and I'll let it go."

"BECAUSE EVERYONE LEAVES!" The statement was torn from her throat so violently, that the words were left lying bloody on the floor.

I felt a tearing sensation in my chest. A pain that I'd never felt before, even in the wake of Julie's death. I realized that it was the feeling of my heart truly breaking. Not for myself, but for someone else.

Taylor's breathing was ragged. "Sometimes, they choose to leave." I knew then that she was talking about her father. And in that moment, if the man had been standing in the room, I knew there was a good chance I would have killed him. "And, other times… Other times, they have no choice. You know they fight so hard—with everything they have—not to leave you alone. But they're torn from you anyway."

My breaking heart shattered. Splintered for the girl who felt so alone in the world. I took a step towards her, but she held out an arm as if warding off a wild animal who wanted to tear her to shreds. "Don't."

I froze. "Please." My voice was as gentle and non-threatening as I could make it. "Please, let me hold you."

That's when Taylor broke. As if the simple offer of human kindness and comfort was too much for her to bear. She merely collapsed, her knees knocking against the hardwood floor with a brutal sound.

I sank to the ground next to her, not waiting for voiced permission to hold her. I just wrapped my body around hers, and the second she felt my presence, she clung to me with a ferocity that stole my breath—her arms clinging to my neck, her legs encircling my waist as I knelt on the floor.

Violent sobs wracked her body, and it was all I could to do to absorb them. I held her as tightly as possible without hurting her. She needed someone who would never leave her. I could be that. I would be her friend, her constant shadow, her shoulder to cry on for as long as she wanted me. I would be more if she let me. It might not be forever, *she* might choose to leave, but it would be worth the pain if I could heal even a part of this precious girl's soul.

I don't know how long we stayed like that. My knees throbbed and my back ached, but I didn't move a muscle. Eventually, Taylor's tears slowed. I trailed a gentle hand up and down her spine, hoping it would encourage her to calm further.

I knew the moment she came back to herself because she tensed. I squeezed the back of her neck. "Don't do that. Don't freeze up on me now. Don't shut me out. I'm honored that you let me in, even if I did kick down the door."

Taylor exhaled a breath, and it tickled my neck. Her face was still firmly pressed there. "I don't know what to say."

"You don't have to know." I pulled back to gaze into those bewitching blue-gray eyes, rimmed red from crying. She flushed and turned her head away. I placed a single finger under her chin and brought her face back towards mine. "No more hiding."

Her throat bobbed. "Okay." There was a moment of silence where we simply stared at one another, both of us with our walls completely down. "I don't know what to do now," she whispered.

"I bet you're exhausted. How about I put you to bed?"

Taylor nodded, a light pink staining her cheeks. "I have a favor. You can totally say no if it's too weird."

"What is it?"

"Will you sleep with me?" Her voice wavered as if she were fighting against a new rush of tears. "I don't want to be alone tonight."

I knew how much it had cost her to say those words. To make that request. And I was fucking honored. "I'd be happy to."

Carefully, I got to my feet with Taylor still wrapped around me like a sloth on a tree branch. I navigated around the living room furniture and finally made it to the master bedroom. Gently, I set Taylor down on the mattress. I pulled back the covers, and she quickly crawled under them. The light in the room was low, and I made quick work of shucking my shoes, pants, and button-down. I wouldn't risk ditching my tee or boxer-briefs.

Silently, I slipped beneath the covers on the opposite side of the bed and flicked off the lamp. The light from the full moon shone through the window to highlight the apples of Taylor's cheeks and the fairest strands of her hair. I opened my arms. "Come here."

Instantly, she rolled into my embrace, her back to my front. I kissed the top of her head. "Sleep. I'll be here when you wake up."

CHAPTER
Twenty-Eight

Taylor

I AWOKE TO A PINK SKY AND STRONG ARMS SURROUNDING me. I froze for a moment as memories from the day before assailed me. I felt as if I had lived twelve lifetimes in twenty-four hours.

One of the arms around my waist tightened, pulling me flush against a wall of muscle. A trail of tingles shot through my nerve endings and grew in intensity as I felt something harden against my backside. Instinctively, I wiggled my hips.

A growl sounded behind me. I stilled, my heart rate ratcheting up a few notches. "Be very careful, Short-stack. I've had your tight little body pressed up against mine all night. My restraint is about to snap."

My brows lifted. "I thought you didn't want this." The image of Walker pushing me away when I kissed him had played over and over in my mind the past few weeks. I still felt an echo of the pain the action had inflicted.

Walker's hand flexed against my hip, sending a jolt of arousal to my core. "I didn't mean it the way you thought." He rocked his hips against me, and I let out a little moan. "I'm very clearly attracted to you. I just knew it wasn't the right time for us. And I wanted more than a drunken hookup from you."

My eyes widened, and my heartbeat picked up speed. "What do you mean?"

In a flash, Walker was on top of me, hovering over my body. Not a single part of him touched me, and yet it was the hottest thing I'd ever experienced. "What I mean is—I want to explore what this thing is between us. Neither of us can know what the future will bring." He ran his nose up the column of my throat. I trembled. "I think we should take things one day at a time, see where the road leads."

He sucked my earlobe between his teeth. "Because I am sure as fuck exhausted from not giving in to you." I began to pant, it was pathetic. In a matter of minutes, he'd turned me into a quivering pile of need. "What do you say, Taylor?" He rose above me again so that I was staring into those gorgeous greens of his. "Want to see how hot this fire burns?"

I fisted his t-shirt and pulled him to me with a force that surprised us both. Our lips crashed together in a battle for dominance. Each of us wanting to see how far we could push this chemistry between us.

Walker's tongue slipped between my lips, tangling with mine. His taste was like his smell—it had a quality that was uniquely him—and I knew it would spoil me for all other men. I didn't care. I tugged at his shirt, needing it off, needing as much skin-to-skin contact as possible.

The piece of clothing sailed to the floor, and then his hands were yanking at the hem of my tank. I sucked in a harsh breath when Walker's thumbs trailed over my nipples as he lifted the shirt higher. He paused when the cami rested just above my breasts. "So fucking pretty. I want to see what shades these pretty nipples will turn when I suck on them."

His words sent a spasm straight to my core. My fingers dug

into his muscular shoulders, and they flexed in response. "So stop staring and do something about it."

Heat and challenge blazed in Walker's eyes. His head dipped. "Careful what you ask for…" he said and then took one of the peaks into his mouth with a force that had me bowing my upper body off the bed. This was no slow seduction. This was a full-on assault.

Fire licked from my nipple to my clit, and he hadn't even touched me there yet. I let out a barely discernable curse. Walker chuckled, sending another slew of sensations through my body. "Ready to beg for mercy?"

"Never." It came out as a half pant, half plea, and both parts said I was a dirty liar.

"We'll just see about that." With those words, Walker turned his suckle into a nibble, and with each rake of his teeth across my tender flesh, another jolt of lightning shot to my center.

He would be the death of me. I needed to fight fire with fire. I forced myself to release the vise-like grip I had on his shoulders and began raking my nails up his back in the same alternating pattern of pleasure and pain he was exerting on my nipple. Walker let out a guttural groan as I reached his head and grasped a handful of his hair with my hand.

Pulling his mouth away from my breast, I brought it to my own. "I need more."

Another flash of heat and challenge seared those green depths. "I'll give you more, but I'm taking my fucking time."

I grinned, but I had a feeling it was slightly feral with need. "Take your time next time."

"You make a damn good case for quick and dirty." With that, he tore my tank top the rest of the way off my body and went to work on my sleep shorts. He pulled them down with a speed I didn't know he possessed. His gaze zeroed in on the juncture between my thighs, and I fought the urge to squirm under his intense stare. "You're bare." His voice was rougher than it had been just seconds before.

I cleared my throat. "I, uh, like it that way."

Walker's hands gripped my thighs, pulling them apart, leaving me completely exposed. His eyes never left my center. "I like it, too," he said, a devilish smile spreading over his face.

My hands fisted the sheets as his hands slowly crept up my legs, closer and closer to the place I wanted him most. When he stopped just shy of where I needed him, I bit down on my lip. Hard. Walker's gaze moved to my face. "Tell me you want this."

My eyes widened, and I released my lip. "I want this. Want you. Now."

He jerked his chin in a nod and gave me a swift kiss. Walker trailed the tip of his thumb down the valley between my thigh and center. I held my breath. He dipped the digit between my folds, and I couldn't hold in my moan.

Walker's touch was feather-light. He explored each dip and curve and as his eyes stayed focused on my face. I realized he was studying my reactions, discovering how to drive me higher. Each circle and swipe brought him closer to my opening, but he didn't venture to that bundle of nerves that I knew would make me detonate.

He eased a finger inside me. His strokes were lazy, as if he didn't have a care in the world. But I was still in a hurry. I bucked my hips against his hand, and he stilled his movements. "Now, now. You in that much of a rush? You want it all?"

"I want you inside me already. This is nothing"—I sucked in air—"but a poor imitation"—another breath—"of what I'm really after." That did it. The last thread of his control broke.

Walker left my body. For a moment, I thought he was pissed and leaving, but then I saw a flash of silver in his hand. A condom. He tore the wrapper with his teeth, and it was ridiculously hot. His other hand went to his boxer-briefs, pulling them down and shaking them off.

My jaw went slack. He was perfection. I watched in fascination as he rolled the condom over himself. I swallowed hard. He was large. So big, I knew I would still feel him tomorrow. But there was also something about him that was beautiful. I didn't think I'd ever considered a penis beautiful before, but Walker's was. His skin was so smooth, the ridges so perfect, I fought the urge to lick my lips.

Walker took three strides and was back at the bed. "Ready?"

I nodded. My gaze traveled over Walker's entire body. He was strung tight, like a bow in danger of snapping. I swallowed again. He leaned over me, brushing a gentle thumb across my nipple. I shivered. "Tell me if it's too much," he whispered.

"I will," I replied faintly.

His tip nudged my entrance, and I felt a pull in me so strong, it was like being sucker-punched, as if my body already knew his and craved the touch with everything it had. I pulled in a sharp breath, and Walker's eyes narrowed on mine. I nodded, trying to urge him on. He pushed inside me with a slow glide, the movement forcing my eyes closed so I could soak up the sensation.

Walker stilled, and I was grateful. It took me a few moments and some deep breaths to adjust to his size. A fingertip circled the peak of my breast, and my eyes flew open. "So fucking beautiful." This time, he was staring at my face when he said it.

My cheeks burned, and my body seemed to melt. The stretching turned to heat. "Move," I begged. "Please, move."

Walker dipped his head, brushing his lips against mine, and then he moved. Slowly at first, and then picking up speed. My hands clutched at his bunching bicep muscles, beginning to slicken with sweat. I wanted to feel as much of his skin as possible. My fingertips started to explore each curve and dent of muscle. His skin was silk over hardened steel.

I trailed a hand through the dusting of hair on his chest I'd lusted after at the lake, pulling some just a bit. Walker let out a garbled curse, and his thrusts grew more frantic. Unbridled. The rhythm chaotic yet exactly what I needed.

My arms fell to the bed, yet again feeling forced to fist the sheets to grab hold of something that could tie me to the Earth. Walker dragged a sandpaper-rough thumb across my clit, and the cord that had been steadily tightening within me snapped.

My walls clenched around Walker, and he let out another curse, thrusting twice more before collapsing on top of me. We lay there panting, both still twitching with aftershocks. After moments passed, I groaned. "Move. You're too heavy."

Walker chuckled but rolled us, taking me with him so that I was now lying on top of him. My cheek rested against his pec and vibrated with each beat of his heart, strong and steady. Slowly, my breathing evened out. "That was—" I began.

"Explosive?" Walker finished.

I pulled my head back and rested my chin on his sternum. Walker's gaze traced over my face. "You're not going to freak out and run on me, are you?"

My whole body tensed, and Walker groaned. "Don't do that. Unless you want me to fuck you again right now."

My eyes widened. "You could go again?" How was that even possible?

He grinned. "You could have me ready to go just about any-time and anywhere." I buried my face against his chest, feeling my cheeks heat. "I really don't want to do this, but I gotta get rid of this condom."

Right. I nodded against his chest, and he rolled me yet again. This time, he slipped from my body. I felt the loss of him acutely, as if a part of me were missing. I shook off the ridiculous notion and reached for my tank and shorts as Walker's tight ass disap-peared into the bathroom.

By the time he returned, I was fully clothed. His gaze raked over me from tip to toe. "I liked the other get-up better."

"Most guys do prefer naked."

Walker climbed onto the bed, backing me up against the pillows. "We need to make sure we've got a few things straight."

I sucked in a breath. "Okay…" My head spun at what he might be about to lay on me. This was a one-time thing, never to happen again? He wanted me to move to Oregon permanently and have a million of his babies?

Walker's eyes bore into mine. "You and I are going to see where this thing leads." I pressed my lips together. "We're not going to worry about all the possible what-ifs. We are going to roll with things. I'm going to have you. Often." My lips stretched into a slow smile. I liked that plan. "I'm also going to be here for you." My heart stutter-stepped. "No matter what does or doesn't happen between us in the bedroom." Another skipped beat.

"And you are going to talk to me. Let me into what's going on in that pretty little head of yours." He tapped a finger on my temple and then let it trace down around my ear. I shivered. Walker pressed his mouth to my forehead, then to each of my eyelids. The gesture was so sweet, so tender it made my heart ache. "Do you think you can do that for me?"

I took a deep breath. This was it. Could I roll with this, with him? Not knowing where we might end up? Having a good idea that the outcome might hurt a hell of a lot? There was something I needed to get out into the open first. I sank my teeth into my bottom lip before speaking. "Jensen told me about Julie."

Walker's expression gentled, and then he sat next to me on the bed. "I would have told you about her myself, she just hadn't come up." He traced the hem of my sleep shorts with his finger. "She was my first love. If she'd lived, I think she would have been it for me. But what we had,"—his eyes met mine—"it never got the chance to grow out of that puppy-love stage."

My heart hurt for him, for the loss of what might have been.

"I'm sorry you lost her."

Walker brushed his lips against mine. "Thank you. Life doesn't always take us on a path we understand, but I know that even with the moments you think will break you, there's always something beautiful waiting. *If* you keep pushing on." He tucked a stray lock of hair behind my ear. "So, you think you can risk taking this journey with me? See where we end up?"

I stared into those green irises rimmed in blue. There was fire in them. Flames that singed my soul. Something that was too tempting to leave alone. Even though I knew I'd likely end up burned. "I can do that."

Walker released a breath I hadn't noticed he'd been holding. "Thank fuck." I giggled. Freaking *giggled*. It was girlish and very unlike me, but I couldn't help it. Walker's eyes playfully narrowed in my direction. "Oh, funny is it? Hilarious that you've got me tied up in knots, my dick hard enough to pound nails whenever you're around?"

I bit down on my bottom lip and shrugged. "Sorry?"

"You're not sorry," he growled and then dove in to tickle my sides.

I shrieked with laughter until he touched a tender spot from my tumble down the ravine. I froze and sucked in a pained breath. Walker immediately pulled back, frowning. "Shit. I completely forgot. Are you okay?" He pawed at my tank top. "Let me see."

I let out a frustrated sigh. "I'm fine. Just a little sore."

"I'll be the judge of that." Walker gently lifted my shirt. "Turn around so I can see your back." I did as he instructed, knowing it would go quicker if I just gave in. "Fuck. You've got a real nasty bruise and a few deep scrapes."

"I cleaned the scrapes last night," I said, trying to put him at ease.

"Well, I wasn't exactly gentle with you this morning, so you need to let me clean them for you again."

I pressed my lips together to keep from laughing. "All right, Dr. Cole. Do your worst."

He placed a kiss at the base of my neck that sent tingles down my spine and slipped off the bed. When he returned, he had his boxer briefs and tee on and held a large first-aid kit.

"Was that here?" I asked.

"Yup, in the kitchen, beneath the sink."

"Good to know."

"Planning on injuring yourself in the future?"

I snorted. "Well, I am trying to teach myself to cook."

"Are you now?" I felt a cold alcohol pad touch the small of my back and jumped. "Sorry about that." Walker blew on my skin to ease the sting. "You know, I'm a real good eater. I eat just about anything, so I could be your guinea pig while you're trying to learn."

This time I snickered. "You might regret that offer."

"I promise you, I won't." He kissed the top of one of my shoulders. He was careless with his displays of affection. Not in a bad way, just in a way that said he had a deep well of love and care in him that was so full, it was overflowing. It wasn't surprising when I thought about it. He had amazing parents, a hilarious grandmother, a protective sister, and a precious nephew, who all loved him deeply. Not to mention, a town that adored him. He had a lot to give.

I relaxed into the knowledge. It helped me to keep from freaking out about his frequent lip touches and gentle caresses. It was just Walker. I didn't need to read anything into it.

His roughened fingertips spread some sort of ointment across the scrapes on my back. I turned my head to the side, catching a glimpse of his shoulder. "Thank you."

"I'll be here to take care of you anytime you need."

"You can't promise that," I whispered.

Walker squeezed my arms and placed a kiss on the back of my head. "I can promise anything I want to. But if it makes you feel better, I'll just say, I'll do everything I can to be here when you need me."

A tightness took over my body. I both desperately wanted to sink into that reassurance and run as far away from it as possible. I settled for something in the middle. "How about I just thank you for taking care of me this go-around?"

"That works for now." Walker rose from the bed and grabbed my hand so that I stood with him. "Now, why don't I make us some breakfast before I have to head into work."

I breathed a sigh of relief that he wasn't suggesting I try cooking for him now. "That sounds perfect."

CHAPTER
Twenty-Nine

Walker

A KNOCK SOUNDED ON THE DOORFRAME OF MY OPEN office door. "Were you just whistling?" Tuck asked, disbelief lacing his tone.

My head snapped up, and I forced the shit-eating grin I'd been wearing off and on all morning from my face. "Maybe."

Tuck studied me intently as he crossed to one of the chairs opposite me at my desk. "You seem…chipper. Way too cheerful for someone who had his ex go missing, and the girl he likes shot at just yesterday."

A muscle in my cheek ticked as a pang of guilt hit me at the reminder that we still had no leads regarding where the hell Caitlin was.

Tuck's eyes narrowed. "You got laid!"

"Would you keep it down?" I gritted out as I stalked around my desk to shut the door. "I don't think the entire office heard you."

"You did. You sly dog, you. I find the girl, and you swoop in all hero-like and catch her when she almost faints. No wonder you got in there." I smacked Tuck upside the head as I walked back around to take the seat behind my desk. "Ow. What was that for?"

I settled in my desk chair. "That was for being an idiot."

"What? Your best pal in the world can't be happy when his boy gets himself some? Especially some that is as smokin' as Taylor."

My jaw clenched. "Don't talk about her like that."

Tuck's eyes flared. "Understood. I get it, I do. This one's different."

I scrubbed a hand over my jaw that was beginning to ache. I was trying really hard to do exactly what I had instructed Taylor to do: take things one day at a time. Not think about what the future might hold.

But what I did know was that I had never had sex like that before. A fire had licked through me that I knew might never get extinguished. So, I was going to do my damnedest to get Taylor to stay in Sutter Lake, to really let me in. It might be an uphill battle, but I never backed down from a fight.

I met Tuck's stare. "It *is* different with her. There's something…I don't know…" I pulled at the collar of my shirt. "Something special about her."

A grin split Tuck's face. "I'm happy for you, brother. Really fucking happy."

"Don't get too excited. She's slippery. Like a horse that's been hurt. Skittish. No sudden moves, if you catch my drift."

Tuck nodded, but before he could say anything else, another knock sounded on my door. "Come in," I called.

Clark poked his head in. "Perfect. I was just about to call Tuck after I spoke with you, Walk."

"What's going on, Chief?"

Clark strode towards the empty chair, gripping the back of it so tightly, I thought it might snap. Shit. This was not good. "Some hikers found another body."

I sucked in a sharp breath. It felt as if the air were made of tiny shards of glass that shredded my throat and lungs. "Caitlin?" I asked, my voice rough. We hadn't ended well. She'd been a bitch to Taylor. But I knew she would've gotten over it, gone back to the sweet girl I had known growing up. My chest tightened when I thought of her parents.

Clark kept his gaze on me steady. "It's looking that way. I know the two of you had history. I'm sorry, Walk."

I straightened in my chair. "You're not taking me off the case, are you?"

Clark shook his head. "No. Maybe I should, but you're the best I've got. You're not family, and you weren't currently seeing her. I can bend the rules."

I jerked up my chin. "I appreciate that, Chief."

"You can thank me by catching this son of a bitch."

I didn't let my eyes move from his. "We will."

Clark released his death grip on the chair. "Get on out to the crime scene." He gave us the details of where the body was located, along with instructions to keep him up-to-date, and then headed back to his office.

What freaked me out the most was that the body had been found so close to where we had discovered Taylor. I roughly pocketed my phone and shut off my computer with enough force to send the machine rocking.

Tuck's meaty palm came down on my shoulder. "You gonna be able to keep your head straight with all this?"

"Yep," I said through my clenched teeth.

"Good. We need you on your A-game."

As we headed out to Tuck's truck, my phone buzzed in my pocket.

Taylor: *Want to brave dinner at my place tonight?*

Emotions warred within me. Part of me wanted to beat my chest in victory that she had reached out to make plans. The other part felt guilty as hell for any bit of happiness I might be experiencing currently.

Me: *I'd love to, but I have to warn you, I might be shit company. On my way to a tough call-out.*

Within seconds, there was a reply.

Taylor: *Zero pressure, but maybe I can take care of you for a change. You don't have to talk about it. Just come eat. Hopefully I won't give you food poisoning.*

I let out a bark of laughter, and Tuck's gaze jumped to me. He raised an eyebrow, and I just shook my head.

Me: *Sounds perfect. I'll text when I have an idea of when this might wrap up for the day.*

Taylor: *Great. See you later.*

Me: *Tonight, Short-stack.*

Tuck didn't press me for details when I climbed into his rig, and I was grateful. I did not want to venture into the land of feelings with Tuck. I soaked up the silence, attempting to get my mind focused on the task ahead.

The trailhead was littered with law enforcement vehicles when we arrived. As Tuck threw the truck in park, I spoke up. "I sent an officer to Frank Pardue's cabin. There was no answer. His truck is there, but no signs of life. I told my guy to stay put till Frank comes back."

Tuck ran a hand through his hair. "That fucker's slippery. I doubt he's going to come waltzing home when there's a squad car parked outside his front door."

"If he doesn't come back by the end of the day, we'll get more creative, okay?"

Tuck opened his door. "All right, but I'm telling you, he won't show."

I rolled my eyes as I climbed out of the rig. Tuck always wanted to play commando. If he had it his way, he'd be stationing men around Frank's property in full camo gear with night vision goggles. Sometimes, waiting a guy out worked just as well.

Tuck and I hiked up the trail, each of us training our eyes on the surrounding underbrush, looking for any signs of a struggle or clues to what might have happened. It took us over an hour to reach the place where our people had set up shop.

Greg spotted us coming up the trail and headed right over. "It's another bad one. What the hell is going on, Walker?"

I forced my body to stay relaxed, to not show any outward signs of distress or anger. "I don't know, Greg. But we're going to find out."

"I hope we can do it before anyone else gets killed," he said with a shake of his head.

I swiped at my brow. Though we had headed into fall, it was mid-day and still warm outside. "Do we have a positive I.D.?"

Greg paled. "I thought you were notified. It's Caitlin."

My gut burned, but I fought to keep my mask of composure. "I knew it was likely, but I hadn't heard for sure."

Greg's Adam's apple bobbed as he swallowed. "The, uh, body is pretty fresh," he said, wincing. "I was able to identify her. It's pretty bad, boss. Are you sure you want to see it?"

My eyes narrowed on him, and he took a step back. I appreciated my officers having my back, but I didn't want any of them questioning my ability to handle a situation.

Tuck stepped forward. "He'll be fine. Could you point us in the right direction?"

"S-s-sure," Greg stuttered, and I felt a little bad for the kid. "Scene's that way, about half a mile."

I jerked my chin at Greg, and Tuck and I moved away from the trail. I let my mask slip for just this half mile. Let my jaw tighten, my fists clench. I would have let out a scream, but I didn't want the people around us to hear. Life was so fucking unfair sometimes.

I caught sight of a group of people fanning out around a

roped-off section. Techs were scouring the area, looking for evidence. Carly and her assistant were bent over what I assumed was the body. I steeled myself for the worst. I still wasn't prepared.

The first glimpse of Caitlin knocked the air right out of my lungs. Her neck was bent at a horrifying angle, her hair spread around her like a halo. Her skin was a sickly grayish color and had a sheen to it. This was nothing like the girl I knew. So full of life, even if that came out as anger at times. I fought the shudder that wanted to course through my body.

I was thankful when Tuck spoke because I was still struggling to find my words. "Hey, Carly. Got a time of death for us?"

The medical examiner's head turned at the sound of her name. "We've got to stop meeting like this, boys. Still not firm on T.O.D., but I'm guessing sometime in the last twenty-four to forty-eight hours."

I cursed under my breath, and Tuck went on alert next to me. Carly straightened from her crouched positioned next to Caitlin's body. "There something I need to know?"

Tuck ran a hand through his hair roughly. "We were not far from here yesterday. Less than twenty-four hours ago. We were looking for Walk's, uh,"—he eyed me—"girlfriend, I guess you'd call her." Carly's brows rose, her eyes sparkling with humor. Tuck continued speaking, and the humor soon fled Carly's gaze. "She got lost while on a hike on Creek Line trail. Then she got shot at. Took a tumble down the ravine."

Carly's head shot towards me. "Is she okay?"

I swallowed thickly, having come to terms with the fact that Taylor had most likely been shot at by Caitlin's killer. "She's fine." The words came out harshly, but Carly, used to working around men, took no offense.

She gazed around the surrounding woods. "I'm glad. You think whoever shot at her killed this young woman?"

I stared down at Caitlin's ravaged form. "I think it's likely. Why don't you walk us through your best guess as to what happened."

Carly nodded and squatted next to Caitlin. "These are just my preliminary findings. Things may change once I've been able to complete a full exam."

"Understood," I said, impatient for her to give me more information.

She continued. "Let's start at the beginning. See these marks here?" Tuck and I nodded as we took in the bruising around Caitlin's wrists. "She was bound in some way for several hours. Possibly days."

I cursed. Tuck remained stonily silent. Carly moved on. "I believe she was,"—she paused for a moment—"hunted down. Either she escaped, or the killer let her go, only to catch her again. She was shot. Here." Carly pointed to a wound on Caitlin's hip. A shot there would make running almost impossible.

Rage pumped through my veins at the thought of how terrified Caitlin must have been. "But that wouldn't have killed her." I forced the words out.

"No. It didn't. I would say the killer caught up with her and snapped her neck." Blood roared through my ears at Carly's words. "It's similar to the way a hunter would snap an animal's neck if they wounded it but didn't make a kill shot."

Tuck's and my eyes immediately clashed. "Pardue," we said at the same time.

I searched the forest around us. "We have to find him. And fast."

CHAPTER
Thirty

Taylor

"'M ake spaghetti,' she said. 'It'll be easy,' she said." I mumbled to myself as I stirred furiously at a pot of sauce. It wasn't the right color. It looked more brown than red. I sighed, attempting to blow the hair out of my face since I didn't have a free hand.

I'd called my bestie for help when some evil spirit had overtaken my body and forced me to text Walker and ask him to dinner. Carter had squealed with glee when I told her about my plans. Or should I say the evil spirit's plans, because I didn't know what I'd been thinking. Carter had immediately shot off a link to a recipe she promised would be so simple, even *I* couldn't screw it up. As I glanced down at the brown sludge, I wasn't so sure.

I peeked at the clock on the stove. Shit. Walker would be here in twenty minutes. I turned off the heat and dashed towards my bedroom, peeling off clothes as I went. Stepping under the shower's spray, I nearly shrieked. It was freezing. I gritted my teeth and forced myself to power through as quickly as possible.

My attempt to get ready in approximately fifteen minutes resembled a cross between a hurricane and that Tasmanian devil cartoon. I rummaged through my closet, throwing everything I wasn't looking for on the bed. Finally, I found my little black dress. It was that ideal dress every girl had to have in their closet. It was the perfect combination of sexy and sweet. You could style it down or dress it up. It was my go-to in times of tremendous stress. I.e., now.

After pulling on a matching set of black lace lingerie, I tugged the dress over my head. I'd have to settle for having my hair up in some sort of messy bun because I had no time to do anything to it. With a quick swipe of eyeliner, a couple of coats of mascara, and some sheer lip gloss, I was as good as I would get. And just in time for the knock on my door.

I blew out a long breath. Everything would be fine. Just as long as my attempt at dinner didn't kill Walker, everything would be okay. This wasn't a big deal. Just two people having dinner and, hopefully, some really hot sex afterward.

Another knock sounded, and this time, it was followed by a deep voice. "Stop freaking out, Short-stack, and let me in."

I let out a huff of exasperation at Walker's psychic powers and strode to the door. Pulling it open, I asked, "Are you ever going to stop calling me Short-stack?" The exasperation was forced. I loved when he called me that.

Walker shot me a devilish grin that set off a shiver somewhere deep inside me. "But you are short. Short and fucking adorable."

His words made my cheeks heat. "Come in," I invited, opting to avoid the nickname business altogether.

Walker stepped into my space, grabbing me around the waist and bringing me flush against his muscled form. "Gonna kiss me hello?" His eyes twinkled, but there was something underneath the gleam. Sadness or anger, I couldn't quite tell.

I stretched up on my toes and brought my lips to his. He smelled of soap, some woodsy cologne, and that thing I couldn't quite name. Someone needed to bottle the combination. They could make millions, no…billions. I inhaled deeply as Walker deepened the kiss, tangling his tongue with mine. He groaned as he pulled back.

I studied his face, my gaze trailing over the lines of stress and that unidentifiable emotion in his eyes. "What's wrong? Is it the call you were out on?" My mind had been toying with that thought all day, imagining millions of horrible scenarios.

Walker's eyes focused on mine with an intensity that scared me just a little. "Promise me if I tell you what happened, you won't run on me."

I tensed in his arms. It was bad. Really freaking bad from the look in his eyes. "I won't run." My voice was stronger than I felt.

"It was Caitlin. Some hikers found her body not far from where we found you yesterday."

My body felt hot and then ice-cold. I shivered, and Walker's arms tightened around me. "So, the person that shot at me was probably…" I couldn't even finish the thought, it made me nauseous.

"We don't know anything for sure, but it's a strong possibility." I nodded numbly, and Walker squeezed me again, bringing my gaze back to his. "Please don't run. But I do want you to be careful. Keep these doors locked. No activities by yourself. Even swimming at the ranch house, I want you to make sure someone's around."

I swallowed against the lump in my throat. "Okay. Are you okay? I'm so sorry, Walker, I know Caitlin was…" I didn't know quite how to finish that sentence.

Walker's jaw tightened. "We weren't," he started. "It was never serious. At least it wasn't for me. It was more so for her. And I feel a hell of a lot of guilt over that now, but there's nothing I can do about it. The only thing I can do is find this son of a bitch and lock him away. That, I *will* do." The vehemence of his words left no room for doubt.

"I know you will. Walker, if you're not up for this tonight, we can do it another time."

He shook his head and pulled me tighter against him. "This is exactly what I need. You and food and laughter. It's the perfect distraction for the shit swirling in my head. Plus, I want to taste what you've cooked up."

Anxious butterflies took flight in my belly, and I twisted my ring around my finger. Before I could say anything, Walker took hold of my hand, bringing it to his mouth and placing a kiss where my fingers met my palm, right on the ring. Of course, he would notice the nervous habit, the psychic sorcerer. "Come on, lead the way," he instructed, linking my fingers with his.

How long had it been since someone had held my hand like this? A long freaking time. I hadn't dated since my mom got sick the first time, and before that, I had been on one seriously long dry spell. It felt strange, but at the same time, comforting. My heart rate kicked up a notch, and those butterflies flared to life again. It was like I was in the seventh grade all over again, and Mitch Allen was holding my hand for the first time.

I gave myself a mental shake. *Get it together, Taylor.* "I'm, uh, not sure how well it turned out. The color's not exactly right."

Walker squeezed my hand. "It's not about how it looks, it's about how it tastes."

"All right…" I wasn't overly optimistic about the taste either. I'd already set the table, so while I dished up bowls of pasta, Walker poured us both drinks. My stomach churned as we both sat.

I watched with no small amount of anxiety as Walker took a bite of the pasta. His eyes widened a bit, and then he let out some sort of *mmm* sound. "This is good, Taylor. Really."

He almost *never* used my actual name. I eyed him skeptically and took my own bite. It stayed in my mouth for a total of two seconds. Just long enough for me to taste a combination of salt, charred tomato, and something that was way too spicy for a pasta sauce. I spit it back out into my bowl, coughing and spluttering. I frantically chugged my water, trying desperately to rid my mouth of the horrible taste. "I can't believe you swallowed that. Or were able to say it was good with a straight face!"

That was all it took for Walker to burst out laughing. "I'm sorry. I really wanted to like it. I want to be supportive."

"No one would like that!" I shrieked. Walker only laughed harder. "It's not funny. I've probably poisoned us both. We've only got hours to live."

"Oh, quit your dramatics and come here." Walker reached out a hand for me to come to him, but I just shook my head like a two-year-old. "Come on."

I huffed but rose from my chair. As soon as I was within arm's reach, Walker tugged me into his lap. He brushed his lips against mine, and I scrunched up my nose. "What?" he asked.

"We both need to brush our teeth or use some mouthwash or something. I can't kiss you when you taste like that awful spaghetti."

He chuckled and squeezed my waist. "Okay. We're going to use some mouthwash, and then I'll take you out to dinner. How about that?"

I stared down at my lap. "I really wanted to do something nice for you." The words were almost a whisper. My heart ached at how painful and unfamiliar it felt to be vulnerable with someone like this. It had been so long.

Walker placed a finger under my chin, lifting it up and forcing me to meet his eyes. "You did. You tried something new, something you've been wanting to learn, and you let me in on the process. So it doesn't taste like a gourmet meal. You gave me the gift of letting me into your world, which is everything I've been asking for. The only thing that would be a disappointment to me is if you shut me out or gave up trying. You're not going to do that, are you?"

I pressed my lips together because I had the urge to do both of those things. Walker squeezed my side again. "Promise me now that at least once a month you will try a new cooking experiment, and that you'll let me be here when you do. We'll taste-test it, and if it works, great. If it doesn't, I'll take you out to dinner."

My cheeks heated at his sweet thoughtfulness. "Okay," I whispered, suddenly shy.

"Good. Now, let's go get some burgers or something."

I climbed off Walker's lap and pulled him to his feet. "Anything, as long as it's not spaghetti."

CHAPTER
Thirty-One

Walker

MY OFFICE CHAIR SQUEAKED AS I LEANED BACK, typing out a text.

Me: *Dinner tonight at my place? I'll swing by and pick you up on my way home.*

Within seconds, three little dots appeared.

Taylor: *As long as you're not going to force me to assist with the cooking.*

I chuckled to myself. In the weeks that had passed, Taylor and I had fallen into a routine of sorts. Typically, it involved me cooking, and Taylor doing everything she could to avoid the oven or stove.

Me: *The only thing you need to do is pour the drinks, Short-stack.*

Taylor: *Sounds like a fair trade. I might even reward you for a meal well done…*

My pants suddenly felt a little bit tighter. I shifted in my seat. My need for Taylor was insatiable. I'd fucked her in the shower mere hours ago, yet here I was, dying to have her again.

I scrubbed a hand across my stubbled jaw. We'd kept our word to each other and not spoken about where this thing was headed, but Taylor hadn't mentioned plans to return to LA at the end of her lease. I had every intention of making it as difficult as possible for her to leave, and as easy as saying the word *yes* to stay.

I shook my head and returned my focus to the papers in front of me. A final report from the medical examiner's office on our two murder victims. It gave me nothing I didn't already know. I'd been holding out hope that Carly might find some clue that would give me a direction to run in, but there was nothing.

The entire case was stone-cold. We'd combed through every piece of evidence at least twice, in some cases, three times. Tuck and his Forest Service team had searched the woods for places a demented killer might be hiding, but they'd had no luck. The chief was getting antsy, and the town was freaked. I totally understood. I was frustrated as hell.

A knock sounded on the frame of my open door. "What's that angry look on your face for, big brother?"

I stood, ushering Jensen in with a wave of my hand. "What are you doing here, Little J? You hate visiting me at the station." My eyes narrowed. "Is everything okay?"

"Everything's fine." Jensen shut the door behind her and sank into an empty chair. "Can't a sister come pay her favorite big brother a visit at work?" Her smile was mischievous, and I didn't trust it for a second.

"You want something." I sat back in my chair, waiting for her to lay it on me.

"Maybe…" she said, drumming her fingers across her lips.

"What is it?"

The drumming paused. "Well. I've noticed that you and a certain resident of the guest cabin have both been unnaturally chipper lately. Especially given all the crazy happenings around here." I straightened at my desk. Taylor and I hadn't been hiding our relationship, but we hadn't been flaunting it either. The last thing I wanted was to scare her off by having the townspeople or my family start asking when we were getting married. Jensen kept right on going. "That wouldn't have anything to do with a little hanky-panky, would it?"

My face scrunched. I did not want to talk to my sister about who I was sleeping with. "Jensen, who is or isn't in my bed is none of your business."

A huge smile spread across her face. "I knew it! If you weren't sleeping with her, you'd tell me straight out. And if you were sleeping with her, but it was just some harmless fun, you'd tell me that straight out, too. You *like* her. And I mean *really* like her." She clapped her hands together with glee. "You two are perfect for each other!"

I raised a hand as if to ward her off. "Hold on there. Do not freak out, go crazy, and call up Taylor, telling her you need to start planning a wedding. I do not want you to scare her off. She's still gun-shy." Understatement of the century.

Jensen's face softened. "I'm not going to do anything to screw this up. Why do you think I'm here, at the place that smells like stale coffee and gives me the creeps, giving you the third-degree instead of bringing a bottle of wine over to Taylor's and trying to pry the truth out of her?"

She exhaled, seeming to gather her thoughts. In a quieter, more serious tone she said, "I know she's still scared. She's better overall. She opens up more, spends more time with the family without me having to con her into it. But I can still see the fear in her eyes."

My chest tightened at Jensen's words. She was right. Taylor was letting us all in more and more each day, but she had a long way to go before her walls were entirely down. J leaned across the desk and squeezed my hand. "I like her, Walk. I really like her. Don't let her shut you out."

I gave my baby sister a gentle smile. "I won't."

Jensen released my hand and leaned back in her seat. "Good."

"Now, tell me what's new with you. How are things going with Bryce?"

A faint blush tinged my sister's cheeks. "They're good. We're taking things slow. Super slow. That's good, for the most part." A shadow of doubt crossed her face as she scrunched her nose in that adorable way she always did when she was unsure of herself. "I just hope that's not a sign that he doesn't actually like me all that much."

I hated that Jensen had this kind of self-doubt. It made me want to pummel the asshole who had left her high and dry as soon as he found out she was pregnant. Alone and pregnant at nineteen, she'd been terrified, and it had done a number on her self-confidence. It was rare that she allowed those doubts to show to anyone, and I was glad that Taylor wasn't the only one letting me in.

I cleared my throat, bringing Jensen's gaze away from her hands in her lap and back to me. "Taking things slow just means that he respects you. I think that's nothing but a good sign."

J sighed. "You're my big brother, of course, you love that he's not trying to get in my pants."

"Too much information, J."

She let out a giggle. "All right."

"I do want to get to know him better, though."

Jensen eyed me skeptically. "That's fine, as long as you don't threaten him with bodily harm."

I grinned. "Not unless he deserves it."

She shook her head. "Why don't we go on a double date?"

Warmth filled my chest at the thought of taking Taylor out on a proper date. Showing everyone in Sutter Lake that this gorgeous girl was mine. "I'll ask Taylor if she's up for it."

Jensen beamed. "Awesome. All right, big bro, I'm outta here."

As she stood, another knock sounded. "Come in," I called.

The door swung open hesitantly. Ashlee poked her head in.

"Sorry to bother you," she said, dipping her chin, a blush on her cheeks.

"That's all right," I assured.

"Hey, Ashlee," Jensen greeted. "How are you?"

"I'm just fine. And yourself?"

"Doing great. Just paying the knucklehead a visit, but I'll get out of your hair. See you later, Walk."

"Bye, Little J," I called after her as she headed out. She looked back at me and stuck out her tongue, showing her disapproval of the nickname. I chuckled and turned my gaze to Ashlee. "What's up?"

"Barry Stevens is here to see you. He wanted to get an update on Caitlin's case."

I instantly sobered. I couldn't imagine what the poor man was going through and hoped I never had to experience it myself. "Show him on back."

Ashlee nodded and escaped down the hall.

I put away all the sensitive files on my desk and locked my computer screen. Just as I shut a desk drawer, Barry's harrowed face appeared in my doorway. "Come on in, Barry. Can I get you anything to drink?"

He moved slowly as if he had aged decades in the past few weeks. "No, thank you. I just wanted to come by and see how things were progressing. We got a call that they were finally releasing Caitlin's body to the funeral home."

Sympathy filled me, but I fought against the urge to let it show on my features. A man as proud as Barry Stevens wouldn't want to see that now. "Unfortunately, there's not a lot I can tell you at the moment. We are pursuing every avenue available to us to find out who did this."

It was true, we were doing everything we could. There just wasn't much to show for it. Tuck and I had finally tracked down Frank Pardue, but after hours of questioning, there was nothing we could hold him for. He was still the number one suspect in my mind, but he claimed that he had been off hunting dozens of miles away when Caitlin was killed. With nothing to prove or disprove his story, we'd had to let him go.

Barry gave a stilted nod. "Well, I just had to check."

"I understand. You come by anytime you like, but I promise I'll call as soon as we have anything we can share."

He stood slowly. "Thank you, Walker. You're a good man." My chest hurt at those words, guilt swamping me as I remembered my last encounter with his daughter. "You'll come to the funeral, won't you? It'll be this weekend."

I swallowed against the sudden dryness in my throat. "Of course, I will."

Barry gave another nod. "I'll see you then."

"See you," I replied, leaning back in my chair as I watched his pained footsteps lead him out of my office. I had to find the monster who destroyed this family.

CHAPTER
Thirty-Two

Taylor

I EASED MYSELF BACK ON THE DOUBLE LOUNGE CHAIR ON Walker's back deck, tucking my feet under the wool blanket he left out here just for me. The view was amazing. During the day, you could see all the way to the town below. Tonight, I could see rolling hills and fields in the twilight as glimmering stars began to appear in the sky.

Inhaling deeply, I soaked in the crystal-clear night air. It was amazing just how relaxed I felt here. How at home. If I was honest, it freaked me out a bit. But I pushed those thoughts aside, deciding instead to focus on gratitude for this night—this moment.

A plank in the deck creaked. "What are you thinking about so hard over there?"

I turned my head to see Walker striding towards me, two open bottles of beer dangling from his fingers. "Just thinking how much I love this spot."

He settled next to me on the lounge, handing me a beer and casually throwing an arm around my shoulders. I snuggled into his side, soaking up his warmth. "I'm glad you like it. I had the architect orient the house so the back deck and master bedroom would have this view."

I tilted my face up towards Walker, drinking in the shadow on his cut jaw and his sharp features in the moonlight. "I don't think I knew you had this built."

"My parents gave me and my sister each a couple hundred acres to build on, hoping it would be lure enough to keep us close." He absentmindedly ran his fingers through my hair as he spoke, sending small shivers down my spine.

"But Jensen lives at the guest house next to the ranch house," I said, thinking of the adorable two-bedroom cottage Jensen and Noah lived in.

"She just keeps her horses on her land for now. It was easier when she got pregnant and while Noah's still young. She's close to my parents and Gran so they can help out. But you never know. If things keep progressing with Bryce, she might be building a house before long."

I shot up, spilling a little of my beer. "Are things getting serious between them? She hasn't said anything to me."

Walker grinned. "Don't go getting too excited. They're taking things slow. Jensen did say she wanted us to go on a double date with them."

"You told her about us?" I fought the urge to duck my head, feeling suddenly shy about it all. He hadn't pushed for us to go public in any way. I hadn't been sure if it was because he didn't want to rush me, or if he wasn't sure we would last. There was even a small part of me that worried he was somehow ashamed of me.

Walker must have sensed my thoughts like the psychic sorcerer he was, because he tugged me to him, taking my beer and putting it next to his on the side table. He positioned me directly on top of him, wrapping his arms around me in a tight hold. "I love that you're mine." I relaxed the smallest bit. "If it was up to me, I'd be screaming it from the rooftops. I just haven't wanted to ask for too much, too soon."

I let the beat of his heart and the warmth of his words ease the rest of the tension in my body. "We can tell people." My stomach flipped. That meant his family would know. The town. People would want to know my business because he was one of Sutter Lake's golden sons, one the entire population claimed as their own. "What if people don't like me?"

Walker's arms tightened around me. "I think everyone will adore you. But if anyone's mean to you, I'll beat them up."

I snorted. "You're a cop. You can't beat up someone just because they don't like me."

"The hell I can't." I rolled my eyes heavenward, which he, of course, couldn't see. He held me even tighter. "So, you want to go on a proper date with me?"

"Well, I'll have to think about it, Deputy Chief. I might need to wash my hair that night."

"You little minx." Walker's arms turned from offering a comforting cocoon to becoming tickling monsters.

I shrieked like a hyena as I squirmed and rolled, trying in vain to escape his grasp. "All right! All right! I'll go on a date with you."

The tickling subsided. "That's what I thought."

His smug tone had me vowing retaliation, so I did the only thing I could think of with my hands pinned to my sides. I bit him right on the pec.

"Fuck, Short-stack! That hurt." His voice was a mixture of shock and humor.

"That's what you get for being a smug bastard."

Walker released his hold on my arms and dipped his hands beneath my shirt. "Smug, huh? I'll show you just what I'm so smug about."

My heart rate kicked up a notch, and my breath came quicker as he unhooked my bra. "Oh, really? All I hear is a lot of talking. I'm not seeing much action to back up your claims. I guess, sometimes, you just have to do the heavy lifting yourself." I peeled off my top as if to prove my statement, letting my bra fall to the ground next.

Walker's eyes zeroed in on my breasts, his hands following suit. "God, I love your tits." His thumbs brushed over my nipples in tandem, and I sucked in a breath. Walker, always the consummate student of my body, noted the reaction. He began tracing patterns around the buds, varying his tempo and pressure. It wasn't long before I was panting.

I tugged at his shirt. "Need this off."

Walker rose up to allow me to pull it up and over his head. "Patience, Short-stack. I like playing with you," he said as he lay back down, his hands coming to my breasts again. No matter how many times we were together, he always wanted to take his time, and I was forever in a rush to feel him inside me.

Walker's fingers plucked at those buds now, and I felt a zap of pleasure in my core. I arched back, sinking into the feeling. Since I was straddling him, the movement brought me right up against something very long and very hard. I moaned. I was wearing a skirt, so only the thin fabric of my panties separated me from the ridge in his jeans.

I rocked against him as he pinched harshly. I trembled, biting down on my lip. Walker's hands left my breasts and skimmed up the outer sides of my thighs, dipping under the flouncy material of my skirt. "So fucking smooth. What do you put on your skin to get it this soft?"

"Just. Lotion," I panted.

"Smooth as fucking silk." He shot up, taking one of my nipples into his mouth and sucking deeply. At the same time, a finger stroked me through my panties.

The sound that escaped me was some unintelligible combination of a moan and curse. My hands went to his hair, tugging it and holding him to me at the same time. He nipped me, and I tugged harder.

Walker released his hold on my nipple, pulling back before bringing my head down to meet his. He took my mouth in a soul-consuming kiss. I swear I saw stars behind my eyelids as his tongue stroked mine, and his finger continued to tease me. "God, you taste like heaven," he said against my mouth. "I want you to ride me. First my face, and then my cock."

My eyes widened. I talked a good game, but I wasn't usually the one in charge. Walker ran a hand up and down my spine. "I'll guide you."

I bit my bottom lip but nodded. Walker reached into his pocket, coming back with what looked like a pocketknife. "I was a boy scout. Always be prepared." My brows pulled together, unsure of where this was headed. He flicked out the small knife. "I hope you're not overly fond of this pair of underwear."

And before I could get out a word of protest, Walker cut one side of my panties and then the other. "You're buying me another pair," I huffed.

Walker sent me a devilish grin and then disappeared beneath my skirt. "Don't worry, it'll be worth it." His words vibrated against my center, and a shiver shot through me. His tongue traced me from my opening to my clit, lazily exploring every part of me. Each stroke drove me higher. Each teasing flick of his tongue made me quake.

I was moments from coming apart at the seams when he stopped. "Don't come. I want to be inside you when you do."

I let out a strangled curse. "Then get in me now."

Walker chuckled. "Always such a demanding little minx."

I paused, staring down at Walker, his lips shiny with my arousal. His green eyes blazed with fire. "I'm on the pill," I whispered. He froze. "I've haven't been with anyone but you for a very long time. I've had physicals since. I'm clean."

Walker's hands tightened around my waist and rose up to take my mouth in a long, slow kiss. I could taste myself on his tongue. "I got tested last week. I'm clean. Can I take you bare?"

I nodded. This was huge for me, and we both knew it—trusting Walker with this. He rested his forehead against my own. "You're mine."

"I'm yours," I breathed. I unfastened his belt, flipped open the button, and slowly pulled down the zipper. I helped him shimmy out of his jeans and boxers as he pulled my skirt down over the curve of my backside.

Walker's hands caressed the skin there, slowly moving his palms to my hips. He guided me towards him at a snail's pace, never once taking his eyes from mine. His tip teased my entrance, easing inside me. The stretch was a delicious burn. I wanted to get lost in the sensations, but I never once allowed my eyes to close, I kept them riveted to those green orbs looking back at me.

The rhythm we found was slow, and for the first time, I didn't want to rush. I didn't want to hurry to the top of the rollercoaster. I wanted to enjoy every dip and bend in the ride. I wanted to feel it all. And I wanted it to last forever.

Eventually, the pace changed. Walker shot up to retake my mouth. I cried out into the kiss as my walls quaked around him. He groaned his response as I felt his release. In that moment, I knew the fortress I had built around my heart was beginning to crumble. It scared me to death, but being without him frightened me more.

Sweaty and sated, we fell back against the lounge. Only the sounds of our slowing breathing and the night insects surrounded us. The smell of the pine trees wrapped us up tight.

Walker trailed a hand up and down the ridges in my spine. I kissed his pec over where his heart might be. "You're mine, too," I whispered.

"I'm yours, too." I felt his words everywhere, and a small, broken piece of my heart knitted itself back together.

CHAPTER
Thirty-Three

Walker

THE SQUEAKING OF A WOOD-PLANKED STEP HAD ME jolting awake. Taylor and I had opted for a night under the stars instead of crawling into my bed. Now, reacting to my sudden movement, she moaned and stretched. My dick hardened. *Not the time, buddy.*

My eyes scanned the back deck and the fields below. Nothing. A throat cleared. "Well, good for you two. It's about damn time." My grandmother appeared from under the eaves of the house.

I groaned. "You have got to be kidding me."

Taylor blinked, the last remnants of sleep clearing from her eyes at the sound of voices. "What's going on?"

I pulled the blanket up a little higher around her, even though she was wearing my t-shirt. "That's what I'd like to know. My grandma decided that six a.m. was the perfect time for a little visit."

Taylor squeaked, her eyes shooting behind me to my grandmother. Who waved. Fucking waved. "Well," Irma huffed, "I wasn't expecting you to have company, and I know you're always up early. But I'm delighted, just delighted that you two have figured this thing out."

Taylor started to giggle. The giggles turned into belly laughs as she rolled closer to me, burying her face in my chest.

I tilted my head back, looking at the sky for patience. "Grandma, why don't you go into the kitchen while Taylor and I get ready."

The grin on my grandmother's face told me she was up to something. "Oh, no, I don't want to interrupt your morning." I snorted. *Yeah, right.* "I'll just let Sarah know to expect Taylor for dinner tonight." I opened my mouth to argue, unsure if Taylor was ready for primetime with my family, but then I shut it again just as quickly with one look from my gran. "No more hiding out, you two."

Taylor poked her head up over my shoulder. "We'll be there."

Warmth flooded my chest. This was real. And good. Taylor was trying. Pushing the boundaries of what she was comfortable with to make room in her life for me. I pulled her closer, kissing the side of her face.

"Wonderful," Irma said. "We'll see you at six. I'll just show myself out."

"You do that," I called.

"Watch your tone with me, young man."

Taylor started giggling again. The vibrations only made my cock strain harder against my boxer briefs. When I heard my grandmother start up the golf cart she shouldn't be driving, I launched from the lounger, throwing Taylor over my shoulder. My hand dipped under the tee she wore to palm her smooth, bare ass. She shrieked and then moaned.

"We're going to the shower. We're going to erase the past fifteen minutes and start this day the way we should have."

"And what way is that?" she asked, voice husky.

"Me eating you until you scream, and then you coming on my cock."

She squeezed my ass, and I almost dropped her. "Such a way with words," she said with a laugh. "But I like the way you think."

"Good." I set her down on the tiled floor of the bathroom and got to work.

I made her come twice in the shower and once while *helping* her dress before leaving for the station. It was a great way to start the day.

Taylor sat beside me in my truck, staring down at her hands, twisting that ring on her right hand. She'd been quiet since I'd picked her up. Too silent.

I reached over, stilling the staccato movements of her hands. I laced my fingers with hers and squeezed. "Want to tell me what's got you running in circles in your head?"

She blew out a breath and mumbled something about psychic sorcerers.

"What was that?"

"You're some sort of psychic sorcerer. You always know when something's up with me. It's freaky."

I chuckled and gave her hand another squeeze. "I'm a cop. I know by someone's body language when something's not right. And I know your body pretty damn well."

Taylor pressed her lips together, seeming to fight a smile. But something dark still lurked in those blue-gray depths. Her shoulders slumped. "The last time I was with your whole family...I had a nightmare that night. It really freaked me out. I just don't want that to happen again."

My chest tightened at the doubt in her words. I pulled my truck over to the side of the road. Turning, I took her face in my hands. "First of all, thank you for telling me. Second, I'm going to be with you all night, and you haven't had any nightmares when I've spent the night before, right?" She nodded between my hands.

I hated that being around my family brought all her fears to the surface, but I was proud as hell that she'd faced them down. I kissed her softly, tasting a hint of the beer we'd shared before leaving her place. "I'm with you. Always."

Her eyes blazed with blue heat, the type of flame you knew would leave third-degree burns. But, damn, it was beautiful to watch.

She fisted a hand in my shirt, pulling me to her, and slamming her mouth over mine. The force of the kiss took me by surprise. There were things she couldn't say. Things that scared her. But she said them with her lips, her tongue, her body.

I groaned into her mouth before pulling back. "Are you seriously going to make me walk into my parents' house with a hard-on?"

Taylor's eyes widened and then danced with laughter. It wasn't the blue heat, but I knew it was what she needed to go into the house with a light heart. "Sorry about that," she said with a laugh.

"Let's just hope I can get it under control in the three minutes it takes to get there. Do me a favor and be less gorgeous, would you?"

She chuckled. I squeezed her knee and tried to think about baseball stats, all the paperwork I had to catch up on, anything.

We pulled up to the ranch house, the windows lit up against the evening sky. I threw the truck in park and went around to open Taylor's door. I helped her out and then pulled her to me for a fierce hug.

I loved that she fit so perfectly against me. Her head ended up tucked right under my chin, like the adorable short-stack she was. Her curves seemed to hug my planes of muscle just right. I inhaled her scent, it was a combination of honeysuckle and the underlying notes that were uniquely Taylor. I could never get enough.

I kissed the top of her head. "Everything's going to be fine. Just remember, they already love you."

Taylor let out a sigh and then tilted her face up so that her chin rested on my sternum. "Thanks for putting up with my crazy."

I grinned down at her. "Anytime. Plus, you being crazy just means you'll fit in with the rest of my family."

A smile spread across her face, and I closed the distance to brush my lips against hers.

The sound of a shouted, "Tay Tay!" broke the trance as Noah bounded down the front steps. He launched himself at Taylor's middle, and she caught him easily. "Tay Tay, I read the book about the boxer all by myself! Mom didn't have to help me once!"

Jensen appeared behind him. "It's true. He didn't even need a single hint."

Taylor squeezed Noah's shoulders. "That's amazing. Does that mean it's time for a library and bookstore visit for some new books?"

Noah bobbed his head up and down enthusiastically. My jaw fell open. Was this the same nephew who had dragged his feet, making up any excuse in the world to avoid reading?

Jensen elbowed me in the side. "Shut your mouth, you'll catch flies." I snapped my jaw shut, and she chuckled. "Taylor's worked miracles with him, I swear. She has a gift."

I studied Taylor in the throes of conversation with Noah. She was great with him. I wondered what it would take to get her to consider teaching at one of the local schools. As I turned that over in my mind, my mom appeared in the doorway. "Get in here, dinner's almost ready, and I need my gossip time with Taylor."

A soft smile, one I knew was reserved for my mom, appeared on Taylor's face. I reached out and took her hand in mine, linking our fingers. "We're coming."

It only took about sixty seconds for Taylor to relax. As soon as Taylor saw she had my mother's approval, we lapsed into easy conversation and laughter at Noah's antics.

"So," my gran began as we dug into the feast my mom had prepared. "When are you going to give me some more great-grandchildren? I'm not getting any younger here."

Taylor turned red as a tomato, and I choked on my beer. Jensen started cackling with laughter. Noah just looked between Taylor and me, little-boy brows pulled together in confusion. My father cleared his throat. "Now, Mom."

"Don't you, *now Mom* me, Andrew. You know I have a gift for knowing when something's right. When two souls are meant for each other. And these two are it for one another. What's the point in pussyfooting around?"

"Irma!" my mom scolded.

"I speak the truth," Gran huffed.

I thought I could see the panic rising in Taylor. Her fists were clenched around a napkin, her breathing shallow. Fuck. She was going to run on me. Then Taylor did something that shocked the shit out of me. She burst out laughing. Deep belly laughs that shook her whole body. Soon, the entire table joined in, even Noah, who had no idea what we were laughing about.

Taylor dried a tear from the corner of her eye. "You certainly don't mince words, Miss Irma."

"What would be the point? I only got so much time left." Gran reached across the table to pat Taylor's hand. "You're good for my boy here. And he's good for you. Just remember that when the time comes and things get hard or scary. It's always worth the fight."

Taylor sucked in a breath. I ran a comforting hand across her back and squeezed her shoulder. "All right, Gran, you've had your say. Can we get back to eating?"

"Yeah, hurry up and eat everyone," Noah chimed in. "There's

chocolate cream pie for dessert, and that's my favorite."

Jensen rolled her eyes. "Every dessert is your favorite."

Noah's expression took on a pondering quality, then he nodded. "Yeah, that's pretty much true. Everything but stuff with coconut. That's just gross."

Taylor let out a light laugh, and I was relieved to see her eyes bright and untroubled. "I don't like coconut either."

"That's 'cause you're smart."

The entire table broke into laughter. Taylor leaned into my side. This was Heaven, right here. My girl pressed up close. My family all around. Laughter tinging the air. Good food filling my belly. I hoped with everything I had that I could hold on tightly enough to make it last.

CHAPTER
Thirty-four

Taylor

I SMOOTHED MY HANDS OVER MY BLACK PENCIL SKIRT AS I got out of Walker's truck. I didn't want to be here. Really, *really* did not want to be here. I wanted nothing to do with anything close to death or loss. And a funeral was right smack in the middle of that mess.

What I did want was to be there for Walker. And, let's face it, I'd been pushing all sorts of limits and challenging the rules I'd placed on myself over the past couple of years. Walker squeezed my hand, tugging me to him. "Thanks for being here."

Here was the funeral of his ex-girlfriend. I wasn't sure it was appropriate for me to be here, but Walker had asked, and I couldn't deny him. I brushed my lips against his in a kiss that was more about comfort than passion. "No problem."

Walker squeezed my hand. "I know it's a big deal for you. And I want you to know that I understand that."

I pressed my lips together, unsure of what to say. I went with a nod, just ducking my head. Walker curved an arm around my shoulders and curled me into his side. I soaked up his warmth and strength as we prepared to face what lay ahead.

As we crossed the parking lot of the local church, a high-pitched voice shrieked from our left. "You did *not* bring her here." A bottle-blonde toddled towards us on shoes with heels so pointy, they would surely be classified as deadly weapons. She was familiar. Recognition dawned. This was Caitlin's bitchy friend from the bakery. Great. Just great.

"Bridgette," Walker said in a low but firm tone. "This isn't the time or the place."

Bridgette huffed, tossing her blonde locks over her shoulder. "That's for damn sure. You showing up is bad enough, but to bring your floozy with you? You might as well spit on Caitlin's grave."

I winced and bit the inside of my cheek to keep my temper in check. Apparently, this girl was all about the drama. Walker's grip on my shoulder tightened. "Bridgette, that's enough. I know you're hurting, but this isn't the way to deal with it."

Bridgette lifted her chin in the air as if she were better than anyone who might deign to be in her presence. I fought the urge to roll my eyes. The woman narrowed her gaze at Walker. "This has nothing to do with *me*. This has everything to do with you and that trampy whore."

Uh-oh. That was going too far for Walker. Even if your best friend had recently been murdered, it seemed you did not call me a trampy whore in Walker's presence. He released his hold on me and took two angry strides towards Bridgette. "Get this through your apparently tiny brain, my relationships are none of your damn business. Now, cut the fucking crap before I find something to arrest you for."

Bridgette's jaw fell open. "Y-y-you can't do that. My daddy will have your job for even threatening something like that."

Walker snorted. "Your dad might be rich, Bridge, but he has zero pull in this town. No one likes him because he indulges your spoiled ass and thinks his shit doesn't stink."

Her mouth gaped open and closed like a fish's. Walker shook his head and exhaled a long breath. "I'm sorry you lost your best friend, but it's no excuse to attack someone who's done nothing wrong."

"She's done everything wrong!" Bridgette's gaze shot to me, anger flaring back to life. "*You,*" she seethed, "you ruined everything. Walker was about to ask Caitlin to move in with him before you strode in and stole him away. You should be ashamed of yourself. Better yet, you should just leave. No one wants you here."

I held my tongue, even though I wanted to give this chick a piece of my mind. Bridgette was now a shade of red that I was pretty sure meant a stroke was imminent. She cocked her arm back as if she were about to slap me, but a hand caught her around the bicep. "We have got to stop meeting this way, gorgeous," Tuck said, sending a devilish smile my way.

Walker stiffened. "What did you just call her?"

I rubbed a hand up and down Walker's back. "All right, all right. Enough with the drama already. If you haven't noticed, we've got ourselves a bit of an audience." I tipped my head to the side, towards a group of at least twenty people who were gathered at the front of the church, including, I winced, Walker's entire family, Bryce, and Ashlee. Shit. I waved, attempting to reassure them. Jensen gave me a thumbs up. I fought the urge to laugh.

"God, help me," Walker begged.

I smiled up at him. "Well, we are about to walk into a church, this seems as likely a place as any for him to hear your call."

"I think my prayer should be 'God save me from smartass women.'"

"Sounds like a good prayer," I agreed.

Tuck let out a bark of laughter. "You two are meant for each other."

Bridgette whirled on Tuck, smacking him in the chest. "Oh,

shut up, you fool." And then she stormed towards the church, still the color of a tomato.

Tuck turned back to Walker and me. "Well, that was a fun way to start the day."

Walker took my hand in his but used the other to smack Tuck on the backside of the head. "Hey!" Tuck protested. "What was that for? I just saved your girl from getting bitch-slapped."

I leaned around Walker so I could meet Tuck's eyes. "Thanks for that, by the way."

"No problem, gorgeous," he said with a wink.

Walker slapped him again. "*That* was for being a flirty fucker. Stop hitting on my girl."

Tuck grinned. "What? You worried she'll finally see the error of her ways and leave your sorry ass for a real man?"

Walker threw an arm up in the air. "I give up. You're hopeless."

"You're both hopeless," Sarah said as we reached the church steps. "And you're embarrassing Taylor, so behave."

A gentle smile formed on my face. I loved Sarah, she was the best. There were still times when she did things that caused my heart to pang because it reminded me of my mom, but mostly, she was a comfort. A way to experience the same kind of care my mother gave to everyone in her orbit. Sarah dipped to kiss my cheek. "I hope you gave that awful girl a piece of your mind."

I let out a soft laugh. "I didn't even need to, your son had that pretty well covered."

Her eyebrows rose. "Glad to hear it."

We all filed into the church. Walker, Tuck, and I slipped into the row behind the rest of the Cole clan, Walker refusing to let Tuck sit next to me. I pressed my lips together, staring at my lap, not trusting myself not to smile or laugh.

When I lifted my head, my gaze landed on the dark coffin at the front of the church. Pain sliced through my heart as memories of my mother's funeral slammed into me. She'd opted to be cremated, so there hadn't been a coffin, but everything else—the flowers, the sea of black, the sounds of sniffling—was all heart-wrenchingly familiar.

My heart picked up its pace, my breathing growing quicker, more shallow. I wasn't sure if I could do this. It was too much, too soon. A hand took mine, guiding it to a chest. Walker's voice sounded over the blood roaring in my ears. "Breathe with me. Just copy how I breathe."

It took a few false starts, but I finally followed his instructions. I'm not sure how long it took, but my heart rate began to slow, and my breathing evened out. "Sorry," I whispered.

Walker traced tiny circles on the back of my hand, which was still planted on his chest. "What did I say about apologizing? Plus, I'm the one who should be saying I'm sorry. I never should have asked you to come."

I swallowed thickly. "I wanted to be here for you."

He squeezed my hand and then lifted my chin with a finger so that I was forced to meet his eyes. "You are here for me. You made me smile on a day when I thought that would be impossible. And when I feel your body next to mine, my soul settles somehow. I feel…at peace. So, you are here for me in every way I need."

I brushed my lips against his. "I'm glad," I whispered. Walker wrapped his arm around me and, as the pastor began to speak, I got lost in my own thoughts. I thought about how I hadn't needed to run as much lately. How well I slept next to Walker. How the peace I felt when I was with him was the same serenity I experienced when I lost myself in the water.

It scared the hell out of me that this man could come to mean this much to me so quickly. I closed my eyes and offered up a silent prayer. *Please, God, please don't take him from me, too.*

CHAPTER
Thirty-Five

Walker

MY BODY JOLTED AWAKE AS MY PHONE RANG OUT from Taylor's nightstand. She moaned. Sadly, not the kind of sounds I loved hearing from her. This was an angry, frustrated moan. She batted at my chest. "Make it stop."

I chuckled, hitting the screen of the phone. "Cole."

"This is Harry at dispatch. We have a report of an attempted kidnapping. Officers are on the scene, but we thought we should call you, given everything that's been going on."

I was suddenly wide-awake, my body on high alert. "You did the right thing. Where'd it happen?" I was already climbing out of bed, searching for the clothes I'd shed in a mad dash to get both Taylor and myself naked as quickly as possible last night.

"Three blocks south of the saloon. Corner of Hillhurst and Pine."

I buttoned my jeans while cradling my phone between my ear and shoulder. "Tell them I'll be there in ten."

"Will do, Deputy Chief."

I slid my phone into my pocket and pulled my shirt over my head. Glancing back at the bed, I saw that Taylor was sitting up now, fully awake and biting the inside of her cheek. She was breathtaking. Hair all mussed from sleep and me having my fingers tangled in it. Her skin glowing. But her eyes…her eyes were filled with fear.

I crossed to her in two long strides. Cupping her face in my hands, I brought it close to mine. "Everything's going to be okay."

"What's going on?" she whispered, her voice still raspy with sleep.

"This happens sometimes. Not regularly, but every now and then. A case where they need a senior officer on-scene. So, I gotta haul my ass outta bed, away from my girl, and give them a hand." I didn't want to tell her the details. I didn't want to freak her out any more than necessary. She'd already had a tough day, she didn't need this.

Of course, she pushed. "What happened, Walker?"

I kissed her hard on the mouth and then sat next to her on the bed. "An attempted kidnapping." Taylor's pretty mouth fell open. "The victim is fine, but I need to go see what's going on."

Her hands shot out quicker than I'd ever seen her move, and she clung to me, arms around my neck. "Please, be careful."

The funeral had taken a toll on her. I never should have asked her to go with me. It was too soon. There were too many bad memories, and now she was freaked the hell out. I rubbed a hand up and down her spine. "Everything's going to be fine. I promise. I just need to take a few statements and put some pieces in place."

Taylor sagged against me in relief. "Okay," she breathed.

I kissed the side of her face, her temple, then her forehead. "You're mine."

I felt her smile against my throat. "I'm yours."

I pulled back, studying her face. She still looked concerned, but there was no longer panic in her eyes. I glanced at my watch, three a.m.. "This will take a couple hours, and then I'll probably just stay at the office. But I'll call you when things are wrapped up to let you know everything's okay."

She nodded, pressing her lips together. "Thanks."

"Of course." I rose from the bed, crossing to the closet to grab my badge and gun. Taylor had insisted I get a lock box if I wanted to keep a gun at her house. The thought made me smile.

Holstering my weapon, I crossed back to Taylor and brushed my lips against hers. "Talk to you in a few hours."

"In a few hours," she said softly.

I made my way out of the cabin, making sure the door was locked behind me, then jogged to my truck. It took me less than ten minutes to get to the scene. What I found there shocked the shit out of me. Sitting huddled on a bench, shaking like a fucking leaf, was Bridgette. Kelly, one of our few female officers, was consoling her, while a medic checked Bridgette's pulse. A few other guys milled around.

Hopping down from my rig, I strode towards Bridgette and Kelly. I slowed my pace as I got closer, not wanting to frighten Bridgette any further. I carefully took a seat on the bench on Bridgette's other side. She didn't move, didn't even look at me. I met Kelly's gaze. She just shook her head.

This was not good. I turned to the medic. "She in shock?"

The guy, who looked all of eighteen, nodded. "I'd say that's a pretty good guess. She'll respond if you ask her questions, though."

I scrubbed a hand over my stubbled jaw. "Bridgette, can you tell me what happened?"

Her head slowly and jerkily turned towards me. "I-I was walking to my car from the saloon, and someone grabbed me from behind. Put a hand over my mouth. I tried to kick him, but I couldn't. So, finally, I bit his hand and screamed." She lifted a shaky hand to point at two guys talking to another officer. "Those guys saw and came running. Whoever had me, he-he shoved me to the ground and took off."

Kelly spoke up then. "No one got a good look at the guy. He was wearing a ballcap. They said they'd guess a pretty large build."

"H-he told me not to scream. That it would be worse if I fought him." Tears tinged black with mascara tracked down Bridgette's cheeks. "His voice. It-it sounded familiar, but I can't place it."

My spine went ramrod straight. This had to be the same guy who killed the hiker and Caitlin. Had to be. This was too small a town to have more than one violent psychopath. "Bridgette, I want you to think real carefully over the next couple hours and days. See if you can't remember where you've heard the voice before."

"O-okay."

I jerked my chin at the medic. "I think you should take her in, let the docs take a look at her."

"Was already planning to as soon as you were done with your questions."

"Thanks." I crossed to the other officers and got the same story from the two guys who were here from Portland to do some fly fishing. They were freaked and didn't have any additional information.

I drummed my fingers against the side of my thigh. If this was the same guy, where would he go when he was spooked? I swirled ideas around in my mind before landing on one. He would go to where he felt safest. His comfort zone. His hunting ground.

"Hank," I called to one of the officers. "I want you and Kelly with me. We're going to check out the area around Creek Line trail."

"Now?" Hank asked, his eyes widening.

"Now. If this is the same guy, he's going to retreat to where he feels safe. The woods. We have to find him on his turf." I called dispatch and let them know I was taking a couple of officers to follow up on a hunch. "Let's roll out."

Hank and Kelly hopped into their squad car, and we headed for the Creek Line trailhead.

We were all sweaty and exhausted, even though the sun had yet to rise. Our group paused to suck down some water, and for me to study my GPS. I had guided us towards the area directly between where the first and second bodies had been found. I hoped that we would find something, anything that would point us in the direction of our guy or his hidey hole.

Our trek through the woods had been mostly quiet. I gave Hank and Kelly silent props for not uttering even one word of protest, even when, two hours in, we'd still found nothing. Zero signs of life. I blew out a breath. "I want to check out one more spot. If there's nothing, we'll call it a night. Thanks for sticking with me."

"Of course, Deputy Chief," Kelly said, taking another swig of water. "We can stay out here as long as you need."

"Just want to check out the area north of the creek, closer to the mountain."

Hank nodded his agreement, and we all took a moment to adjust our gear. Silence again reigned as we made our way off the trail and towards the creek. After finding a downed log to cross on, we began the incline up the other side. A tiny glimmer of light flashed in the corner of my eye. I froze, holding up a hand for the others to follow suit. "Turn off your flashlights," I said as a low order.

My eyes strained to see in the darkness. There it was. A small, flickering light. From what? A lantern? Fire? I let out a slow breath. I had two choices. I could call it in, wait the hours it would take to assemble the SWAT team, and hope this guy didn't get away in the meantime. Or, I could go in with Hank and Kelly at my back. It was a risk either way.

I checked the gun at my hip. "We're going in. I'm going to call in backup, but I don't want to risk losing this guy while we wait for them to assemble and hike in. You are to use *extreme* caution, and I am going to take point."

Hank's and Kelly's postures both straightened. "We're with you, sir," Hank said.

I jerked my head in a nod and made the hushed call. Turning back to Hank and Kelly, I hoped I was doing the right thing. "All right. Let's do this. Follow my lead. No lights. Try to make as little noise as possible."

No light and careful feet meant slow progress. It took us nearly half an hour to get up the hillside. We grabbed onto tree roots and rocks to pull ourselves up when needed, and as we got closer to our destination, each of our breathing was ragged. We were filthy, exhausted, and covered in scrapes, but we were going to get this bastard.

Just as we crested the top of the ridgeline, a loud crack sounded. It was deafening against the silence of the pre-dawn forest. I didn't have time to react before a burning sensation filled my chest. The force of the bullet sent me sailing backwards, crashing into the dirt.

Curses filled the air around me. "Stay down," I wheezed. "Active shooter."

"This is going to hurt, sir," Kelly said before leaning all her weight against my wound. It was as if a hot poker lanced through my chest.

I heard Hank's muted voice on the satellite phone, something about an officer down. My vision began to tunnel. "Oh no, you don't," Kelly yelled. "Stay with me, Walker."

I tried to force my focus, to narrow it in on her. "Tell Taylor—" I began.

"Nope. You're going to tell Taylor whatever this message is," Kelly began. "But I guess you can practice on me."

My lips tried to pull into a smile but failed. "Tell her...love her." Just before my world went dark, my mind was filled with nothing but images of Taylor's face. Her bewitching blue-gray eyes. Her wide smile. Her golden hair, framing her beautiful face like a halo. If I was going to go, at least the last thing I saw was pure beauty.

CHAPTER
Thirty-six

Taylor

THE WORDS ON THE PAGE BLURRED AS I ATTEMPTED TO read the same paragraph for probably the fifteenth time. I snapped the book closed and picked up my phone for about the one-hundredth time. Nothing. No missed calls or texts.

My stomach churned. Something wasn't right. Walker should have called by now. My eyes bore imaginary holes into my phone's screen. I tapped the message icon.

Me: *How'd everything go?*

Me: *Just making sure you're okay.*

Me: *Please just send me a quick text letting me know everything's fine.*

My morning tea roiled in my stomach. That's it, I was calling Jensen. I hadn't wanted to worry her, but I was now officially freaking out. I had just tapped on her contact when I heard tires on the gravel of my driveway. My breath whooshed out of me. It had to be Walker. I was going to smack him really fucking hard for scaring me this badly.

I rushed to the door, yanking it open and stepping out onto the porch. I was halfway down the steps before I realized the car wasn't Walker's. It wasn't one I knew at all. The driver's door opened, and it took me a couple of seconds to recognize Tessa as the form who exited the vehicle.

My heart stuttered, skipping several beats before settling into a rapid rhythm. Tessa started towards me, her steps measured, her face pale and her expression worried. I fell backward, my ass landing with a jolt on the stair. There was a burning sensation in my chest I'd only felt once before. I shook my head back and forth with a fierceness that made it ache.

Tessa crouched in front of me, careful not to touch me. "Jensen asked me to come and get you. She got a call while we were setting up for the day." She paused. "I'm so sorry. Walker's been shot. He's at the hospital now, but it's bad."

Her voice was incredibly gentle. It didn't matter. Her words still inflicted a level of pain I'd never thought to experience again. I had taken great care to make sure I never had to go through it again. But I'd gotten lazy, careless. I'd let my walls crumble, and now I was paying the price.

Tessa rose slowly and extended a hand. She had a fluidity of movement that was beautiful. It's funny the things you noticed at times like this. The world seemed to be moving in slow motion. "Can I help you up?"

I said nothing. Just stood and started towards Tessa's car. Gravel bit into my feet, but I didn't care.

"I'm going to grab your shoes and purse," Tessa called. I still said nothing. Just slipped into the passenger seat.

Tessa was back in a flash, placing my purse on my lap and easing my feet into a pair of flip flops before circling around and getting in the car herself. We drove in silence, with nothing but the roaring of my blood in my ears to keep me company. Thirty minutes later, Tessa swung her car into a parking space at the hospital. I numbly reached for the door handle, pausing only briefly to get out a strangled "thank you" to Tessa.

She nodded. "Of course."

We made our way towards the double doors of the emergency room. My steps faltered as the angry red letters shone down on me. I hadn't been in a hospital since the night my mother died. I gritted my teeth so hard, they made an audible noise, but I forced myself to keep walking.

Tessa led the way to some sort of reception desk. She spoke softly to a woman behind the counter, and I didn't try to listen. "They're in a waiting room upstairs."

We took an elevator up two floors, and Tessa found the room we were looking for. It was full to bursting with people. Just the sight of them all made me nauseous. My breaths came more quickly. Jensen spotted me and flew from her chair, throwing her arms around me as her body was wracked with sobs.

I forced my arms to encircle her. To do the kind thing. I felt like a robot.

"He's in surgery," Jensen said between sobs. "It's really bad. He was shot in the chest. They said they'd tell us more when they know it."

I tried to coax out words of reassurance, but I had none. Jensen led me towards her parents, who looked ravaged. Completely wrecked. Their only son's life was hanging in the balance, and there was nothing they could do. Jensen placed me between herself and Sarah. Sarah reached out to grip my hand tightly. She seemed to have no words either.

The room was mostly silent as we waited. Muted conversations started up and then died off. People got up to place or receive phone calls. There were lots of individuals in uniform. Bryce arrived with Ashlee, and Jensen collapsed into his arms, dissolving into sobs as he held her. I gripped the arms of my chair tighter.

A woman in a Sutter Lake PD uniform approached me. "You're Taylor, right?" I nodded hesitantly. She swallowed roughly. "I was with Walker when it happened." My entire body tensed. "He, uh, he wanted me to tell you something."

I shot from my chair, sending it flying back against the wall. "NO!" I shouted. "No! Don't you tell me what he said, because he is going to tell me. Walker is! Not you."

Just as I was about to launch at her, Tuck strode through the door, looking disheveled and dirty. "What the hell is going on in here?" He caught me around the waist and moved me back. "What did you say to her?" he accused the officer but didn't wait for her answer. He kept pushing me towards the door.

By the time we reached the hallway, my entire body was shaking, and I could barely walk. Tuck gave up trying to guide my movements and instead lifted me up in a bridal-style hold. I shoved my face into his neck. The tears came now. Hot and angry and terrified.

Tuck set me down on a bench at the end of a quiet hallway, still keeping one arm curved around me. "He's a fighter, Taylor. He's going to make it." Tuck's voice was thick with unshed tears.

I said nothing, just clutched the shirt of Walker's closest friend with a ferocity that scared even me. I had to turn it off. All the emotions threatening to overwhelm me, I had to shut them off. I couldn't do this again. I ground my teeth together, squeezed my eyes closed, and prayed for a release from the pain. Exhaustion must have overtaken me, because the next thing I knew, my eyes were blinking open at the sound of Tuck's and Andrew's hushed voices.

"I went to the scene," Tuck started, a hardness to his tone now. "Tried to track the bastard, but he's good. I lost him in the creek."

Andrew ran a hand through his disheveled hair. "I can't believe something like this is happening in Sutter Lake."

I pushed off Tuck and moved into a sitting position. "Is there any word?"

Andrew gave me a gentle smile. "I was just coming to tell you.

He's out of surgery. He's in rough shape, but they expect him to make a full recovery." The tears wanted to come again, but I refused to let them. Andrew pulled me to my feet and into a tight hug. "He's going to be just fine. We can go in and see him once they've settled him in a room."

I nodded against Walker's father's shoulder and then pulled back. "What happened? Do you have any details?"

Andrew's jaw went hard. "He was shot in the chest, right above his heart. An inch lower, and I don't think he would've survived." I shuddered violently. "Amazingly, the bullet missed all the important stuff. His heart, any arteries, his clavicle, all fine. He does have a collapsed lung, but that should be fine with some rest."

An inch. One single inch was all that had come between me and total devastation for the second time. I forced those thoughts from my mind. "When can we see him?"

"They're moving him to a room now. He'll be out of it for several hours, though. Jensen and Sarah are going home so they can check on my mom and Noah. Hopefully, they'll get a couple hours of sleep. You should do the same. Come back after you've had some rest."

I shook my head fiercely. "No. I'm staying. I know I might not be able to see him right away, but I'm staying."

Andrew patted my hand. "We'll make sure you can see him."

Andrew, Tuck, and I followed a maze of hallways until we found the correct nurses' station. A portly woman with a kind face showed us to Walker's room. "He's all settled in. Now, he looks a little battered, but I assure you, he's going to pull through just fine. Just push the call button and buzz us if you need anything."

The beating of my heart quickened as we approached the doorway. When I crossed the threshold, that horrible burning in my chest came back. The fire that threatened to take me to my knees. I sucked in an audible breath, trying to force air into my lungs.

There were tubes and machines everywhere. And that damned sound of a heart monitor beeping away. I reminded myself I should be glad I could hear the beeps. Walker's heart was doing its job. It was strong, and he was going to be just fine. I let Andrew and Tuck approach him first. I was the interloper, after all. The new addition to Walker's life. They'd been with him practically since he'd breathed his first breath.

Tears tracked down Andrew's face as he bent to press a kiss to his son's head. The gesture was so tender, it had me taking a step back and staring at the pattern on the linoleum floor. When he was done, Tuck took his turn. Taking the time to whisper what looked like a vehement promise in Walker's ear before backing away.

I was up. My eyes locked on the rhythmic rise and fall of Walker's chest as my feet brought me closer and closer. Suddenly, it wasn't Walker I saw lying there, but my mother. Her weak heart slowly giving out as the rise and fall of her chest grew shallower and shallower. I squeezed my eyes closed and shook my head to clear the image. Walker was alive. He was *alive*. I repeated it over and over in my head. He was alive, and that was the only thing that mattered right now.

I let myself sit in the chair next to his bed because I didn't trust my legs not to give out on me. I scooted it as close as possible. Carefully, oh so gently, I lifted his limp hand, the one that was free of tubes and wires. I traced the rough tips of his fingers, soaking in their familiar sandpapered feel.

Emotions warred within me. Half of me wanted to crawl into the bed with him and get as close as possible. Force his heart to keep beating. The other half of me wanted to run. Run fast and far and never stop. I hated myself for that second piece.

I focused on the feel of Walker's hand in mine, the beeping of the heart monitor. I forced myself to be strong. I stayed. I didn't run. Even though I was scared spitless.

Minutes turned to hours, and still, I didn't move from my spot. Finally, fatigue began to war with my eyelids, and I laid my head down on the side of Walker's bed, not losing my gentle grip on his hand. Sleep claimed me within seconds.

A feather-light sensation on my head woke me. My eyes fluttered open, taking a moment to adjust to the light. A hand brushed along the side of my face. I shot up. "Walker!"

There he was, eyes fully open though ringed in dark circles. He looked as though he'd been through a war, and I guess in a way, he had. He was still the most beautiful sight I'd ever seen. "Hey, Short-stack," he said, his voice even rougher than usual.

I stood. "Are you okay? Do you need the nurse? Some water? Anything?"

Walker let out a low chuckle that turned into a wheezing cough. "I'm fine," he said, his face laced with pain.

My brows pulled together tightly. "You don't sound it. Let me get a nurse."

He grabbed my hand, his hold strong. "They've already been in to look me over while you were asleep."

My eyes widened. "And I didn't wake up?"

A grin pulled at Walker's lips. "You were out like a light. You even let out a couple adorable snores."

My hands flew to my mouth. "I didn't."

His grin widened. "You did." He grasped the edge of my shirt and tugged me closer to the bed.

I bent down and, with the gentlest touch I could manage, I brushed my lips against his. "Are you in much pain?"

Walker's eyes bore into mine with an intensity that stole a beat of my heart. "It's manageable." He traced circles on the back of my hand with his finger. "I won't lie, there were a few moments there where I wasn't sure I would see your pretty face again." The burning sensation was back again, and I bit the inside of my cheek. "There are some things I want to tell you—"

"Not now," I interrupted, my heart giving a painful squeeze. "When you're feeling better, we'll talk about anything you want to, but right now, you need to rest."

Walker's eyes roamed my face, peering into my soul like always. I worried that he would call me on my brush-off, but he didn't, he merely tugged me down into another lip touch. "You're mine."

"I'm yours." The words sliced through my throat as though they were made of razor blades. I was his. But I didn't want to be. I didn't want him to own my heart and soul. Because I knew now that if I lost him—I'd never survive.

CHAPTER
Thirty-seven

Walker

I PUSHED UP TO A SEATED POSITION ON THE COUCH SO THAT I could get a better view of Taylor in my kitchen. The injury to my chest barely hurt. Weeks had passed, and there was now only a slight pulling sensation when my muscles bunched and flexed. I'd have to log a few sessions with a local physical therapist to make sure everything was as it should be, but then it would be back to work. I'd be confined to a desk at first, but I'd be back in the field before long.

Each day, I got stronger. Each day, I healed. And each day, Taylor pulled away a little more. She made excuses not to share my bed, saying that she was afraid she'd bump my wound in the night. Every time I tried to deepen a kiss, she retreated. Today, she'd taken me to my latest doctor's appointment, and I'd gotten the all-clear to return to the majority of my activities, including sex. I'd been thrilled, mentally planning all the ways I was going to take her when we got home.

Taylor had immediately rushed into the kitchen, saying she needed to make me lunch. I watched her staccato movements as she put together sandwiches, one of the few things even she with her cooking curse could prepare. It was as though she were on alert for a possible attack from any direction.

I got it. I really did. Taylor had lost so much, and just when she let her walls down, and began to really let me in, I'd almost died on her. It would take time for her to see that I wasn't going anywhere. But I had all the time in the world.

My front doorbell rang. "I'll get it," I called before Taylor could stop what she was doing. A frown pulled at her mouth, but she didn't argue. I made my way to the door, pulling it open to find Ashlee standing there with a plate of cookies in her hands. "Hey, Ashlee."

Pink tinged the woman's cheeks. "Hi, Walker. I just wanted to check on you, see if you needed anything, and bring you some cookies."

I gave her a gentle smile. "That's very kind of you. Come on inside." I stepped back to allow Ashlee to enter and closed the door behind her. "We can put these in the kitchen, Taylor's in there making a couple sandwiches." I led Ashlee down the hall towards the kitchen. "Short-stack, Ashlee's here, and she brought cookies."

There was a look on Taylor's face that I couldn't quite decipher. Some cross between pain and frustration that made no sense, but she greeted Ashlee warmly. "Hey, Ashlee. That's so sweet of you."

Ashlee ducked her head. "It's no problem. I don't want to interrupt, I just wanted to check in. Walker, do you need help with anything? Need me to bring you anything from the office or anywhere else? Or I could bring over some home-cooked meals? I'd be happy to help out in any way I can."

Taylor gripped the counter, her knuckles turning white. The pieces clicked into place. She was jealous. I had to fight the chuckle that wanted to escape my throat. "I'm good, Ashlee, but thanks for the offer. I'll be back to work in a couple days for desk duty."

Surprise and relief shone in Ashlee's eyes. "Oh, that's wonderful. I'm so glad. I'll just leave you to your lunch and see you in a few days."

"I'll see you out." I ushered her out the door, waving as she hopped into her car. Heading back to the kitchen, I let the smile I'd been fighting take over my face.

Taylor looked up as I entered. "What's with the dopey smile?"

I crossed to her, pulling her into my arms. "You were jealous."

Taylor's face scrunched up adorably. "I was not."

"You were, too. And it was fucking cute."

She tried to extricate herself from my arms, but I held firm. "I was not jealous. Now, will you please let me go? I'm trying to finish lunch."

I dropped my arms. "What is going on with you? I've tried to be patient, to let you work through this on your own, but I think it's time we talk."

Taylor's shoulders stiffened. "I don't really think there's anything to talk about."

"How about the fact that you'll barely let me touch you? How about that?"

Her head snapped up, and I saw fire in her eyes. "I haven't wanted you to hurt yourself."

"Well, the doctor cleared me, what's your excuse going to be now?" I asked, throwing my arms wide.

Taylor flinched at my movement. "I just need some time."

"Time for what?" I was not going to let her use this as an excuse to push me away. I refused.

"To think. I need some space to figure out what I want."

"Well, which is it, Taylor? Time or space?" My temper teased the surface, and I knew I needed to keep it in check.

She twirled the ring on her finger. "I don't know, maybe both."

"That's bullshit."

"I'm no good for you, Walker." Her words were soft and filled with such grief, they broke my heart.

"What are you talking about?"

Tears pooled in her eyes. "I'm a mess. Can't you see that?" She swiped at her face, and I fought back the urge to pull her into my arms. "You got hurt, and all I want to do is run away. Do you know how fucked up that is? I think I might love you, and yet all I want to do is get as far away from you as possible at the time when you need me the most."

My heart stuttered at her confession, warmth filling my chest. "Taylor, baby, that is totally understandable given what you've been through recently." I reached for her, but she stepped out of my grasp, shaking her head back and forth.

"No, it's not! You deserve better. Someone like Ashlee, who'd love nothing more than to be by your side through it all."

"What the fuck? Seriously, Taylor, what the *fuck*? I do not want, nor have I ever wanted Ashlee. I want *you*. You're mine, remember?"

"I'm broken, Walker."

"Well, then all your beautifully broken pieces are mine."

Taylor's body visibly shuddered at my words. "I think I'm going to go back to LA for a while."

My spine went ramrod straight. "No. You go, and I'll follow your ass."

Her shoulders slumped. "Please." There were tears in her voice. "Please, Walker, I need to get my head straight."

My teeth ground together with such force, I thought I might crack a molar. "I'll give you space to get your head straight, if you promise me you won't leave."

Taylor blew out a slow breath. "All right." Her eyes, full of tears, met mine. "I'm going to go now…if you're okay on your own."

I wanted to scream at her that I wasn't fucking okay on my

own, but I resisted the urge and nodded instead. She disappeared into the guest room she'd been staying in, I assumed to get her stuff, and I just stared at the two sandwiches assembled and placed on plates. Footsteps sounded, drawing my attention.

There she stood, duffle over one shoulder, so eager to walk right out of my life. "I'll call you when I figure things out." I nodded, and she headed for the door.

"You know I love you, right?"

She froze. "I know." The words sounded so unbelievably tortured.

"To the depths of my soul. I'll give you time, but don't think I'm letting you walk out of my life so easily."

Taylor's head jerked in a nod as her shoulders shook with sobs, but she didn't turn around. Instead, she walked right out the door.

CHAPTER
Thirty-Eight

Taylor

Tears clouded my vision as I drove down the gravel road back to my cabin. What the hell was I doing? I had no freaking clue. All I knew was that I needed space. I needed to retreat to the safety of my bubble, a place where there was no one it would destroy me to lose.

I wanted to run somewhere Walker would never find me, but I would have to settle for holing up on my couch with a blanket pulled over my head. I swung into my driveway, and my jaw clenched. There was a large SUV parked to the side of my house, one I didn't recognize. The last thing in the world I wanted was to be forced into polite conversation with anyone, especially a stranger.

I pulled down my car's visor. Shit. I was a mess. I did my best to dry my tears and wipe away the tracks of mascara on my face. There was nothing I could do about the red eyes and cheeks other than put on my sunglasses. Grabbing my bag, I opened my door.

My eyes scanned from the strange SUV to the front of my house. A figure reclined on my front steps, a baseball cap pulled low, sunglasses on. Was he taking a nap? Then I noticed a guitar case leaning against the wood railing of the porch steps, and it all clicked into place. "Liam?"

The figure shot up to sitting and then moved to stand. "Hey there, Tay. How would you feel about a house guest? I really needed to get out of Dodge, and it had to be under the radar—" He paused mid-ramble to study my face. "Are you okay?"

That was all it took. I promptly burst into tears. And not the pretty kind. These were snotty, hiccupping sobs. Liam wrapped me in a tight hug. "Hey, hey now. Everything's going to be okay. Whatever it is, we can fix it."

"N-n-no we can't." I cried into Liam's shirt.

"What could be so bad that it's not fixable?"

"I-I-I fell in love with someone."

Liam pulled back, lines creasing his brow. "You fell in love with someone?"

I nodded.

"And that's bad?" he asked.

I nodded again.

Liam burst into a fit of laughter that had him leaning back to let it out. Rage flooded my veins. So many emotions had been pumping through my body for the past few hours, I was on over-load. So, I didn't take the time to think or calm my temper like I should have, I just wound my fist back and socked Liam right in the stomach. "It's not funny, asshole!"

Turning on my heel, I stormed into the house, leaving Liam wheezing in my wake. I went directly to the kitchen and opened the freezer to pull out a bottle of vodka. I filled a glass with ice, a healthy pour of alcohol, and a dash of lemonade. Taking my drink, I walked out to the back deck and sank onto one of the rockers.

It felt like a million years ago when I had sat out here after a nightmare and decided that Sutter Lake would be my home for the next little while. In reality, it had only been months. So much had changed, yet I found myself longing for how things used to be. Alone was the only state of being that was safe. I had now learned that lesson the hard way for the second time. I could have friends, but I couldn't open my heart to create a family. The risks were too great.

The sliding door opened behind me, but I didn't turn around. I kept sipping my drink, staring at my beautiful view and listening to the water below. Liam sat in the rocker next to mine. Only the sound of the bubbling creek filled the air as we rocked.

Eventually, Liam blew out a long breath. "I'm sorry I laughed." I said nothing in return. "Do you want to tell me what's going on?"

I turned, looking at Liam for the first time since he'd sat down. "First, why don't you tell me why you're here. Aren't you supposed to be recording an album right now?"

A muscle in his cheek ticked, and he took a pull of the beer he had apparently helped himself to. "Some news is about to break that will send every blood-sucking paparazzi in a thousand-mile radius to my doorstep, so I thought it would be good to get out of LA for a while. Go someplace no one would expect to find me."

I studied Liam's face, a pang of guilt hitting me in the belly. He looked awful. He hadn't shaved in days, and dark circles rimmed his bloodshot eyes. "Everything okay?" I knew it wasn't, but I hoped he'd open up if I asked outright.

He tilted his head back, staring at the crystal-blue sky. "Not really. And it doesn't help that I have an album due in a couple months and haven't written anything decent in almost a year." His head came back down so that he was again staring out at the horizon. "I think it's time for a change of scenery. Do you think I could stay a while? Maybe this place will inspire me."

"You can stay as long as you want. But to be honest, I was thinking of going back to LA."

Liam's head snapped in my direction. "You just told me that

you had fallen in love with someone. And now you're saying you want to go back to LA?"

It was my turn to stare out at the horizon. "It's complicated."

"Is he married?"

I scooped a piece of ice from my glass and pelted it at Liam. "No, you ass. You know I don't mess around like that."

He shrugged. "The heart wants what the heart wants."

My chest squeezed at that painful reminder. "I don't want my heart to want anyone. Or anything."

"Tay," he said softly. I refused to look at him, not wanting to see the pity in his eyes. He grabbed hold of one of my hands and gripped it tightly. My eyes shot to his. "It doesn't work that way."

"I'm not strong enough."

Liam squeezed my hand fiercely. "You are one of the strongest people I know." I bit my bottom lip hard to hold back the tears that wanted to fall. I wasn't strong, I was a fucking wimp. I didn't want the possibility of any more pain inflicted on my heart. Liam sighed, recognizing the doubt in my eyes. "Tell you what, why don't we get wasted, and you can tell me all about this love of yours that has you wanting to run for the hills?"

A snort escaped me. I'd definitely need lots of alcohol if I was going to talk about Walker for any length of time. "I'm in." Maybe Liam could show me a way out of the mess I'd gotten myself into. At the very least, the alcohol might numb the pain. I stood. "We need shots."

Liam's eyes widened. "Shit, this must be one hell of a story."

"You have no idea."

CHAPTER
Thirty-Nine

Walker

"YOU AREN'T SERIOUSLY BRINGING A MUG OF COFFEE into my tea shop, are you?" Jensen's voice rang out over the handful of early-morning customers at The Tea Kettle.

I took a long sip from my travel mug and grinned. I was not a tea drinker. I needed a strong hit of caffeine in the morning. Jensen rounded the counter, leaving Tessa to help the customers in line. She shook her head as she walked towards me. "Some supportive big brother you are."

I ruffled her hair before she could duck out of my hold. "Hey, now, I buy your baked goods."

"True," she admitted. "Is that what you're here for now? A nice scone?" she asked, arching a brow at me.

I shuffled my feet absentmindedly. "I just wanted to come and check up on my baby sister." It was a total and complete lie, and she knew it.

Jensen ushered me forward with a wave of her hand. "Come on, I'll grab us breakfast, and we can eat in my office and catch up."

I breathed out a sigh of relief. My sister was a good one. She knew I needed her advice about something, and she wasn't going to make me beg. "Sounds good. I'd take one of those ham and cheddar scones if you got 'em." They were the best.

Jensen grinned over her shoulder. "I think I can scrounge something up."

I headed to the office while Jensen ducked behind the bakery case. Pushing open the door, I crossed to one of the worn, over-stuffed chairs in the corner. The office fit the mismatched quality of the rest of The Tea Kettle. Nothing was an identical set, yet somehow it still worked.

Jensen bustled in moments later with a selection of biscuits, cakes, and scones. I rubbed my hands together. "Looks delicious, Little J."

"Thanks," she said with a small smile. Jensen had worked so hard to make this place a success, and I was damn proud of her. "So, what has my big brother walking into my tea shop before seven a.m.?"

The mouth-watering bite of scone I had just swallowed suddenly turned to lead in my stomach. "Taylor and I...we're, uh, having some issues, and I wanted a female perspective." My face felt hot.

Jensen's eyes narrowed in some sort of combination of concern and anger. "What did you do?"

"Why are you so sure it was me who did something? You're *my* sister, aren't you supposed to be on my side?"

Jensen let out a little huff. "I'm on both your sides. And I assumed it was you because she's been doing nothing but taking care of you for the last three and a half weeks. She's barely left your side."

"Well she's left it now," I said, a hint of anger tinging my tone.

Little lines creased Jensen's brow. "What do you mean?"

"She wants to go back to LA."

"What? How is that possible? She loves it here. She loves *you*."

I rubbed a hand over my stubbled jaw, feeling the now familiar sensation of pulling where my stitches used to be. "That's the problem."

"Would you please stop talking around the issue and tell me what the hell is going on?" Worry filled her eyes, and I knew Jensen's patience was at an end.

"Me getting shot really messed with Taylor's head. She's been trying to keep it together, but she's freaked."

"Does she want you to quit your job or something?"

I gave my head a little shake. "No. She wants to end things altogether. She said she just needs some time, but I know her. That's an excuse for her to retreat and hide. If she goes back to LA, I'll never see her again."

Jensen's jaw tightened, but I pushed on before she could speak. "She's terrified, J. I've never seen someone so fucking scared. I broke through those steel-reinforced walls. Half of her loves that I did it, and I'm pretty sure the other half hates me for it." I broke my scone into tiny pieces. "I don't know what to do."

Jensen's expression had softened. "You can't give up. Whatever you do, don't leave her alone. I know that's what she's asking for, but it's the last thing she needs. You need to show her that no matter what she does, you won't let her push you away."

I straightened my shoulders. Jensen was right. If I left Taylor alone, she would only think of all the reasons we shouldn't be together. All the reasons it was dangerous to love me. I needed to show her that this love, this *life* was worth the risk. I pushed up from my chair and bent to place a kiss on my sister's cheek. "Thanks, Little J. I can always count on you."

"Always," she said. "Give me two secs, and I'll wrap up some things for you to take over to Taylor's."

My sister knew me so well. She knew I wouldn't delay in getting to Taylor. "Thanks, sis."

"If anything will give you a way in, it'll be her favorite tea and some baked goods."

I let out a chuckle, my first laugh since Taylor had walked out my door yesterday. I had a plan, I had an in, and I wasn't taking no for an answer.

I pushed the door to my truck closed with an elbow as I balanced Taylor's tea and a massive bag of treats in my hands. I rolled my shoulders back, readying myself to do battle if necessary. I slowed a few steps from the porch. There was an SUV I didn't recognize parked next to the house. California plates.

Shit. Had she called someone to come and get her already? I really fucking hoped not. But if she had, I was going with them. I was taking Jensen's advice and not leaving Taylor alone for a second. I bounded up the porch steps and pressed the bell. Nothing. There were zero sounds of stirring coming from inside the house.

I pressed the bell again and followed it with a strong knock. Still nothing. A lead weight once again settled in my gut. What if something was wrong? I pounded on the door. "Taylor! It's Walker. If you don't answer the door in sixty seconds, I'm coming in."

I set her tea on the porch railing while I searched my pocket for my key ring, I had an extra set for the cabin on there. Before I could get them, the door swung open. "Jesus, do you know what time it is?" Standing in the doorway in nothing but boxers, hair tousled in a way that said he'd been having a little too much fun last night, was Liam Fairchild. Fuck.

I said nothing. Liam blinked against the sun, letting his eyes adjust to the light. "Oh, hey man. Walker, right?"

"Right." My voice was rough as burlap, and my mind spun, going in directions that made me want to puke up the baked goods in my stomach.

"Who is it, Liam?" A sleepy voice I recognized all too well said from inside.

"It's Walker."

Taylor appeared in the hall, hair a teased rat's nest, and wearing nothing but an oversized t-shirt. What in the actual fuck? My jaw turned to granite, and I was sure my eyes were raging. Taylor's eyes moved from me to Liam and back again. "I thought I told you I needed some time?"

My breath came in quick pants. "And you spend that time half-naked with some guy?"

Taylor's eyes turned hard, blazing with that blue fire I loved so much. "Excuse me?"

"You heard me."

"How I spend my time is none of your damn business! I told you I needed time and space to figure things out, but you never listen! You just push and push and *push*! Why can't you respect what I ask for?"

"You want me to respect what you ask for? Fine. I'm outta here. I don't need this shit." I pelted the bag of goodies at the shirtless rock star still standing in the entryway. "Here, help yourself, though it seems you already have." I spun on my heel, taking a swipe at the cup of tea still balanced on the rail. It flew into the drive, splashing everywhere.

I jumped into my truck and tore out, sending gravel flying. I only made it half a mile before the need to empty my stomach overtook me. I swung to the side of the road and heaved into the tall grass until the only thing coming up was bile.

I knew Taylor was terrified. That, I could handle. I could go as slowly as she needed, coaxing her every step of the way. But I never expected betrayal. Not from her. The image of Taylor and Liam half-dressed flashed in my mind. Suddenly, I was retching again. If only I could rid my heart of Taylor the same way.

CHAPTER
Forty

Taylor

"WHAT THE FUCK, TAY?" LIAM'S WORDS STRUCK out like a whip.

I leaned back against the hallway wall and slowly sank to the floor, my entire body trembling. What had I done?

Liam crouched in front of me. "Taylor, why did you let him think something had happened between us? That is beyond messed up."

Tears filled my eyes and began to spill over. "It's the only way he'll let me go."

"Fuck." Liam turned, sitting next to me on the floor and pulling me in to his side, his arm around my shoulders.

"He deserves better than me. I don't think I can do this, Liam. I'm scared all the time, and I don't think that's going to change." Just saying the words aloud brought on a flash of memories, but this time, they weren't of my mother wasting away in a hospital, they were of Walker. Images of his large, vibrant body filled with tubes, of the gauze covering the wound on his chest. I shuddered, and Liam pulled me closer to him.

"You are one of the best people I know. So loving. So giving. But you've been slowly disappearing into nothing since your mom got sick. You don't laugh as much, and we have to battle for you to let us in. Hell, we practically had to kidnap you to go on vacation with us last spring." I exhaled a slow breath, knowing he was right.

Liam squeezed my shoulder. "But Carter said the last couple of months when she talked to you, you sounded more like your old self. I was at her and Austin's one night when you called. Taylor, she burst into tears when she got off the phone with you. She said it was the first time she'd heard your real laugh in over a year. Not the polite one you use because it's appropriate. Your *real* one."

Tears continued to fall. I knew exactly the conversation he was talking about. I had been telling her about a dinner at the Coles', recounting some story about Irma. I'd had tears in my eyes then too, but only because I was laughing so hard. Walker and the Cole family had brought so many wonderful things to my life. But I was so scared. Would it be worth the pain if I lost one of them?

Liam squeezed my shoulder again. "We love you, Tay. We want to be there for you. But you can't keep running. You can't keep pushing everyone away."

I let my head fall to my knees. "It's the only way I know not to hurt."

Liam's grip on me tightened until I was sure it would leave a bruise. "You're lying to yourself, Taylor. Pushing people away doesn't mean it won't hurt if you lose them, it just means you'll be lonely until they're gone."

I gritted my teeth. Liam was wrong. I felt a measure of peace when I was alone. When it was just me and the water, swimming until my muscles shook with fatigue. Or when I was alone with the road, my feet pounding the packed earth until my lungs burned. That life could be enough for me.

Liam released his hold on me. "I'm going to be honest with you because I think you need a wakeup call. You're wasting your life away. You have so much to give. You're an incredible teacher, and you have such a way with kids. You were an amazing caregiver to your mom, you could give that gift to someone else. You used to be one of the best friends someone could hope to have."

I clued in to the *used to be* part of his statement and cringed. Liam pushed on. "But, honestly, this past year, you've been a crap friend." My head snapped up, but Liam held up a hand. "I get it. You've been through something horrible. And in relationships, we all have times where we take more than we give. It's natural. But it can't go on forever. Get your head out of your ass and realize you're not the only one dealing with shit before you lose the only people you have left."

With that, he rose. "I'm going to take a shower and get dressed. Why don't you do the same, and then I'll make us some breakfast. Maybe you'll be ready to really talk then."

I bit the inside of my cheek but nodded. Liam's and my talk last night hadn't really been a true discussion. It had quickly devolved into us taking shots and me yelling about what a good-looking, pushy bastard Walker was.

I sat on the floor for another few minutes, breathing in and out, the air feeling harsh against my lungs. I knew it wasn't the air causing the sensation, it was the harshness of the truth. I played the last two and a half years back in my mind. My friends had been amazing. So incredibly supportive. But had I given any of that back? I wasn't sure.

That uncertainty gutted me. I had no idea what my future held, but one thing was for certain, I needed to repair my friendships. It was clear that Liam was messed up about something, and I had barely noticed.

But Liam was here now. In Sutter Lake. A place I knew held

peace and the power of restoration. I would be there for him and support him in whatever ways he needed. I was done getting stuck in this pity spiral. I thought about how good it had felt to help Noah learn to read. It was selfish, but helping others, getting some outward focus, that was the way forward.

I pushed up from the floor and headed for my shower. I stripped off the massive t-shirt I was wearing. Walker hadn't been looking at me closely enough, because if he had been, he would have realized that the shirt was his. Wearing it to sleep helped me feel close to him, even when he wasn't next to me. My heart clenched with a painful spasm.

I stepped under the spray and let the steaming water pound down on my body. I wished it could wash away the many mistakes I'd made over the past two years, clear away the hurts I'd caused. But the only one who could do that was me.

Turning the dial, I switched the water off and stepped out of the shower. I made quick work of drying myself off and slipping on some yoga pants. I bit the inside of my cheek as I looked at my t-shirt options. My fingers trailed over the worn cotton of another of Walker's shirts. I couldn't resist it. I pulled it over my head, taking time to inhale the familiar scent of his detergent and a lingering hint of his cologne. I squeezed my eyes closed, attempting to relieve the pain. It didn't work.

I toed on a pair of sneakers and headed out into the living room, steeling my spine in preparation for my talk with Liam. It was time for me to do some major apologizing and some real listening.

The main living space was silent. I didn't see him in the kitchen and, poking my head out, I noticed he wasn't on the porch either. I listened harder. There were no sounds of the shower still running in the downstairs guest room. "Liam? Are you getting ready?" Nothing.

I knocked on his door. "Liam?" Still nothing. I slowly pushed open the door, not wanting to catch an eyeful. The bed was empty, filled only with rumpled sheets and scattered pillows. I peeked in the bathroom. The shower floor was wet, so he had been in there.

I made my way back towards the kitchen in search of my phone. Maybe he was more pissed than I thought and left. I had a lot to make up for. I rounded the corner, and my heart plummeted to my toes.

Lying sprawled out, face-down on the floor, was Liam. "Oh my God, Liam!" I ran to him and crouched at his side. I felt for a pulse. All the air in my lungs whooshed out of me when I felt the rhythm against my fingers. Carefully—oh so freaking carefully—I rolled Liam onto his back.

With one hand behind his head, I leaned over so that my face was right next to his mouth. I breathed another sigh of relief when his breath tickled my cheek. *Not dead. His heart is beating. His lungs are inflating. He's not dead.* I leaned back and, for the first time, felt a sticky substance on my hand. I pulled it carefully from behind his head and gasped. My hand was covered in blood.

My entire body shook as I rose and reached for the landline on the wall. Red smears appeared on the nine and one. I tried to even my breathing. Everything would be okay. Help would come. What the hell had happened? My eyes searched the kitchen in front of me. Had he tripped and hit his head on the counter? How long had he been lying here?

"9-1-1, what is your emergency?" was all I heard before a hand covered my mouth, and an arm encircled my waist, yanking me away from the phone. My heart raged against my ribs, beating wildly out of control. Was this what it felt like to have a heart attack?

I kicked back, trying to get at my attacker. I couldn't get purchase. And whoever this was, wore leather gloves, so my attempts to bite the hand covering my mouth were in vain. I screamed louder against the gloved hand, hoping—*praying*—that the operator would hear me.

A moan sounded from the floor. Liam. Shit. Fuck. *Please don't let this asshole kill Liam.*

A face pressed against mine, lips moving against the shell of my ear as I felt a prick in my side. "You should have left Sutter Lake like you said you were going to. I really didn't want to hurt you, but now I have no choice."

The world began to go wobbly. But the voice... The voice tickled the memories at the back of my quickly fading mind. I knew this person.

CHAPTER
Forty-One

Walker

I OPENED AND CLOSED MY FIST, WINCING EACH TIME I FLEXED my hand. I really hoped I hadn't broken it. After puking my guts out on the side of the road like a total pussy, I'd found my mad. Making a quick trip home to brush my teeth before heading to the office, I'd also found the time to punch a hole in my wall. Fuck. I'd need to patch that tonight.

Opening my bottom desk drawer, I poured a couple of Tylenol into my open palm and tossed them back with stale coffee, grimacing at the lukewarm liquid. My desk phone blared to life. "Cole," I barked. My entire office was giving me a wide berth after I had torn through here earlier, so I knew it had to be important.

"Walker, it's Harry. We had a weird call into dispatch..." He let his voice trail off.

"Okay?" I asked, completely unsure why this warranted a call to me.

"See, no one spoke when I answered."

"You know where the call is originating from, just send a unit out there to check it out." Harry had been on the job for almost twenty years, he knew the protocol. What the hell was up with him?

"That's the thing, it's coming from the guest cabin on your family's ranch." The world seemed to dip into some weird slow motion at his words. The guest cabin. My ranch. Taylor. Before I could find my voice, Harry kept talking. "Now, I think I'm hearing a low moaning in the background. I sent a unit out there, but I thought you should have a heads-up."

Of course, I should have a heads-up. Harry should have gotten to the point fucking quicker. "Thanks, let the unit know I'm on my way."

I tore through the office, not unlike I had that morning, but this time, my panic was at an all new level. What the hell was going on? I skidded to a stop at my truck, fumbling with my keys and cursing myself as I yanked open the door. Flipping on the sirens, my tires squealed as I swung out of the parking lot.

I don't think I'd ever made it to the ranch so quickly, even when I had gotten a call that Jensen was in labor. My mind ran through every possible scenario. Fuck, what if Liam had a temper and had hurt Taylor? He didn't seem the type, but I didn't really know him. I'd kill him if he touched a hair on her head.

Gravel flew as I slammed on the brakes and threw my rig into park. I ran towards the house, taking the steps two at a time, identifying myself as I entered.

"We're in here, Walker." I heard Kelly call from the kitchen.

I thundered down the hall, skidding to a stop at the sight in front of me. Hank was supporting Liam as the musician sat up, looking dazed as Kelly, donning gloves, pressed gauze to the back of his head. "What the hell is going on? And where is Taylor?" The small amount of patience I had been holding onto snapped, and I was losing it.

"We're not sure," Hank answered calmly. "Can you tell us what happened, sir?"

Liam's eyes struggled to focus. "I-I-I'm not sure. I was walking into the kitchen to make breakfast for Taylor…" He trailed off as if trying to remember. "We had a fight. She let Walker think we slept together." His gaze moved to me now as if he had just realized I was in the room. "I didn't sleep with her, man. She's like my sister. We got shitfaced, and she talked about you all night. She's in love with you."

Something in my chest seized and then released. They hadn't fucked. She loved me. It mattered, but not as much as what the hell had happened to her. "What happened after you went to cook breakfast?" I urged Liam on.

He looked from me to the stove, searching his memory. "I put the pan on the stove and turned to get something out of the fridge. Then…wham, someone hit me over the head with something."

"Most likely with that skillet," Kelly said, inclining her head to the pan that rested on the counter.

All of a sudden, Liam's eyes bugged out, and he started to struggle against Hank's hold. "He took her! Someone fucking took her! I couldn't really see, it was blurry, but someone was dragging her out of the house. Fuck! I just laid here while someone fucking took her!"

My blood turned to ice. There was only one person who could have done it. I went on auto-pilot. I pressed a button on my radio. "Dispatch, this is Deputy Chief Cole. I need to report a kidnapping."

After calling it in, I retraced my steps, studying the gravel drive to the best of my ability. It told me nothing. Just as I was about to punch the porch railing, sirens sounded. An ambulance, followed closely by an SUV with its lights flashing. The chief's vehicle. I gritted my teeth. I was going to have a fight on my hands to stay on this case.

I pulled my cell out of my back pocket and hit Tuck's contact.

I was going to need help, and Tuck was the best tracker I knew, not to mention he wouldn't give a damn if I'd been kicked off the case. The line just kept ringing. No answer. I cursed but waited to leave a message. "Call me. Now." That's all that was needed, I knew Tuck would respond as soon as he could.

The ambulance pulled up in front of the house, and two medics jumped out. I pointed at the front door. "They're in the kitchen, it's straight down the hall." The two guys jerked their chins in affirmation and headed inside with a stretcher.

I clenched and unclenched my fists as the chief strode from his car towards me. "Walk, what's going on?"

I opened my mouth to speak, but the words didn't want to come. It was like, if I spoke them, then the whole nightmare became true. I cleared my throat and focused on my training. "Taylor's been kidnapped. A friend that was staying with her, Liam Fairchild, was assaulted. EMTs are in with him now, along with Kelly and Hank."

Clark gripped my shoulder. "You hanging in there, son?"

"I'm fine, sir. But you know it's this psycho that's been terrorizing our town. We have to call in SWAT."

A look of pity filled Clark's eyes, and my jaw hardened. "I'll put SWAT on standby, but we have no clue where to send them even if I do call everyone in."

I roughly ran a hand through my hair. "Send us into the forest, the same area we know he frequents. It's at least a place to start."

"First of all, you're still riding a desk, you haven't been cleared for active duty. So, even if this case weren't a complete conflict of interest, which it is, you'd still be out."

My teeth ground together as my nails dug into my palms. "You would seriously keep me out of this? That girl that's missing, most likely in the hands of a fucking psycho murderer? She's the love of my fucking life!"

The chief drilled a finger into my chest. "That's exactly why I'm keeping you out of this. Your head isn't on straight. I promise you, I will work this one myself, and I'll do you the courtesy of keeping you in the loop."

Clark's words gave me zero reassurance. No comfort. The only thing I wanted was Taylor back in my arms. A chance to make things right between us. My chest burned. I needed that chance. And the only way I knew to get it was to work the case myself. No one would be as diligent as I was. No one would give their blood, sweat, tears—and life, if needed—but me.

I shook my head at Clark and headed back inside. I needed to see if Liam had remembered anything before I took off to search on my own. By the time I made it to the kitchen, Liam was strapped to the stretcher. "Walker, tell them I don't need to go to the hospital. I need to be looking for Taylor. We have to find her."

I placed a hand on his shoulder. "You got your head cracked open, man. You need to go to the hospital." I met his still somewhat dazed eyes. "I will do everything I fucking can to bring her back safe."

Liam nodded, and the action made him wince. "We need to get him to the hospital," one of the medics said.

"Okay, just give me one second," I said, pinning the medic with my most intimidating stare. He shrank back, giving a small nod. "Did you remember anything else? Did you see anything? Hear anything? Hell, even smell something?"

Liam's brows pulled together in a combination of concentration and what I was sure was pain. "He was tall. At least a full head taller than Taylor."

My chin rested perfectly on the top of Taylor's head when I hunched, so the guy was probably around my height, maybe a little shorter. "That's good. Anything else? Hair color?"

"I think he was wearing a hat… Fuck!" Liam smacked the gurney he was lying on. "I can't even help you ID the guy."

"You gave me something, and that's better than nothing." Liam simply shook his head as if disgusted with himself. "I've gotta get outta here. They're not going to let me work the case the traditional route, so I'm going to color outside the lines a little."

"Walk—" Hank started to say at my admission.

I held up a hand to stop him. "I won't be alone, but I can't have guys in uniform with me either." Both Hank and Kelly looked pissed and worried, but I didn't have time to reassure them. "I'll call if I find anything."

With those parting words, I took off in a jog, moving out of the house, down the front steps, and towards my car. Just as I was pulling the truck door open, my phone buzzed. I glanced at the screen. Tuck. I hit accept. "Fucking finally. I need your help, man."

CHAPTER
Forty-Two

Taylor

COLD. BONE-CHILLING COLD. THAT WAS THE FIRST THING I became aware of. The second was the pounding in my head and an insatiable thirst. I forced my eyelids open. They felt like sandpaper, gritty and harsh against my tender eyes. It took a few moments for them to adjust.

Where the hell was I? I tried to clear my jumbled brain, my eyes roving around the dark space, looking for clues to jog my memory. Dirt floor. Rock walls. My breaths came quicker as the first taste of panic licked at my skin. No true source of light. Just a low-level ambient sort of glow.

I squeezed my eyes shut for a brief moment. I held a hand against my chest and imagined it was Walker's and that he was again showing me how to slow my breathing. My eyes flew open as memories slammed into me. Walker showing up at the house. Me allowing him to think the wrong thing. My fight with Liam. Liam lying helplessly on the floor. A hand on my mouth. And then—nothing. Just blackness.

I scrambled back in a half-crawl until my back hit the stone wall of what must be a cave. Jagged pieces of rock dug into my skin. My head snapped back and forth in either direction, looking for any sign of movement. Was I alone?

My heart rattled against my ribs as I fought to control my breathing. Passing out wouldn't get me anywhere. My eyes strained against the darkness. I could make out basic shapes. The curve of the rock surfaces. My gaze stuttered over a lump on the ground. Was that a rock? I studied the shape for several minutes, trying to make it out while attempting to keep my breath even and slow. I had nothing. No idea what it could be.

I licked my dry, cracked lips. I had to see what it was. Slowly, I crawled towards the darker shape, not yet trusting myself to stand, let alone walk. I inched closer, and my breath caught in my throat as I froze mid-shuffle. It was a person. Friend or foe? Friend or foe? What if it was my attacker playing some ghoulish game? Or worse, what if there was another prisoner in this chamber?

I bit down hard on the inside of my cheek, the metallic tang of blood filling my mouth. If someone was hurt, I had to try and help. My arm shook like a leaf as I reached out towards the form. My fingers grasped a flannel-clad shoulder. Nothing. I swallowed hard and gently rolled the person to his or her back.

I shot back with a gasp, holding onto my scream with everything I had in me. Staring back at me was a man I'd never seen before, his face bleached of any color, eyes open wide, unblinking. A bullet hole sat squarely in the center of his forehead.

My stomach heaved, but there was nothing for my belly to empty. I hadn't eaten since the day before. What time was it now? How long had I been gone? Was anyone looking for me?

My heart cried out for Walker with a ferocity that had me gasping. He was the only thing I wanted in that moment.

Footsteps echoed off the hard stone of the cave, and I skittered back against the wall. My eyes darted around frantically, searching for some path of escape, somewhere to hide. There was nothing. My chest constricted in a vise-like grip. I couldn't seem to get air into my lungs.

The sharp edges of the rocks cut into my palms. I tried to focus on the pain instead of my rapidly beating heart and my inability to catch my breath. A beam of light cut across my body, zeroing in on my face. I threw a hand in front of my eyes on instinct. The light burned.

"You're awake. Good." That voice. It was so familiar.

I slowly lowered my hand and let my gaze adjust to the brightness in increments. As it did, my body turned to stone. No. It couldn't be. My heart spasmed. This would kill Jensen. "Bryce?" My voice came out as a croak.

"Hey there." He crouched down three feet from me, and I pushed back harder against the wall.

The jagged edges of the stone piercing my body felt like a warm embrace compared to what I might receive at this man's hands. "W-what's going on?"

A feral grin stretched over Bryce's face as he toyed with the flashlight in his hands. "Come on now, Taylor, don't play dumb with me."

My fingers dug into the dirt floor of the cave. "I-it was you? You killed Caitlin and that hiker?"

The grin turned into a smirk. The same kind of expression a guy would wear if you'd asked if he lifted something particularly heavy. "Not just them. Lots more. Some you may have heard about, many more you haven't." My mind flashed to the woman from Willow Creek Walker had told me was missing, and my heart broke a little more.

"They were easy prey. Not even really a challenge." Bryce rested his chin on the lens of the flashlight, the beam casting creepy shadows over his face. I shuddered. "Though you did throw a little wrench in my plans when you wandered off the trail. You almost interrupted me while I was dealing with Miss Caitlin."

I bit the inside of my cheek to keep from crying. I did not want this asshole to see me break, he seemed like he would get off on it. Bryce shone the beam back at me. "Something tells me you're a fighter. You might actually be some fun." He edged just a bit closer, and I held my breath. "I haven't had a real challenge in far too long."

Bryce reached behind his back, and my world slowed. Was he reaching for a weapon? Was this the end? Walker's face filled my mind. His rugged jaw, almost always covered in stubble. His piercing green eyes that could set me aflame with one look and put my soul at ease with another. I'd never get a chance to tell him how sorry I was. To tell him how much I loved him.

A water bottle flew at my head. My reflexes, still a little slow, barely reacted in time. Bryce rose. "Drink up. And eat this." He tossed a granola bar at me next. "You'll need your energy for the hunt to come."

The hunt. "What does that mean?"

Bryce turned, a glint in his eyes that spoke of arousal. "It means, I'm going to let you go."

My heart rattled in my chest, its rhythm chaotic.

"But then, I'm going to catch you. I'll wound you first. Somewhere non-lethal. Maybe the shoulder like your nosy boy-friend. You'll be bleeding then. That will slow you down. I'll take my time tracking you. You won't be able to hide."

My fingers dug harder into the ground, my nails snapping. Bryce's deviant grin reappeared. "You won't know how to hide. You're a city girl. You should have stayed there."

I wanted to rage against him, rake my nails down his face. Scream at him that I did belong here. Here with Walker. Bryce's grin widened. "A little of that temper wanting to come to the sur-face I see. Good. That'll make things interesting. We'll have lots of fun, you and I. And then I'll snap your fucking neck."

With that, Bryce strode towards what must have been the mouth of the cave. When he disappeared from sight, my body began to shake. The trembling was so strong, I could barely hold onto the bottle of water. Silent tears tracked down my face. Hugging my legs to my chest, I bit down on one knee to keep myself from letting loose my sobs.

My chest burned with the weight of my fear. Burned with the pain of possibly losing Walker and everyone else I loved. Forever. How many minutes, hours, days had I wasted giving in to my fear? Allowing it to control me. I thought I had been controlling it, keeping those around me at arm's length as a way to push the terror of losing someone else down. But really, the fear had held all the strings.

I cursed myself for being so stupid. For being such a coward. Images danced in my mind. My first glimpse of Walker that had stolen my breath. The sound of his laugh. Falling asleep to the strong beat of his heart at the movie. His callused fingers trailing up my bare back.

The burning sensation in my chest grew stronger. I let the feeling sink deeper, spread throughout my body.

Things snapped into place as if I had suddenly been given the final piece of a puzzle I'd been missing for years. A part that changed the entire image. I simply needed to relish the burn. The pain that would always fill your life if you loved fully and deeply. That pain was proportional to love and joy and all the other wonderful things you might be lucky enough to fill your existence with.

My mother's gentle smile filled my memory. Would I have traded any of the million moments of pure joy I shared with her for less pain at her passing? Never. I would experience the worst of that pain every day for the rest of my life for just one of those precious seconds. But that's what I had been doing. Preemptively erasing those moments with Walker by pushing him away. Hoping that if I didn't let him too close, it wouldn't kill me to lose him.

I'd been lying to myself. All I had succeeded in doing was losing time with him that I would never get back. Time I would give anything to have right now. The tears fell faster and harder. I would allow myself this moment to break down, to let everything out. All my pain. All my grief. And then I would figure out how to fight.

I would fight for Walker. I would fight for myself. I would fight for our future. I would give my all for a lifetime filled with joy and pain, abundance and loss. A life with him.

My tears began to slow. I straightened my spine, wiping at my face with the bottom of the t-shirt I wore. Walker's tee. He was with me. I pressed the material to my nose and inhaled deeply. The scent of his cologne was even fainter now, marred by dirt and sweat. I *would* take in that smell again. I swore it to myself.

I exhaled a shaky breath and reached for the water at my side. The first thing I needed to do was build up my strength. I needed it to fight. My hands still trembled as I opened the bottle of water. I listened for the crack of the seal. The sound of the little plastic tines popping was music to my ears. At least the water wasn't drugged. Or so I hoped.

I forced myself to take slow, careful sips, even though I wanted to guzzle the thing down. Slow meant giving my stomach a chance to get accustomed to having something in it again. I felt around on the floor of the cave for the granola bar Bryce had thrown at me. It took a minute to find the small, plastic-wrapped treasure.

This would be more of a risk. There was no way to know if he'd laced the bar with something, I'd just have to hope that the sicko truly got his rocks off from the *challenging hunt*. I shuddered just thinking the words in my head, but I forced myself to move forward in my actions.

I tore the wrapper around the bar, happy to feel that my hands were a bit less shaky. I took a small bite. The combination of chocolate and peanut butter, normally a favorite of mine, barely registered. I counted ten chews before swallowing, then took another small drink of water. I repeated the process until the granola bar was gone and the water was down to its last dregs.

My gaze roamed the cavernous space. I could see things more clearly now, my eyes having adjusted to the lack of light a bit more. I searched for a loose rock, small enough for me to lift easily but large enough to do some damage. After precious minutes wasted searching, I had nothing. Bryce must have checked out the space before leaving me here with the dead guy.

The dead guy. I gathered all the courage I could muster and inched towards the man with the vacant stare. I had to see if there was something on his body that I could use to defend myself. Careful not to touch his graying skin, I turned each of his pockets inside out. The only thing I found was a wallet.

I flipped through the worn leather billfold. Nothing. I squinted at the driver's license. Frank Pardue. Wasn't that one of Walker's suspects? Had he been working alongside Bryce, or was he just in the wrong place at the wrong time?

I shook my head forcefully. It didn't matter. I needed to focus on a way out of this mess. I sat back down, wanting to conserve as much energy as possible. My fingertips traced patterns in the dirt as I tried to think back to the one self-defense workshop I'd taken.

Carter had dragged me to the free seminar that had been held at the gym her husband, Austin, owned. It had been two years ago, and I struggled to remember what the instructor had said. Never let them get you to a secondary location. *Well, too late for that.* Go for the soft targets: eyes, throat, junk.

That was something I could work with. I gathered dirt into

my hands as a plan formed. I played various scenarios over and over in my head as I waited. All the contingencies I could think of. I stood, practicing the moves I would need to make—first slowly, focusing on precision, and then faster.

Footsteps echoed against the stone, and I froze, my entire body seizing up. I shook out my arms and legs, forcing the muscles to release the majority of their tension. I perched on the edge of a boulder. I tried to make it seem as though I were as relaxed as possible.

I hung my head, letting my hair cover most of my face so that I could get a peek at Bryce but still hide my expression. I began sniffling and then let my shoulders shake as though I were crying. I needed him to see me as weak. A girl who had crumbled from the strain of it all. Not someone who would fight him tooth and nail with everything she had.

The footsteps came closer. I could do this. Bryce's shadowy form appeared. "You've got to be kidding me." He continued striding forward. "I thought you might have some promise, but here you are, sniveling like a child."

I let my shoulders shake harder. "W-why are you doing this?"

"Why am I doing this, she wants to know," Bryce said with a sneer. "I'm doing it because I like it. I'm doing it because I can. And I'm doing it because girls like you, who show up where they don't belong, need to be taught a lesson."

His words twisted my stomach. There was pure evil leaking from his tone. "P-p-please don't do this." It killed me to give in to my voice trembling even if I was using the waver to my advantage.

"They all fucking beg. It's so damn pathetic. 'Please don't kill me, I'll do anything.'" Bryce let out a harsh laugh. "Do you know that a lot of them offer to suck my dick, fuck me, anything. I hadn't expected that. Like I would want their whore selves."

Bile churned in my stomach, but I forced it down. I just

needed him to come a little bit closer.

"What, you're not going to offer the same?" I said nothing, just bided my time, keeping my head down. Bryce took another three steps forward. "Come on, you whore yourself out just fine for Walk—"

His words cut off as I sprang up, throwing the dirt I'd gathered in my hands at him, as close to his open eyes as possible. Bryce let out a strangled curse as his hands automatically flew to his face. I used that split second of distraction to grasp him by the shoulders and plunge my knee into his groin.

The sound that came out of him was a garbled cry. He dropped to his knees. This was it. I was going to make it. I was going to escape. I braced to run, making it one and then two strides before a hand clamped around my ankle and jerked. Hard.

My legs flew out from under me, and I slammed into the ground below. Light burst in my vision as my jaw slammed shut. I cried out in pain.

Bryce dragged me back towards him, the rough ground tearing at my skin. "You fucking bitch! You'll pay for that." He was on top of me then, sitting astride my pelvis. My breathing came in quick pants—so fast, I had no hope of slowing it.

Bryce leaned over, closer to me, studying my face. Then, he burst out laughing. The sound grated against my skin as tears leaked from my eyes. "I knew you'd be fun," he said, slapping my cheek twice without any real heat and then winding up and hitting me again with such force my teeth split my lip.

Blood filled my mouth as I gasped to catch my breath. Bryce seized a fistful of my hair, pulling it taut. "You've made things interesting, but now I have to level the playing field. Things must be fair when we enter the fight, don't you think?"

Stars danced in my vision as he tugged harder on my hair. "DON'T YOU THINK?"

I could only moan in reply. My vision seemed to be fading

in and out. My mind felt foggy, as if I didn't have a firm hold on reality.

Bryce kept a firm hold on my hair with one hand while he reached behind himself with the other. I blinked rapidly at the item he retrieved. The blade. Acid choked my throat as I felt him harden against me. He loved this. Terror was his drug, the thing that turned him on more than anything.

I bucked against him with the little strength I had left, doing anything I could to get him off me. It got me nowhere. Bryce simply chuckled. "Stop moving, or I might slip and make things worse." I froze. "You'll still have a chance to run from me, don't worry." He slowly lifted up my shirt, and tears stung my eyes. "Don't move a muscle. I'm only evening the playing field. This is what's fair."

I squeezed my eyes closed. I wasn't strong enough to fight him off. I could only hope that he wouldn't kill me immediately. That I'd have a chance to outrun him. The flat side of the blade pressed against my stomach. I filled my mind with thoughts of Walker. I traced every detail of his face with my memory.

The knife bit into my skin, slicing along my belly in one long line. I held my breath and saw the magical blue rim of Walker's green irises. Another slash of the blade. "X marks the spot, Taylor. Now, I have something to aim for."

Pain overrode all of my senses, but I held on to my vision of Walker. My mind held the memory, my soul called out for his heart, and as darkness took me, I relished the burn.

CHAPTER
Forty-Three

Walker

MY TIRES SCREECHED AS I PULLED UP TO THE FOREST Service station. I swung my truck into a parking spot. Grabbing my phone, I slammed my door with such force, I was surprised it didn't crack the window.

As I jogged toward the station's front door, I tried not to focus on the what-ifs, but it was impossible. Was Taylor cold right now? Hurt? Dead? My entire body locked. She couldn't be. Some part of me was sure that I would feel it if she were. She had to be alive. And I would find her. This wouldn't end the way Julie's story had.

I shoved open the door and jerked a chin at the young guy behind the front desk. The kid's eyes widened at the rage that was clearly emanating from me in waves. "Tuck's in the conference room. He said to send you back." The guy's voice trembled just a little.

"Thanks." I was already taking off towards the back room.

I pushed open the door without knocking and found Tuck studying a set of maps that covered the conference room table. His head snapped up at the sound of the door. In two strides, he grasped my hand and pulled me in for a tight half-hug. "We'll find her." His voice was gruff. He knew how much Taylor meant to me.

I was so thankful for this man who was more brother than friend. I swallowed against the emotion gathering in my throat. "I know we will." I released Tuck and stepped towards the table. "Tell me what you're thinking."

Tuck knew the woods better than anyone. He was my best hope of finding Taylor. "I've been studying where we found the bodies in relation to the surrounding access roads, trails large enough to fit an ATV...anything that would help this guy get around quickly."

"Find anything?" I couldn't disguise the hope in my voice. I checked my watch. Time had to be running out. My jaw clenched as an image of Taylor filled my mind, her head thrown back in laughter, blue-gray eyes twinkling in the light.

I needed her with me. Needed a chance to make things right. If I got her back, I swore that I would do what I should've done all along: never leave her side. She could push me away all she wanted, but I wasn't going anywhere.

Tuck drummed his fingers against the wood table, drawing my attention back to the task at hand. "It doesn't make sense."

"What do you mean?" I followed the direction of his gaze to a specific area on the map.

"I think we need to check out Pardue's property again. It's the only area that has a road that would give the killer easy access to both hiking trails while avoiding the more populated trailheads."

My muscles tensed. I clenched and unclenched my fists in an attempt to relieve some of the pressure. It didn't work. "You think it's him?" We'd had the guy in an interrogation room. Gone at him for hours. I would never forgive myself if we'd had him in our grip and let him go, allowing him to hurt Taylor.

Tuck's gaze met mine in a hard stare. "I think we need to

check it out."

"You know this is totally off the books, right? If something goes wrong, we could both lose our jobs. Or end up in jail."

"Don't be a little bitch." Tuck slapped me on the back. "Like I'd let you go into this on your own." His serious stare morphed into a slight grin. "Always trying to steal all the glory. Sometimes, I need to rescue the damsel, too."

I wanted to smile, but my lips refused the action. "All right. We gotta leave our service weapons. Do you have something else here?"

Tuck snorted. "Who do you think you're talking to? I've got my rifle in my truck, and my Glock in my desk."

Of course, he did. "Okay, let's head out then. We'll take my truck."

"Control freak," Tuck called over his shoulder as he headed to his office for his personal weapon.

I was grasping onto any semblance of control I could, even if it was something as simple as being the one in the driver's seat. Taylor's face flashed in my mind again, sunlight glinting off her golden strands as she stared out at the ranch. I would get her back.

Tuck reappeared, holding two bulletproof vests. "Better safe than sorry."

There was a slight twinge in my chest where the bullet had struck. I resisted the urge to rub at the spot. "Not a bad idea."

Tuck's jaw tightened. "Are you sure you're ready for primetime?"

I tore one of the vests out of his hands. "Don't ask stupid questions." I would be back on active duty next week anyway, and no one, not a single person on this planet, could keep me from looking for Taylor.

Tuck grunted in response, but I took it as his acceptance. We made our way to my truck and took off for Pardue's land.

We were mostly silent during the drive. I took the time to go over every single piece of evidence in my mind, every gut feeling and hunch, trying to see anything I might have missed. I came up with nothing.

As we got closer, I glanced at Tuck. "Think we should check out the house first?"

Tuck's jaw worked as he pondered. "Probably wouldn't be a bad idea."

"We don't have a search warrant. We're not even on duty."

"Don't need a warrant if we have probable cause."

"True." The idea of hearing a scream had me clenching my teeth together and gripping the steering wheel harder.

I made the turn toward Frank's house. The tires crunching gravel announced our arrival. There would be no element of surprise here. Hopefully, that didn't shoot us in the foot. I parked at the front of the rundown cabin, my eyes searching the area. "His car's here."

Tuck's gaze scanned the front of the house. "Don't see him, though."

"Let's go see what we can find." Tuck and I bumped fists the way we always did before SWAT missions. A routine that had always brought good luck before.

We both slipped from the car, neither of us attempting any sort of covertness—that ship had sailed. We strode up the porch steps, eyes taking in every detail possible. I pounded on the front door. The only response was the whispering of the leaves in the wind. I knocked again. "Pardue. It's Walker. I need you to give me a minute." Nothing.

I shot a sideways glance at Tuck, whose gaze was focused on the ground. He crouched, touching a finger to something. His hand went to his weapon, and I knew he'd found something. I followed suit, unsnapping my holster, my hand circling the grip of my gun. "What is it?"

Tuck stood, lifting his finger so I could see. "Blood."

My chest tightened with a painful squeeze. *Please, God, don't let it be Taylor's blood.*

Tuck's eyes were already following a trail I could barely see. "It leads away from the house."

I tried to feel relief. We had a clue. A direction to head in. I felt nothing but sheer panic. "We need to call this in. Get some crime scene techs out here." I would take all the help I could get, I wasn't an idiot.

Tuck was already moving, though. "Just let me see where this leads before you have twenty guys here messing up my trail."

I gritted my teeth. "Fine. Hurry up." I'd give him five minutes, and then I was making the call.

I watched Tuck in silence, my insides rioting at having to wait to do something, *anything*, to help Taylor. He moved carefully, eyes tracing a path invisible to most. Within a few minutes, we'd made it to one of the paths that headed away from the cabin and into the woods. "They went this way. You can call the team in now, but you and I should push on. More people will just get in my way."

He didn't need to tell me twice. Nothing could have kept me from following that path. I pulled out my phone to call the chief as Tuck studied a map on his GPS device.

Chief answered on the first ring. "Where are you?"

"At Frank Pardue's. Tuck and I found traces of blood on the front porch. You need to get a team out here now."

"We're on our way. Stay put." Frustration rang out in the chief's tone. I got it. I really did. But that didn't mean I was going to follow his orders. There was too much at stake.

"Can't. Tuck's found a trail. We gotta follow it."

"Goddammit, Walker! You're not working this case."

"I know I'm not. I'm just a civilian out looking for his girl. We'll be on public land. You can't stop us."

Chief let out a series of colorful curses. "At least tell me the direction you're headed in. I'll send the rest of the SWAT team after you."

That I could do. Backup was always welcome, just as long as it didn't hold up my progress. I quickly explained which path from the property we were heading down and in which direction.

"Just be careful." There was emotion in the chief's voice. I knew he saw me as a second son, knew he was worried, but I had to keep going.

"Will do. Talk soon." With that, I hung up. "Let's go."

We headed down the trail, which was just wide enough for an ATV to pass through, going slowly so Tuck could make sure we were following the right tracks. How he knew, I had no idea, and I wasn't going to slow him down to ask.

For the next hour, we kept up the painstakingly meticulous pace. I was pretty sure I had ground my teeth down to nubs. Suddenly, Tuck jerked to a halt, holding up a hand to stop me. His eyes darted away from the path before us, and his gaze moved to the woods on our left. He scanned the trees. I strained to hear any sounds that seemed out of place. Nothing jumped out.

Tuck turned back to me, speaking in a hushed tone. "They veered off the trail here." His brows pulled together in a combination of concentration and worry. "There are a series of caves about five hundred yards off the trail in that direction. That has to be where he took her."

A riot of emotions erupted within me. Hope that we were close. Fear that we were too late. Terror at what the asshole might have done to Taylor in the hours that he'd had her. I pulled my gun from its holster. "Let's go."

The great thing about working with Tuck was that we required very few words to communicate. *Let's go* was all that was needed. We both understood that Tuck, as the tracker, would take the lead. We knew that as much silence as possible was necessary. And finally, there was a soul-deep understanding that we would do whatever it took to get Taylor home safely. I trusted Tuck with that most of all.

Our movements up the mountainside were quicker now that Tuck had an idea of where to go. Before long, we had made it to the edge of the tree line, halting so that we would still have cover while we decided our next move.

There were three cave openings before us. Two smaller ones and a larger cavern, but any of the three could easily hide people. I glanced at Tuck, looking for his take on where we should start. He pointed down towards the outskirts of the forest. About twenty yards away was a camouflage ATV.

My heart picked up its pace. They were here. I sent up another silent prayer, begging for Taylor to be all right, promising anything I could think of in exchange for her return, safe and whole. A muttered curse coming from the middle cave had my gaze shooting to the opening, and my body going on high alert.

The cave itself was dark, and I couldn't make out who was speaking. I could only see a form striding back and forth near the mouth of the cave, the person muttering to themselves. My eyes jumped to Tuck. There was only one way to do this. Full out assault. In the thirty feet separating us and the cave's mouth, there were no trees or boulders to provide cover.

I jerked my head in the direction of the cave, and Tuck gave one swift nod of assent. We took off at a dead run. Ten feet in, the figure's head swiveled in our direction. I raised my weapon. "Don't move, this is the Sutter Lake Police Department. Show me your hands."

Of course, the guy did the opposite, tearing off back into the cave. He moved with a speed and agility I didn't think Pardue would possess at his age.

"Fuck!" I pushed my legs harder. "I don't think that's Pardue."

"No shit, Sherlock," Tuck retorted, matching me stride for stride.

"Any clue who it is?"

"Not a one." We slowed as we reached the cave, each hugging one of the walls so no one could get the jump on us. "We need to be prepared for the possibility of more than one assailant."

I gripped my gun tighter. The last thing we needed in this equation was another unknown. We crept down the natural hallway the cave formed, letting our eyes adjust to the lack of light.

"Walker and Tuck to the rescue, huh?" The mocking jeer echoed off the stone.

I froze, betrayal and disgust coursing through my veins. My gaze sought Tuck's from across the cave. The whites of his eyes flashed with a ferocious rage. We both knew the owner of that voice. Had shared beers with him. I had told my sister what a great fucking guy I thought he was. Had practically shoved her in his direction.

I had to tamp down my fury, get control so that I could get Taylor out of here. Get her to safety. Then, I could lose it.

"You're too late. I've already started my game, and you can't play."

My entire body locked. I refused to think about what that might mean. I had to press on, and I couldn't let Bryce get in my head. I motioned for Tuck to keep moving.

A light shone from somewhere ahead, a flashlight on its side I realized, illuminating a cavernous room at the end of the cave. Ominous shadows danced along the walls, but I only had eyes for one thing. Taylor. Her eyes were closed, and even in the dim light, I could tell she was deathly pale. My heart stopped beating until I saw her chest rise and fall.

Bryce had pulled her against him as he leaned against a boulder in the corner of the cave. One arm held her to him, while the other held a knife to her throat. Taylor's eyes fluttered, and she let out a low moan when Bryce jerked her against him.

In that moment, I knew I would kill Bryce. There was no way I would let him out of the cave alive. A fire raged within me, my insides burning with the need to get to Taylor. "There's no way out of this, Bryce, not unless you put down that knife and let us take you in."

Bryce let out a dark chuckle. "I don't think so, hero boy. Either both of you put down your guns, or I will slice this pretty little throat in front of me."

I forced myself to ignore Bryce's taunt and checked my angles. There was only one option. A headshot. A target that was half-hidden behind the girl I loved more than life itself.

Tuck's footsteps sounded to my right. "I need you to be real sure if you take a shot, Walk. Because if you miss and hit a cave wall, we could have several tons of rock coming down around us."

A hysterical yet excited giggle came from Bryce. "Maybe we'll all die together. That would be a good ending to this little story. Do it. Come on, Walker, end all our misery."

Bryce was completely gone. There was no talking him down, even if I didn't want him dead. My eyes darted to Taylor's face, leached of all color. It was now or never. I breathed in slowly, holding the air at the top of the inhale. Blood roared in my ears as the whole world slowed. I squeezed the trigger.

The crack reverberated off the stone of the cave. Bryce's head snapped back as he flew back into a boulder. Tuck and I sprinted forward as Taylor's body crumpled to the ground.

Tuck went for Bryce, knowing I needed to go for Taylor. "He's dead."

I already knew it, but I still felt a minor release of tension at the words. I rolled Taylor to her back. "Fuck! Get the flashlight! I need light!" Because what I hadn't been able to see while Bryce held her against him was that the front of her dark t-shirt was covered in blood. A t-shirt, I noticed absently, that was mine. My chest burned.

Gingerly, I pulled the material away from her middle, the cotton tacky with blood. Tuck shined the light on her stomach and cursed. Her butchered flesh stared back at me, taunting me for not quite being quick enough.

Tuck grasped my shoulder. "We need to get her outside so we can call in a chopper."

I nodded. I slipped a hand under Taylor's knees and the other behind her shoulders. Tears stung my eyes. She was so light. My little short-stack. She had to make it. I said the words to myself over and over, willing each sentence into her as though I could make the statement true just by the ferocity of my belief. Tuck led the way out, shining the light to guide my path.

Fading light shone from the mouth of the cave. I gently laid Taylor on the ground while Tuck immediately pulled out his sat phone and began barking orders into it. I quickly stripped off my bulletproof vest, then peeled off my t-shirt. Tuck threw me a water bottle that had been clipped to his pack.

Again, I lifted Taylor's blood-soaked shirt. I poured water over her wounds, hoping I would be able to better see what needed tending. What emerged had me fighting back rising bile. A crude X marred her beautiful skin. Blood seeped from the gashes, and I pressed my shirt to the wounds.

Taylor's eyes fluttered again as she let out another low moan.

"Taylor, baby, open your eyes. Come on, Short-stack."

Her eyes cracked open, just slightly. Her beautiful blue-gray depths were dulled by pain. "Walker?"

"I'm here. I'm right here, and I'm not going anywhere." Taylor's eyes started to close again. "No you don't, stay with me."

Her lids opened once more, just barely, and just long enough for her to say, "Love you."

Then there was nothing.

CHAPTER
Forty-Four

Taylor

IT WAS THE SOUND THAT BROUGHT ME AROUND. THAT FAINT beep, beep, beep, that drew me back to the land of the living. The closer I got, the more aware I became of the pain. My head throbbed as if a heavy-metal drummer were practicing on my skull. And there was a hot, burning sensation emanating from my belly.

My eyelids felt as though they carried five-pound weights on their lashes, but I so desperately wanted to open my eyes. After several fruitless attempts, I was finally able to crack them open. The movement felt like something was scratching against my tender irises.

The light in the room was blinding. I blinked several times, trying to get my eyes to adjust. Slowly, my vision returned, the room going from blurry to focused. The sounds became clearer. The hum of an overhead fluorescent light. The beeping of a heart monitor—a heart monitor. Hospital. I was in the hospital. Why?

Suddenly, memories slammed into me, stealing my breath. I gasped against the shocking intrusion, fisting my hands in the blankets on the bed. The back of my hand stung at the action, the

IV line that was connected there pulling. I was okay. I was safe. But what about everyone else? Liam? Walker?

My memories of Walker in the cave seemed hazy at best. Was it even him? Or had my mind concocted the whole thing? The hopeful delusion of a girl who thought she might be dying.

My gaze searched the room. Empty. I was alone. The thing I had fought so hard to be, was now the thing I hated more than anything. Tears stung my eyes. It was too late. Too late to make amends with my friends. And too late for Walker.

I didn't blame him. He thought I'd slept with another man. I'd pushed him too far, one too many times.

My chest heaved. I tried to control the motion since it only caused my pain to flare, but I couldn't seem to catch my breath or control my sobs.

The door to my room swung open. Walker strode in looking like a fierce avenging angel from some post-apocalyptic novel. His clothes were rumpled, his face smeared with dirt, and he was pissed. "Jesus, get a nurse, would you?" he called over his shoulder.

My heart rate sped up, my sobs only worsening.

Walker's face morphed from angry to concerned in a split second. "Short-stack, you're safe. It's okay. Everything's fine now." He grasped my cheeks in his hands. "Breathe with me, just breathe."

But I couldn't. What was happening? He was here. Why? "You're here." The words came out as a croaky rasp.

Walker's brow creased. "Of course, I'm here. Come on, baby, breathe with me."

"Liam?" I asked with a wheeze.

"He's fine, he's just down the hall. Everyone's okay. Just breathe."

My eyes drank him in as my breathing finally began to slow. He bent and placed his lips firmly against my forehead, staying there for several moments. I soaked up the warmth of his lips against my skin. I wanted to stay in this moment forever. I didn't care about the pounding in my head or the burning in my stomach as long as I had Walker's lips on my skin. If I could hold onto that, I could handle anything.

It was that thought that had fresh tears spilling over. "I'm so sorry. So, so sorry."

Before Walker could respond, a nurse bustled in. "Well, hello there, Miss Lawson. Glad to see you awake." She eyed me and Walker. "Sorry to interrupt the lovers' reunion, but I need to take a quick look at your vitals."

She made notes of the readings on different machines and checked the various tubes I was connected to. "Everything looks good. Can you rate your pain for me on a scale of one to ten?"

I bit the inside of my cheek. "Maybe a four?"

The nurse gave me a gentle smile. "I'm pretty sure you're lying, but we can wait for another dose of pain meds if you'd like. Just press the call button when you're ready, or I'll be back to check on you soon." I nodded in agreement, and she turned to leave.

As the door closed with a quiet snick, my eyes found Walker's again. They seemed pained. Did he dread telling a girl in a hospital bed that their relationship was over? My stomach churned.

Walker sank down into the chair next to my bed. He gently took the hand that was free of the IV between his own. My eyes stung with tears again. "I really am so sorry—" I didn't know what else to say, couldn't seem to find adequate words to convey everything I felt, all I had realized.

Walker shook his head and then lifted my hand so that my palm rested against his rapidly beating heart. "I'm the one who owes you an apology."

My eyebrows rose. "What are you talking about?"

"I knew you were scared, terrified really. I never should have let you push me away. I left you alone, and you were taken." A single tear crested over his bottom eyelid. "And I didn't find you quick enough…"

Walker's words trailed off as I shook my head vehemently, wincing at the pain the action caused. "You found me. I'm *alive* because of you." More of the moments in the cave had begun to come back to me, and I knew if Walker hadn't gotten there when he did, I would likely be dead.

Walker's jaw was granite-hard, his words seeming to be ripped from his throat. "But I didn't get there before he hurt you."

I pushed my hand harder against his chest. "I'll heal." The statement was simple but true. I would heal. And if I had Walker by my side, I knew that recovery would happen quickly.

Walker's gaze locked on mine with such intensity, my heart stuttered in its rhythm. "I love you. You snuck in and stole my goddamned heart, but I hope you never give it back. Please give me the chance to love you." His eyes pleaded with mine.

My heart seized and burned. A sensation that was nothing but pleasure and peace this time. "I'd love nothing more than to be loved by you and to love you in return."

Walker dropped his hold on my hand and grasped my face again, this time brushing his lips against mine. It was a feather-light touch, but one with the deepest of meanings. "You're mine."

"I'm yours," I whispered against his lips.

Walker pressed his mouth to mine again. "And I'm yours, too."

"Yes, you are." Warmth flooded my entire body. This beautiful, strong man, who never gave up fighting for me, was mine. I flashed a huge grin.

Walker gave me a slow and sexy smile. "I might have to share you for a little bit, though." I blinked up at him, confused. He let out a low chuckle. "The waiting room is filled to the brim with people just waiting to see you."

"Really?"

"Yes, really. Carter and Austin hopped on a private jet as soon as they heard what had happened and have been going between Liam's hospital room and the waiting area. My entire family is there, a large portion of the SLPD, Tessa, even Arthur, Clint, and the rest of the bridge club is out there."

Pain flashed in Walker's eyes at the mention of his family, and my own face lost its grin. "How's Jensen?" I couldn't imagine what she must be going through right now. My heart ached for her.

"In stoic denial, I'd say." He rubbed a hand over his stubbled jaw. "It's not that she doesn't believe Bryce did those things. She does. She just…I don't know, is playing off that it has any sort of impact on her. She's focused solely on you."

I reached for Walker's hand again, needing to draw strength from him to ask the next question I needed an answer to. "I-Is he dead?" That part of my memory was still hazy. I was pretty sure I remembered Walker shooting him, but I had no idea if that shot had been fatal.

Walker's teeth ground together. "He is." He seemed to struggle with how to express what he needed to say next. "I'm not sorry for it. Bryce never would have stopped. There was no other option. He was sick. I'm not sure why, but maybe Ashlee will be able to fill us in on the missing pieces once she's able to come to terms with it all."

Oh, God. Ashlee. I couldn't imagine how this must be rocking her world. "Is she—?" I started to ask, unsure of what word to use because of course she wasn't okay.

"She's hanging in there. She's been in the waiting room, too. Wanted to make sure you were going to be okay."

"Walker, that poor girl."

"I know," he said, his voice gruff. "He was the only family she had left. Her dad took off when she was twelve, and Bryce was fourteen. Her mom drank herself to death."

My stomach churned again as tears pricked my eyes. Walker brushed his lips across my temple. "We'll get past this. All of us. Together."

A knock sounded from the door. "Come in," Walker called.

The door swung open, and a disheveled Ashlee appeared. Her eyes were red and swollen, and her face was incredibly pale. She shuffled in, one hand grasping the bag that was over her shoulder, the other shaking slightly by her side. The door closed quietly behind her.

Ashlee's wide eyes swung from Walker to me. "They said you were awake." I wasn't sure how to respond or what to say to someone who had just recently discovered that her brother was a serial killer. Ashlee just bobbed her head slightly. "That's good. I needed you to be awake for this."

With a shaky hand, Ashlee pulled something from her bag. The world slowed. I wished I could blame it on the pain meds or the blow to my head, but no. The world slowed because Ashlee had a gun. A weapon that was now pointed directly at me.

CHAPTER
Forty-Five

Walker

I SLOWLY STEPPED TO MY RIGHT, EFFECTIVELY BLOCKING any shot Ashlee might have of Taylor. What the hell was happening? Ashlee's hand shook. Not a good thing when that hand was holding a gun. Tears streamed down her face as her eyes hopped from Taylor to me and back again.

I held out a hand in a placating gesture, while mentally cursing the fact that my weapon had been taken by a crime tech as part of the investigation into Bryce's death. I knew I'd be cleared, but they just had to take my fucking gun. Now, I had no weapon. No way to defend Taylor. I stalled for time. "What's going on, Ashlee?"

"She's not supposed to be here." Ashlee's eyes were wide, almost feral, and they were fixed on Taylor with the ferocity of a cornered wild animal. "She's a liar. Did you know that? She lied to make me think she wasn't a threat. Lied to hide that she wasn't after you. But she was! From the first minute she got here."

"And you!" Her eyes shot to me again, and she shook the gun at me for emphasis. "You killed my brother! The only person who ever really loved me."

Her voice had a keening quality to it now, her grief right on the surface. "You were supposed to love me. Why, Walker? Why couldn't you love me? What's wrong with me?" Ashlee's tears fell harder, streaming down her cheeks and dripping from the end of her chin.

My mind whirled, trying to put the pieces together. "I had no idea you felt that way. Why didn't you tell me?" How had a seemingly innocent crush turned into this?

"LIES! You knew!" The gun rattled again.

The beeping of the heart monitor increased in speed, and I knew Taylor was panicking. I had to find a different track. "Ashlee, I didn't know, I promise. I thought we were friends. We are, aren't we?" It was a total lie, but I didn't know what else to do other than plead complete ignorance.

Ashlee cocked her head to one side as if pondering what that might mean. "Friends?"

"Yes. Friends." I searched for where I should go from here. Where could I take this conversation that would help me understand what the hell had happened and how to get us out of this situation? "And friends are honest with each other, right?"

Ashlee cocked her head to the other side. She wiped her tears away with her free hand, still not dropping the gun. "Yes..." Her voice was quiet now.

Quiet was good. Quiet meant calm. And I needed her to keep from making any sudden movements that could cause the gun to accidentally go off. I pushed on. "Can you tell me what happened?"

"She ruined *everything*." Ashlee was back to a keening wail again. Shit.

"What do you mean?"

"You were supposed to be with me. We're perfect for each other. And I've worked so hard for so long to get us together."

My muscles locked. "How have you worked to get us together?"

She looked at me like I was an imbecile. "I got rid of them, of course."

My chest tightened along with my fists. "What do you mean you got rid of them?"

Ashlee's eyes hardened. "Bryce liked killing. He mostly did it away from here to protect me, but when I needed someone to disappear, he would do that." More tears spilled over her lower lids, but I no longer felt that pull of compassion towards her. "Bryce always took care of me. Did you know that our dad beat us?"

I'd heard rumblings that Mr. Elkins had been a nasty drunk, but there had never been substantiated claims that the police department could act on. Then he just disappeared. Everyone thought he'd just abandoned his family, but maybe that wasn't the case. I shook my head. "I didn't know, Ashlee. I'm so sorry."

"Bryce would always take the beatings for me, whenever he could. They were so bad and always for no reason. Finally, Bryce said we had to stop him." Ashlee sniffled, wiping at her face with her long sleeve. "He used to chase us into the woods. This time, Bryce said to lead him to a specific area, so I did. Bryce had hidden a shovel out there, and when I ran by, Daddy trailing after, Bryce killed him."

More of the pieces began to fall into place, and my blood ran cold.

"See, Bryce was good. He protected me. Always. Always. Always. He protected me, and he wanted me to have what I wanted." Ashlee's eyes turned in my direction. What she wanted was me.

"I would tell him who I needed to be gone, and he would do it. See, he killed to protect us, but then something broke in him. He liked it." Her face fell. "Too much. I told him to only kill the bad people, and he said that's what he did."

Caitlin and a random hiker counted as bad people? I wanted to ask but didn't. Taylor? My body vibrated with the rage currently coursing through me.

Ashlee was oblivious, she just kept right on with her tale. "When I heard you were going to propose to Julie after she graduated, I knew I had to stop it."

My eyes fell closed for the briefest of seconds. I finally had the answer I'd needed for over a decade. The thing that would allow me to put Julie to rest completely. I'd known her killer, and I'd ended his life. And I would bring Ashlee to justice, as well.

A weird combination of emotions flowed through me. Heartbreak at the taking of an innocent life for the most selfish of reasons. An innocent who had meant so much to me in my young life. Relief followed closely on its heels by guilt. Relief that Julie would have her justice and that losing Julie had meant I was free to find Taylor—the woman who truly set my soul aflame. And guilt for feeling both of those things.

I pushed those thoughts aside as Ashlee kept talking. "I told Bryce, and he said he would take care of it. He did." The rage reignited in my veins. All the years of betrayal... It was almost too much to bear. "You didn't really date seriously after that, so I didn't really have to do anything. I know you just needed time to sow your wild oats. And I was giving you that."

Ashlee's eyes snapped towards Taylor, anger flooding her expression. "But then Caitlin got greedy. It wasn't enough to just date you. She wanted to marry you. She wanted what wasn't hers. I heard her in the bakery."

My mind flashed back to the scene Caitlin had made that morning at the shop. Ashlee and Bryce had both been there. Was that all it had taken to set Ashlee off?

"Then *she* had to come." Ashlee shook the gun in Taylor's direction. "That liar. She said nothing was going on between you two, but the whole time, she was trying to snare you. I knew it!"

I took a step towards Ashlee, keeping one hand outstretched. "We can figure this out. There's a solution, I promise you. We just have to find it."

Ashlee's head bobbed up and down in a jerky nod. "There is. She has to die." I froze mid-step as Ashlee's eyes and the gun swung from me to Taylor and then back to me again. More tears fell from her eyes, her shoulders heaving. "And you have to, too. You killed Bryce. Why? Why did you have to do that?"

I was going to have to tackle her and hope for the best. Fuck, I really didn't want to get shot again, but there was no way Ashlee was giving up on this crazy mission she was on. My eyes were drawn to a spot behind Ashlee at a small movement. The door was creeping open. I really hoped it was a cop from the waiting room and not some unsuspecting nurse.

I forced my eyes back to Ashlee, not wanting her to be clued in to the intruder behind her. I needed to keep her talking. "I'm sorry—" I blurted. "I didn't know the whole story. If I had known what happened to you and Bryce, I wouldn't have killed him." Lies. Total lies.

"It's too late. You did, and now I have to defend him. Protect him like he did for me, even if it's too late." She cocked the hammer on the gun, and my muscles coiled in preparation to leap at her. Suddenly, she crumpled to the floor in a heap. Left in her place was Liam, standing there decked out in a hospital gown and those socks they gave you with the rubber dots on the soles, holding a fucking bedpan.

My jaw fell open. "Did you just knock her out with a bedpan?"

Liam grinned. "It seemed only fair. Her brother cracked my skull open with a skillet." His face grew serious. "Are you guys okay? She was fucking crazy. I could hear her all the way out in the hall."

I crouched, lifting the gun from where it had landed on the

floor. "You might want to grab some on-duty officer and an orderly."

Liam nodded and ducked back outside to get some help. I turned to Taylor. Her eyes were wide, and her face was as white as a sheet. I rushed over to her, panic licking at my veins. "Are you okay?"

She nodded woodenly. "She's crazy. But at the same time, I feel horrible for her, she's led such a messed-up life." Taylor's gaze went from Ashlee on the floor to me. "Is it over now? Please tell me it's finally over."

I set the gun down on the table next to the hospital bed. "I hope to hell it is." Brushing my lips against hers, I cupped her face in my hands as police officers and medical staff burst through the door.

CHAPTER
Forty-six

Taylor

THREE WEEKS LATER

STRONG ARMS ENGULFED ME FROM BEHIND. I LET OUT A little moan as I burrowed back against the hard, warm body behind me. "Too early. Let me sleep."

Sleep was coming much easier now. I never would have thought that would be possible just weeks after almost getting hunted down by a serial killer, but it was. I'd had a couple of nightmares that first week when I was still in the hospital, but Walker had been right there beside me, never leaving me to face the darkness alone.

He talked me through whatever was on my mind. Held my hand, stroked my hair. He spent every night in a narrow cot beside my hospital bed. But since returning home, he'd held me each night, and no more nightmares had come.

A chuckle sounded from right next to my ear, and then teeth nipped at my lobe. The action sent a zing of sensation down my spine. I was awake now. Walker's low and husky voice sounded. "The doctor cleared you for all activities, didn't he?"

A slow smile crept over my face. I'd been to my final doctor's appointment yesterday and had gotten a clean bill of health. It had been a full day of doctoring and running a few errands that we'd been putting off, so by the time we got home, I was exhausted. I'd fallen asleep on the couch and had only awoken when Walker carried me to bed. There'd been no sexy times. Only a love affair between me and my pillow.

I pushed my backside against the growing bulge in Walker's sleep pants. "He did clear me for moderate activities...including bedroom-type things." My voice was thick with the last remnants of sleep and growing desire. I hadn't had Walker inside me in what felt like forever.

Walker's hand dipped below the waistband of my sleep shorts, and I sucked in a breath as he teased my folds. A growl sounded in my ear. "You're already wet. Fuck, I love that."

A very unwelcome knock sounded at the door. "What?" Walker barked.

I giggled.

"Uh, breakfast is ready. If you're not too busy." I'm sure if we could have seen my bestie's face, it would have been flaming red. Carter and Austin had stayed in Sutter Lake for the last three weeks, baby Ethan in tow. They'd wanted to help Liam and me recuperate. We'd had matching severe concussions, though Liam's was a little worse than mine. The wounds on my stomach, while awful-looking, weren't actually that deep. They'd probably scar, but there was no permanent damage. I was incredibly grateful.

"We'll be out in a minute. Thanks, Carter," I said, still fighting laughter. I loved having all the people I cared about most in the world at the cabin with me. It made for tight quarters, but I loved the feeling of having them all as close as possible. It had been a time of healing and repairing of relationships for all of us.

Walker, on the other hand, was just about done with the cramped living space. He growled in my ear again, but this time out of frustration instead of arousal. "I am taking you to my house today."

I chuckled, the action causing delicious tingles to overtake me since Walker's hand was still between my legs. My laugh turned into a moan.

Walker nipped my ear again and removed his hand. "Soon." He kissed my neck. "Very soon."

The way Walker could play my body with the barest of touches was criminal. I groaned and forced myself into a sitting position.

Walker was by my side in an instant, his brow creased. "Are you okay? Is something hurting you?"

My face softened, the frustration melting away. "I'm fine." I brushed my lips against his. "Just pouting because I wanted a lazy morning in bed with you."

Walker grinned and pulled me to my feet. He pressed his warm lips to my forehead, and I soaked in the feeling, warmth filling my entire body. He pulled back, tucking a stray strand of hair behind my ear. "I have something I want to ask you."

I studied his expression. It was hopeful, with some excitement and a touch of nerves mixed in. "Okay…"

"We haven't talked about the future much." My stomach tightened. We really hadn't. We said that we loved one another all the time now, but that hadn't transitioned into *future talk*. I'd wanted him to broach the subject first. The old-fashioned Texan in me shining through, I guess.

Walker pressed on, his eyes drilling into mine. "I want you to stay." My shoulders sagged in relief. "And move in with me." He brushed his lips against mine. "Make a home with me."

My insides twisted in the best possible way, my stomach dipping at the promise of building a life with Walker. "There's nothing I'd like more."

His eyes searched mine for any hint of doubt, but I knew he'd find none.

A smile broke over my face. "I've actually been looking into what I would need to do to get certified to teach in Oregon."

Shock washed over Walker's face, and I smiled wider. "Really?"

"Really."

Walker pulled me tighter against him. "That makes me real fuckin' happy." He pressed a hard kiss to my mouth that softened as his tongue swept in. He slowly pulled his lips from mine. "I love you, Taylor."

I'd never grow tired of hearing it, especially when the blue blazed in his mostly green eyes, the way it was now. "Love you to the moon and back." It was something my mother used to say to me, and I'd taken to saying to Walker. I figured she'd like that I did.

His eyes softened. I'd told him that it was something I'd shared with her, and he'd said he was honored to share it with us both.

"Come on, guys! Finish banging so we can eat already!" Liam's voice rang out from somewhere outside our door.

The growl was back as Walker declared, "We're moving you out today."

I giggled, throwing my arms around him and burying my face between his pecs.

We quickly dressed, brushed our teeth, and made it out to the dining room.

Liam gave Walker and me a devilish grin. "Well, well, well, if it isn't the two lovebirds." He let out an exaggerated kissing noise, and I elbowed him in the gut. "Hey! I'm still wounded."

I snorted. "You're as wounded as I am, which is not at all."

Liam grinned. "I don't know, my head still hurts a bit. Think one of those cute nurses would make a house call?"

Both Walker and I groaned. Liam had had the entire hospital staff aflutter with his presence, especially the young nurses. Luckily, his charming personality had endeared them all to him, even the straight men, so the press never found out about him being in Sutter Lake.

Liam knocked shoulders with me. "Come on, help this poor injured soul put the silverware out."

I laughed, and Walker headed into the kitchen, shaking his head. "I can't listen to this fool anymore."

"That's gratitude for you," Liam called after him. He tipped his head down to me. "I save both of your lives, and this is the thanks I get."

Now it was my turn to shake my head, but my lips were tipped into a smile as I moved around the dining room, setting down knives and forks. Helping Liam set the table, I was suddenly struck by the full-circle moment. Almost a year ago now, I had stood in a similar place, doing this very same thing. Getting ready to tell my closest friends that I was planning to move to Sutter Lake for a year. Now, that year was potentially forever.

Liam pointed a butter knife in my direction. "You've got an I'm-up-to-something smile on your face, Taylor. What gives?"

I bit the inside of my cheek. "Nothing."

"You're a horrible liar."

The rest of the crew poured into the dining room. Walker and Austin carried heaping piles of food, while Carter carried little Ethan in her arms.

"Why are you calling my girl a liar?" Walker asked as he set down a platter and came to put an arm around my shoulders. "You keep saying you're still injured, but you're asking for an ass-kicking."

Austin snorted. "He's always asking for an ass-kicking."

Liam clutched his hands over his heart in mock-affront. "I'm hurt. Truly. Taylor here," he said, pointing the butter knife at me again, eyes narrowing, "had that I'm-up-to-something smile on her face, but she wouldn't tell me why."

All eyes came to me, and my smile only got bigger. I turned my gaze to my shoes.

"Something is up," Carter agreed. "Tell us what's going on."

"Let's sit," I urged, and everyone hesitantly took their seats. Walker took my hand under the table.

Carter's jaw fell open. "Are you pregnant?"

It was bad timing. I had just taken a sip of orange juice, and it spewed out of my mouth as I choked. Right onto Liam's plate.

He looked thoroughly disgusted. "Gee, thanks."

I ignored Liam. "I'm not pregnant! Why would you think that?"

Carter bit her lip. "I don't know, you're all glowy and happy."

"Those are kind of knocked-up vibes," Austin agreed.

I glared at them both. As excited as I was for the future, I was not ready for a baby yet. I turned my gaze to Walker, who was shaking with silent laughter. No help from him. "Walker asked me to move in with him. I'm staying in Sutter Lake."

Carter beamed, handing Ethan to Austin and coming around the table to pull me up and into a tight hug. "I'm so happy for you." She squeezed harder. "I'm sad for myself, not having you back in LA, but so happy for you."

I pulled back from my bestie, tears glistening in both of our eyes. "I'll come visit, lots. And you'll always have a place here."

"Actually, we might have our own place here," Austin broke in.

My eyes widened, going from Carter to Austin and back again. "What?"

Carter's lips tipped up. "I had a feeling you'd be staying here, and Austin and I thought it would be nice to have a place where we could get away from the craziness of LA. Why not Sutter Lake?"

I let out a high-pitched squeal, dissolving into some sort of dorky happy-dance with Carter.

Liam stuck a finger in his ear as if he were trying to clear it. "Damn, woman. First, you spit on my plate, and now you're trying to make me go deaf."

I ran around the table, giving Austin a huge hug and kiss on the cheek. "Thank you." Then I continued on to Liam, hugging him and pinching his cheek. "What about you?"

He swatted my hand away. "Well, I was actually thinking about asking if I could stay here a while. I need a break from LA. What do you say, Walker, think your family would rent me the place?"

Walker studied Liam, probably wondering the same thing I was. *What was he hiding from in LA?* We'd never gotten around to that heart-to-heart, but I'd make sure that happened sooner rather than later. "We'd be happy to have you stay on," Walker said.

I grinned and clapped my hands like a five-year-old. All my favorite people in the same place. Walker pulled me down to his lap and kissed me soundly.

"Ew, gross, we're about to eat," Liam whined. Austin chucked a biscuit at him.

"I'm glad you're happy, Short-stack." Walker kissed the end of my nose.

"I'm the happiest."

Shoving the last drawer of Walker's dresser—no, *our* dresser—closed, I flopped back onto the bed. All my stuff was moved in. Well, the little I'd had sent to me from Texas. I'd have to get everything I had in storage sent up here, too, but there was no need to tell Walker that his home was about to be inundated with dozens of boxes of girlie things.

My eyes traveled around the space, taking everything in. This was the place I would make my home. It was gorgeous, with its high, beamed ceilings and wide-planked floors, but it could use a bit of a feminine touch. I grinned to myself as I wondered how

Walker would react to decorative throw pillows.

I stared up at the ceiling, mentally planning a trip to one of the cute little home décor shops in town. Walker's voice drifted in from the deck off the master bedroom as he talked on the phone. My shoulders tensed as I recognized the tone of concern in his voice.

I sat up, shoving myself against the pillows as Walker strode through the door. His eyes were pinched, and he scrubbed a hand down the side of his face. I patted the spot on the bed next to me. "How is she?"

Walker sat down on the edge of the bed, toeing off his boots and scooting up until he was reclined against the pillows, as well. He sighed. "She's pretending everything's fine, but I know it's not. I hate that she won't talk to me."

Walker and I were both worried about Jensen. She'd broken down in tears the first time she saw me in the hospital, apologizing for bringing Bryce into all of our lives. None of this was her fault, but she couldn't see it any other way and had completely shut down. Now, she refused to talk about Bryce or what had happened.

Walker traced circles on the back of my hand. "Do you think she's mad at me for killing him?"

I sat up with a start. "What? No, Walker." I grasped his hand in mine. "She hates him for what he did. She probably would have killed him herself. But Jensen blames herself. We just need to keep telling her none of this was her fault, even if she can't hear it right now."

Walker's jaw hardened. "I wish I could kill him all over again for what he's putting her through."

Walker had been cleared of any wrongdoing in Bryce's death, and Ashlee had been committed to a criminal psychiatric ward a few counties over, but the siblings' presence was still sending ripples of pain throughout the community.

I squeezed Walker's hand, not having adequate words to ease his pain. He tugged on my arm, pulling me to his chest. The rhythmic beating of his heart, the steadiness of it, brought comfort.

I pressed a kiss to his t-shirt-clad chest. "I wish I had the words to make it better."

Walker's lips brushed the top of my head. "You make it better just by being here, right like this."

I lifted my head so that my chin rested on his sternum. There was so much love in his gaze, and I was overwhelmed by my need for him. My mouth met his as I climbed up the bed to straddle him.

Warmth flooded me as his lips caressed mine in a dance that was a mixture of comfort and heat. I rocked my hips against his, and Walker let out a groan as his eyes fell closed. I rocked again, and they flew open.

He tugged at the bottom of my shirt, pulling it up and over my head. His gaze traveled from my face then traced a line down the column of my neck to my breasts and lower. The look in Walker's eyes hardened, and I tensed.

He traced his fingers, feather-light, over the raised scars on my belly, still an angry red. "I'm so sorry this happened. So fucking sorry I didn't get to you in time."

I placed two fingers under his chin, lifting it so that his eyes met mine. "You did get there in time. I'm here. I get to make a life with you. That's what matters."

With a growl, Walker flipped me onto my back so that he was between my legs and hovering over me. My breath caught in my throat as he cupped my cheek. "I love you so fucking much." His words were a fierce battle cry.

Walker trailed a hand down my neck, moving lower and lower at a painfully slow pace. I leaned up as he reached behind me to unhook my bra. His gaze zeroed in on my nipples, and he bent to pull one into his mouth. He lapped and laved as I squirmed beneath him, pressing my thighs together to try and get some semblance of relief. It didn't work.

Walker released my tight bud from his lips and kissed each one. "My favorite color, this dusky shade of pink when you're turned on and your nipples are straining to get to me."

My core tightened at his words, and I dipped a hand under his tee, trailing my fingers over his taut skin. Walker trailed his tongue lower. So very gently, he kissed his way down one scar and then the other.

My breath caught at the tender gesture. The warmth that had flooded me at his lips' first touch caught fire now, giving me that beautiful burn. The blaze that caused my heart to clench and my nerve endings to sing.

"I need you," I whispered.

That was all it took. Walker pulled down the shorts I was wearing with a speed that was almost alarming. He tore his t-shirt off and had his pants on the floor within seconds.

I took a moment to drink him in—the broad shoulders, perfectly formed muscles straining with need. My eyes found his. "You're perfect."

He pounced, his mouth devouring my lips, tongue stroking mine. Walker pulled back, uncertainty flooding his face. "Tell me if anything hurts."

"I will."

Walker cupped my face, his eyes boring into mine. "Promise me."

My heart squeezed. "I promise."

His tip bumped up against my opening.

"Please." It came out as a half word, half moan, and I didn't even care.

In that deliciously slow tempo he had turned into an art form, Walker pressed in. The pressure built, and when he was fully seated inside me, I felt him everywhere. From the tips of my toes straining against the mattress, to the top of my head arching back into the pillow. He zinged through every nerve ending, danced through every vein. He was in me now and forever.

My fingers pressed into his shoulders while I wrapped my legs around him so my heels dug into his ass. I loved feeling the bunch and bow of his muscles beneath me as he slowly moved. The delicious drag of his cock against my walls was heaven.

Each pass seemed to drive him deeper and build the spiral of sensations higher. My skin seemed to tingle everywhere, vibrating to the tempo that Walker set with his thrusts. His pace increased, and a fine sheen of sweat covered us both. When he finally drove so deep he bottomed out, I couldn't help the sharp intake of air.

Walker's eyes fell closed for the briefest of moments, and then his lips were on mine with a hunger I'd never felt from him before. It was as if he wanted to connect us in every way possible, see how deeply he could instill himself in me.

I cupped his face as he pulled back, sucking in air. "You're everywhere. I love you, Walker."

"You're mine." His words were choked.

"I'm yours." I brushed my lips against his. "And you're mine."

"I'm yours."

My heartbeat stuttered at the emotion in his eyes, in his voice, radiating throughout his body. It was that emotion raining over me that sent me spiraling over the edge. Everything came together in a way I had never experienced before. His touch. His words. His heart. The orgasm sent such powerful waves through my body, I saw stars.

My inner-muscles clamped down so hard, I thought it might have caused Walker pain. He let out a curse I couldn't quite discern as his back arched and he thrust even deeper, releasing everything he had.

Walker collapsed on the bed, rolling us so that I was now on top of him, both of us panting. I tried to grasp onto reality as I came down from the otherworldly high.

Walker's heartbeat thrummed against my cheek. I placed a kiss directly over it. "Thank you for letting me belong to you."

He squeezed me harder against him, brushing his lips against my hair. "Never letting you go. We're going to build a beautiful life together."

epilogue

Taylor

ONE YEAR LATER

I PUSHED OPEN THE FRONT DOOR, CALLING OUT AS I DID. "I'M home! Are you here? If you are, pour me a large drink because I've had quite the day."

"In the kitchen," Walker called back.

I slipped off my heels by the front door and headed towards Walker's voice. "Timmy Jenkins stuck an open glue stick in Sally Peters' hair."

I heard Walker's low chuckle before I saw him. "He must like her."

I rounded the corner and drank in the sight of my gorgeous man. "It's not funny. We couldn't get it out, so I had to call her mother to come get her and take her to a hairdresser."

Walker pressed his lips together in an attempt to stifle his laughter. I was back to teaching, first as a substitute last year, and now as a full-time second-grade teacher right here in Sutter Lake. I loved it, even with dramas like today.

I melted into Walker as he wrapped his arms around me.

"How was your day?"

"Boring. Nothing but paperwork and a couple tourist speeding tickets." He might have sounded annoyed with the lack of action, but I knew Walker was happiest when his town was sleepy. He pressed his lips to my forehead. "Come on, I want to take you somewhere."

I tipped my head back. "I'm exhausted, can't we just stay in tonight?"

Walker brushed his lips against mine, and I sank into the kiss. His tongue swept into my mouth, and I groaned. "You're not playing fair," I said, pulling back.

He sent a mischievous grin my way. "You'll be glad you let me steal you away. I'll even take a couple beers with us so you can have that drink you're craving."

"I think I've earned two."

Walker chuckled. "Deal." He grabbed three beers from the fridge and led me back out the front door, barely giving me enough time to slip on some flip-flops.

Once in the truck, Walker typed something into his phone. "Sorry," he said. "Tuck had a question about a case."

I leaned back in my seat, putting my feet up on the dash. "So, where are you taking me?"

Walker slipped his phone into the cupholder and turned over the ignition. "You'll just have to wait and see."

He was always doing things like this for me. Surprising me with dinner out or taking the boat around the lake, even just finding a new place for the two of us to go running together. Within a couple of minutes, I saw that tonight, he was taking me to our spot.

A smile played on my lips as we crested the hill to the overlook Walker had taken me to the very first time we'd gone running together. It was my favorite place in all of Sutter Lake. We came here often. Sometimes, on a run, other times we'd bring a picnic lunch, or like tonight, a couple of beers and a blanket.

I reached over, squeezing Walker's muscular thigh and pressing my lips to his cheek. "We're just in time for sunset."

His gaze met mine briefly before he turned back to the gravel road. "Glad you let me steal you away?"

"Very glad," I whispered into his ear before sucking the lobe into my mouth.

"Damn, woman, you're going to make me wreck my truck."

I giggled but released my hold, sitting back in my seat. Walker pulled to a stop and got out, grabbing a blanket from the cab. He opened my door and helped me hop down from the entirely too tall truck.

I grabbed the beer from Walker's arms as he went to spread the blanket out under a beautiful Aspen tree. Walker leaned against the tree's smooth trunk and patted the ground between his legs. I needed no further encouragement and hurried over, settling between his thighs.

I held up two beers, and he used the bottle opener on his keychain to pop the tops. We were silent as we sipped, just watching the sky put on a dazzling show and soaking up the simple joy of being together.

Just as the sky turned a breathtaking shade of orangey-pink, Walker's lips brushed against my ear. "Love you more than life, Taylor." The corners of my mouth tipped up, warmth filling my chest. His lips swept over my temple. "You make me happier than I ever thought I could be."

My heart began to pick up its pace. Walker kissed the side of my face again. "I love belonging to you and having you belong to me. I want to make that official."

A black leather box was placed in my lap. "Open it," he whispered.

Hands shaking, I placed my beer down and lifted the lid. The last remnants of sunshine made the ring's gem glimmer and dance, the hue of the sky making the diamond almost look pink. It was beautiful and so unique, with an antique setting that almost looked like twining vines, holding a massive center stone.

Walker lifted the ring from the box. "It was my grandmother's. She said she'd be honored if you wore it." Tears began to fill my eyes. "Let me give you a family." The tears crested over then, spilling down my cheeks.

I turned my head so that I could meet his gaze. "You've already given me one."

"Is that a yes?"

"A million times yes."

Walker slipped the ring onto my finger. A perfect fit. Then he cupped my cheeks, wiping away my tears with his thumbs. "Luckiest man on this Earth."

I grinned so widely, I thought my face might split in two. "I love you. To the moon and back. Always."

I'm not sure who closed the distance first, but our lips met, and the kiss seemed to go on for ages. Lips and tongues and hearts and...forever.

Walker pulled back and flashed a smile that told me he was up to something. "One more thing." He put his fingers to his mouth and let out an ear-splitting whistle.

"What in the world—?" My words were cut off by a stampede of loved ones: Walker's entire family, all my best friends from LA, and a few other familiar faces.

A small figure was the fastest. Noah pumped his arms as he ran up the hill and launched himself at Walker and me, landing with an *umph*. "Tay Tay! You gonna be my aunt now?"

I burst out laughing. "You bet, buddy."

"Yes!" he shouted, pumping a fist in the air.

I grinned up at a smiling and slightly teary Jensen. "I'm so happy for you two," she said. I knew she was, but the happiness in her eyes couldn't disguise the bone-deep pain I knew was there.

My beautiful, fierce Jensen was the one holding people at arms' length now, and I didn't know how to fix it. She needed someone as determined as Walker had been with me to break down her walls.

Walker stood, pulling Noah and me up with him, and we were engulfed in hugs and well wishes. Irma elbowed her way through the crowd. "Outta my way! I gotta see how my ring looks on my girl." Walker let out a chuckle as Irma broke through.

She beamed, grabbing my hand and holding it up to the light. "It's perfect on you. I knew it. Didn't I tell you all they were the ones for each other? Maybe now you'll all start respecting my premonitions a little more."

The small crowd broke into laughter as Andrew and Sarah stepped forward. Sarah pulled me in for a tight hug and then cupped my face in her hands. "I know I'll never replace the amazing mother you had, but I am honored to have you as a daughter."

Fresh tears spilled down my cheeks as Walker pulled me back against him. I looked around, meeting the eyes of everyone who was so dear to me. "She'd be so happy, you know. This would make her happier than anything. To know that even after losing her, it brought me to my new family."

In that moment, I knew, my mom was here. She always would be. I lifted my face to the sky and whispered, "To the moon and back."

THE END

ENJOY THIS BOOK?

You can make a huge difference in Beautifully Broken Pieces' book life!

Reviews encourage other readers to try out a book. They are critically important to getting the word out about a book and mean the world to every author.

I'd love your help in spreading the word. If you could take a quick moment to leave a review on your favorite book site, I would be forever grateful. It can be as short as you like. You can do that on your preferred retailer, Goodreads, or BookBub. Even better? All three! Just copy and paste that baby!

Email me a link to your review at catherine@catherinecowles. com so I can be sure to thank you. You're the best!

BONUS SCENE

Want to find out what happens when Taylor learns she's pregnant? By signing up for my newsletter, you'll get this bonus scene. Plus, you'll be the first to see cover reveals, upcoming excerpts from new releases, exclusive news, and have access to giveaways found nowhere else. Sign up by going to the link below.

www.subscribepage.com/BBPbonus

ACKNOWLEDGMENTS

I love reading every book's acknowledgments, and if you've stuck around this long, maybe you do, too! There's just something about getting a peek into the author's process. Who helped them along their journey, who inspired their words, and any other glimpses they might give us. What can I say? I'm nosy.

Beautifully Broken Pieces grew out of my own loss. My story is not Taylor's, but I drew from my own experiences to try and capture some of Taylor's raw moments of grief. If you've read this book and lost someone close to you, consider this me giving you a hug through the pages of this novel. Be kind to yourself and never be afraid to express your loss however you need to.

So many people helped me make this book a reality, but the first thank you always has to go to my mom. She gave me my insatiable love of books and is my biggest supporter. Thank you for everything, Mom!

Can I tell you a secret? The indie romance community is pretty dang amazing. I'm so incredibly grateful for the women who have been supportive in every possible way; from answering a million questions to sharing my books to giving desperately needed pep talks. Alessandra, Julia, Devney, Emma, Grahame, and the ladies of KB 101…thank you from the bottom of my heart.

To my fearless beta readers: Trisha, Emily, Angela, Ryan, and Emma. Thank you for reading this book in its roughest form and helping me to make it the best it could possibly be!

So many people helped bring this book to life and made it

shine. Susan and Chelle, thank you for your editing wisdom and helping to guide my path. Hang, thank you for putting up with my millions of tweaks and creating such a breathtaking cover. Stacey, for making my paperbacks sparkle. And Becca, for creating trailers that give me chills.

To all the bloggers who have taken a chance on my newbie author self...THANK YOU! Your championing of my words means more than I can say. And to my ARC team, thank you for your kindness, support, and sharing my books with the world.

Ladies of Addicted To Love Stories, you're my favorite place to hang out on the internet! Thank you for your support, encouragement, and willingness to always dish about your latest book boyfriends. You're the freaking best!

To my own personal cheering squad: Lyle, Nikki, Paige, and Trisha, thank you for endless encouraging conversations and lots of laughs. So grateful to have you in my corner.

Lastly, thank YOU! Yes, YOU. I'm so grateful you're reading this book and making my author dreams come true. I love you for that. A whole lot!

ALSO AVAILABLE FROM
CATHERINE COWLES

Further To Fall

ABOUT
CATHERINE COWLES

Writer of words. Drinker of Diet Cokes. Lover of all things cute and furry, especially her dog. Catherine has had her nose in a book since the time she could read and finally decided to write down some of her own stories. When she's not writing, she can be found exploring her home state of Oregon, listening to true crime podcasts, or searching for her next book boyfriend.

STAY CONNECTED

You can find Catherine in all the usual bookish places…

Website: catherinecowles.com

Facebook: facebook.com/catherinecowlesauthor

Facebook Reader Group: bit.ly/AddictedToLoveStories

Instagram: instagram.com/catherinecowlesauthor

Goodreads: goodreads.com/catherinecowlesauthor

BookBub: bookbub.com/profile/catherine-cowles

Amazon: www.amazon.com/author/catherinecowles

Twitter: twitter.com/catherinecowles

Pinterest: pinterest.com/catherinecowlesauthor

Made in the USA
Middletown, DE
04 April 2024

GHOSTS OF THE
SCATTERED
KINGDOMS

GHOSTS OF THE SCATTERED KINGDOMS

WHERE SHADOWS REIGN: BOOK ONE

WADE GARRET

Ghosts of the Scattered Kingdoms © 2021 Wade Garret
Cover art and typography © 2021 Alejandro Colucci
Page design by A.M. Rycroft
Edited by Lily Luchesi, Mike Myers, Tim Marquitz

First Printing: 2021

ISBN 978-1-7346486-3-8

Epic Publishing
www.epic-publishing.com

Special discounts are available on quantity purchases.
For details, contact the publisher by email at publisher@
epic-publishing.com or at the following address:

Epic Publishing
370 Castle Shannon Blvd., #10366
Pittsburgh, PA 15234

To the stories and people that got me here,
I say thank you and I love you.

The following wire was secured with
Baudot Coding.

Mr. Black *-STOP-*
Mina Genza must die *-STOP-* The cult
must not gain another Master *-STOP-*
If it does, the situation in Collezia
will force our hand *-STOP-* You have
succeeded where others have failed
-STOP- Do so again *-STOP-* She dies at
all costs *-STOP-*

Senator Grace
September 14, 323 of the Third Age

1

A woman screamed, followed by the *cha-thunk* of hard metal biting into damp wood.

The crowd cheered and raised their torches to the night sky beneath swaying boughs.

Mr. Black rode down the overground forest road, coming up on the rear of Coven Hall. He already knew what he'd find between the hall's abandoned towers, forever collapsing in on themselves, their soggy walls and parapets little better than mortar mites and moldy bones.

Listening to the crowd, gauging their purpose, the man in black shook his head.

As he closed in, the cries for slaughter and bellows for reprieve grew louder and more ferocious from the other side of the vine covered trees. The strangling debris concealed him from the onlookers gathered to witness the joyful executions at one of the Feld Gods' oldest sacrificial sites.

We do keep them fed, don't we?

The *thunk* of the executioner's axe again splattered across the keep's leaning stonework.

Like a spider, a cold wind crawled down Mr. Black's aching neck. The collar of his winter duster and soot-black tricorn should've shielded him from the nagging chill but, as with a heavy rain, little bits always get through.

The quick, creeping invasion teasing the small hairs at the base of his neck left a lingering swirl within him. A daunting pool, full of endless memories and righteous guilt. Trepidations that gnawed at an eternal knot within him that wouldn't break, no matter how often he wished it.

"Mel?" It was just a moment, a brief lapse in his concentration, but it was enough to open the void.

Reins loose, he was drawn back in time. Confronted by old and bitter truths. Long, silent slings and arrows hurled by the Sabbat, consequences still blood-sworn to his failures regarding the Collezian cult's current leader. Lady Mina Genza who, strangely enough now, best mirrored this most ancient capital's dilapidated court-yard and once lavish gardens that spread out before him beneath the forest canopy.

My, how the mighty have fallen.

Did anyone still living know the true name first given to this land by the Eyldeyryiens?

"Ellizium," said Black to himself.

Tilting in the saddle once returned to the present, Mr. Black quickly counted twenty or so townsfolk, some with young children asleep in their arms, standing in the night's stillness before an impromptu stage. The entire makeshift structure was anchored with heavy rope and rusty shanks to what remained of Coven Hall's east wing, where above which, long ago, the roof caught fire.

Atop the stage stood roughly a dozen harshly bound misfortunate persons of no interest. They were a mixed bag of puppets. Men and women. Young and old. With means and without. Despite their differences, though, Mr. Black recognized a single theme shared by many of their terrified, doe-eyed faces.

If he were a gambling man, Mr. Black would've wagered they were all soon for the same unthinkable realization. That not one of them had any idea how they got themselves into this mess. Truly, even now, some continued to plead that all of this was just a bad dream or a case of mistaken identity.

Alone, this sort of phenomena wasn't such an oddity for any victim to profess during their final moments as they soiled themselves before the gallows. The occasional innocent losing their head was certainly an understandable practicality of this sort of work. Not just here but throughout the corrupt league of bastard princedoms in the Scattered Kingdoms. However, so many at the same time in a single place, gathered and tried, if they were tried at all, in the darkness beneath where once stood Wodan's Altar?

Mr. Black chuckled bitterly to himself as his horse stepped back and shifted its weight, finding a better spot for its right foreleg on the mostly buried cobbles beneath the pine needle and leaf littered dirt road.

The once well-groomed stallion became more

particular about that injured leg.

Mr. Black knew it was getting worse as he patted the horse's croup and withers reassuringly, little interested in those idling on the opposite side of the rickety executioner's platform at the far end of the stage near the makeshift stairs.

The handful of locals huddled there had come to oversee and officiate the evening's brutal entertainment: civic and cultural leaders, spiritual pretenders, and officials of the berg's watch, of which the shrouded executioner was most likely a deputized member.

Iron Front of the great Gol army once... What would their fathers say now?

Weathered and tired, Mr. Black growled a series of coughs and low-spoken curses, causing a few of the almost bewitched citizens toward the rear of the crowd to notice the rider in black. They didn't, however, look his way for long.

The masked executioner raised her red ax again.

A man shouted a hopeless plea.

Cha-thunk.

Wet splinters flew, and another reed basket wobbled with the sad, wet weight of worthless prayers. The rabble's shouting and roaring merged excitement and sorrow into one. The morbid congregation was sickening.

This whole country is going to the same Light-forsaken end, thought Black. Then a curious itch beneath his brow begged him to look over his shoulder.

Mr. Black waited. His hand twitched, reins tight between his fisted gloves. He tensed, ready to gallop, then breathed to steady his nerves. He listened again. Sniffed the air, then closed his eyes and, slowly, the impulse to draw or loose one of the many weapons concealed about his person dwindled into the night.

There was nothing. Not for miles. Not through the forest or back up the mountains.

Not for days had there been anything or anyone behind him on the road down from Collezia.

Mr. Black was sure of it, and yet, he couldn't shake the instinct, the little voice that'd kept him alive all these years. The sensation spoke to him through the ghostly breeze blowing across the gallows. It told him that, maybe somehow, the Enemy could've gained on him since he'd destroyed Senator Grace's last message.

Mr. Black chewed on his dry lip and overgrown mustache and spat the sourness out.

Perhaps they were already there, ahead of him, in Pehats Berg?

Cha-thunk!

The image of the vhendo's feast left to freeze in bloody stumps returned to him.

Gut tightened. Teeth clenched. He smelled the distant fires that drove the people from their homes, the fresh snow near the mountain stream choked with the monster's collective kill. He remembered the spongy, blue-gray corpses as they bobbed silently, innocently in the rushing water. Others, those more recently dragged onto the bank by predators late to the vhendo's gorging, had turned a rancid white-green.

Mr. Black blinked, and the circling owls waiting for their turn at the banquet vanished.

Cha-thunk!

Beasts from Beyond the Black now served Lady Genza's will, yet that sect wasn't reported to have enough power to—

Cha-thunk!

Mr. Black focused, and clarity slowly pierced through his weariness. He grudgingly accepted it was all his fault. There was a break in the chain or a loose link. Either way, someone had talked. A bribe? A debt?

Cha-thunk!

"That bitch knew," Black muttered, sinking deeper into the aged saddle.

He spurred the horse softly and moved down the road, back into the obscurity of the overgrown forest, away from the ruins of the once grand hall and those born to die cold and unknown in the mud for sins or deeds they'd neither had the sword or mind to resist.

Death comes for us all.

Mr. Black had to adapt. Survive. Information was now the mission priority. Without it, he might never get another chance to rip out Lady Genza's treacherous heart and feed it to her, and that was a promise he meant to keep.

2

Black stiffened as an old ward passed over and through him. It dispersed from his awareness as he crossed Ellizium's forgotten border, lost beneath the mud, before ducking below the broken archway showing the sign for Pehats Berg ahead.

Approaching the berg's outer watchtower, he eyed every distant roof and slit wall position before catching the irregular shape in the wet grass at the base of the post just off the gateway. Bael rats, most likely. Disgusting creatures. And like his mother used to say, "Once they're in, they're in to stay."

He discreetly checked the bandage on his horse's flank, disguised to keep the stallion's weakening state a secret from any guard or civil servant who might bar his passage. Disease was one of the few things not taken lightly in the Scattered Kingdoms. Generations of piled dead awaiting the flame made it one of the few things everyone agreed on.

The bite wound was deep. The medicine failed.

The poison would spread.

Lucky for him, his wounds from the vhendo weren't so severe.

Beside the gate left ajar, opposite the maggot-infested door where bullies and highwaymen often harassed locals on their way to and from various caravan companies, lived the town's first line of defense.

The watchman was fast asleep in a chair inside the shack, spear cuddled in his arms.

The rusted-out thermal condenser on the table inside the watch station wouldn't last the winter, and the bolter at the old man's feet was equally condemned. His tattered cloak and hand-me-down shield, combined with such makeshift lodgings, spoke all too well to Mr. Black that this was the best Pehats Berg had to offer. Pity.

Inside the wall, which was more like a giant fence at certain points, Mr. Black came upon a small cropping of Snickering Ashes. The thorny trees were decorated with red nooses left to dangle from its heaviest branches. One was currently occupied by the corpse of a woman who'd been branded a witch.

Mr. Black turned his horse away as it appeared she'd already set to rotting. Crows feasted on her eyes, mouth, and other tender bits of soft flesh.

The Faith of the Ten Pillars was all but gone in the Scattered Kingdoms, and yet Light Bringer customs were still religiously observed.

I need a drink.

The Two Sisters Inn wasn't far, but Mr. Black had to make a pit stop, so he did, and then headed there. The popular inn was in the center of the berg, about a stone's throw from Goran's stables. Goran's family rarely asked questions, especially when boarding was paid in full. Two days was enough to cover odds and ends and not excite curiosity or potential thievery from the family, times being what that were.

The man in black slipped the stable boy, Harold Cross, another coin and bit for future damages, disguised as a tip for attention to detail while tending his horse.

Little Harold caused Mr. Black to pause just as the stall swung closed behind him. Most folk ignored or generally looked down on the backward youth because, why should he be any different from his kin? Black knew better what the handicapped were capable of. His sister taught him that.

In that brief moment before the door closed, Mr. Black saw Goran's youngest grandson tend to the saddle and harness the way a coroner tends to a victim bound against their will. With each strap and buckle, little Harold became more entranced by whatever it was he could see or feel beyond the leather and iron.

Black grinned as little Harold poked at the secret bandage.

Perhaps this simpleton wasn't so stymied. Perhaps he had some Tuch?

The door closed, and Black was gone.

* * *

The Two Sisters's original logo, unlike those remaining neon travesties once glorified by the berg's carpetbagger entrepreneurs come south after the last great war, swayed by hook and chain above the first floor. The white letters on the black board peeled and cracked from water damage.

At three stories and twenty-one rooms, the Two Sisters was the largest lodging in town. Wide bricks and scatterwood boards gave it a fat, heavy base. Beard moss and spiraling root ran all over it like most other buildings. Truth be told, the brush grew so fast and hardy it was more crops than weeds.

Mr. Black was all but midnight, eyes barely noticeable beneath his tricorn when he entered the inn's front door. Men hardly glanced at him as they passed, women in arm and ale in hand. Smoke slithered overhead, playing between the rafters and slow fans.

Despite the odor of bodies packed tightly and sins not always committed behind closed doors, the aroma of roasted meat and vegetables somehow endured, if only a little. And Mr. Black was hungry.

Moving through the bar, he removed his fingerless gloves and slipped the tarnished silver band from his left hand to his pocket. A precaution of habit over necessity so far from the Isles of El'shwn. Yet, he sometimes felt guilty how it cheated his sister's memory by hiding his failed oath. He stopped to rub his aching drawfingers. The tabs within his gloves were almost worn through.

A pair of warm lips gently brushed his ear. "Arium."

Mr. Black grinned.

Again, the husky voice tickled his cheek. "Arium Black."

"Good to see you, too, Daphnia," he replied to one of the owners of the Two Sisters. "Give Jezzy a kiss for me, won't you?" If the tall redhead with legs to kill for were there, he'd have rather done the kissing himself. Odds were, though, she was somewhere below the inn, grease on her chin, tinkering with devices few but her sister would ever see or understand.

Daphnia spotted a not-so-discreet Sleeve Stinger on him. The secret forearm weapon seemed too close for comfort as one of her most profitable girls passed by, making her way to another gentleman with heavy coins in his pockets.

Daphnia took Black's hand. "We must speak."

"Later."

"I'm afraid, old friend, you do not have much time." After another glance, Daphnia left him.

She was right. Switchboards never lie. Neither do pigeons from abroad. Soon enough, he'd receive another wire or urgent report and be gone again. There was always another dispatch. Another cause or secret mission and, with it, another chance at losing Jezzy's heart.

Alone again, Mr. Black returned to his thoughts. *Two hours.*

It'd be contagious then, or worse. The stable master would be the first to go when the horse turned, if the stallion didn't just die. Then little Harold Cross, due to how his family always gave him the shit work.

Two hours.

"Evening," said the barkeep.

Mr. Black unbuttoned his surcoat and directed his gaze to the cedar casks, not the copper and brass kegs near the jerky automaton washing glasses in the corner. He would've spoken, but he wasn't sure who listened. The barkeep fetched a pint.

Patrons at an adjacent table watched him. With his back to them at the bar, Mr. Black quietly spied on their conversation. After a moment, their greedy, hushed voices reached his ears over the guests dancing near the stage where the piano man played. By now, most of the inn's other customers had gone back to disregarding him altogether but for one reason or another, this batch of seated drunks continued to find him curious. Impressive.

The hour was late. Any good man's day was long over. Were they drifters? Guild?

Mr. Black sensed their lowness, how their lives were lost to the toil of the physical world. If it came to it, he wouldn't think twice about killing them or anyone else in his way. For as the old saying of his profession went, "Sooner or later, Death'll get his parley."

For Mr. Black, it was always the mission alone that mattered. He'd get his chance to repay Lady Genza for every life lost fighting the Sabbat. Of that, he was sure, but first, he needed answers. Direction. This venomous bitch had more than fang and claw at her disposal now, and that's what'd sent him south.

He sipped his drink after slipping the barkeep a bit of cold metal. Sckag. The full lager chilled his hand. It was crisp and light over the tongue, heavy and bitter in the finish. One pint was never enough.

Setting the warm pint on the shiny bar-top, Mr.

Black removed his tricorn. His wild hair fell over his eyes, the longest locks brushed behind his ears, extending past his wiry beard and neck-scruff.

Another rich sip. He licked his lips. His mind wandered again.

So many. Still, they came...

He'd lost the black bastards weeks ago. Still, the questions persisted: Was it a trap for him, or had he finally succumbed to fear for the first time in his life, seeing a trap instead of coincidence? Were the nekctu in Pehats Berg? Had the Enemy's soulless elite outmaneuvered him? Could she have gotten word to them?

The ambush on the banks of the frozen stream had cost him thirteen arrows, two daggers, and a toebag of fume powder. The explosion outside the cave nearly killed him. He had no choice, though, but to wake up the hibernating bulldog bear. Put the giant animal between him and them. Otherwise, the vhendo would've overrun his position, and Lady Genza would likely be torturing him to death right now.

I'm alive.

Another hearty gulp of sckag dismissed the regret of a peacemaker absent from his hand. Unlike the vhendo, dark thoughts slowly germinated by his own dwindling humanity weren't so easily abated; a con he'd convinced himself of for years now, though, in this case, a peacemaker might've turned the tide.

A few songs later, some he quietly sang along with his fellow miscreants, Mr. Black found a soft chair far in the back of the inn's drinking room to rest in. It wouldn't be long now. Margaret never kept him waiting unless that's what Jezzy or Daphnia wanted. She was one of the Two Sisters' best gals. Always good at getting his unspoken messages out.

With a little sleight of hand as she crossed the dancing area, cutting between fellows soon to brawl over a particular blonde, Margaret received the token in her palm from Black. A small, childish trinket. That was it. Without a word or any further detail, she knew exactly what to do and where to go and whom to summon.

Reclining in the cushioned chair, Mr. Black ran his fingers along the arm's loose seam. The floral pattern and olive branches were masterfully detailed. The motif's ancient history was unlearned or forgotten by most, considering the last of the Eyldar were now myth and legend to most people, but not Mr. Black. The fact it remained in Pehats Berg, in this broken and bloody place, made what little hope he had for tomorrow burn brighter.

I should take off my boots, let my socks dry by the fire.

He mused about Jezzy while he waited: chuckling, then wincing. With his sore ribs and freshly stitched wounds, he'd be little use in bed. He closed his eyes, tried to remember what comfort felt like, and was again tricked by his own mind.

They know I've seen the bloodlines.

The vhendo had nearly caught him by the time he made it to the cave after following the river. By two legs and four, they'd come at him. Crashing through anything in their path. Some vhendo he'd never seen before, and his arrows couldn't penetrate them. If their hides were so damn tough, were they really machines? Hybrids?

They know. It gives them hunger. It's what they want.

Despite the amusement of song and drink and the nightmares he now analyzed for missing clues to his current predicament, the man in black nevertheless remained aware of the conversations and flow of people around him.

Because of the various mixed dialects and liquored tongues, though, he only caught bits of the troubling news openly shared beneath mouthfuls of smoke, meat, and ale.

Roughneck travelers had passed through the wade-towns along the Worsa, the highway stretching far north, beyond the Rift, to Maygar and even Collezia, the Pillar Kingdom. More traffic everywhere. That's all the gabbers talked about.

The fact was, the White Knights of Carolinyea, the Holy Kingdom's capital, were on the watch. They were restless. What drew them out? Answering this question was only a piece of his mission. Several regiments were already in sight of Maygar's domain when last he'd heard. In response to this, Maygerian forts near their eastern border along the Vahast had summoned their best soldiers. The Ram Corps division.

Black's stay in Fort Ulkir some months ago had ended after he found out his friend, Lord Dhovemurn, the High-Captain, was missing.

Garrith, you bastard.

Who would gain from the disappearance of one of the Ram's most formidable swordsmen?

Mr. Black swallowed another mouthful of ale. Something was on the move. For months. Years? How long had the Enemy held the list of names before it was destroyed? Was it the only copy? How many, like him, were betrayed?

When the serving automaton finished bussing a nearby table, Mr. Black ordered a meal of bread, potatoes, and a hearty portion of what turned out to be questionable beef. Afterwards, he partially dozed in the chair while his training kept his senses vigilant.

When the inn's front door opened again sometime later, he knew it was Leeann who entered. She was late. Once Leeann was seated in the chair next to him, he asked, "Have you eaten?"

"No," replied the girl.

Though twelve, her voice was fearless, belying her rather timid appearance. Her apron was a dirty lemon color. Her field-frock a patchwork of cotton, wool, and burlap. An old string secured her dusty-blonde hair.

Summoning Margaret now that she'd returned to the Two Sisters, Black ordered Leeann a plate of morsels piled higher than his had previously been. Anywhere else, such a meal would've cost several times what he paid but, in this inn, he often compensated more with information than coin. The kind of information, which, more often than not, ended with bloody knives.

Leann's food arrived, and he hid his sullenness when she awkwardly gripped the utensils. Like most children in her situation, she often ate huddled next to fizzling fires and mangy dogs. There was hope, though. He still had so much yet to teach her—about the ways of his world, the way of the Fifth Finger, and other tricks of his ancient trade.

Leeann ate with a feverish hunger.

Mr. Black's eyes tightened with dark thoughts. He grimaced into the fire.

"It's good," said Leeann. She then switched from the Common Tongue, Latorin, to her native language, Scar, to show her sincerity. "Brah'sebah."

Once Leeann finished, Mr. Black said, "Tell me everything."

"He's here," she gulped. "At my master's home, talking to Mr. Halgin just like you said."

Black took note of the men near the inn's north window. They'd been glancing sidelong at him since he'd ordered her supper. It was only going to get worse. In time, it'd become famine. Mr. Black rubbed his scraggly beard. It had been treated a few days ago for lice. "Lord Rohndolphn?"

Leeann nodded.

Remembering the last time the lord's name was mentioned, and in what circles, Mr. Black leaned closer to the fire. The Sabbat, the twisted network born of the Enemy, the Father of Lies, was spreading. "How many men? Does he carry Duke Talhgho's seal?"

"No," answered Leeann. "Prince Urhal's. I saw it. The lord had it in his fist when he beat my master." The joy of Mr. Halgin's weakness wasn't in her eye but her overall demeanor, and she was justified.

Zahargan Marcus Urhal? This was more than Mr. Black or his employer expected.

Was all the Eastern Mark rising? Was this the root of another Crown War? Was Zahargan Marcus Urhal reaching to be Hae Zar—uniting the Eight Marks of the

Scattered Kingdoms under one royal banner in order to wash clean the tragic history of seven brothers, blood-heirs of the First Breakers?

What were the chances Lady Mina Genza's faction in Carolinyea was connected here?

"Where's he now?"

"With my master."

"What else have you seen?"

"Nightmares. Is it true about Wodan? That he's doing this?"

"The gods are dead."

"My sister asks me—"

"Aydolph's sword was pulled over thirteen centuries ago," said Black.

Leeann looked up then, as if she had more to say.

"Tell her all's well. You shouldn't listen to so many stories."

Mr. Black knew what this season often did to people, how the Faithful poisoned the well as the snows fell. The harshness tempted these poor people in this gray place to turn on one another, transforming the numerous myths of the Breakers into something worse than monsters. All for the Faith's pious coffers.

"That boy, Bringtum's son, he likes to scare little girls."

Leeann nodded.

Eyes closed, Mr. Black laid his head against the back of the chair. "Where do you play after chores?"

"In the Mahar," answered Leeann. "Why?"

Knowing what battles were fought there, blood spilled by the Jackal's Sword, why fay willows and thunder oaks didn't grow on the eastern side, Mr. Black said, "Mind your mother. I know she told you not to play there."

Leeann nodded her agreement again.

"How many men are with Rohndolphn?"

Leeann hesitated, and then said, "Three."

He suspected she meant four, like she thought she saw another but couldn't be sure. An Areht, perhaps a shimmer. Black's remaining weapons wouldn't kill a shimmer, at least not easily.

Black grilled her on how they came, from which street, how many horses or carriages if any, and what arms. Leeann remembered more than any of his other innocent little birdies. It was her talent. The reason she'd eventually leave this place for greater hunting grounds when he finally took her under his wing and drafted her into service.

After Leeann answered all his questions, Mr. Black gave her three coppers and one silver. It was likely the most money anyone in her family had ever held. The silver was for a proper burial if things went wrong. The rest of the metal was for her.

Coins exchanged, Mr. Black turned away to smoke.

The pipe he took from his inner pocket was near a foot long when assembled. A silver pattern had been carefully carved into the bottom of the bowl, but the crisp edges were faded now, the true image all but gone, except to him. The pipe was a gift from long ago. A better time. When he was a different man.

Leeann waited quietly while Mr. Black ruminated between smoke and song. She closed her eyes, listened to the piano as a large woman stepped up on stage and sang "The Song of Luken Glenn." After the first chorus, a gaunt, sour-faced man armed with a fiddle joined in. His quick fingers were the only sign he'd any joy left in his life.

When the song finished, Black spoke from smoke-filled lips, "It's time for you to go. Remember, take the long way home."

Leeann stood and left. The applause covered her exit.

The band took up a faster, happier song next called, "Bright Barley." A common favorite. With the guitarist guiding the singer now, the fiddler faded into the background.

Plans were already in motion. Like once before, he'd have to make it up to the sisters for what he was about to do. What he *had* to do. From his duster, Mr. Black removed a small leather pouch, but instead of tobacco, it was an alchemical powder.

Once sprinkled over the inn's few smokeless fires, the mixture would transmute. The mechanical heat would release an invisible vapor into the air where its potency would be multiplied and further enhanced by ale, liquor, and the intoxicating nature of insatiable women, as well as other drugs used in the dark by a handful of the purveyors of the establishment's delicate delights.

Jezzy stood at the landing of the stairs, protecting her nose and mouth with a special blue flower.

Mr. Black paused but didn't turn, though he knew who tracked him now.

Looking down at him, Jezzy's eyes said, "You owe me."

There is no rest for departing dreams or nightmares

veiled by sunrise.

The blue petals slowly turned a dark crimson, and just before Black was lost to view, Jezzy whispered, "Breathe deep and forget me." She wouldn't, though, and not because of the secret bound within the flower he'd gifted her, either.

Black didn't leave the side door of the inn open for long, just enough to establish his gentlemanly guile for the fairer sex as his only reason for holding it wide. Really, he wanted an extra second to ensure Jezzy's filter did its job.

Out on the street, the smell of firewood and fresh mud flavored the night's cool breeze.

Mr. Black quickly ducked into a damp alleyway, then on into the next narrow where, above him, empty clotheslines hung like frosty spider webs. He moved like a shadow around another corner of waterlogged brick homes with poorly patched mortar.

Two steps. That's how far ahead he thought he was in this dark game. Then Lady Genza had stolen one from beneath him. Tripped him up. Made the game her own. Now, he sought to regain the lead, turn the table.

"Fucking Sabbat," whispered Mr. Black.

Finally, he reached his weapons stash, stowed away before little Harold Cross tended to his weakened horse. He'd tucked the bundle of equipment and other valuables behind a mossy lump of bricks easily removed from the alley. Over the years, this particular hollow had become his usual drop-point. Anything left behind was expendable.

He wouldn't risk touching the sword now, though.

He'd removed it from his belt shortly after entering the berg proper, since such weapons tend to draw unwanted attention. Nevertheless, he had to let it know he was there. Reassure it. Peace restored, Mr. Black was confident he only required the dagger at his back and his trusty bow to watch over and protect him.

The recurve bow of baloxen horn and snake eye wood was flawless, sleek. Almost Eyldeyryien. The wide handle, crafted by some of the most skilled fingers in the Borderland, gave the rich, oiled frame overwhelming distance and power. And with only the dead to vouch for it, none but he knew how deadly a second it was to the modern windrifle or the smaller peacemaker.

He notched an arrow and hurried to the target's home.

Mr. Black moved quickly, negotiating his way through and around a handful of buildings with manicured façades and trimmed hedges. His target lay at the end of a private road. Once there, he paused to gain the best attack point. Only two of the nearby homes on the block would provide the flanking positions he needed. The first would require a lure to work.

Much like the others, Mr. Halgin's residence was two-storied, with smokestacks at both ends. Five rooms defined the interior when last he'd visited the girls some years ago: cellar, kitchen, audience room with the back quarter closed off for private dining, a modest storeroom where staff slept in shifts to better hear their master's bell and, of course, the grand bed chamber.

Corruption pays.

The lord remains? There were only three mounts tied

outside the front, though.

Perhaps Leeann was right, but where was the third bannerman's horse? The rear?

The sentry outside the door remained motionless. Only his green cloak and tunic fluttered in the breeze caught between the nearby buildings.

Mr. Black removed four caltrops from his belt compartment, aimed them at the horses' hooves. The metallic clinking was enough to break the silence on the well-kept street.

The guard stepped down from his sentry position on the porch beside the overhang post and crossed in front of what little light escaped the home's front window.

Too late.

The sentry's horse twitched its tail at the sound of the caltrops, then did exactly as Black expected. It shifted its back hoof, stepping on the pointy metal. Neighing and snorting, the horse stomped and kicked liked mad to shake free the barb lodged in its hoof.

Moving closer to him now, Mr. Black saw the guard wore no more than a chainmail shirt. He also saw enough of the emblem on the sentry's back to tell he was of the Eastern Mark. An outsider. A nobody. Just another soldier who wouldn't be easily remembered this far from home.

The man calmed his horse and reached for the injured leg.

Black felled him with an arrow through his eye before he found the caltrops.

Mr. Black then crossed the empty street and heaved the corpse onto the wounded horse's saddle, fixing the dead man fast to the saddle. Then he untied the other horses and, with a quick slap to their backs, sent them running down the road.

The trap was set. He again melded into the mist surrounding the houses on the block and waited.

One down, three to go.

The front door of the house swung open, and the light from within spread across the yard.

"Damn!" Pressing his head to the neighbor's exterior wall was all Black could do to resist yelling.

There wasn't a shimmer or an Areht, as Mr. Black thought there might be, but there were four guards—not three as Leeann had said. If he could find the fourth man's horse, it would serve him later since, apparently, tonight was going to be a long night indeed.

There was no movement behind the house since none of the three remaining armsmen appeared eager to test their fate in the wet darkness. One of the men called for the fourth now absent from the front of the house.

No, that's not it.

They continued to wait for something despite no reply.

Where's Rohndolphn?

As Mr. Halgin appeared behind the guards, Mr. Black realized the fat man *was* the prize. More than that, he was bait. The lord was gone.

It's a trap…

Mr. Black's bowstring sang, and the arrow whistled clean through the mist and darkness straight into the face of the first man protecting Mr. Halgin. The broadhead arrow pierced the man's left cheek, bone shattered. The force knocked him clear of the porch and down onto the decorative fence surrounding a bed of dead flowers and unkept soil.

Men shouted. Swords were drawn, but not fast enough. Mr. Black let fly another arrow from his midnight bow.

The second guard gurgled out a bloody gasp through his throat, for the arrow had nearly pinned him to the wall.

Panicking as he tripped over the second man to fall dead, the last conspirator spun 'round to kill poor Mr. Halgin but, before he could, Mr. Black stepped from behind him, seemingly from the blackness itself, slit the man's throat and split his ribs.

"*Madu thi mhrgrul bakas hi sic thi-dor.*" Latyn, the First Tongue descended from the First Fathers, carried its own power of stoicism which, in this case, translated to *May the dead shun you at the door.* Mr. Black finished passing sentence in Common, whispering, "May you walk forever in darkness."

Mr. Halgin, eyes wide, mouth gaping, wandered nervously toward the bloodied flower bed.

"You," Mr. Black pointed at Halgin, "take a body. Let's get them inside."

"Who are you?" Mr. Halgin said, quick and furious.

Mr. Black wondered if perhaps the fat man's bravery was fueled by the fact the bloodshed wasn't legally attributable to anything he'd done, at least not this time. However, a second look from the man in black, dripping with other men's gore, quietly compelled the master of the house to act despite himself.

Exploiting the chaos, Leeann, who'd just arrived

after taking the long way back to the residence, acted without word from Mr. Black and ran inside the house to retrieve the skeleton key hidden in the service closet.

Ceann, Leeann's younger sister, peeked out from behind furniture after hearing the commotion, then ran out the back door to gather Mr. Black's things from where he always stowed them, sometimes with the occasional gift, depending upon what time of year he'd last passed through. This time, though, Ceann was after one item in particular.

Such a good girl. Mr. Black never had to give the same hand-sign twice.

He winced. The pain inside, his curse, would only worsen without the damn thing at his hip now that blood was spilled. However, it sometimes acted like a beacon to the Enemy, the Unclean One's servants. Only when it was hungry, though, which is why he rarely teased a feeding or baited it with violence of any kind. It was a fickle thing.

"She knew," Black muttered, knowing there wasn't much time.

Leeann returned a few moments later from unlocking the house staff, including her parents Maria and Benzan, from the cellar. Since Lord Rohndolphn's trap failed, it was best the others quickly and quietly gathered their belongings and sneaked away to the more populated portions of the berg. However, with the girls' future still in limbo, their parents remained quiet at the rear of the common room of the house to assist their new patron anyway possible.

Mr. Halgin tried over and over in the sink-basin but

couldn't clean the blood from his nails or the specks tarnishing his pristine, dark maple vest and white shirt. His trousers were stained at the knees from lifting the bodies. He repeatedly glanced side-eye at Benzan and Maria.

When Mr. Black directed the girls' parents to drag the bodies onto the rug in the common room, Halgin bristled. Of course, Mr. Black wasn't being rude on purpose. In truth, using the rugs was the only way to cover his tracks with so little time. Later, the dead would be rolled, loaded, and taken away by carriage and mule. Forests, especially those surrounding Pehats Berg, had ways of dealing with the ugliness of murder, and the girls knew just where to *lose* the corpses.

"Here, Mr. Black." Ceann handed him the bag from the alley and quickly sat on the bench near the coat rack beside the front door.

Mr. Halgin paused. Was that a name just said?

Leeann eyed Ceann.

Black said nothing.

"By all the saints! Do you know who these men were?" Halgin said, his face tense.

Black opened the bag.

"Do you know who I am? What do you want?"

Mr. Black felt weak at the question. Long had it been since he was asked his thoughts, wants, or needs. He just served. The question put him at odds with his mission, not to mention the passionate alternative personalities and loose ends in his head. The ones keeping him alive or happy when he required it. It was madness. It was survival.

Honestly, he wanted it to not be his problem. He wanted to go home. He wanted her to not have died. He wanted to not have seen the fires. He wanted to forget like everyone else as years and years passed, but it was partially his fault. So, he had to wait. Endure. For the promise wasn't yet his.

Absentmindedly, Black muttered an old phrase, "Faces in shadow and shadows with faces."

He took the sheathed longsword strapped to the outside of his pack and refastened it about his waist, covering the hilt with his coat. Too late, though. They saw the white-silver tip of the sheath, as well as the clasp where hilt and sheath met, called the shield. It was cracked now, yet the proud leather still held the eye because of its age.

Clearly, the sword had passed through many hands over many lifetimes.

Mr. Halgin repeated, "What do you want?"

Maria gripped Benzan's arm tighter.

This short burst of lordly strength seemed to have refreshed the fat merchant, yet a truly insightful glance, such as Mr. Black's, revealed the lord's considerable uneasiness. He had gotten far on bluff alone, so why not now?

"I want what was said to you this night."

Mr. Halgin feigned ignorance.

"You're not Sabbat. You're barely a Black Thumb. The message wasn't meant for you."

Maria and Benzan took fright at such statements, though now they knew why Mr. Halgin often did business in unseemly places, especially at odd hours of the night.

Before now, it was simply assumed Mr. Halgin's affairs weren't exactly legal, given the nature of his associates and various investments across the berg, but few would've guessed he'd dealings so wretched as to be openly called a Black Thumb.

Mr. Halgin did not dismiss the accusation.

"You might've heard their names…" Mr. Black paused for, in that moment, Mr. Halgin's face and demeanor bled through time, seeping through others he'd questioned over the decades on this long road of lost souls bought and paid for by the Enemy in all its incarnations. "But I know you wished you hadn't. Tell me what was said."

"Sir! The children."

The vile irony of Mr. Halgin's empty compassion eluded no one, though, for he was a master of false conviction.

"Tell me," said Black, cold and sharp, "before the vhendo come!"

Benzan pleaded to Black, voice raised, "Sire?"

Leeann and Ceann froze, but not exactly out of fear. Their hands didn't tremble.

"You will not say such things in my presence!" Halgin's expression insisted his servant do something, anything, to quiet the bloody intruder or there'd be Hel to pay. Lashes or worse.

Mr. Black smirked. He saw the glutton turning thoughts over in his head.

It was obvious to everyone now the fat man wondered who this rogue was to assume such influence and power? A hired sword?

Halgin demanded to know if the man in black was working for a rival—another who came here long ago to scavenge what riches could be made off the backs of the Scattered Kingdoms' suffering. Was he a knifeman?

Recently, members of Pehats Berg's council had discussed the idea of re-inviting the Children of the Pillars to talk, perhaps to truly rejoin the struggling community. But Mr. Halgin spoke out against it and won. Less profit in fixing the problem than poorly treating it.

Staring through Halgin's fragile strength, Mr. Black could almost read his troubling thoughts. Had a choice been made to suppress the secret authority granted him by other leaders throughout the berg by assassinating him?

"They're on their way," said Mr. Black, slowly, with the mechanical surety of a rewound clock.

The plump man turned, heavy sweat soaking through his pits.

"What wounds they suffered won't slow them for long."

Mr. Black wondered how many the bulldog bear had killed outside its cave in the mountains before finally the vhendo overtook it. Were Lady Genza's pets days, hours, or minutes behind him now? How much did he want to terrify Mr. Halgin?

After seeing the fervent trust her girls had in Mr. Black, Maria discreetly reassured her stout but gentle husband, who was only thinking of his family, that the man in black was a good, if dangerous, man—just as Benzan had said to her many years ago when first approached by the assassin on his way back to the Silver Isles.

Unbeknownst to everyone but the girls, Mr. Black drew one of his many daggers.

"After they feed on the flesh of their dead…"

Mr. Halgin swallowed hard.

"They will come," said Black, face-to-face with the pompous man.

Mr. Halgin was nearly in tears. "Do you have no decency?"

Mr. Black grabbed Halgin by the throat and lifted him to his tiptoes, clutching his glinting dagger somewhere below. "What did Rohndolphn say?"

As the two men jostled, the pommel of Black's sword again came into view.

Halgin's eyes further widened at the flash of silver.

"Tell me!" Black squeezed harder. Halgin's face purpled.

Benzan reached out, but his girls stopped him. They were resolved to assist their teacher.

"You're Horran?" gasped Halgin, the words barely escaping his blue lips.

The ancient title was meaningless.

Neither Maria nor Benzan blinked at the useless term spoken so far from the Silver Isles.

Black's bloody passion went darker still as he squeezed. "What truth did you hear in lies?"

Tears streaming down his face, Mr. Halgin was shattered within. He was close to pissing himself. He gurgled out enough words for the man in black to be sure his witness was no longer a threat but a willing, whimpering informant.

Mr. Black released him. The fat man fell hard to the floor with a sad *thud*.

"Lord Rohndolphn's gone mad!" gasped the ex-master of the house after he'd somewhat recovered.

"How?"

Halgin coughed, his throat rough. "He's going to betray Duke Talhgho."

Of course, a man of Rohndolphn's pedigree would never be satisfied with his station, let alone his position within the Sabbat. Such ambition for a viscount.

Mr. Black knew this meant Countess Kseniya and her mistress Lady Nadezhda were already dead in their bed. Rohndolphn had no more use for their numerous betrayals. He wondered what other civic officials were compromised now.

The fat man wheezed, "Prince Urhal promised him a terrible gift."

"How do you know this?"

"It was all in the letter."

"What else?"

"I didn't see," explained Mr. Halgin.

Apparently, his nervousness about their scheme had shown, and that's why Rohndolphn beat him earlier before Leeann. That's when Halgin became bait.

Black glanced at the girls, then back to Halgin. "What gift?"

"A blood rite." Halgin continued to sob, fear now superseding pain.

In response to Halgin's blasphemy, Maria made the sign of the Ten Pillars and the Circle of Saints on her forehead and chest. Benzan fumed with anxiety and dread at the notion of such gross wickedness having lurked so close to his children for so long.

"He said this?" asked Mr. Black. "There's proof?"

"The future, unnatural power, it consumed him." Eyes glazed over, Mr. Halgin quieted. It was evident the weight of his servitude to the Sabbat finally induced shock.

He seemed to drift then, lost in the foulness of his own past deeds and concessions. For this wasn't just a game played by wicked men to deceive and subvert their lessors for coin or land but an act of the truly evil and damned. The cost for such crimes extended beyond the grave, so the Faithful said. Debts he willfully ignored his whole life. Until now.

Frustrated and angered by his new songbird's weakened constitution during this moment of personal crisis, Mr. Black, with no time to waste, mercilessly stomped his boot on the prone merchant's right hand just below the wrist.

"Mercy!" cried the fat man.

If Black wished it, Halgin would've lost doughy fingers to the hidden razor edge of his boot.

"Sire?" Maria raised her hands, pleading for peace. "Please!"

"Which rite?" Black now applied all his weight to the fractures beneath rosy flesh.

Tears streaming, Halgin gritted his teeth. His bottom lip was smeared with blood.

"We're going to play a game," said Mr. Black. "It's called, Don't Lie to Me."

A few minutes later, after rattling off a series of

phrases and terms in languages beyond the crying merchant's comprehension, Mr. Black recognized a change in his captive after a specific word: "*Tzimetskēs?*"

"I-I don't know." Halgin slumped over, his swelling hand finally freed.

Mr. Black waved Ceann onward.

She approached the fat man with a snifter of bourbon. Mr. Halgin shot it in a single gulp.

Creeping farther down the rabbit hole, Black added, "*Desmödleri?*"

Mr. Halgin nodded, his ruined hand folded over his sweaty, dirty belly.

Least it's not an Areht.

Confident of the bloody, lecherous weapon against him now, Black paced the room.

Leeann and Benzan assisted Mr. Halgin from the floor to the table opposite the small bar, where the decanter of bourbon waited atop a pewter serving platter. Mr. Black poured bourbon into three crystal glasses. Ceann offered one to her former master. Their father split his share with Maria. Mr. Black then poured the parents another splash of courage while everyone waited for him to speak again.

"The prince commands nekctu now?"

Halgin drained his glass before answering. "Just one."

Maria and Benzan held their children tighter with each dark revelation.

Mr. Halgin's eyes strayed to the portrait of his wife and two girls, the family he destroyed.

Marcus' daughter! The evidence was vague but nevertheless rang true to Mr. Black.

He heard reports nearly a year ago about Princess Patrycja Urhal's untimely illness and death, yet little else was detailed, no mention of her body being removed or otherwise missing from the family crypt beneath her father's castle.

"You've seen her?"

"Yes, I was among the greeting party when she first arrived that night."

Mr. Halgin briefly described how the princess came by steam-railmotor, on industrial service tracks long abandoned at the edge of the berg. Duke Talhgho's mechanoids and best tinkers had labored in secret for weeks to prepare the station and tunnels along the previously unusable route.

Black now wondered what other preparations the duke or Prince Urhal had made.

"Pehats Berg will soon be marshaled for the whole Eastern Mark."

The war has already begun. Black squeezed the hilt of his sword.

Could Prince Zahargan Marcus Urhal have somehow convinced his cousin, Prince Utrid Atticus Urhal, to betray the Scattered Kingdoms' peace? What of the third Urhal in the west, Prince Ragnarr Ergantius?

"You know what that means?"

Mr. Halgin shuddered at Mr. Black's quick glance. For the potential unification of all Urhal lines, the Breakers descendants, sons of Gol's last true sovereign, were the greatest source of bloodshed the Seven Marks had faced since Ergantius usurped the Western Kingdom from Ajax over four hundred years ago. And now, the

Sabbat and their Father of Venomous Oaths was again kicking the hornet's nest. To what end?

"What now, sire?" asked Benzan.

Too many questions. Too many threads. Not enough information. Not enough time.

She knew…

Could the Sabbat's information network be so good?

Doing some quick math in his head, Mr. Black figured he barely had an hour, maybe more, before all Pehats Berg knew what happened here, including the condition of his horse, which the towns folk would then have to deal with. And if Lady Genza's vhendo weren't already closing in on the berg for her own reasons, the corrupted transformation and resulting death of his stallion would certainly only hasten their arrival.

"Where's Duke Talhgho now?" Black asked.

* * *

Leeann and Ceann didn't look back as Mr. Black rode off to deal with the new threat, which they imagined was still somehow connected back to Black's original failed mission: Lord Rohndolphn's assault on Wychstone Manor.

With the limited weapons he had and only the mare left behind Mr. Halgin's home by one of the dead soldiers for company, there was a good chance the girls would never see Mr. Black again. Though this wasn't the first time they'd thought as much.

Even so, their instructions were clear: gather their things and make for the jail; speak only with Simkus.

Once Mr. Halgin was arrested, Maria and Benzan naming him a conspirator against the Scattered Kingdoms, the new sheriff would deputize as many able bodies as possible and make haste to Wychstone.

The survival of Pehats Berg would depend on it.

3

Mr. Black raced away from the well-to-do neighborhood. The buildings with manicured façades and trimmed hedges blurred like everything else into night. He took the shortest way through the market square, which was once an open arena for deadly civil disputes when the last king of Gol still reigned. The open space was eerily quiet, the carts and their owners gone since shortly after sundown.

Far from Two Sisters or any other nightlife, the streets were empty as he rode, except for a few sweepers and stilted lamplighters ready to be as done with this night as Mr. Black was. Though they didn't know him by name, they nodded their respects as he rode past. Such honors befitted an elder agent of death and duty hurtling through the night on a quest not of his choosing.

When he found the cemetery not only locked with heavy chains but also guarded, Black cursed his luck and urged the mare to double-time between the dangerous patchwork of modest homes and mercantiles just beyond Pehats Berg's main fair, where all manner of ill deeds often transpired.

After the last respectable dwellings ended, Mr. Black continued to zigzag the commandeered horse through irregular slums, partially attached vacancies, and the occasional collapsed structure, toward the east point of the berg proper, called Labor's Ro.

Why that way?

Well, with the gates closed at this hour, and since he was in no position to fight with anyone or anything that might be looking for a man in black, especially now after leaving so many of Rohndolphn's men dead outside Mr. Halgin's home, Mr. Black decided to play the one card still up his sleeve.

Momma Bwulyaa. She was the only one who could get him beyond Pehats Berg's perimeter and on to Wychstone Manor, where he would hopefully arrive in time to save Duke Talhgho from Lord Rohndolphn's double treachery.

The question was, would she care enough to let him pass?

Perhaps it's been too long.

As the tight streets quickly devolved from stone to brick to cobble to dirt, Mr. Black realized his new mount wasn't really a cavalry mare. Her gait wasn't as aggressive as it should be. Nor was she a palfrey or courser because she didn't easily respond to common rein commands. In fact, it seemed galloping at night was almost unnatural to her.

Ahead of him stood the Darby, one of Pehats Berg's last relics. Completed ages ago, the bridge spanned the widest curl of the Red Bern before it rejoined the Blue Bern and flowed east. It connected the last point of the berg to what was left of its initial logging center, including various core industries that came later, during Pehats Berg's youth, when the stone-and-metal perimeter walls were first constructed. Many of those facilities now loomed like great dead things along the riverbed.

The mare was uneasy as they crossed beneath the iron skeleton. Despite the assemblage of wood rot and rust, the Darby was built to last. It could likely still be raised and lowered for barges moving along the river within the berg's outlying walls.

Mr. Black even noted the equipment tracks still rutted beneath the boarded-over planks. The hidden transport system hinted at a time of great resources few citizens could imagine today.

Once across the river, Mr. Black was confident the nag, which he now believed was a mixed breed of rouncey, hadn't been a soldier's horse for long. Perhaps only a few months. Six at most. Similar to her previous owner, she was likely plucked from some humble stall, given a fighting saddle, then trotted into line with other amateur banner-bearing horses.

Her greenness gave Mr. Black a timetable to build from as he considered what the Urhals had set in motion against the other Marks of the realm.

Easing her to a slower walk to avoid the always present dangers lurking in Labor's Ro, Mr. Black assessed the other side of the borrowed mare's greenness. He'd no idea how she'd act in combat. Would fire or loud noises spook her? Would she throw him at first blood once they reached Wychstone?

Then he grinned because none of that mattered as he turned, descending deeper into the marrow of Labor's Ro. All that mattered now was if she'd stand her ground before Momma Bwulyaa's bloodthirsty wolfhounds. Of course, he couldn't see them anywhere, which he knew meant they'd already sensed him and waited to surround him.

Mr. Black whistled calmly. The shrill sound traveled far in the cool, damp air.

Slowly then, along the walkways connecting the various tanners, seamers, skinners, clangers, butchers, bakers, blacksmiths, whitesmiths, and so on, beastly forms rose from their lurking slumber. Deep within the dark, vague four-legged shapes seemed to come and go as one terrible monster.

And that's when they started to growl.

The shaggy beasts had distinct snarls, and Mr. Black could easily tell them from the mongrels deputies and volunteers used to patrol this side of the berg's oldest quarter with. As rare as they did. More often than not, when the law came looking so deep into Labor's Ro, it was to arrest and repossess not protect and serve.

Bred to hunt bulldog bear, white moose, and steppe elk, the hounds were great in size. Two in particular, though, perhaps more dire wolf than hound, were easily two-thirds as tall as the mare. No doubt that's why she was frightened by their stalking approach, muddy eyes and flashing teeth seeming to slip and vanish within the shadows.

But instinct is a funny thing, a joke Mr. Black knew well, which is why he laughed when one of the younger pack hounds circled them twice before finally nipping the mare's hindquarters. The beast didn't expect she'd raise her back leg and kick her clear across the street, but that's exactly what the mare did.

When the dust settled, the great hound could only groan and moan.

"Momma Bwulyaa!"

As the pack readied to rip the man in black and mare to bloody bits, a distinct tessen fan thrashed through the air. The unique metallic sound stopped the wolfhounds at once. A second flutter of the hand-fan made them sit, the largest hound complying last as though to ensure its mother's will.

"Evening, Momma," said Mr. Black once his mount ceased rearing.

"Haven't seen you around," replied a voice from somewhere in the darkness. "Why's that?"

Black casually searched the area. "Business, I suppose."

"Tricky thing, business." She made a clicking sound with her teeth.

"Yes, and tonight, it's urgent."

"Always is, Black."

He spotted the ember of her cigar then. She'd palmed it before now, the smoke filtering up her sleeve.

Good girl.

From the narrow between Son's Port Bottling and the Crooked Lane Ware Company, an elderly hāfu woman appeared. She moved slowly and had long, thick, twisted gray braids and heavily tattooed hands. She wore a faded burka over a foreign-colored sarafan. Often dressed like a wandering derelict, few people would ever know how powerful and dangerous Momma Bwulyaa was. It was one of the things Mr. Black admired most about her.

"Good to see you, Momma."

She crushed the spit-soaked cigar and tossed the last sparks into the alley before muttering, "Liar."

Momma Bwulyaa flashed her infamous iron smile. Every matte-black tooth was a reminder of sacrifice and vengeance a lifetime ago and a world away, in the Five Towns. Almost the far side of the world from where they were now, and though a child then, no one dared ever call her a half-breed again.

"I need—"

"Need?" Momma Bwulyaa wrapped her burka tight against her frail body.

Momma's wolfhounds stirred at her intonation, the largest showing her teeth. Her youngest son stepped into view.

"Hey, Black." The lad leveled a zhuge model repeating crossbow at him.

"Evening, Cirilo." Black didn't recall the scarification down the center of Cirilo's head, nor the rings in his lips or ears. The young man had changed a lot in only a few years or so.

Ignoring them, Momma Bwulyaa kneeled low, patted her knees. She cooed and smooched to summon her wounded hound. Black was relieved when the wolfhound, though whimpering, finally crossed the street to its loving mother.

"Lucky," said Cirilo, repeating crossbow still on target.

Before Black could agree, Momma Bwulyaa said, "I been looking in on those girls for you for some time now. Good girls."

"I know, thank you."

"The fat toady, though…"

"Has been dealt with."

Momma stood up. It seemed the pup would live. "That why you back?"

"Not exactly."

"Business, but is it Areht or your own?"

Momma Bwulyaa considered anything from the Silver City or its senate Arehthood business. That made it bad for her business. She didn't walk between worlds anymore. She was alone, selfish, and that's how she liked it.

"Both," answered Black.

"He got heat, too, Momma," added Cirilo.

"Yes, I bet 'e does." Her wide smile revealed equally matte-black gums.

The boy said, "We was wondering about that dead soldier, them horses."

"Not all plans pan out." The North Gate was but one of Black's intended escape routes before Mr. Halgin's confession changed his mission entirely.

"Quite the spider, aren't you?" Momma winked.

Cirilo licked his lips and said, "Them spooked horses were crazy, man. Wrecked all sorts of shit. And once that soldier fell off…tsk-tsk-tsk. That mook bastard was mush when they found him near North Gate."

Black nodded. Such a waste.

"They killed them horses, mercy really," said the boy.

Black figured they'd be either lame or almost by the time the guards got control of the lot. Shame.

"Them girls love you," said Momma Bwulyaa.

"Yes, Momma."

"They trust you."

Black tilted his head down. Eyes lowered still.

"I don't trust you," said Momma, trying to see through the shadow created by his tricorn.

Not anymore.

"I don't like you."

"I apologize, Momma."

As if she'd whispered some joke, Cirilo snickered.

Mr. Black waited till Momma Bwulyaa accepted his sincere regret, then told her what he'd come for. "I want to use the Tunnel."

"Kill him now, Momma?" Cirilo's finger floated over the trigger.

The wolfhounds bristled again, but Mr. Black's mare remained steady.

The old woman licked her metal dentures, then spat. "What you need it for?"

"I've got to get to Wychstone."

"You didn't answer my question."

"Rohndolphn is going to murder the duke."

Momma Bwulyaa's cutthroat expression began to change then. Her eyes narrowed as the corners of her mouth slowly relaxed. It was as if all the stained and bloody pieces of the puzzle she'd been toying with for however long snapped into place.

Mr. Black didn't like what he saw. "You knew I was coming, didn't you?"

Momma Bwulyaa's demeanor gave nothing away.

"How?"

She laughed.

"You know what Heimont planned?"

Momma scratched at something in her ear. Mr. Black tried to take some meaning from it but came up empty.

"The plot against Tarvarys?"

Momma winked. She'd never say the duke's first name aloud in public. Speaking so disrespectfully on the streets could get one's head thumped by the watch or even the citizen patrol. Of course, Momma was in no fear of that, neither from Lord Heimont Rohndolphn nor his lap dog, the sheriff. Nevertheless, she believed in customs and decorum and rank, the presentation of power that sustained the order of things.

She was a Duchess of the Under Court herself.

Cirilo said, "Time is money, and money is—"

Momma Bwulyaa hissed at her disrespectful son, but she wasn't quick enough.

Customary manners becoming tiresome, the hour growing ever later, Mr. Black opened his coat so both rouges could see the sword at his hip. He drew the handle out but a few inches from the scabbard.

Immediately, the entire pack, minus the two dire-wolfhounds, scattered from the street as though the night itself had transformed into a starving predator. The largest female, though, out of pure instinct for Momma's wishes, knocked Cirilo down. The hair-trigger of his zhuge repeating crossbow went off, firing three bolts harmlessly into the air.

Impressed by the indifference of the mare, Mr. Black re-sheathed his sword.

"He's much to learn," said Momma.

"So does the little girl I once knew."

Cirilo clambered from his backside and dusted himself off. The wolfhound pack returned, still skittish. Cirilo appeared uncertain at his mother's hounds' reaction.

"The Tunnel," said Black.

"You won't make it."

Momma Bwulyaa's glare was edged by a type of anger that never quite dulled. Yet, her smile seemed fluid, relaxed perhaps by fond memories she'd never shared with another soul.

Thus, Mr. Black replied, "Then you'll finally get to spend that silver I gave you."

At last, as if by a wave of contrition, Momma nodded to her youngest son.

Cirilo darted into the alleyway and returned a few moments later at the head of a rotorikisha.

Once his mother was comfortably seated in the decorative little carriage built for two, drapes closed, Cirilo began to pedal. When enough heat was created through his sweat and the turning of the wheels, the tongs below his seat became red, and the compressed boilers and intricate gear-piston system took over turning the chain. The machine made a heavy thrumming sound as it raced away.

The Five Towns' marvel soon doubled its speed, even uphill.

The pack of wolfhounds ran after their mother, and Mr. Black followed.

* * *

"Why's he so special?" Cirilo asked as they headed north along the river.

"Because," said Momma Bwulyaa, retrieving a fresh cigar and matches from a compartment in the cab, "being cursed is nothing if not an adventure."

4

Riding at a modest pace through the foggy pitch, Mr. Black trailed the gangster queen and her feral bodyguards along the declining riverbank to an area commonly referred to as the Junkyard.

All sorts of scrap from across the berg, especially the two-thirds of Labor's Ro sitting above the Junkyard, had accumulated here over the years. Curiously, though, each pile was neatly sorted and stacked high overhead as custom demanded. No one really knew why, though. Perhaps to be more easily digested as the mounds and pillars of garbage rotted away, becoming one with the bloody and bastardized landscape so close to Pehats Berg's original gate.

A safe distance from where the Red Bern became a truly deep ravine diverting into ancient caverns below a great hilltop at the end of Labor's Ro, just one of East Gate's natural barriers, Cirilo stopped the rotorikisha and quietly dumped its tanks.

A plume of steam flushed out several feet in every direction, creating an even thicker fog over the water before the wind caught it, pulling it up and out the ravine. Cirilo softly cycled down the contraption so the guards at the gate wouldn't hear and come investigate the goings on at the bottom of the ravine.

Momma Bwulyaa exited the vehicle and began climbing stone steps leading to a caged stairway halfway up the cliff-face. As Mr. Black dismounted, she entered the once restricted stairway, leaving the gate open behind her. She trusted his mare could negotiate the slick climb as well as her wolfhounds could.

Following after his mother, Cirilo laughed as he watched Mr. Black try to lead his mare along the edge of the wild river. The mare didn't seem to want to cooperate, though, especially since it seemed she was aware of the great blacked-out building high above the water Momma Bwulyaa had just entered.

Mr. Black gently stroked her ears and whispered a few phrases he'd learned when he was a child.

At the top of the steps before entering the building, Cirilo looked over his shoulder, back down the pathway shrouded by gnarled roots and weedy grass grown out from the cliffs. He wasn't laughing, though, his smile quickly replaced by bitterness. Black and the mare were gaining.

The caged enclosure at the top of the steps from the river led up several flights to a massive, moss-covered structure that straddled the Red Bern. Even in the dark, the building was obviously once an impressive work of engineering. Also, at roughly half the size of the Darby and compressed between both cliffs, it was lucky to still be standing. The far end of the ancient building had collapsed on itself several generations before Momma Bwulyaa ever came to Pehats Berg.

It was considered by some an act of bravery, if not desperation, to approach the partially slouched complex jutting out from the middle of the cliff for fear the last support columns, arches, and support wires beneath it, spanning the river, would finally give and the whole damn thing would split and crash into the water.

Where better to hide a smuggling operation?

It was the same thought he had the last time he needed to use the maze hidden in the bowels of the mission, far, far below East Gate at the edge of Labor's Ro. Something was different now, though. From the stairs, he smelled the heavy scent of spiritual oils and lavender, the boiled honey and ground white chili leaves, the faint mercy of burned snakeroot and gooey, liquefied nightshade. There were other medicinal materials as well, many not commonly used by even rogue herbalists in the Scattered Lands.

Nearing the entrance to the mission following the final flight of stairs that led up from the river, a hostile exchange erupted between Momma Bwulyaa, Cirilo, and another man whose voice Mr. Black couldn't identify. From his tone, Mr. Black figured he was older than Cirilo, but perhaps by no more than a dozen years at most.

"You are not sure if they followed him," said the man, "but you brought him here?"

"He needs the tunnel," said Momma.

"There are a dozen ways into the catacombs. You did not have to come here."

Cirilo said, "True, Father, but only a handful are so accommodating."

"What?"

The largest she-wolfhound bristled.

"The letters from your order were right," said Momma. "He's confirmed their suspicions about Lord Rohndolphn and other suspected Black Thumbs."

"I do not care!" the priest shouted.

Momma Bwulyaa flashed her iron smile, surprised by the man's dismissal of confirmed heretics and worse, as gathered by the Faith's secret ranks across Pehats Berg, "Fine, this is business then."

"Tricky thing, business," replied the priest.

"Light Bringer or not, remember who you're speaking to," said Cirilo.

"No. You remember who I am speaking *for*. These people are my mission."

"Rai," said Momma, "if he doesn't get to Wychstone, before sunrise—"

Rai sneered. "That was not our arrangement. The risk is too great."

"Tha accepted perils and tests of faith greater than you can imagine, and she would've—"

"Do not tell me what my mother would have done! She would not have put the lives and souls of this mission in such a position. Certainly not for a damned assassin you slept with."

Cirilo immediately grabbed Rai by his coat and slammed him against the sheet-metal door.

Rai grunted. The door's weak hinges made a loud screech.

"I warned you," said Cirilo.

Did he fully realize what'd just been said about his mother? Black wondered as he took another step into the crowded hallway joining the caged stairwell to complex jutting out from the cliff-face. "You have Iha's grace for seeing into people's hearts then?" Black slipped his precious silver ring from his coat pocket to his breast pocket before anyone realized he was there.

Momma Bwulyaa clicked her teeth, and Cirilo released Rai.

You've always had it, too, haven't you?

Mr. Black identified the Order of the Faithful associated with Rai's greca as a small branch of mendicant hospitaler. The waist vestment of Saint Ingmar, fastened about the priest's gray coat over his otherwise common clothes, was a telltale sign of the sect's central Ten Pillar dogma.

That wasn't why she sent you away so young, was it?

"Come no closer, Horran of the Isles. You are not welcome here."

Cirilo recoiled at the phrase.

"Welcome or no," said Black, "I'm coming through."

The Horran were living legends. Truth be told, they'd become mythologized across much of the Scattered Kingdoms since last anyone was so openly declared.

Cirilo blinked at the fable standing before him.

Rai stepped forward and pressed his hand against Black's chest to bar him from the inner keep of the alien building.

See my heart then, Light Bringer.

"Don't," said Momma as Father Rai discovered the silver ring Mr. Black had removed from his finger during his earlier visit to the Two Sisters.

"What is this?" Father Rai, ready to assert his will and faith upon any Agent of the Arehthood so far from the Witches of the Silver Tower, plucked the ring from the assassin's breast pocket.

"Let go!" shouted Momma the moment the sterling relic touched Rai's flesh.

Mr. Black whispered back, "He can't."

Rai's pupils swallowed his brown eyes. The wolfhound whimpered and cried.

Struggling as though the ring smoldered in his palm, Father Rai was consumed by the emotional resonance within the sacred loop, the weight of which caused him to kneel, his fist uncontrollably pinned to the floor of the platform, another unforeseen consequence of a trap made possible by arrogance as well as ignorance.

"Help him," said Cirilo, who could only watch as Rai, submerged in an invisible wash of astral echoes, moaned, and shuddered on his knees.

His existence spilled over like a wine glass filled beyond limit. The sensation was terrifying to Rai because the countless imprints upon this tiny, yet tortured article, were beyond his control or understanding. For from the ring came a consuming and never-ending deluge of other lives, secret histories, and all without time or clarity to anchor himself to. Even if Father Rai knew how.

"I'll not be happy if he dies." Momma patted her faithful pet.

As if in reply to Momma's warning, the grace of Eyoh's blessing interceded, saving Rai at the point of drowning. Because he was a Light Bringer, a beacon among the Faithful, Eyoh's power within him freed his pupils from glossy black voids, transforming them into white hot mirrors.

Perhaps there's hope yet, thought the man in black.

However, just when it appeared Rai had weathered the worst of it, settling into a place where he might discern context from the memorialized timeframes astrally welded to the glimmering heirloom as it spoke to him, a second trap was triggered. The bottom of the ardent river making up Mr. Black's past, fell out beneath the young Light Bringer, becoming fathoms of freezing darkness that swallowed all light and warmth.

Black winked at Momma Bwulyaa when Rai hit the floor.

"He's unconscious," said Cirilo.

Mr. Black leaned down and removed the vestment of Saint Ingmar from Rai's waist and tied the lightly lacquered rope about the guard of his sword, securing it in place so there was no room for the weapon to be drawn.

The last and largest of the wolfhounds, now that the others had already pushed through the metal doorway into the mission, moved to do the same beside her mother, keeping far away from Mr. Black and his sword.

"What's that for?" Cirilo asked.

Tipping his tricorn back, the rogue assassin replied, "Precaution."

Momma knew better, though, because Mr. Black

wasn't a practitioner of the traditional Shinzo discipline of Kendin. Nevertheless, a sword-lock in this case, because of what they both knew lay beyond the veil leading into the hospital, was a good idea.

"He'll return it when he wakes," said Mr. Black, cautioning Cirilo as he reached for the ring.

Momma Bwulyaa, followed by her pet, led Mr. Black and his mare into the Mission.

Inside the great refuge for the sick and forgotten, dim candlelight and sputtering lanterns illuminated the equivalent of *thoughts and prayers* for those without means. Makeshift curtain walls sectioned off countless rooms, each filled with numerous beds in dismal condition, burdened by a variety of infirmed people.

The air felt muggy to Mr. Black. Everything smelled of congealed salt and slick filth no matter how many roof hatches were open or how often the floors were scrubbed. Despite all the treatments, he knew plenty of the patients who'd arrived at the Light Bringer's doorstep were simply running out the clock.

Mr. Black could see their families waiting for the morticians and gravediggers that would arrive in a few hours. There was no doubt about it, the mission was where the poor, huddled together, hoping for divine intervention, came to die in Pehats Berg.

"You alright?" asked Momma Bwulyaa.

Mr. Black sensed part of the sword become agitated at his hip beneath his coat, the same unnatural aspect of the blade he'd used to scare off the wolfhounds earlier. Thankfully, the article tied about the hilt seemed to buffer the essence within the metal, which had increased greatly in power due to the immense amount of suffering in the air.

"We'll be away soon," said Momma.

She closed several curtains before Mr. Black and the mare passed before the suffering.

Just beyond the center of the Hospitaler's Mission, behind where some of the patients were recovering and doing well, Mr. Black noted a small sub-trackway, not unlike the sunken rails beneath the Darby, running the length of the room.

The trench, once used to move heavy equipment, was about ten feet wide and five feet below the floor. Mr. Black could see most of it was hidden beneath the floorboards, though, as the Mission overtime had built overtop whatever this building was in centuries past, it had converted much of the sunken space for their needs.

Mr. Black pondered the sub-level tracks that once led to the building's exterior section before it collapsed. Father Rai had done a good job building over the rails because Black couldn't say for sure what they used to transport, given all the Faithful had done to repurpose this industrial depot into a place of healing and mercy for those who only death could truly release from such poverty.

"This way."

Momma smiled as her pet took the lead, a lantern swaying from its jaws.

After reaching the far right wing of the Mission's first floor, Momma Bwulyaa slid aside a camouflaged portion of the corrugated façade. Plaztacrete showed beneath. Solid stone so smooth it was once liquid.

How it got there, or when, or why, no one knew. Similar to the Darby.

Assisted by the light from her faithful pet, Momma Bwulyaa preceded Mr. Black and the mare as they descended through more plaztacrete hallways. Step by step, they marched deeper into the secret sub-levels of whatever the mission had been in ancient time; passages so effectively hidden from the world, the actual depths were long forgotten beneath Labor's Ro. Some forty feet above their current position below ground.

"Just here," said Momma Bwulyaa when they arrived at what appeared to be a cargo lift.

The service M-noid, which both operated and was the lift, responded to Momma's proximity with a slow spinning yellow warning light.

The sandblasted automaton was integrated into the operator's position aboard a diesel cargo lift, which Momma encouraged them all to enter, after which the M-noid closed the gate behind them. As expected, since Momma Bwulyaa knew her trade well, there was just enough room for Mr. Black, her, her wolfhound, and the mare to fit comfortably.

The M-noid and diesel lift were new to Mr. Black. He'd been alone the last time he ventured into the tunnels and hadn't bothered with the lift. Nevertheless, if his wits served him, he figured it was likely the river, in combination with a giant wood-burning furnace that now powered the industrial bucket and cage slowly cradling them into the dark, down into the structure's first basement.

As he watched the ticker *click* arrive at a depth of

about one hundred feet, Mr. Black now suspected a Tinker of some skill must've fallen into Momma Bwulyaa's debt in recent years. He smirked. That's how she upgraded the previously ragtag system of mechanical counterweights and pulleys. That, or perhaps a rogue Areht.

No telling how the M-noid came into the mix, though, since it was difficult enough getting common goods from the Silver Sea surrounding the Isles of El'shwn, which made Mr. Black wonder what other things the Duchess of the Under Court might've smuggled to and from Pehats Berg, given the weight the M-noid was capable of hauling.

"It's loud." Mr. Black wondered where and how many dynamos were in operation.

"This isn't normal business hours," answered Momma.

Of course, not all guises work all the time. Not even ones so elaborate. So, if any citizen patrol or formal deputy came snooping around the mission and discover the smuggler's pass and the modified lift leading into an area carved out below Labor's Ro that shouldn't exist, they'd quickly find another deterrent.

Inside the lift door was posted a royal plague notice. Anyone with even the most mythologized or faintest knowledge of Scattered Kingdom history, the Black Thumb Purge, or the Crusades that followed, would be familiar with it.

However, if said warning, focusing on major historical outbreaks, such as wax tongue, rose mouth, and cherry belly, failed to convince a snooper about the severity of their potentially life-threatening breach, there was also a writ, sealed by the Hospitaler crest, that listed in great detail a dozen currently terminal patients kept in seclusion beneath the mission. The list arranged the poor wretches by sex, age, and blight; all destined to live out the last of their days, however few, in the mission's basement, never to see daylight again.

What made this harsh warning so useful to someone like Momma Bwulyaa? The fact it was true. Just another reason why she always carried Iha's scarf in her pocket when doing business below ground. Mr. Black, on the other hand, buttoned his duster all the way to the top and tucked his chin behind the Areht glyph secretly placed within the folds of weatherproof fabric and leather.

The lift came to a hard stop. "Watch your step," said Momma, flipping a two-handed lever.

A series of glow rods and spliced-in vacuum-tubes slowly flickered to life.

You've been busy, thought Black as he reached for the lantern dangling in the wolfhound's mouth and extinguished it.

Yet another reason why Momma Bwulyaa was always bloody wary of arousing Arehthood suspicion. Such inventions and shortcuts were things the Areht never liked being in the hands of others without their prior approval or supervision. A rarity. Especially anything so linked to the Ten Pillars Faith.

Shortly after exiting the roll-up door past the lift, the mare began sneezing and snorting. Momma Bwulyaa laughed. Her wolfhound barked. It took the horse a few moments to get accustomed to the stale, dusty, cave-like air swirling with pockets of burning oil. A cobweb-covered sign bolted to the plaztacrete wall took much of the horse's snot.

Mr. Black passed his fingers across the gooey sign, and some illegible script appeared beneath the dust. The old characters suggested a vague link to Scar Tongue. There always seemed to be those tiny dots taped into the corner of such plates or markers. Mr. Black couldn't really translate the archaic script but was confident enough in one word he'd seen in other parts of Uropà's forgotten underbelly: Metro.

"I've never noticed that," said Momma.

Mr. Black nodded for her to continue onward. They descended three more levels.

"Quick now," said Momma when they passed by a patient's room with an iron door painted with a green X. Through a small square window, Black saw a novice wearing a combination plague gown and respirator mask, attempting to remove skrul boils from a screaming infant.

"I'll need a few things," said Black, hand firm on the pommel of his sword, touching the article of Saint Ingmar. He ceased when they could no longer hear the wailing child.

"Lucky for you, we've had a good year," said Momma.

Of course, Mr. Black was never surprised by the fact, no matter the shortage of food, medicine, or even coin, weapons, drugs, and powder always seemed easy enough to come by.

A few moments later, the wolfhound gently tugged on Momma's coat. The old woman ignored the beast till she felt teeth, then turned to playfully question her beloved harasser but, instead, paused to ponder the real reason for the wolfhound's prodding.

"Black?"

He stood still in the middle of one of the secret labyrinth's interconnected corridors, but he faced the opposite direction where Momma Bwulyaa led them.

Mr. Black was no longer concerned with getting to Wychstone Manor hastily. Nor was he particularly intrigued by the two Children of the Faith who wheeled out a shrouded stretcher laden with a bloated corpse. It was being removed from one of the secluded cells, no doubt headed for the crematory, which was in another area.

No, Mr. Black's purpose and full attention was focused on the last man to emerge from the room following the deceased. It was clear he'd been crying into his hands for some time. Leaving the mare to idle in the hallway, Mr. Black approached the grieving man as he knelt upon the prayer stool provided for him outside the room.

"Emil?"

"Mr. Black?" His beard was far less bushy when last they'd seen each other.

"Why aren't you on duty? What're you doing here?"

"My mother—"

Lifting Emil to his feet almost in anger, Mr. Black asked, "Where's your wife?"

5

Leeann and Ceann removed their coats and packs and finished what was left of some watery soup in a pot. Then they did as they were told. They waited patiently on the bench by the door, with its rusty hinges and dusty security-arm beam, while their parents made the necessary report to Deputy Gabija Simkus over hot tea.

The temperature continued to drop. Ceann became colder and tired of the tiny spinning top she'd taken with her and put it away. She was careful not to let Leeann see it, for it was really hers.

Ceann then wrote her name in the frosted glass pane. Her script was always better than Leeann's, whose interest was focused on the dual-barreled snaphaunce muzzleloader and combo powder-ball bag resting on the shelf behind the sheriff's desk. It was the largest weapon of its kind she'd ever seen.

The girls had known Deputy Simkus all their lives.

She was independent. Assertive. A real leader.

An obvious choice for Mr. Black to rely upon.

Ceann smiled as Gabija helped her parents document everything Mr. Black had instructed them to say. It all sounded very official, very legal, and very corrupt. Maria helped Benzan formally sign his name as the deputy respectfully looked on. Ceann always thought Deputy Simkus had kind eyes.

"Where's Emil gotten to?" Benzan asked, knowing the two were often inseparable.

"He's on leave in Dalegrad," answered the deputy. "His mother's taken ill."

"Not serious I hope?"

"Maybe green gut." Deputy Simkus shook her head.

"What happened?" Maria asked.

"After a poor hunt"—one of many the deputy didn't have time to elaborate on—"his mother came across what she thought was an old bear cache partially buried in snow. From Emil's last letter, his mother didn't appear to know what the animal was, but she couldn't turn down the meat. Their smokehouse was nearly bare when her husband arrived."

"Mose and Valter?" asked Maria as she looked about the room.

"They're fine. They're with my sister's family."

It was clear Deputy Simkus appreciated Maria's concern for her young sons.

Relieved, Maria mouthed a quiet prayer praising the Ten Pillars.

Across from the girls in the jail's main holding cell, Mr. Halgin continued to coddle his broken hand.

His rubbed his head. He moaned as if he'd vomit any moment while eyeing Benzan with a painful glare and muttering, "Perhaps those last few weren't such a good idea?" However, given his predicament, no one in earshot could blame him for draining the last of the bourbon decanter before they'd left for the jail.

Ceann had never seen the inside of the jail before. She wasn't with Leeann the time Mr. Halgin ordered her to stand witness against one of his previous housekeepers, who he swore was stealing from him, which she was of course, because Mr. Halgin was a cheapskate. Leeann confirmed nothing of it to the magistrate, and despite her knuckles being rapped and her backside bruised for a week afterward, she never thought to recant her sworn statement to the legal assembly.

Unlike most public property in Pehats Berg, the jail, a modest two-story brick building, seemed rather comfortable inside to Ceann. The iron stove was fully intact, stacked tall, and burning well with more freshly cut logs waiting in the corner. Rows of cabinets and crowded bookshelves were neatly sorted along the walls. The three desks for active-duty staff were sealed in thick polish, and the floor had been swept and mopped as recent as that morning.

Ceann wasn't sure what she expected the jail to be like, especially considering how frequently clients of local seedy establishments, particularly the Two Sisters, were often detained for various crimes, including nefarious deeds. All in all, though, the jail didn't seem such a rough place to be holed up in.

Her mother and father looked over at her as they

sipped the last of the hot tea the deputy had poured them.

Leann seemed to recognize the simple-minded, childlike thoughts behind Ceann's sweet, wide eyes, and hinted to the pocket doorway behind and to the right of the sheriff's desk. Of course, Leeann knew what was back there. She'd seen it. And that was exactly the point she wished to make clear to her sister, who hadn't.

Remembering how Leeann had called it a real dungeon, Ceann swallowed hard.

Leeann grinned. Mr. Black always said the unknown should be considered dangerous, never presumed innocent. Also, to know entry and exit and the dangers between. And it just so happened in this case Leeann had Mr. Halgin, as well as her own lightly scarred knuckles, to help her never forget one of Mr. Black's best lessons.

Shaking off Leeann's teasing, Ceann did as her father waved her to do and refilled the kettle on the cook stove with water taken from a bucket sitting nearby. She guessed the pump was somewhere down the hallway Leeann had reminded her of.

Suddenly, the front door opened, and Sheriff Fyodor Kozlov entered.

Instead of greeting Deputy Simkus or the girls' parents, the sheriff shut the door and immediately went and stood before the occupied holding cell. His troubled eyes sifted through Mr. Halgin's weak and shaken demeanor. The fat man displayed his broken hand. The sheriff didn't flinch but rather scowled.

Like most men of this region of the Midlands, Sheriff Kozlov was thickset, with a broad beard, wide chest, and tree trunks for legs. His great cloak concealed much of his tweed uniform, except his freshly polished boots and the dimensions of the bulging, bludgeoning weapon on his right hip, extending roughly to his knee.

"Sir?"

After stepping in the little trail of mud Sheriff Kozlov tracked in, Leeann sensed Deputy Simkus was a little more than surprised at the speed the sheriff had received her message from Deputy Dmytro who, as she looked, wasn't following close behind.

Deputy Simkus turned from the sheriff to Benzan, who blew the last of the drying powder clean off the writ.

Maria's smile tightened, a nervous reaction to Simkus's obvious attention to the semi-confidential document, but she managed to steady her teacup.

Leeann wondered if she was wrong about Deputy Dmytro's destination.

She didn't see firsthand the message Simkus rushed to write, but it wasn't long after they had arrived at the station the deputy had scratched out her orders. And the two consulted for a bit with Maria and Benzan outside the jail before Deputy Dmytro took the letter and rode off.

Sheriff Kozlov unbuttoned his cloak and tossed the loose portion over his right shoulder, exposing the back of his vest which, unlike Deputy Simkus' uniform, was more hauberk than leather and cloth.

No honor among thieves, thought Leeann.

Deputy Simkus rested her tea on her desk and approached the cell, hands casually on her hips. Her left fingers teased the sheathed dagger at her belt.

Reading Leeann's expression, Ceann was equally apprehensive.

Why didn't Deputy Simkus re-holster her truncheon, which still lay beside her keys on the desk? She'd removed it before taking her parents' statements.

Ignoring the mail vest, Leeann considered the sheriff's no-longer-concealed mace. The bludgeon was roughly half a silver meter long, secured by leather clasps, looped through a metal ring on the right side of his belt. The weapon's head was impressive, with its seven solid iron spikes. The bold-looking status symbol seemed like it could easily knock a hole in any door or kill a man with a single swing.

Sheriff Kozlov rubbed his neck as he asked, "What's the prisoner said?"

Simkus answered, "Nothing really."

"When's Horvat due?"

Simkus heard Mr. Halgin do his best not to snicker. It was well known he and the magistrate were old friends.

Maria glanced out the window. Two horse-mounted men arrived outside the jail.

From the look on her mother's face, Leeann knew neither man was Deputy Dmytro.

Deputy Simkus' eyes narrowed. "Magistrate Horvat's still dealing with the Snješka murder out in Lux." Some of the tenant farmers ignited a little uprising, and their landlord's eldest daughter had paid the price.

"No matter," said the sheriff. "The fat man will keep awhile here."

Deputy Simkus asked, "Dmytro didn't tell you?"

The sheriff shook his head.

"He sent a letter for Magistrate Jurić down the Blue Bern."

Sheriff Kozlov slowly drew the red-stained letter from his cloak's inside pocket. "He didn't say much a'tall."

Deputy Simkus licked her lips. "I thought you were at home?"

"You know me, Gabija. Always need a stiff-one to get the blood going."

Not all plans pan out, thought Leeann as she eyed their packs near the door.

As the refilled teakettle softly whistled, Maria looked again.

Now, there were even more armed men arriving on horseback outside the jailhouse. Some were known in the berg, at least in passing. The rest most certainly weren't from around these parts. Everything about them was wrong.

Ceann, who usually poured Mr. Halgin's drinks, caught the faintest scent of a different liquor slowly wafting in from the doorway, trailing the sheriff. The aroma was smoky. Likely with holiday caramel and spice afternotes.

Heavy footsteps shook the floorboards outside the jail, followed by more commotion in the street. Sensing his wife's growing fears, Benzan took a firm yet somewhat nervous hold of the chair behind Deputy Simkus' desk.

With another sniff, Ceann was confident in what she now smelled. It was the only bottle of rum Mr. Halgin ever really drank. But it wasn't special just because it was brewed by Duhrgan brewmasters deep in the Rift, far to the northeast of the Scattered Kingdoms. Really, it was special because there were only two women in all Pehats Berg Ceann ever bought it from and, most times, the sisters didn't want to part with the luxury.

"He's one of them," said Leeann.

She finally discerned what bothered her about one of the sheriff's faint footprints.

It wasn't just mud he'd tracked in, there was blood about the heel. That's why his boots were otherwise freshly polished. Just one of the Two Sisters' many amenities. Seems something caused the boot-shiner either to miss a spot or, more likely, the sheriff was forced to depart the inn quicker than expected.

"Doesn't matter anymore," said Sheriff Kozlov, scratching the side of his head.

Accepting Deputy Dmytro's demise, Simkus put herself between the sheriff and the girls. "Halgin didn't name you."

The sheriff looked from Deputy Simkus to Mr. Halgin and back.

"You happy now, Fyodor?" asked Mr. Halgin.

Deputy Gabija Simkus' eyes welled with anger. Fury for every slight she overlooked, every little greasy corruption or sick touch she let pass. It wasn't Pehats Berg's fault it had so many rats, that's just what thrived in sewers filled with rot and shit. Her husband Emil said as much over the years, but she hadn't listened. With every promotion, she hoped for better. Wanted better. Now, she knew better.

Mr. Halgin sighed. "Kill her."

The door flung wide then, the wood creaking through the fame.

The sheriff's men entered. Swords drawn. The sheriff turned.

Simkus slashed her dagger at Kozlov's sweaty jugular, a near miss; she gashed his chin and mouth. Blood sprayed across his face. Then she punched him in the nose. The cartilage snapped. Blood poured over his slit mouth.

She forced Sheriff Kozlov, his eyes tearing, beard shiny red, into the cell bars.

The much larger Kozlov snarled, eyes bulging. He jabbed a stiff right hand into Simkus' face, then punched her in the gut several times with his left. Her ribs cracked, and her guts heaved with sourness.

"Let me out!" shouted Mr. Halgin.

Deputy Simkus felt the world go gray and fuzzy. She fumbled her knife but managed to grab it before it dropped. Her head felt cold and distant. Even so, she swatted the sheriff's stiff arm away and stabbed his left forearm though to the bone. She retreated, or so she thought, before he howled, whirled back, unslung his mace, and jammed it into her throat.

Mr. Halgin continued to bang on the bars. "Let me out! Fyodor, let me out!"

Buckled now, struggling on her hands and knees, Simkus flailed her blade at the sheriff, but he dodged it easily, bent over, and laughed in her face. She flopped on her side, and glared up at him, wishing she had the strength to kill him.

"I warned you, Gabi."

Hot, violent, vengeful tears ran down her cheeks.

The sheriff teased the edges of his mace across the floor. "I warned you not to marry Emil, didn't I?"

As a final insult, Deputy Simkus spat bloody black chunks on the sheriff's boots.

Sheriff Kozlov splattered her skull all over the jail wall.

Mr. Halgin pointed at the girls, catching the sheriff's eye. "Don't let those brats escape!"

Squinting through watery eyes and the pain of a bloody broken nose, Sheriff Fyodor Kozlov paused to assess what'd happened in the rest of the jail during the minute or so it took him to murder Deputy Gabija Simkus.

When the front door burst open only a minute past, Benzan immediately hurled the deputy's chair with all his might into the first two men through. Neither of whom were ready, and though one raised his shield, the shattering force sent them sprawling. The sheriff's chair was next out the door for good measure.

Taking the opportunity gifted by her love, Maria quickly shut and locked the front door and secured the bar.

With the front secure, Benzan grabbed Simkus' truncheon from the floor.

Leeann and Ceann grabbed their packs from the vestibule, snatched the keys from the deputy's desk, lifted the muzzleloader, powder, and ammo from the wall, and rushed out the rear door after their mother.

"Fyodor!"

Sheriff Kozlov turned round to the fat man, who

pointed the other direction.

"Watch out!"

Benzan pounced on the bloodied sheriff. He swung the truncheon, splintering Kozlov's left kneecap. The partially blinded Kozlov roared and grabbed his knee. Benzan swung again and crushed the little bones in the sheriff's right ankle.

Benzan abandoned the front door, which was secured from within by the wooden bar, just as the rest of the sheriff's men, still outside the jail, crashed through its window. Yet Benzan, as though oblivious to the shattering and cursing, suddenly dropped Simkus' cracked truncheon in exchange for the former sheriff's mace.

The bloody father of two then levied the full measure of the spiked weapon through the traitor's chest. The sight of Kozlov's ribs being crushed through to his spine so blood and other gore pooled on the floor caused Benzan's new foes to pause despite having him clearly surrounded and outnumbered.

"Father!" cried Ceann.

Mind like a razor as she summoned all her focus, Leeann bolted past her hollering sister and ran down the hallway behind the sheriff's desk toward the rear of the jailhouse, which was really an anteroom.

Leeann ran past a wall mounted wall pump and a water closet and found two more metal doors at the rear of the tight corridor. One was a cellar door. The other had separate locking bars in front of it. She knew the one on the right led to a dungeon, and the other led to the walled off square behind the jail.

"Mother!" cried Leeann.

Between the doorway, Maria chanced a final glance to meet her husband's loving gaze and capture one last moment. She screamed instead at the madness and violence swarming him, then slammed the pocket door and locked it.

Ceann, tears streaming, took the keys from her mother's almost lifeless fingers and ran to Leeann's aid.

"Here," shouted Ceann, tossing the keys to her sister.

After three or four tries with the tarnished keyring, Leeann finally found the right one. And, of course, it was black.

The heavy door rattled open, and the two small girls assisted their distressed mother outside.

"Break it off in the lock," Maria said, shakiness abating.

Ceann quickly shut and locked the bars, then returned the key to the door's exterior lock. Using the butt of the powder rifle, Leeann snapped off the bit of jagged metal. Finally, Maria slouched against the door in the darkness and sighed, tears streaming. As with the pocket door, it wasn't much of an obstruction, but maybe it'd buy them enough time.

Maria hugged the girls and kissed their foreheads. "I love you girls."

"We love you, Mom."

It began to mist again. Starlight came and went between the drifting cloud cover.

After catching her breath, Maria tricked Ceann into helping load the snaphaunce double-barrel rifle. Leeann looked around at what'd once been a pleasant courtyard.

The brick foundation of a gazebo or pergola lay in the middle of the quiet space.

Leeann hadn't notice it before when, long ago, Mr. Halgin had goaded her into bearing false witness, but as her eyes adjusted to the night, she caught the remnant evidence crowded out by the surrounding walls and tightly packed buildings. The outdoor area was mostly barren gravel, some of it overgrown with twisted trees, weeds, and brambles clinging to life.

The once-painted pavers had weathered and cracked since being converted into a makeshift training square for the deputies, which Leeann guessed made sense since it also doubled as a gray stage for official trials and pious executions worthy of the effort.

The irony that only thorn bushes and poisonous flowers continued to thrive in the shadow of the soggy walls surrounding the rear of the jail wasn't lost on Leeann. Mr. Black's little humorous lessons seemed to be everywhere these days.

The metal door suddenly rattled in its frame.

"Mother?" shouted Ceann.

Debris fell along the molding, powdering the misty air. The snarls and cursing of men roared between their efforts to beat and kick down the door.

"Where you going?" asked Ceann, her breath steaming.

"Rope," replied Leeann.

She ran for the rundown storage shack in the corner of the enclosure.

"Good girl." Maria smiled when Leeann tossed a portion of the rope over one of the larger tree branches swaying in the wet breeze above the wall. Then she fed the line till both ends could be knotted together.

Stone cracked around the frame.

The former sheriff's mace punched a single spike through the metal.

"Wait," said Ceann. "What's that for then?"

Leeann dragged her little sister by the arm to the other side of the square to where the wall was tallest. Much taller than the other two sides, but the brickwork had swollen and separated from the mortar because the gutters along the adjoining building were in heavy disrepair. Most importantly, it was opposite the tree branch with the diversionary escape rope dangling in front of the storage shack.

The door dented around the handle. Halgin's men would soon bust it open.

Maria turned and faced the alleyway. "Hear that?"

Ceann paused to listen as Leeann removed and tossed their shoes over the wall with their packs.

Maria cocked both barrels. "They're coming over."

Leaving but a few men to assault the sabotaged door from within the jailhouse, the others had gotten smart and doubled back around. They came running down the narrow alley, which deadened closest to the partitioned section of the wall where her girls now scrambled to safety.

"Climb damnit!"

Leeann pushed Ceann up the wall.

"I'm trying."

"Use your toes."

"I am," cried Ceann as she struggled up the damp

bricks.

More debris fell from the doorframe. The hinges started to give.

Leeann quickly climbed past her little sister now more than halfway up the wall.

Maria ducked and knelt beside the swinging rope. She noticed candles in a few of the windows above them. Apparently, the commotion in the jail hadn't gone unnoticed by some of the nearby residents and third-shift workers. Some gaped down at them through the yellow light, hazy glass windows. Others, realizing what they were about to witness, quickly turned their backs.

Just as Leeann pulled Ceann to the top of the slick wall, the door handle broke off and clattered onto the ground.

"Mother!" shouted Ceann.

Boom! Maria emptied one barrel at the first man to peek over the courtyard wall. The shot clipped the edge of the stonework; nevertheless, it tore much of the soldier's face off. His shiny helmet was ripped clean off his head. It landed in the trees above him.

"I didn't see where it came from!" called one of the men.

Maria's heart raced as she scanned for the next bit of metal to catch stray starlight. This wasn't anything like hunting hare or grouse with Benzan, but it wasn't much different, either. Not really. Not if she wanted her children to live. So, that's what Maria harnessed as the lingering pan-smoke burned her eyes, contorting her stomach.

"Let go!" Leeann struggled to force Ceann over the other side of the wall.

It was odd but also perfect amidst the chaos. As the girls argued through clenched teeth and red cheeks about the wall and the small gap between the nearest buildings, Maria was strangely reminded of all the mischief they'd ever made. All the games they played. She couldn't believe how grown they were. How tough they were. How unlike her they were.

A final heavy swing of the mace split the jam, sending the broken lock airborne.

Leeann and Ceann were just babies, Maria's beautiful babies, and yet, they already outgrew her. It's why her trigger finger felt awkward and cold while they were less affected by the chaos and death. She could see it then, even feel it somehow as their futures materialized somewhere deep in her mind, the truth almost hypnotizing her between the cold shadows, softly falling rain, and misty starlight.

The realization was beautiful and complete. Plucked out of time. Hers alone.

As the wall and neighboring buildings failed to choke the life from the little vegetation growing about the courtyard, so too would Leeann and Ceann survive. Not just today, but until the berg was but a memory.

However, such will to thrive, to fight against all things bent on their destruction, had its price. It was then Maria knew that, by the time Ceann was half her age, her girls would be nothing like her or Benzan and everything like Mr. Black. And it wouldn't be long after that till they forgot, willfully or not, everything before Mr. Black first came to Pehats Berg. In a sense, from this point onward, the girls would no longer be hers but his.

Could she live with that? What else could she ask for? Be thankful for?

Crack!

Maria felt a sudden pain in her side. She looked down. Blood seeped through her.

Startled by the ball-shot that cut through Maria's side, knocking her down, Leeann and Ceann tumbled together over the wall in quiet horror. Leeann threw a hand over Ceann's mouth and clamped her own mouth shut to avoid revealing their location.

"I got her," bellowed one of the killers before dropping over the wall.

Like a wraith of ignited pan-powder, another soldier stepped through the ruined doorway to make sure the other man was right. That Maria was dead.

She wasn't. Mortally wounded, dress soaked red, Maria dug deep to steady her nerves. Control her fears.

"I see you now," said the man.

"But I saw you first," answered Maria. Boom!

Knocked flat on his back, the armsman gasped at the amount of blood and pain roaring from his shattered hip. He cursed and cried as he tried for his weapon, but balked because, to recover the stunted braunbess he dropped, he'd have to roll onto his wound.

Maria grinned at his pain and incoherent violent threats.

A third thug, the one who smashed through the door with his newly acquired mace, exited the rear of the jail. Unlike with Benzan, it was clearly written on his face how he hoped for a different sort of satisfaction before murdering Maria.

Watching the big bastard moving cautiously toward her as she struggled with the muzzleloader's ammo, Maria leaned against the darkest and mistiest section of the wall beside the shack. Her lungs were ready to burst. She wheezed and spat blood. Yet, despite the sweat pouring down her back and the burning fire seeping from the hole in her gut, she felt oddly at peace in the rain and shadow.

"Find her," shouted another of the sheriff's men. "Before the bitch can reload!"

Barrels cocked, calmness settled upon Maria's weary, wet shoulders.

Men rallied over the wall and through the doorway, weapons drawn. Swords, shields, arms, and armor glinted in the darkness as each killer got closer.

"Shit!" shouted the mace-wielding mercenary the moment it gave away his position.

Boom!

Crack!

Boom!

6

Leeann slowly blinked through the tiny snowflake dust on her eyelashes. "Ceann?" She tasted blood in her mouth. Perhaps she'd bitten her tongue, but she wasn't sure since her head pounded. Fresh sleet gathered on her lips. She licked them clean to moisten her throat. "Ceann?"

Shifting from her muddy side to her damp chest, it occurred to her that her feet weren't wet and cold like everything else; somehow her shoes and socks were on. That's when her body remembered what her mind forgot in its stillness.

Leeann inhaled a deep breath and choked. Her injured arm radiated from the marrow. Her shoulder throbbed. Her hand was black and blue and tingled as though coated in itchy sand. And through the pain, just like Mr. Black had taught her it would, everything came rushing back: the courtyard, the fall from the highest section of the wall, the reckless landing as she twisted to protect Ceann from the impact waiting somewhere at the bottom of the gap between the jail and the building beside it.

Reliving those brief moments in a flash of frosty lightning, in the shadows of a building wintery haze, alone, her parents dead, her sister missing, Leeann did her best not to sob and give up, succumbing to her numerous pains.

"Ceann?"

The world continued to spin and separate. Pain radiated all over.

"Where are you?"

She got up on her knees, dislocated shoulder held still, and spotted Ceann.

Their pack tossed away so not to be easily spotted in the moonlight, Ceann lay a dozen or more feet ahead. She was face down in the street behind a row of refuse crates, sniveling and mumbling to herself between deep, labored breaths.

"Ceann!" Leeann crawled to her little sister's side.

"Leeann?" Ceann's raised head up from red verglas and pink rainwater.

"Are you okay?" Even barely able to move her shoulder, Leeann righted her sister.

"You're awake?" said Ceann.

Leeann delicately separated the ruby mess from the nasty goose egg above her little sister's right eyebrow. She then realized something was missing. "Where's your pack?"

"Couldn't take both."

Leeann winked. "Your shoes are on wrong, you know that?"

Ceann giggled, though painfully. "I found yours first after the fall."

"I was wondering how that happened. Thank you."

Ceann's eyes welled. "Don't, I almost wore them."

Leeann flinched as her little sister gave her a great, consuming hug.

She'd waited alone for their mother to come over the wall, until she didn't. Ceann then did her best to lug Leeann's unconscious body to safety.

"Is it bad?" asked Ceann, now aware of the pain her hug caused.

"It's not good." Leeann wiped the residual sweat from around Ceann's face and neck.

"I'm sorry." Ceann carefully hugged her big sister again.

Leeann added, "I can't believe you dragged me all this way?"

"If there was a barrow, I would've used it."

Though tears fell, both girls smiled.

Leeann knew they were now roughly a dozen blocks from the Dailborka residence, where the Bringtums served another wealthy merchant the way her own family had previously served Mr. Halgin. That meant if they hustled and stayed off the main streets, they'd make it to the Two Sisters while it was still dark.

"You went the long way?" said Leeann.

"It's what you would've done."

No, thought Leeann as she glanced back the way they'd come. *I would've carried you.*

"Mother and Father?"

"We've got to get moving," said Leeann, wiping away Ceann's tears.

After helping Leeann set her shoulder the way they'd seen Maria aid Benzan years ago, resulting in more tears and clenched curses, Ceann slung their heavy pack over her shoulder and carefully climbed onto Leeann's back.

"Wait," said Leeann. "How did you know to get us to the Sisters?"

"Mr. Black called it a castle once."

"He did, didn't he?" replied Leeann.

"Well, well…" someone said from the darkness.

The unknown man caused Ceann to clutch at Leeann's neck the way a startled cat might.

"I'll be sure you two princesses get there safe 'n sound." The thug, masquerading himself as a soldier of the realm, stepped from wherever he'd been lurking since tracking them over the courtyard wall. He carried a lithe ax over his shoulder.

Leeann felt like she was already dead, strangely weightless. If she could think coherently in this captured moment, she'd rather the pursuer slit their throats or crush their skulls with his foreign-styled ax than take them alive. Anything but that.

"Leeann?" whispered Ceann as her nervous, watery eyes darted about.

"Now," he said, stepping around to face them, "you sweets are coming with me."

"Leeann?" Ceann's frightened gaze drifted ahead, above the buildings.

The soldier licked his lips. "Don't worry, though, we're still going to the Sisters."

"No," answered Leeann.

"Leeann?" Ceann's jaw now chattered.

"What?" replied the man.

"No," repeated Leeann louder. "We're not going with you."

"Little bitch."

Testing Ceann's ankles about her waist, her little sister's arms about her neck and good shoulder, Leeann tried to determine which way to make a run for it.

"That's good—you try it."

His eyes grew with violent pleasure. Mr. Halgin would settle for one, as long as the other was dead. Either way, their condition upon delivery wouldn't matter. Having just marched with the First Urhal Ranger Company so many miles from Corvel in the east of the Scattered Kingdoms, he was due a bit of excitement.

"*Leeann!*" Ceann's scream was pure, primal.

From somewhere in the dark frost above them, a monstrous silhouette took shape atop an adjacent building scaffolding. It then took flight.

Ceann shut her eyes as they were knocked down by a great, swooping gust that cleared the street of old wooden boxes, loose trash, anything weighing less than the girls' combined mass. Leeann covered their heads against the terrible flurry of debris spawned by its leathery flesh and ebony feathers, which also muffled any other sounds between the buildings for a moment, save for the erratic flapping of the unknown monster's huge wings.

Unlike her sister's, Leeann's fear didn't cripple her. Sure, her heart beat like thunder in her ears, and she, too, felt like screaming as they were knocked down, Ceann hugged her head in blind, hysterical panic. Nevertheless, Leeann remained transfixed by what little she could discern in the wet, wintery mixed darkness.

He's still alive, thought Leeann.

Her anxiety fueled an odd curiosity as she watched the monster, relatively oblivious to them since pouncing, crushing much of the man's body, and feeding on the wiggling mess pinned beneath its six-inch talons.

Hidden by the mercenary's cloak, Leeann guessed the jack plate was an unexpected annoyance to the monster's four, heavily spurred wings. At least until it manipulated its lower wings, folding the patagium membrane so the resulting bone structure best resembled great shredding, probing antennae.

Leeann blinked through her terrified fascination as grit and gore splattered her face.

The monster made a mixture of chortling and hissing sounds as it moved about its food.

Remaining as still as possible, Leeann watched as the byrnie about the dying man's arms and legs irritated the nightmare in the alleyway, as evident by the little starlight that partially captured its atrocious maw's inability to snap the limbs clean and swallow the morsels whole.

Ceann shuddered as more blood and bodily fluid splashed across the cold, wet street.

Regardless of her little sister's nonverbal protests,

Leeann knew they couldn't escape. Not yet. So, she hugged Ceann tighter, mouthing sweet, tear-laced words to her so neither would piss themselves for fear. Because, at any moment, that which was mostly concealed by the darkness in the alley, might become aware of them. And though earlier Leeann wished for a quick death over capture, she now wanted very much to live.

After a few exploratory pecks, the monster's extensive beak finally broke through the dead man's skull. The soupy *crunch* was a sound Ceann was sure to never forget. A second, smaller mouth with tiny, sharp teeth, emerged from somewhere inside the shadowy monster's gullet. Not knowing why, Leeann instantly envisioned a bat's mouth, the ivory razors briefly glinting in imaginary moonlight.

"Don't let it eat me," moaned Ceann into the base of Leeann's neck.

"Shhh," replied Leeann, her sister's hot tears and snot oozing down her collar.

With the precision of a vise, the monster gripped the dead man's head in place with its beak while its smaller, more flexible mouth devoured whatever sloppy chunks of brain its long green tongue tore free.

Thankfully, much of this horror was blocked from their view not only by shadow and a growing wintery mix of sleet and snow, but also by the monster's dominant wings, which it continued to use to better position itself about the corpse as it fed. On the other hand, the sounds of every gulp, crunch, chew, and wet slurp weren't muffled in anyway.

Leeann continued to watch the monster feed, too

frightened to move or escape.

Patience, Mr. Black's toughest lesson, was the only weapon Leeann had left.

Just then, as though they'd a mind of their own, a peculiar grin crept over Leeann's lips. Why? Because Mr. Black was right. The monster, which Leeann now figured was half the size of a female griffin, at last decided it would rather finish its meal from the safety of a nearby rooftop than the damp, cramped alley.

Ceann stiffened as the monster readied for flight by stretching its most avian pair of wings.

"It's almost over," whispered Leeann.

Too bad the young man then slipping away from his sleeping lover didn't decide to exit the elderly bachelor's front door and not quietly depart with a lantern through the side service partition, which opened onto the dark street just behind where the girls lay prone.

Because instead of encountering a few, fifteen-stone bael rats or maybe a knifeman waiting to rob him on his guilt-ridden stroll back to his unsuspecting family, he stumbled upon something far worse.

So unimaginable was his horror given crisp, warm clarity, that he soiled his pants.

"Leeann?" said Ceann after hearing the newcomer stop his approach.

"Don't. Move," Leann warned the dumbstruck civilian as quietly and calmly as she could.

The cheating lover screamed and dropped the lantern.

"Shit!" Ignoring her own wounds, Leeann immediately rolled with Ceann to avoid the liquid fire and broken glass sprayed across the alley by the monster's terrible black leathery wings during takeoff.

Crystalized against the night, wings beating, beak thrashing, the flying abomination appeared as some kind of mutated offspring of raven and bat. It chirped and cackled furiously, clutching and pawing at the dead soldier's body with a pair of stunted, humanlike arms that extended from the folds of its sparsely matted and feathered chest.

Vhendo, thought Leeann as it crashed about between the tight buildings.

The vhendo was violent and erratic in the air, hissing at the fire, which seemed to have momentarily blinded some of its freakish eyes no longer camouflaged by the grisly mane about its callused neck and shoulders.

Enraged, the vhendo threw down the corpse from an adjacent two-story roof before giving a terrifying series of squawks at the fleeing children, just as they shouted, "Move! Move!" at the wandering lover still stupefied by the flying vhendo.

Like her sister, Ceann knew by its color the cheap animal-based lantern oil wouldn't burn for long despite how hot and bright the flames licked at the cracks in the polluted street or the wood grain along the building's wet shutters. On the other hand, Leeann knew something Ceann didn't. With how intense the fat-oil burned, there was a good chance at least some of the vhendo's greasy underbelly plumage and wiry hair would ignite.

At least, that was Leeann's hope as she burned her hand as she snagged and hurled what remained of the broken lantern, still gushing sizzling oil, at the blood-thirsty vhendo circling toward them.

"Burn, you ugly bastard!"

"You got it!" Ceann cheered.

Struck just above its hind legs, the vhendo caught fire. It wailed with pure madness, feathered wings flapping, leathery wings trying to wipe away the flame. Then it fell from the sky and crashed somewhere behind them in a heap of fire, feathers, and gnarled flesh.

It wasn't dead, though. Not even close by Leeann's guess.

The enraged vhendo cawed and hooted and wailed in an eerily human way as it began to get up from the wreckage it created, rolling and thrashing and slamming itself against anything to extinguish the gooey flames quickly burning out over its body.

"Wait for me!"

Leeann ran, and neither sister looked to see if the gigolo followed.

7

Everything was a bouncing, shaking, terrifying mess as Leeann ran with Ceann on her back.

Ceann kept looking over her shoulder and backpack. "It's coming!"

The vhendo flew low over the berg, darting between buildings without landing when able, smashing chimneys to rubble with its mighty wings when not. Debris rained from the sky when it was forced to perch on rooftops to keep track of Leeann, who did her best to cut every corner so the vhendo might lose track of them.

The sounds of pelted cobbles and bricks echoed everywhere through the dampness.

Leeann shouted but didn't slow when fragments of falling housing struck her chest.

"It's coming!" called Ceann.

They cut through a broken fence, ducked around a corner.

Leeann could barely feel her feet. Her shoulders burned. Her arms felt like jelly.

"There!" Ceann spotted the vhendo soaring, searching through the haze of low clouds.

Still not looking back, running with fear and blood in her mouth, sweat and street runoff soaking her clothes, Leeann ran and ran. It was all her body knew to do. It felt like forever as her feet pounded to keep them ahead and out of sight of the still-smoking predator hunting, lurking somewhere in the dark, snowy sky above them.

It wasn't long till they were found, though not by the vhendo.

A few of Mr. Halgin's other hired thugs, traitors to Pehats Berg and the peace of the Scattered Kingdoms, saw the two girls round a cobbler's shop and gave chase.

Of course, giving the vhendo other options was part of Leeann's plan.

What wasn't part of Leeann's plan? The handful of people standing in her way, in the street outside Goran's stables, across and to the left of where her legs finally gave out on her.

What's that noise? Ceann glanced in the direction of the crowd.

"Emil?" Leeann couldn't believe it.

Across and to the right of where the two girls almost collapsed on the street, at the mouth of a dead-end that doubled as a loading dock for the shops along the row, Deputy Emil Simkus was gagging and hogtying two of Mr. Halgin's lookouts.

One was a local loser, petty thief, who apparently sold what was left of his life to the traitors. The other was yet another interloper from beyond the berg. Lastly, there was an unknown man dead at the deputy's feet. It seemed he didn't surrender as quietly as his compatriots. The hilt of a dagger jutted from the base of his neck.

"Emil!" cried Ceann as he saw them.

"Wait," Leeann told her. "It's still out there."

That noise again? This time, Ceann thought it came from inside Goran's stables. She could smell smoke now, just barely, though, like a doused campfire.

Emil smiled at them but signaled them to wait.

The street was still crowded, and Leeann knew there was really no way to be sure if there weren't any more fake deputies or suspiciously armed persons Emil didn't recognize from either the watch or the civilian patrol.

"Hurry," whispered Ceann when Emil finally gave the go-ahead.

Leeann stayed low, her whole body aching even worse as she hunched while running.

"You all right?" asked Emil when they were safely by his side.

Unsure what to say, Ceann only nodded as she slid down from Leeann's back.

Ignoring the crowd and the intimidating hand-cannon now strapped to Emil's chest, Leeann asked what was most pertinent. "How?"

"You-Know-Who told me you'd make for the Two Sisters."

However, when Emil didn't find either them or the inn's two owners after riding with all haste from Father Rai's mission, he'd decided to further investigate on foot the situation Mr. Black briefed him on before Black headed into the tunnel.

"That's when I found these gents," said Emil, explaining how he'd stumbled across the newly deputized loudmouths saying things they now wish they hadn't.

Lucky for him, he didn't need to unsling the carriage drakon from his chest holster during their arrest. Mr. Black had insisted he take the hand-cannon despite not having many rounds for it. When Emil asked why, Mr. Black assured him he'd need it.

Leeann looked around the dead-end. "Is he here?"

Emil shook his head. "Wychstone." He began to drag away his disarmed captives, their various weapons left neatly behind in a row.

"Them?" Leeann pointed to the crowd, many still in their bed clothes despite the weather.

"Not sure." Emil exchanged the shortsword donated by Momma Bwulyaa for the spatha blade seized from his detainees. "Some shouting and loud noises from inside Goran's earlier. Before I arrived. They," he nodded toward the fools now hunkered behind the public troughs, "said a small fire started in the upper lofts after that." He pulled the dagger from the dead man's throat.

Trepidation grating her keen mind, Leeann stepped around, behind Emil.

Sensing Ceann's responsive nervousness, Emil asked, "Your parents?"

As Ceann hid her face in his chest, Leeann only stared, her eyes telling a violent story. An earlier chapter of this bloody night.

As Emil checked the bruise over her right eye, Ceann began, "Gabija… She—"

Emil softly hushed Ceann. "It's okay, sweetie." He smiled, dabbed her eyes, then his own.

Hugging Emil, Ceann felt safe, finally safe and, in that moment, the sound she recently heard coming and going became clearer. Someone was humming.

"No. It's not okay," said Leeann as Emil cleaned the blood from Ceann's brow.

At first, Emil meant to console the older girl as he had Ceann. He couldn't imagine what they'd been through. The death and violence they'd seen. Such horrors no child should endure. They looked like Hel. Then he paused. Something about Leeann's expression changed, cleared his mind, made him wonder if her agitation and shakiness wasn't from fear. Least not any kind he was familiar with as a father of two.

"Vhendo," said Leeann as Emil came close, kneeled to embrace her.

"What?" He immediately thought of his boys, Mose and Valter.

"It's true," added Ceann. "We saw."

"Only one," Leeann clarified, since it could also be used as a plural, "Mr. Black—"

Before she could elaborate about the scout, some of Mr. Halgin's hired swords who'd pursued them since murdering their parents and escaping the jail erupted into the open street whence the girls just came.

The crowd outside Goran's fled the scene.

"What now?" asked Ceann as Emil gathered them and tucked out of sight.

"We kill 'em," said a young man from somewhere unseen.

Emil turned quick on his heels to defend the girls against the unknown speaker. It was a false alarm, though, for the street-hardened rogue with a large repeating crossbow over his shoulder was a friend. He smiled at the quick-acting deputy before swallowing the juice of the cao ma leaves packed thick around his gums.

"Ani!" Leeann leapt to Cirilo and hugged his waist after he emerged from behind the mesh-cage door at the rear of a popular butchers.

"Where'd you come from?" Emil asked.

Cirilo kissed the top of Leeann's head. "Momma thought you'd need help."

"Ani," beamed Ceann. "How'd you get here?"

"My wheels." His rotorikisha was twice as fast with an empty basket.

Emil shook Cirilo's hand. "Lucky you found us."

"Not luck," replied Cirilo as Ceann teased the rings in his lips.

From behind the hāfu warrior, Momma Bwulyaa's largest dire-wolfhound stepped into view.

Emil grinned, accepting there was really no such thing as a dead-end when you probably knew every shortcut and building-to-building access point across much of the berg because that's how you always avoided the watch. Not to mention when being assisted by the wolfhound's ability to track both Emil and the girls based upon known familiarities.

Something was wrong, though. After a few searching sniffs, the dire-wolfhound's ears flattened, and her fur bristled. She slowly bared her knifelike fangs while a deep, hot growl churned in her belly.

"They're not alone," said Leeann, peeking again at the mercenaries.

Of the three men shouting at each other in the street outside Goran's, now they were closer and in the open, only the one with the round shield appeared uninjured. Of the other two, the least wounded was half-carrying the third man, who was nearly lame, his spear now a crutch. His leg and hip were ruined.

Leeann guessed there'd been a fourth man earlier, his corpse now obviously abandoned some streets back given the amount of blood and where it seemed to have splattered in clumps over the tunics of the three surviving murderers bought and paid for by Mr. Halgin and those intent on destroying the peace of Pehats Berg.

"Ani?"

"Yes?"

Ceann whispered into Cirilo's ear, "I heard something again."

Cirilo leaned over close and said, "What was it this time, imōto?"

Leeann pointed. "There!"

Right on cue, the vhendo ceased its stalking as it leapt down from a nearby rooftop. It landed with a frightening *thud* and skidded to a halt. Bristling, growling, it reared and squawked. The apex display was something akin to a roar but, given the combination of twisted animals it most resembled, it was unnaturally worse.

"By all the saints," said Emil, his mind struggling to accept what he saw.

The entire street reverberated and rumbled with

the vhendo's deafening terror cries which, strangely enough, somehow amplified its heavy, putrid, freshly burnt stench. The savage nightmare come to life, then turned and looked. Then it shook and flapped about as if confused by the many tasty morsels. It chirped and cackled, drool flying.

Cirilo felt his toes and fingers go numb but recovered quick enough so he didn't need to sit.

Emil drew his drakon, cocked the wheel. His hands shook.

Just then, the weaker of their captive thugs fainted. The other man pleaded for release since Mr. Halgin's promises were meaningless now, and he shit himself at the prospect of being eaten by the monster.

The dire-wolfhound crouched, instincts telling her how close to death they all were.

The vhendo's rear wings buckled, flight seeming out of reach now. It hooted, thrashed, yet the lingering pain from the lamp oil somehow still worked to its advantage, encouraging it, streamlining its form. It then lunged for the two slower killers.

Leeann spotted a side-sword jutting out its right shoulder, no doubt the fourth man's last act of bravery before being ripped to pieces. Or so she assumed.

Sword or no sword through its shoulder, the hissing terror snatched the lame combatant from the arms of his fellow conspirator and, in a single chomp through the man's throat, beheaded him the way one decapitates a chicken before putting it in a pot.

He's signing, thought Ceann, seeing a faint glow through the windows in Goran's stables.

"We need to go." Emil drew the sword at his hip. The heavy metal calmed his sweaty palm.

"Now," agreed Cirilo.

"We can't," replied Leeann, her hand swatting away Ceann's searching fingers.

She was right. There was no escape.

If Mr. Black wanted it, they would've been long gone, but they weren't. That wasn't the mission, no matter what large, sweeping goal he had for however many moves ahead he was in this unknown game. So, whatever was about to happen was always going to happen, and considering the two forces soon to collide, it was better to be inside the Two Sisters than out in the streets or the wilds beyond Pehats Berg.

Cirilo spotted several arrow shafts breaking the silhouette of the vhendo's still-smoking hide as it dug deeper into the headless man's spine. "We kill it then, right?" Though a touch of violence and madness flickered in his eyes, he wasn't sure the pouch over the small of his back had enough bolts to do the job.

"Maybe?" It was the best Emil could do.

They were all glued, eyes wide, as the second soldier scrambled on all fours across the open street to recover the spear of his fallen man. Shouting, as if that would overcome his apparent fears, he thrust it directly into the vhendo's maw. The blade bit deep somewhere in its darkened face, and the shaft bowed in the middle.

"You want to save them?" asked Leeann, again, ignoring Ceann's pulling at her hand.

"No, imōto," said Cirilo, spitting the milky-white cao ma from his dry mouth.

Emil scanned for somewhere or way to trap the monster. No good. They were screwed.

"You girls—"

"Ceann!"

Leeann bolted after Ceann, but her sister was already halfway to Goran's stables.

Grinning at the bravery of his little sisters, especially the one secretly Tuched, Cirilo stepped out from the safety of the tightly packed buildings and leveled the huge repeating crossbow at the vhendo. "Hey, mooks! Over here!"

"For you, Gabija!" Emil dropped the drakon's hammer.

8

When Leann entered the stables, just a few feet into the darkness after closing the door behind her, the smell nearly knocked her down.

It was sour and salty and wet. The odor was strange, different from the vhendo's, but also heavier than the normal dusty dander that normally lingered in the stalls.

Leeann might've thought it was afterbirth, for she'd helped many pregnant cows and horses and goats deliver, but the similarities ended there, for clearly this wasn't natural. Not from nature in that way. Whatever aline membrane had recently burst caused the hairs all over her arms and legs to stand on end.

Ceann stood just ahead of her older sister, fidgeting in darkness.

Leeann grabbed Ceann by the back of her hair. "Are you mad?" she said, pulling hard.

"Shhh!"

"What're you doing?"

Ceann scrunched her face. "Be quiet."

Eyes searching, shapes in the black and shadow becoming clearer as her eyes adjusted, Leeann realized what they had walked into. "Shit."

The stable's whole interior, from the main room where the Gorans' bookkeeping was done, to the farthest stall saved for those behind on their dues, was the most violent and disturbing scene they could've imagined.

Everything was a wreck. Smashed by unthinkable violence.

All the horses were dead. All the people were dead.

Blood and bowels and hay coated the walls, floors, and ceiling beams. The horses weren't just slaughtered. They were mangled and torn and broken as if a giant grinding wheel had chewed them up and spit them out. The girls couldn't tell for sure, but they guessed a few of them might even have died early, right before the onslaught. Fearful convulsions or sudden heart attacks most likely. Their eyes bulged from their sockets, and their swollen tongues lay limp in foamy, vomit-filled mouths.

"Ceann?"

I hear you. Where are you?

Leeann didn't easily recognize the few corpses, but after relighting one of the lanterns knocked on its side, most of the fuel gone and the glass chimney broken, she recognized members of Goran's family lying among the chaos. Their cold bodies were scattered like muck thrown from a horse's shoe.

"Look," said Ceann. Leeann turned the lantern's

open flame and found Goran.

Old man Goran's body wasn't like the others, which Leeann assumed were killed either before or after the patriarch. He'd been shot in the head.

"What happened here?"

"This way," said Ceann. She ducked beneath where the fire had started in the lofts above.

"The vhendo could still be here?"

Ceann didn't answer, simply kept pace ahead of the lantern's light.

A dozen steps behind her little sister as they slowly moved through the eerie darkness, Leeann paused to notice they were following a trail of gore leading to one of the stable's middle stalls.

"Leeann?"

She quickly came to stand beside Ceann.

Neither was ready for what lay waiting for them.

Little Harold Cross, armed with a click-lock air pistol, his overalls caked in shit and other vileness, sat in the corner of the stall, elbows about his knees, humming to himself as he sweetly stroked the snout of an enormous creature equally bathed in grit, hay, and freshly red entrails.

Though half a size greater than a large draft horse, the creature curled on the floor of the freshly mucked stall appeared not as a chaotic terror to the girls, but as a purposefully calming amalgam of horse, bear, and something reptilian.

Both of its odd-toed paws wielded three great claws. Its forelimbs were long enough to knuckle-walk, and its hindlimbs were stout yet disproportionately stunted. Any of its skin not covered in slick gore or shaggy fur, was protected by coarse yet glossy scales, almost like plate armor.

"Is that?"

"No," answered Ceann, referring to the new creature.

Leeann wasn't sure how Ceann could be so confident, but she trusted her sister.

"Harold?"

Harold gave a sluggish grin. He appeared exhausted beyond measure.

"You heard me singing again?" he asked.

"Yes," replied Ceann.

Leeann turned. "What?"

"You never believed me!" said Ceann, her tears hot.

"Why didn't you say something?" Leeann immediately realized how foolish she sounded.

"I did!"

Swallowing hard, Leeann felt her own tears well.

"Why would I continue to explain? So you could ignore me, make fun of me again?"

A wave of guilt surged in Leeann's gut. "How was I supposed to know?"

Ceann shook her head. "You're my sister."

There'd been little hints over the past few years. Ceann had shown an oddness or peculiarity at uniquely crucial moments. Nothing spectacular. Things not exactly normal, yet still perplexing, which is how she eventually came to befriend one of Pehats Berg's favorite little whipping posts.

It was no secret. Harold's own father, Goran's eldest, once thought about smothering him.

As an example of Ceann's Tuch, she intercepted Black's message to Margaret. The token, a small spinning top, was supposed to be for Leeann to find, but Ceann sensed something when she saw their mother Maria trip and accidentally drop some of Mr. Halgin's dirty laundry on the floor earlier that day. At the time, Ceann watched with deep interest as out of Mr. Halgin's wrinkled pocket fell a single coin sticky with bourbon.

The coin spun as if it might never stop. She had smiled at that. It was when Ceann knew Mr. Black was in Pehats Berg, though she didn't know how or why she was so certain of it. She expected to find a similar coin in Margaret's usual drop-point but, instead, found the top. She decided to keep the trinket for herself. Of course, that was after rushing out to tell Leeann Mr. Black expected her at the Two Sisters.

"Mother believed me. Father, too. Even Mr. Black, but never you!"

"I'm sorry." Confused and exhausted, Leeann tried to console her little sister but was pushed away. "I'm so sorry."

"You believe me now?" Ceann rubbed at her aching forehead.

Leeann nodded, though she wasn't sure what she believed anymore.

"Are you okay, Harold?" Ceann slowly approached him.

"We're okay."

Though mentally drained, Leeann knew Harold wasn't well, and not in the way most people would assume. There was a fine salt-dust on his face and neck.

His eyes were sunken, bruised. He sounded sleepy drunk.

"Your friend's horse was really sick," said Harold, wiping red snot from his nose.

"Mr. Black's?"

"It's all right, though. That's why he left'm with me."

Leeann walked deeper into the stall, careful not to step on the creature's scaly tail.

"Khalix survived the Chimeraosis." Harold yawned. "It's okay. He's not sick anymore."

"It did this, Harold?" Leeann was more than confused.

"His name is Khalix."

Leeann began again, "Khalix killed your family?"

"It wasn't his fault." Harold teased the great creature's ears. "I saved him."

"How?" asked Leeann while Ceann looked on with wide eyes and a big grin.

Harold's answer was a goofy, half-sleepy laugh to himself, followed by incoherent whispering as his eyes at last rolled back in his head. He would've fallen over if not for Ceann jumping forward, bracing him.

"He's Tuched." Ceann assumed it was obvious by now.

Leeann glanced at the air pistol. "Why him, not your family?"

"Khalix will save us."

9

"Leeann!"

Emil slammed one of the stable doors behind him. "Ceann!"

Stepping out from the stall, Leeann waved her arms high overhead. "Emil?"

Spotting her lantern, Emil called out, "Girls—"

The body of the second mercenary crashed through the door behind Emil, snapping it off its hinges and knocking Emil's feet out from beneath him.

Cirilo kicked down the rest of the broken door, entering after the merc. He lifted the crossbow, stretching the fresh gash across his gut, and cursed loudly. Blood was already soaking through his pants. He helped Emil recover his bearings, who then reloaded the drakon.

The ex-deputy had already blown off one of the vhendo's more human-like arms, so they could escape from the streets to the stables. They weren't quick enough, though, which is how the spearman's corpse became a flying battering ram hurled at an unthinkable speed from the vhendo's beak.

Cirilo squeezed the crossbow's hair trigger and let fly another broad bolt. "Come on!"

Despite Cirilo's command though, the dire-wolf-hound wouldn't come. He grinned, as though expecting nothing less than that she'd refuse to yield the street to the monster.

The vhendo chirped, its tongue tasting the air as it circled the loyal pet blocking its way.

"Over here," said Emil as he directed the lone shield bearer deeper into the stables.

Still armed with his round shield and coupled shorts-word, the last of the foreign soldiers staggered his retreat with Emil and Cirilo, for fear moving too fast would again draw the vhendo's attention away from the ichor coated dire-wolfhound just outside what remained of the broken door. Never in his life would he have imagined his survival would depend on a wolfhound's bravery against something so evil.

"Move," ordered Emil. He fired the drakon a third time, creating a small shockwave that buzzed the stable's stuffy interior.

"What's this?" Expecting to find only the body of his dead friend, the soldier stood baffled by the apparent bloodbath they'd walked into.

Feeling the gooey carnage beneath his boots, Emil sighed. "Great."

"Two'll kill everyone," said Cirilo, smirking at the

nearby hay sticky with guts.

"Vhendo didn't do this."

Halfway to Emil, Cirilo, and the Urhal soldier, Leeann quickly explained what'd happened here.

"What?" asked Emil.

"Where's Ceann?" Cirilo looked past Leeann, back to the stall she'd just exited.

Loud barking and snarling drowned out the vhendo's beastly howls. The combination of noises broke the momentary calm. Everyone looked back, toward the feral battle still raging in the space just outside the stables. A moment later and the vhendo shrieked, and then started whimpering. The first they'd heard since it caught fire. The dire-wolfhound had scored a vicious bite or two.

Slumping against one of the burnt supports beneath the stable's loft, Cirilo pressed his wounded belly. "There's rope and chain…"

"Here, let me." Leeann moved to support Cirilo.

"Where's your sister?"

"She's safe," answered Leeann while tending his wounds.

"Can we trap it?" asked the merc, wiping black blood from his shortsword onto his shield.

"Maybe," said Emil, studying the fresh chips along his own blade.

"Burn the stable down around it?"

Cirilo nodded at the building's many corners and support beams while Leeann reloaded his crossbow.

"It might work," said the soldier, pacing back and forth in the glow of the lantern.

"No, it won't," said Leeann.

A heavy gust of wind swept through the stables then, followed by Momma Bwulyaa's favorite dire-wolf-hound emerging from the edge of the lantern light. The noble hound limped on a mangled paw. Her flank had nasty gaping wounds. Her fur was torn bare in some spots. Nevertheless, the impressive pet continued to softly growl even as she went and rested at Cirilo's side.

"Good job, girl." Petting her, Cirilo discovered her tail had also been lost in the fight.

"We're out of time," said Emil.

As the unnatural wind receded, the tiny flame dwindled, choking on what little fuel remained to feed the wick. Leeann's eyes reflected her silent agreement with Emil, though death wasn't their final option just yet.

Concealed in unsettling silence looming just inside the mouth of the stables, the heavily wounded vhendo suddenly let loose a paralyzing caw. The roar was even louder than Emil's drakon. Everyone covered their ears and/or instinctually kneeled in defense of the painful noise, which likely loosened some of the rust off the stable's old bones.

Free of harassment or challenge now, bleeding wings and scorched eyes proof of its resolve, the vhendo stalked its tightly huddled quarry as if having learned a secret passed down through the ages to only the most cunning predators. Those now standing before it were already dead. They just didn't know it yet.

"End of the line," said Cirilo.

The dire-wolfhound stood growling between Cirilo and the foreign Urhal soldier.

Shot. Slashed. Mauled. Burned.

It kept coming.

"The hunt's not over yet." Emil readied himself.

Stung with annoying arrows and bolts, it kept coming.

The soldier struggled but, in the end, he dropped his shield. "We can't fight it anymore." He'd been trying to grin and bear it, but his broken arm finally gave way.

Sensing Emil was low on ammo, Cirilo fired another volley at the approaching vhendo but missed. He cursed.

"We have to fight," said Emil.

"No," said Leeann, shaking her head, "we can't."

Everyone paused until Leeann shouted, "Run!"

Conditioned by wrath and bred to serve an insatiable bloodlust, the vhendo chased them deeper into the stables. Exactly what Leeann was hoping it would do. Despite its numerous wounds, it had to go on. Even the most ferocious predator would've conceded the fight because of its wounds long ago. Not the vhendo. It would never stop.

Cirilo bellowed, "It's almost on us!"

Leeann couldn't believe her eyes upon entering the stall where she'd left Ceann and Harold behind. "Where's Khalix?"

Aware she still held Harold's hand as Leeann returned, Ceann, embarrassed for the first time in her life, immediately let go. She grabbed for the lantern

Leeann whipped around in every direction, trying to locate the giant creature which, for all practical reasons, was nowhere to be seen inside the stall.

"We're dead!"

"Shhhh!"

Once the light was in her possession, Ceann quickly snuffed the lantern's wick.

"What happened to the light?" Emil tripped in the darkness as he rushed in.

Cirilo and the dire-wolfhound were next into the stall. The foreign soldier followed.

"No exit." Cirilo wondered about forcing the vhendo through the stall's open doorway.

"I can't see it," said the panicked soldier. "Is it still behind us?"

"What's it waiting for?" Leeann said.

"Ani?" whispered Ceann.

"You okay?" asked Cirilo once he found her in the dark.

Again, Leeann demanded to know, "Where is he?"

Ceann didn't answer. Couldn't. She simply held her sister's hand.

"Who?" asked Emil in the cramped darkness.

"We're trapped!" shouted the soldier.

"Why's it hesitating?" Leeann calculated the odds as her mind raced with fear and anger.

"Hello, everyone," said Harold after tucking the air pistol into his belt.

"Harold Cross?" Emil asked.

"I'm here," he answered as though replying to roll in the old schoolhouse.

"Here it comes!" Emil put the children behind him as best he could.

The soldier bumped something shaggy and large in the dark and jumped to the other side of the stall. "What's that?"

"He's my friend," answered Harold.

"What?" replied the soldier.

"Now!" cried Ceann.

"We're the bait," whispered Leeann.

10

"Do it!"

At her wit's end with Ceann, Leeann did as she was begged and turned the knob of the lantern. The resulting spark ignited the last of the oil soaked through the wick, catching everyone by surprise, including the vhendo.

It was partially across the threshold of the stall. Almost close enough to touch. Beak open, the vhendo's vile tongue and inner mouth dripped long strings of saliva. It was on the verge of slaughtering everyone in the darkness, but then came the light.

Turning from the sudden glare, Ceann noticed Harold in her periphery. It was only a split second but, in that moment, she knew little Harold Cross had changed. A dangerous yet marvelous curiosity now shaped his gaze, toned his features. No longer was Harold dazed or dreamy-looking, the way some children often are. No, it was like he was waiting for something hidden by the chaos. His face was lean. His concentration effortless. He smiled.

Screeching. Stomping. Tattered wings flapping. The vhendo attacked, claws first.

"Protect us, Khalix."

Everyone froze. That's what you do when you're about to die. It can't be helped. The response is automatic in most people, save for Mr. Black or those like him, familiar with facing death on a near constant basis. That wasn't this bunch. Even Cirilo, who'd seen and done his fair share of terrible things offered by the hearts of men, shut his eyes against the inevitable horror. As did the Urhal fighter, for his crimes since marching east from the Scattered Kingdoms paled in comparison to the darkness now sure to devour them.

However, after those first few jarring seconds, savagely torturous moments filled with consuming violence and the ruckus of crashing debris and splintering wood, presumably as the vhendo tore everyone else to pieces in the madness made visible by the flickering lantern light, it dawned on those still standing, still breathing, that something else had happened.

Something wondrous. Something miraculous.

One by one, they each opened their eyes. The stall was now two. The middle wall and some of the ceiling had been ripped down. Hesitancy and bewilderment abounded their faces for, instead of finding everyone else dead and themselves the sole survivor, each person in their own way slowly discovered the vhendo, sprawled out in the far corner of the now massive stall. It was still. Quiet. Slumped on its side, the way a trophy predator might fall when felled by a better hunter.

"By all the Saints," said the soldier, raising his short sword. "What's this now?"

Emil and Cirilo turned and looked at what the soldier pointed at.

Khalix appeared as a semi-translucent bipedal blur, easily twice the size of the vhendo. He crouched over the dead monster, poking and prodding it. Curiouser still, despite the abundant carnage and new damage to the stalls caused by their brutal and quick confrontation, most of his camouflaged features remained untouched by the vhendo's gore.

"He's my friend," answered Harold.

"Did you know about that?" Leeann asked.

"Not exactly," replied Ceann.

Though it was hard for the men to know precisely what they were looking at regardless of the lantern in Ceann's hand, it was abundantly clear the vhendo had been little match for little Harold's friend. As far as they could tell, anyway, given its greater size and assumed strength, and the fact it seemed relatively unscathed by comparison.

"Your friend, Harold?" Emil sheathed his spatha blade and slung the drakon.

"Best friend," replied Harold. "Aren't you?"

Ceann smiled at Harold.

The Urhal soldier lowered his blade and gazed with almost mythical interest at the vhendo's ruined carcass, then at the joined stall's damaged doorway, ceiling, and walls. He wondered how Harold's friend had removed more than half the vhendo's raven-like skull before digging around and prying out most of its insides through its asshole.

Little did they know just how humanlike the vhendo once was. Till now.

As if to assure Cirilo and the rest of their safety now, at least for the moment, the dire-wolfhound began sniffing the dominant creature's massive forepaws and slightly hooked claws. After a moment, she lapped at each of the foot-long talons, for they were heavily coated in the vhendo's heart-blood and gray matter.

"Wait," said Emil, suddenly aware what the she-wolfhound was doing.

"Qwailou," Cirilo winked. "Do I look worried?"

Allowing reality to settle for a moment, accepting Cirilo knew best about the fortitude of a dire-wolfhound's stomach, Emil's face eventually loosened into a less-than-nervous smirk. Everyone ignored the rich black glaze slowly turning various shades of purple as the vile spray and pooling drops coagulated across both them and the stall.

Smiling now, Cirilo asked, "What's his name again?"

"Khalix," answered the girls, almost in unison.

Cirilo knelt beside the dire-wolfhound. "I like it. It's a good name."

After sniffing over Cirilo and the rest, figuring the threat was gone, the great moropod relaxed its posture. Khalix's serpentine bio-defense mechanism naturally disengaged and, just like that, his unique hide returned to the same muddy colors first seen by Leeann and Ceann when it slept on the floor of the previously cramped horse stall.

"It has to be eight at the shoulder," remarked the soldier.

"I don't understand," said Emil, who couldn't stop staring at Khalix.

Unlike the vhendo, the newcomers weren't instinctually scared of Khalix's true form. Not really. As they witnessed the dire-wolfhound continue to nip at the moropod's mostly reptilian tail, the way she might tease another member of her pack, it was more like they were all in awe of Khalix, a natural reaction when in the presence of nature's power, wonder, and authority perfectly combined in physical form.

"I'm sleepy," said Harold, who then passed out in Khalix's giant forearms.

"Harold?" Ceann moved to his side.

Cirilo quickly checked Harold's pulse. "He be okay."

Khalix pawed and cuddled Harold to him as though he were his pup.

After assisting the unconscious boy to a better position across Khalix's great shoulders, Cirilo said to the noticeably anxious creature, "He needs you, big guy."

Khalix responded by rubbing his wet snout and muzzle over Cirilo's face.

"Big dog," said Cirilo.

Ceann, hands softly trembling, wiped tears from her eyes and flush cheeks.

As though he'd a question, Cirilo glanced at the older sister.

"We stick to the plan." Leeann's eye twitched just enough for Cirilo to see.

"It's why Black sent me," added Emil.

"Is the Two Sisters even safe now?" Cirilo asked as he set his final bolt into place.

"How?" Ceann looked from Leeann to the soldier and back.

All eyes turned on the Urhal soldier. A conscripted killer and foreign mercenary working for any one of Pehats Berg's newly exposed enemies: Mr. Halgin, Lord Rohndolphn, or Duke Talhgho. That is before the duke himself was betrayed by the other two conspirators now vying for power and placement as the Sabbat continued to grow and spread its influence across the Scattered Kingdoms.

"Wait?" The soldier dropped his shortsword. "Wait!"

"Nah." Cirilo raised his crossbow, and the hair trigger did the rest.

"No!" Even though he was within arm's reach, Emil wasn't quick enough.

Lifeless, though standing, the Urhal soldier fell, his body as stiff as a freshly cut 2x4.

"You get what you get," whispered Cirilo, curiously inspecting the fresh blood splatter.

"Son of a bitch!"

"I bet he was." Cirilo strolled toward the red stain with his bolt in the center.

Emil suddenly grabbed Cirilo from the back, knocked him down, and took the crossbow.

"You stupid?" shouted Cirilo.

Emil stepped back from Cirilo. "Leeann?"

"What?"

Neither girl looked to Emil as the dead man bled out through the giant hole in his jugular.

"You can't just kill——"

"Can't I? Look around!" Leeann's eyes shone like stones polished by intense heat.

Ceann moved to protest with her sister, but Cirilo waved her to him. This was something Leeann had to do on her own. Also, in his anger, Emil had further injured Cirilo's gut so, though grinning, he truly needed the help now.

"They murdered our parents."

"I know."

Disgusted and confused by the execution, Emil threw the crossbow back to Cirilo.

"You get one." Cirilo's smile was deadly serious.

"Emil, they would've murdered us," said Leeann.

"So, you saw this man kill your parents? This man?"

"Did you hear what I said?"

Emil calmly paced the stall, but after a few strides up and back, he quietly conceded to Leeann's rightful fury born of the madness that'd led them here. Yet, he paused when he looked down at the dead soldier who, despite whatever else he'd done, in the end helped them fight the vhendo.

"Say it?" said Leeann.

"I'm a deputy," said Emil, "sworn to——"

"Your oath means nothing."

"It can't."

Leeann shouted, "They killed your wife!"

"She died protecting you. She died doing her duty."

"You don't get it," said Leeann, her anger and fear smoldering across her tongue.

Cirilo nodded encouragingly to his little sister.

"This is war now," said Leeann, tears falling. The night's weight closed in.

"My sister's right," said Ceann, though she could clearly see how ashamed Emil still felt.

Leeann added, "When this is over, either we're all dead—"

"Or they are."

Ceann didn't blink when Leeann finally broke the lantern on the lone dry patch of stale hay between the dead Urhal soldier and the vhendo's stinking carcass.

11

Light Bringer Rai finally exited the last hallway of the maze-like basement beneath the Mission. His mole torch blazed blue in front of him, scaring away any critters crawling about the cobweb-strewn passages,

Father Rai hated going down there.

This lowest sub-block complex, last used for storage overflow, was first discovered by his mother, Sister Iha, years before Momma Bwulyaa followed her from their squalor in the Five Towns, far, far to the east of the Scattered Kingdoms.

The Light Bringer descended the nearest and largest subterranean stairway. At first, the bifurcated steps appeared to be composed entirely of bedrock and not plaztacrete. In reality, though, it was molded of various alloys, though long since coated in centuries of heavy sediment, creating the illusion of carved stalagmite.

Mr. Black called out, "How are you feeling?" His

voice echoed across the great hold.

Father Rai smiled into the void beyond his mole torch. "Humbled."

As a man of the Ten Pillar Faith, he'd never reflected on the reasons why the ancient citizens of Ellizium would've designed such a metropolitan traffic center more than a mile below ground, nor had he thought about the grand sections of floating steps since retrofitted into a series of loading ramps by Momma Bwulyaa's smugglers.

Nor had Father Rai ever possessed the academic curiosity to properly consider, until now, the many ancient histories intrinsically linked to the Tunnel's existence so far below Pehats Berg, which is exactly where Mr. Black needed him to be because their discussion to come was going to be worse than the headspace tied to the ring that Rai's spiritual recklessness had tricked him into challenging during their recent meeting.

"I have been told the power is not reliable beyond the infirmary."

After a moment, Mr. Black replied, "Is it not?"

"It can be testy."

"Good to know." Mr. Black wondered why the priest purposefully mimicked Tinker's industrial jargon.

Now that Father Rai was clear of the stairs, underneath and opposite where he'd first exited the mission's nearly forgotten storage areas, he could better distinguish Mr. Black's distant form from the greater darkness.

Duster tossed haphazardly to the side, sleeves rolled back, Mr. Black was crouched on the floor, surrounded by all manner of electrical artifice: liquid tape, freeze spray, a tinker's hand-cranked temp sensor, a babbage wave meter, and others.

The rogue's silhouette cast long and tall across this side of the mammoth substation opposite the stairway, thanks to the acetylene cutter Momma scrounged up for him earlier.

The blowtorch had likely gone missing thanks to one of her crew during a recent salvage operation into the catacombs. Proper tools such as these weren't always easy to come by. Words, if not worse, would most certainly be had if Momma Bwulyaa ever discovered the thoughtless scrapper who *accidentally* left it behind.

Never coincidence or convenience, thought Mr. Black.

Father Rai patted his horse. "I know Momma wishes her mules were more like you."

It was true. The mare seemed oddly at ease underground.

As with Black, she ignored the priest while finishing off the handful of brown apples left for her in a basket on the docking side of what was once a grand concourse stretching several hundred meters in every direction. The flat sprawl was made up of rows upon rows of abandoned subterranean tracks and gritty, filth-covered security lines below, many of which were hidden by gentle streams or sludge washouts.

"I have not been down here in a long time," said the priest.

"Why's that?"

"My mother loved to come here."

"Didn't you when you were a child?"

Not stopping to reply, Mr. Black continued to heat

and chip away at the hardened algae and debris coating encasing a covert access panel beneath what was once a pristinely polished tile floor.

The Light Bringer whispered, "When I became a man, I discarded childish things."

After glancing over the amassed gear lying about Mr. Black's work area—the bag laden with unknown wares, weapons, and other smuggled contraband, all gifted by Momma Bwulyaa, of course—the Light Bringer then offered the silver relic from his pocket. He held out the ring between his fingers with a bit of his greca, so not to touch the heirloom again.

In the combined blue light of his mole torch and the paler, almost cyan light of Mr. Black's cutter, Father Rai's eyes flashed with terrible emptiness and other-worldly confusion. It was only momentary but, as he looked through the ring, Eyoh's Grace began to fill his heart and soul once more.

"Be careful, priest."

"I've so many questions."

Black dialed back the cutter. The tool's white-blue flame became orange and yellow again. "Sorrow is often the gift of true wisdom."

Father Rai smirked at the reworded Pillar text. "But you wear it as a suit of armor?"

"Until I've got eyes in the back of my head—"

With his final hammer strike, the panel retracted.

"Touché," said Father Rai.

Mr. Black undid the vestment of Saint Ingmar from his sword hilt.

"Ah, yes," said Father Rai. "You could keep it?"

"No more need for precaution." Mr. Black extended his hand.

"As you wish."

With Rai's property returned, the Agent of the Isles licked his ring finger before forcing the tarnished band over the knuckle on his left hand, stopping just before his finger-free glove began. He then turned the ring three times about the knuckle, flexing and relaxing his hand, reacquainting himself with it.

"Would it have mattered if I died?"

Mr. Black only momentarily considered the question and didn't answer. He wasn't sure when the last time was he'd calculated the value of one life over another. Consequently, his inability to recall the moment proved his point.

He chuckled to himself, then spat a bit of loose floating grit onto the stone floor.

Father Rai, Hospitaler of Saint Ingmar, shook his head.

Of course, it was a silly question because, in Mr. Black's line of work, life and death and even truth itself only ever mattered on a sliding scale.

"That's not what you came here to ask me, though."

Father Rai meant to speak, he even stepped forward, but Mr. Black had already moved on. He located and disarmed the square keyblock inside the panel, which is all he'd thought about since the fat man informed on the Sabbat.

Mr. Halgin had divulged not only Lord Rohndolphn's plan to betray and murder Duke Talhgho for his own ends within the cult's hierarchy, but also how

Princess Patrycja Urhal, otherwise presumed deceased, had returned to the land of the living, traveling far from her family crypt in the east without fear of the sun.

And all of it, everything, was somehow intertwined in the schemes of Lady Mina Genza, as well as other forces of the False King, whose terrible influence already lay heavily upon the Scattered Kingdoms.

Always shadows, always threads of the same spiral.

Black lifted the corded keyblock out from the secret panel and set it beside him on the stone floor.

Made of what some might consider wonders in this part of the world, a pliable waxlicon and highly sensitive, though partially decayed, bioplazta sheeting, the strange Areht device appeared to still be functional despite its age and disuse.

Father Rai finally asked, "Why are you really here?"

The man in black replied with a single word, "*Ishtar-garï.*"

"Cannibals?"

"Often."

"Carrion?" said Father Rai, roughly retranslating the vulgarity.

Mr. Black thought to elaborate on the country priest's twice-interpreted version of the Nor Folk's uniquely elemental-based language, as divined from the wilderness' first children but, instead, said, "In between."

"What do you mean?"

"Blood in. Blood out," whispered Mr. Black.

"Here?"

Sensing a soft echo in his scabbard, Mr. Black nodded.

"Now?"

The Agent of the Isles made a fist with his left hand in the center of the keyblock. It reacted almost immediately.

Mind racing, panicking, Father Rai watched a yellow beam of light appear at the bottom of the keyblock. It rose slowly and turned vertical, as if Mr. Black's fist provoked further study and analysis.

"War?"

Though used to blood and death, Father Rai had never been within leagues of an actual military conflict. And the difference mattered, for he knew what kind of man he was.

Mr. Black grinned, but it wasn't a humorous grin, more like the expression of a man preparing for something already on its way. Inevitable. Certain. Pain? Yes, more pain. Much more. Then he winked, his grin widening as a sensor of some kind was triggered now that his ring was finally identified by the device.

Thoughts spinning—what could be worse than town criers summoning oaths and banners, women and children resigned to fend for themselves when honor and valor failed against iron and blood—Father Rai stepped back.

The young priest hoped to meet the man in black's eyes and discover some silver lining to this crimson-fueled mystery, the idea of war and death twisted to the point it was the least of their worries. Too bad the Horran's impenetrable stoicism and deepest cynicisms were again preoccupied with cloture beneath his tricorn.

"Mel?"

"What did you say?" Rai asked.

Mr. Black shook his head, realizing he'd whispered the quiet part aloud.

The silence returned without explanation, and only made the priest's thoughts trip into darker realms thick with fear and betrayal beyond the rise of wicked and gluttonous men and the power they sought to dominate each other with. Never mind such efforts were rarely if ever their own. In reality, the price for flesh and mashing teeth has always ever been levied by those under the protection of the lord's patronage.

And that's when it happened to Rai again, but without touching the ring this time.

Between that often misshapen yet sublime codependency tricked upon the mortal masses, where Father Rai's mind was rare to wander because of his strict faith in the Saints and their teachings through the Ten Pillars, he found himself once more reliving some ancient journey to a place outside the Spiral, where the faces in shadow and shadows with faces would forever haunt the man in black, the lone ranger so far from his home.

"The Beasts from Beyond the Black?"

Mr. Black clarified, "Vhendo."

The Light Bringer's pious and somatic gestures slowly lost their utility.

Such power in a single word, thought the man in black.

A knot formed in the pit of Father Rai's stomach as he thought he heard something moving overhead, skittering and scratching among the stalactites and natural outcroppings along the ancient metro station's vast dome ceiling.

"You must name them," said the man in black. It was one of the few lessons taught by the Eyldar, which Mr. Black wished they'd not forgotten.

After a time working the ring back and forth into the lock's jellylike surface, a disjointed emergency pathway appeared, then flickered along the tiled floor. From the tubes of light that didn't instantly burst or burnout, a trail formed. It led off halfway across the concourse, in the direction of the Tunnel.

"Tell me what's happening, Horran."

Hoisting the bag of tools over his shoulder, Mr. Black laughed to himself.

"I know what you are."

Your mother taught you well.

Father Rai pleaded, "Tell me, so I might save them."

"All of them?" Mr. Black asked, tossing his coat to the priest.

Catching the modified winter duster, Father Rai answered, "As many as I can."

"That's the thing, priest."

"What?"

"No one can really save anyone but themselves."

"Wait."

Nervous, limbs twitching with biting caution and confusion, Father Rai trailed Mr. Black along the winking pathway. It eventually stopped before a mammoth column, one of a handful the priest had seen up close while working in the catacombs beneath the Mission, some of the largest support edifices he'd laid eyes on. Mr. Black, on the other hand, showed no unique interest in the column's base cap, which was nearly

100sf in diameter.

"Surely, we can—"

"Seal the windows and doors?"

Father Rai looked toward the ceiling, his prayers seeking refuge in the shadows.

Mr. Black continued, "Bring the pigs and sheep inside?"

Bringer Rai felt sweat trickle down the base of his neck as the skittering and scratching sounds from somewhere above again shifted their emanation point, then faded. They didn't vanish but merged with the shadow, into the deep dark, and there they remained. Watching them. Whatever they were, they were waiting for something, and that made the unknown evermore frightening to the priest.

"It isn't winter that's coming."

"What then?"

Dropping the bag at his feet, raising his left fist, and pointing the ring at the column, Mr. Black looked into and through Rai's eyes and said, "It's ruin."

Sections of the column moved, realigned, coordinating with Mr. Black's outstretched fist. As he watched, Father Rai found himself again grappling with uncertainty and tempered hostility towards the past. The myths and legends. A world once wholly dominated by the Arehthood.

Ruin? The word rolled over and back in Father Rai's mind. He covered his mouth and nose as billowing dust and ancient gas burst from the breach around the no-longer-secret façade. He squinted through the cloud as plates and other pieces decoupled from the column's exterior shell.

About the size of a grand double door, the covert barrier shielding the port finally separated from the mass of stone entirely, compelled by the man in black's manipulation of the ring's unique neural enhancements. Its ability allowed the ring bearer to systematically and virally influence the hold's internal mechanisms and intelligent protocols.

What some Tinkers might call, "The Ol' Wink'n Nod."

"By all the Saints," said the priest.

Concentrating on his work, Mr. Black didn't respond.

"What are you doing?"

Mr. Black wasn't a hundred percent sure what he was doing, so he didn't reply. He was interested in the network devices governing the underground utilities flowing through the hollowed-out middle of this enormous engineering column. It was just one of many points he'd need to access, but only if this central H.U.B still had the juice.

Once the actuators finished sliding the disconnected block-faces to either side of the large opening, Mr. Black asked Father Rai to raise his torch.

"What is it?" Rai asked.

Stepping into the oversized maintenance box, Mr. Black called for his bag of borrowed scrapper tools. Father Rai handed it to him. The priest watched and listened as the self-muttering man in black hunted for the manual override. It was hidden somewhere in the walls, behind the vacuum tubes, coils, belts, gear chains, rods, fuse bulbs, and other strange contrivances, essentially the guts of the column, he'd exposed.

After tearing into it for a few minutes, Mr. Black's ring finally divined the small handle. It could just barely be seen, thanks to the priest's mole torch, behind a bundle of orange wires. Once disengaged, the Agent of the Isles unlocked the service hatch at the top of the box, releasing an Arehthood device roughly two-thirds the size of the original barrier.

"You are no warlock?" asked Father Rai, amazed by the assassin's legerdemain.

"Practical works only." Mr. Black's veiled mirth echoed upward through the work shaft.

As one large, single contraption, the H.U.B. unit effortlessly descended into the maintenance box, then slowly ejected itself outward from the column. Once free of the barrier, the released apparatus repositioned sections of itself, powered by compressed air and stored energies, readying for operational systems check.

Father Rai watched the machine's stiff, almost painful motions and rigid component assembly with suspicious fascination. He was amazed how its self-corrections and articulations appeared so humanlike, particularly the actions one might perform when stretching after being cramped for so long in place. Such personified mimicry was something the priest had never seen in any machine before. This was the most advanced mechanoid anyone in his order had ever been close enough to touch.

The Light Bringer couldn't help himself. "How did you do this?"

Instead of indulging the priest's curiosity, though, Mr. Black rested on the foldout stool mounted to the workstation's underside. It was cold and small. He felt strange, almost out of body, sitting now where in the past he would've stood, keeping watch. Something in the back of his mind then made his eyes dart over his shoulder.

"Are you all right?" asked Father Rai.

Brushing off the Light Bringer's concern, Mr. Black began his work, flipping switches, pressing buttons, turning dials, resetting diodes, and banging on a myriad of essential Babbage gizmos.

"Ruin." The hushed letters scratched over the priest's teeth. The word simply wouldn't retreat from the tip of his tongue or the foreground of his thoughts. Like a bell rung in the dark above uncertain depths, the ripple would never recede while the tiresome arc would slowly meld into the connection he unconsciously searched for. For as with all things, it was only a matter of time.

An image blinked into existence on the H.U.B.'s screen.

"What happened?" Rai asked.

The glow, slow to rise and spread, then cleared away the fuzz and static previously dominating the five green glass terminals mounted with heavy bolts over the H.U.B's workstation.

"Thank the wyrd," said Mr. Black as he punched the hard metal keys.

"What now?"

"I'm hailing a shuttle." From the screen, Black could see the nearest one was more like a train with over twenty passenger cars. He kept looking.

Father Rai winced at the Areht terms.

"The locomotives don't work?"

Again, Mr. Black questioned the priest's need to affect a Tinker's vernacular.

Also, had the man in black meant a steam or coal-powered train—as rare as they'd become in some parts of the world—he would've said so. No point in correcting Rai, though.

Black pushed a few more buttons, causing one of the otherwise-forgotten rails below the concourse to hum. The electric tremor created random popping and crackling bursts of atmospheric static along the heavy track.

The smell of burnt ions filled the air.

Though his gaze remained firm, a slight repose outlined Mr. Black's jaw.

"Not in a century—"

Once the visible route was fully magnetized, anything metal near the line was expelled with incredible force. The resulting power surge sent debris ricocheting across the stone walls of the concourse, so much so the mare, otherwise calm as a statue, kicked its hind legs, snorting loudly.

Father Rai was also caught off guard by the discharge.

"The tube seems to be working fine," said Mr. Black.

The embarrassed priest now glanced over the alien screens as if to understand his error. Certainly, he'd no idea what he was looking for; nevertheless, he demanded involvement to dilute his awkwardness and startled demeanor, which wasn't a great idea. The green symbols combined with the zooming in and out of various lighter green frames in reaction to Mr. Black's dialing, and his constant clicking of keys just made the priest nauseous.

"Gotcha," said Mr. Black. Then he chose a shuttle from the detailed list of conveyances and hailed it.

Half the size of the first maglev Mr. Black discovered in the system's garage bank, it was still much larger than a shuttle. As a bonus, according to its specs, it maxed out at nearly five hundred kilometers per hour, depending on certain variables and track conditions.

However, with such speed available to him now versus traveling the hundred plus miles on horseback, the potential fluctuations in arrival time almost didn't matter. Because, though it would be close, thanks to the tunnel, Mr. Black would make Wychstone before sunrise.

It is still possible to salvage this.

"I know," Mr. Black answered.

Father Rai looked curious as he asked, "Who are you talking to?"

Mr. Black squinted and rubbed his eyes. She was getting louder.

"Who're—"

"It's time for you to leave now."

12

Father Rai was in mid-protest when he noticed a peculiar din in the cavern his ears hadn't picked up earlier and which his mind couldn't let go of. It was almost like the wafting echoes were partly shambling out from the tunnel.

He listened as the shambling slowly became a crawling along the walls, then a slithering through the stone and tiles beneath his feet. The very air became tense with secret whispers and chilling sharpness the more Father Rai focused on the black.

The Light Bringer's fear further contorted the void, reimagining it into something truly separate from the Light of Heven. An ancient portal between worlds, or perhaps one of the very rifts, in reality, the Areht once claimed to travel. Either way, he dared not raise the mole torch toward the tunnel again for fear he'd see something hungry for blood stalking the improbable shadows of other worlds.

Mr. Black again paused to focus on a particular sequence of jade symbols blinking through the layered screen burn. Something was wrong, but he couldn't say what. It didn't help that some of the letters and numbers were beginning to bleed together in the console, making it hard to accurately distinguish the symbols.

Too late now, thought Mr. Black as he monitored the approaching shuttle.

Father Rai toyed with the lacquered rope about his waist.

"Priest?" said Mr. Black, the ring signaling to him the Light Bringer's supernatural intent.

Petition ignored, goosebumps nipping across his neck, the priest's lips moved through the Arel with consecrated precision.

Eyes closed, reinvigorated by the prayer words of his calling, the priest summoned a great spiritual protection, a marrow-deep shielding power against the violent devastation left in the Horran's wake returned to Father Rai's exposed thoughts.

The conflicting resonance fell hard across the priest's senses, doubling its power from the root-word the Light Bringer's unconscious mind couldn't detangle itself from. And once fully amassed in his mind, the gritty, icy spray crashed over him, swallowing places he knew, people and families he'd taken care of and known his entire life.

His life and Black's past became a torrent of horrors.

Eventually, husks and stained fissures were all that survived of the land.

You're never the same, thought Mr. Black.

"The World...of Ruin."

"What was that?" Mr. Black asked, finally stopping his work.

"Cardinal Mandrake's vision." The ancient prophet's name skipped from Rai's tongue like a stone thrown by a child over a still pond. Dogmatic drivers long beaten into Bringer Rai's mind and soul caused the knee-jerk reaction, the mental association, for whenever he needed to visualize one of the most famous converts and divine prophets of the Pillar Faith, the priest only ever thought of the enormous painting in the Citadel.

This was by design, of course, because one of the articles of faith performed by every parishioner across the globe was ensuring all anti-Pillarite depictions or unnatural shadowscreens were removed from public circulation and destroyed.

Much blood had been spilt in this generational endeavor, culminating in the final years of the Inquisition some four hundred years ago.

Thus, the world turned, and history was remade to suit the present. As such, the Citadel's most sacrosanct possession were the largest and most exhaustively accurate, multidiscipline portrayals of Cardinal Mandrake.

The relief's background was captured in charcoal and outlined in ink before the Cardinal's two hundred and ninety-sixth birthday, which also coincided with the birth of his seven hundred and fifty-fourth great-great-grand-daughter.

Central to Pillar doctrine, the three-dimensional work solidified and celebrated the end of the Ill Fire Age, a legendary time before history was young, a period still remembered across the world today in various, yet largely subtle, ways because of the mythologized Eldritch Wars that nearly destroyed the splendor left to Man's charge by Eyoh, following the Eyldeyryien's total abnegation of humanity.

"What do you see now?" Mr. Black asked, for the young Light Bringer's face had softened.

Despite the indoctrinated image's ancestral weight heavy upon Father Rai's mind and heart as he stood motionless beside the assassin, the priest found he'd been transported. Not in body, but through his awareness, as carried on the back of the Horran's shared yet shattered impressions, to El'shwn: Capital of the Silver Isles, Realm of the Seven Cities, home of the Senate and the Arehthood's mighty spire of reason and power.

Beside Mr. Black, in one of the nine gardens somewhere beneath the Silver Tower, in this separated time so long ago now swirling and whirling in the young priest's mind, sat a young woman in a distressed white-iron chair.

I wonder if she'll say anything to you…

Father Rai could almost feel the sunshine as he gazed upon her.

In the young woman's powdery hands atop her properly crossed knees, over her formal Sasahtan with perfect pleats and ageless resiliency, rested a book, the cover of which was adorned with a colorful shadowscreen image of the Grand Areht, the Arch Majistor himself, Rowan Liam Mandrake.

It was odd, though, because Father Rai now found the wraparound book-jacket's photocell portrait of the Cardinal—far removed from the pontifical identity he was otherwise familiar with to be sure—much less enthralling than the young woman's unique esper.

Like most Light Bringers, he'd never seen the glow, yet he knew what it was and why he was seeing it.

For how Mr. Black's ring had transported his mind from outside the tunnel to the Where and When he now saw before him, a similar process was affecting the Areht in this time outside his own. The young woman's body was there in the garden and sunshine, but her mind was elsewhere, which the priest could plainly see due to the visual energy escaping her form.

On the outside, her plainness beguiled her standard Areht uniform, while her sullen features and faded chestnut hair teased an organic fragility. And all the tiny distractions and dead-ends hinted at internal suffering and a weakened mortality, which only the cleverest might ever conclude from her otherwise noble-born appearance. All of it might've fooled others, but not this Light Bringer of Saint Ingmar.

Father Rai knew better because Mr. Black knew better.

Without seeing it, Rai felt it. He remembered it because the image was now his own. Above the young Areht's brow, partially hidden beneath the hood of her uniform, rested a Halo, and such a circlet could mean only one thing.

In that moment, whatever was happening between the two of them (three if one counted the now intruding Light Bringer) in the garden's soft morning haze was being experienced simultaneously by one or many of the Gan, those who reign supreme within the highest ranks of the Arehthood's most erudite masters.

The man in black loved his sister, more than anyone else in the world.

Paused by this revelation, Father Rai now humbled himself in the light of his mole torch. "I'm sorry for your loss."

There were so many losses, too many to count, yet the man in black could easily narrow down a handful of instances, the wheres and whens the ring had likely allowed the Light Bringer to stray. Because, of course, it did. It always acted in line with his goals. It was always party to his plans, even if he didn't create the opportunity for angles beforehand. It didn't matter. She was always with him. Both sanity and madness. Strength and weakness.

"It was a long time ago," said Mr. Black.

"How did the Tribu die?"

"On her feet."

Bringer Rai let that sink in for a moment. "A noble end."

"So I was told," said Mr. Black.

Confident this wasn't an area the assassin wished to expand upon and most thankful for the opportunity to create a better closeness between them through such an unlikely divination, Father Rai finished their moment of commonality with a respectful nod.

Mr. Black winked at the now-enlightened Light Bringer, as a part of himself secretly subdued the almost berserker-like anger bound within the scabbard at his hip. Then he typed vigorously on the workstation's keys.

"What was her na—"

Biting his tongue, Father Rai stepped forward.

Mr. Black's incessant typing became thunderous. The Horran's fingers flew. No longer did he hunt complex or incomplete information within the site's programming or manipulating power flow from its few remaining storage banks housed in similar arrayment towards a final series of goals yet unknown to the priest. No, this was different. That, he'd done this before. Many times, in fact, for the Light Bringer recognized a bit of his own rote skillset in Mr. Black's trained actions.

Then, in a single black-and-white drop-down sub screen, separated from the facility and its primary functions, those boxes still displayed in other active screens within the H.U.B.'s monitors, Mr. Black appeared to have made an outside connection far beyond the boundaries of this subterranean utility complex. Through this private portal, he composed a letter of sorts.

The Light Bringer had never used any such device before to collect his thoughts or to communicate across vast distances, such was a matter of his faith and personal sacrifice. Nevertheless, he recognized the universal compositional structure as Mr. Black drilled through each keystroke without errors.

Between mission notes and objective specifics branched out from his initial target, Mr. Black singled out various details and lists within the letter. Each arranged with dates and times so a pattern would take shape for whoever the reader was. Outcomes were highlighted, including collateral effects and blowback probabilities related to his original mission to execute Lady Mina Genza, senior Sabbat Cult member in Collezia.

All of it was laid bare for the totality of the reader

to absorb, process, and react accordingly.

"Senator Taroun Grace?"

Mr. Black didn't answer or explain the classified document, nor did his fingers slow.

"What is this?" If the Light Bringer had known or thought to ask of the senator's politics, he might've reconsidered his tone, which was heavily inspired by a fortuitous presumption on the priest's part.

"Damnit," muttered Mr. Black through clenched teeth.

Again, the shuttle deviated from the programed route as seen on the map Black had expanded for easier reading. Scratching his beard, Mr. Black hoped this wouldn't affect the internal clock he'd set for himself.

Time...always against me.

Clicking through the screens, Mr. Black figured something, or someone, had compromised the rails again somewhere along what was once known as the Argyle Line. There was no telling when or why the areas broke down, whether it was natural or something more provoc-ative. It was of little consequence in the end, though, for the network had dozens of alternate lines and reroute points along the once vibrant metro grid, which the system was already using now to modify and complete its travel path.

"What are you doing?" Father Rai asked, realizing his torch would soon run out of fuel.

Glancing back to his priority screen, Mr. Black answered flatly, "Making my report."

Bringer Rai held his tongue when he saw new names bracketed off within the black-and-white window: Rhys,

Lidweina, Phernand, Eramis, and Ardose. Each person was either to receive this digital memo directly about the Sabbat's activity between Collezia and the Scattered Kingdoms or learn resulting orders following Senator Grace's reading of the man in black's secret message.

"You are alerting the Areht?"

Mr. Black said nothing.

The unique soft blue of the mole torch sputtered out, becoming a glaring rich orange and yellow blade. Shielding his eyes, Father Rai wondered if this Senator of the Isles had a cabal of his own. Rogue Horrans doing missions outside the full knowledge of the Senate, as well as the Arehthood?

If they were like the man in black, the priest could trust none of the identifiers were actual names. More likely, they were professional monikers given or gained from years of service to the Areht or their masters, the Gan.

Father Rai continued, "That will bring them here?"

"An Ak'kadre was coming one way or another," said Black as he quickly reached out and snuffed the torch with the palm of his gloved hand.

Cast in the green glow of the H.U.B., Father Rai almost balked at how many Areht that could mean. "Why?"

Mr. Black's deadeye glare silently decried how woefully over his head the young Light Bringer was. He'd no idea what forces would soon befall the Scattered Kingdoms, the many hands and claws soon to reach for the yoke and whips that have forever kept this broken nation together. He scoffed at Rai's painful ignorance, saying nothing of what Pehats Berg would resemble once the dust settled. If it survived at all.

"You've proof?" asked Father Rai, venturing deeper into the yet encrypted communiqué.

Seeing fear and not anger in Rai's expression, Mr. Black replied, "I've seen the bloodlines."

"Genesis?" The young Light Bringer couldn't believe he said it.

"I know their names."

Mr. Black recognized a subconscious change in the priest's pantomimes then.

Father Rai wasn't struck with a sense of religious fulfillment, a logical prediction based on the man in black's forthright assertion about the documented truth asleep in ancient blood. No, it was more like he'd heard someone else speaking, someone not Mr. Black, saying the very same phrase but in a different situation. The two moments combined into a unique form of déjà vu, which almost caused his mind to slide back in time again.

Watching this in real time, the Horran knew Father Rai had gleaned more from his memories in the garden beneath the Silver Tower than he'd intended to share. Especially with anyone outside a few choice friends and allies to the cause.

Such a prospect, the lapse in his mental defenses, endangered more than just a small sense of Mr. Black's privacy. If the priest ever fully learned what Mr. Black discovered concerning the fate of his beloved sister and Tribu of the Gan so early into her fealty to the Areht-hood that crisp autumn morning.

"The prophecy, it's real then?"

"Enough for the Enemy to tip its hand," said Black, paraphrasing his old friend James Dun.

The Light Bringer appeared dumbfounded as the enormity of the revelation confronted him.

"Breathe," said the Agent of the Isles.

Father Rai nodded. His pulse calmed, though his brow remained wet.

Mr. Black recouped his duster and stashed it under one of the saddle's leather straps, then prepped the mare for fast and violent travel. He stowed weapons and related items about the horn and packs, as well as on his own person.

Momma Bwulyaa had been most kind to part with a plethora of useful accoutrements and affectations: various explosives, a few special flares, three primed blasters and one repeating wheelblaster, all of which now crisscrossed Mr. Black's body in a bandolier-type harness.

She'd also given him one pneumatic vambrace punchdagger, which he'd already strapped into place on his left forearm, a pair of darū trencher goggles with complementary ear plugs and, finally, a personal gift from the gangster queen herself—a rechargeable CO_2 grapple gun with more than fifty feet of triple braided, silica blended noba spider silk. The rogue had already snapped the handheld tool into the tackle strap above his left shoulder harness.

Bringer Rai felt terrible shame as the assassin made a final pass over his gear, specifically the bow and partially empty quiver, which he might need on his stealthy assault of Wychstone Manor.

Watching Mr. Black's steady composure, the priest's

anxiety and timidity almost got the better of him because, in those moments swirling with danger and darkness more than two thousand years in the making, he almost blamed the assassin for the enormous evils now beset-ting them on all sides.

Mr. Black whistled to the mare, thumb and middle finger just grazing his lips. Thankfully, this was a trick the previous owner had properly trained her to respond to. Mr. Black smiled. His old gambling buddy James Dun always swore how horse whispering and similar glamours first originated in the Borderlands, a gift from before the Old Ones.

Quietly stung by his reflexive, almost instinctual need to condemn the Horran for this day of days his faith was meant to prepare him for, the young priest felt weakness and confusion. He'd never felt lower in his life.

The guilt was shameful, and what made it worse, the priest's Pillar Faith had truly been shaken and changed by the Horran's command of the situation, which by rite and virtue, should've been addressed by his own author-ity, not an extension of the Arehthood. Except, the Light Bringer wasn't ready for this.

None of them were. Not for what was coming.

A small, unnatural light appeared at the far end of the concourse.

"Here we are," said Mr. Black of the approaching shuttle.

Slowly, the whole inner mouth of the Tunnel became brighter and clearer. Scaly and hairy things searched for cover anywhere they could find protection along the once brightly colored metro's smooth surfaces. Metallic sounds filled the cavern as sparks dashed over the tracks when the maglev shuttle's undercarriage dipped too low to the rail it was supposed to fully hover over.

As the shuttle swayed and dipped due to worn portions of the rail's connectivity, causing the whole contraption to somewhat slither like a snake instead of glide like a bird, its headlamps shone even wider and deeper into the greater hold now.

Mr. Black looked to the ceiling, now two-thirds visible, and grinned.

Noting the strange joy in Mr. Black's eyes, the priest followed his curious gaze and saw what had skittered about the dome of the subterranean commuter junction earlier.

At first glance, Father Rai assumed it was vhendo but, in fact, it was the youngest unofficial resident of the catacombs beneath Pehats Berg. At least for a handful of years, given its small size. Moreover, it was the true culprit behind the taunting sounds meant to scare trespassers away from its nest.

"Where's mommy?" Mr. Black asked the stony wall crawler.

The inverted childlike creature with its soft wings, splotchy gray skin, and matching stone-like horns, crawled back toward a particularly narrow outcropping, what could only be a secret access tunnel leading to the heart of the brood.

When the young gargoyle had gone, darkness returned, Father Rai asked, "Will she attack?"

Settling into the saddle, Mr. Black answered, "Not me."

Though he'd never seen one before, Father Rai swallowed hard, because it was well known among the ranks of the Faithful that once, long ago, gargoyles were the servants, protectors, and even spies of the Areht. Before Horran, before Tark Units and other M-noids, it was the gargoyle that often plagued the Pillar's servants.

"Don't be scared," said Mr. Black, adjusting his goggles and earbuds.

"Easy for you to say."

"True."

The priest knew how the flying dogs were often recorded as gorging on the Faithful. At least, that's how they were depicted during the Crusades, when impolite rumors suggesting gargoyles were in fact once kin of the duhrgan people were still spoken in topical conversation, whenever the Faithful discussed the complete conversion of humanity's noble cousins, strategizing how they'd kneel before the Ten Pillars before the end.

Mr. Black then added, "She'd make a quick snack out of you."

"Thanks." The priest glanced about, guessing where she'd ambush from.

"Relax," said Mr. Black as the maglev settled into the station platform and its superconductors powered down.

Each coach, once slick and glossy, now coated in layers of hardened filth, came to rest on the somewhat jerky hydraulic bracing bumpers, which automatically rose from the floor to gently support the train as it came to a stop.

A pop of static and garbled voices echoed briefly across the concourse.

"What's that now?"

Ignoring the priest's question, Mr. Black said, "She'll have a taste for something else soon enough."

"Eyoh, help us." Father Rai could now see what Mr. Black had long guessed. There were already passengers aboard the maglev, not including the feral stowaways biting and clawing atop the roof of the engine car. A few other vile-looking horrors climbed horizontally along the coach's ancient shell of metal and glass, their piercing talons and fangs easily maintaining enough grip to support their fast-moving weight.

Pin teased from high in the saddle, Mr. Black muttered softly, "So it begins."

"What should I do?"

Bursting through one of the passenger doorways came a mass of oily filth dragged from the ruins of many-legged nightmares.

The alpha wasn't the largest Beast from Beyond the Black among the subterranean throng frothing at the mouth of the tunnel. Still, the grotesque, rat-like obscenity, which appeared mostly human below its naked torso, wasn't exactly small either. Nearly as large as Mr. Black's mare, the demonically aggressive vhendo was covered in bristling chitin protrusions from its exposed frontal brainpan to its pincered tusks, and all the way down to the tip of its gnarled tail, which flashed like a scythe some ten feet behind it.

"What do I do?"

"Run," said Mr. Black.

The once human monstrosities snarled and shrieked. The alpha opened its gooey maw, displaying dozens of frightening incisors and bone-crushing molars. Then it howled, a screeching, wailing bark meant to summon the remainder of its scouts still somewhere behind the maglev, in the thick darkness beyond the Tunnel.

"I'll find Momma," shouted Father Rai.

Trencher goggles down, Mr. Black barely whispered his reply. "You do that."

"I'll save as many as I can!"

As the Light Bringer ran frantically to the stairway leading back up to the mission's sub-basement, Mr. Black pulled the pin. However, before the assassin could release the trigger and throw the audiokinetic explosive, a different yet equally overprotective mother came to his aid from the darkness above.

Daunting wings curled and closed behind her pitted, rocky shoulders. The ferocious female gargoyle settled into her prey, pressing the alpha beneath her petrified talons and claws the way a golden owl might after surveying a savory rat it'd long been tracking from its domain in the sky.

The alpha, though crunched and scrambling for purchase, wasn't bested yet.

Momentarily pinned, her claws digging in, the alpha slashed the gargoyle's backside and tore at her left wing with its tail. True, only a few lacerations left more than flaked ridges along her flank but, of those strikes that pierced her craggy hide, they drew rich, red blood.

The matron hissed and growled at the pain, roaring only when the tip of the alpha's tail hit bone.

The gargoyle endured several of these strikes while fighting off other attackers, till she finally had enough of the darting scorpion stinger that continued to find chinks in her armor. So, she ripped it in half.

The alpha cried and spasmed, whining for escape.

The gargoyle turned atop her prey, finishing the infectious predator with a single, spine-crunching bite to the back of its neck and throat.

Not to be upstaged by a former ally of the trade, whose very reappearance and audible dominance seemed to have triggered some evolutionary coherence in the remaining vhendo, Mr. Black threw the thunderstick into the Tunnel.

He laid low across the mare's shoulders as the intensity of the raw light, combined with the concussive explosion amplified by the cavern, was so searingly intense all the vhendo were momentarily stopped in their tracks.

A dozen of the Beast from Beyond the Black took immediate shelter from the burning light, clawing and biting at each other to get clear while many more were briefly crippled in place as they attempted to relieve their burning eyes and ears or whatever sensory tools had replaced the bits and pieces that might've once been human organs.

With perhaps a minute or two gained, Mr. Black quickly drew the twin-barreled powder blaster from the holster nearest his trigger finger.

Crack!

The packed shot struck a vhendo, the third to exit the same coach the alpha had emerged from moments ago, square in its hairy thorax. Mr. Black cursed, blaming his poor kill-shot on the bulky trencher goggles and the vhendo's hybrid exoskeleton. Such is the luxury of hindsight. Even so, the smoking wound staggered the beast, quickly wooing it into a necessary crouching posture as purplish-black blood pooled about its hindlimbs.

Crack!

A second shot from the heavy sidearm sealed the vhendo's fate, thus making it easier for the once-back-woods farm horse to simply trample the obstructing amalgam of mammal and insect as they boarded the maglev's passenger car.

Of course, it didn't hurt that Mr. Black already whispered words of encouragement into her ears, seconds before throwing the thunderstick and spurring her into action, dual efforts delivering them to safety, away from the evil and violence soon to flood the mouth of the Tunnel and up through the Mission, then out to greet the unsuspecting citizens of Pehats Berg's East Gate and Labor's Ro district.

Not all battle plans pan out, little brother.

"I know," said Mr. Black, his bone-grinding exhaustion rearing its ugly head again. His boots felt heavy, his fingers and joints sore. Thoughts drifted out of time and place, between bloody memories and cold delusions.

That is why we train for every contingency.

"I remember," said Mr. Black, the image of his sister fading into the back, beyond the pain.

The automatic doors chimed, signaling the shuttle was ready to leave the concourse and make haste to the underground station nearest Wychstone Manor.

That's when Mr. Black saw the gargoyle wade in and splash among the recovering vhendo.

Bigger than a large man, her body a mix of stone

and coarse flesh, she challenged many of the vhendo all at once with auspicious confidence. Using only her claws, teeth, and the impressive strength of her tail, she twisted, maimed, contained, and killed as many of the thrashing Beasts from Beyond the Dark she could.

What really aided her in this particularly unfair fight, despite the odds against her, was her incredible resistance to the effects of the bomb, both the light and the concussive shockwave. Elemental attributes, so it's been said, that related to the creation of her specialized species long ago.

It wouldn't be nearly enough to survive them, though, not with vhendo still violently clambering through from the forgotten bowls of the metro. The old female instinctually recognized what was coming from the heart of the catacombs, and with a single beat of her thirty-foot wingspan, she took to the air, escaping even the threats capable of leaping a dozen or more feet after her as they tried to snag and bite her forked tail.

"Nicely done, ol' girl," said Mr. Black.

Like a metal monster prodded to move, the fourteen subway coaches and two synchronized engine cars quietly pulled out from the docking station. The initial diesel ignition turned over all power to the superconductors.

As expected, following the shuttle's smoky discharge from beneath the engine cars, the vhendo maintained their primary interest on the fearless gargoyle flying and swooping above the fray instead of on Mr. Black.

"But your duty's not done yet." For that, the man in black felt sorry.

Mr. Black, Agent of El'shwn, raised his sister's ring one final time.

He concentrated on a single thought, and the image was thus shared with the gargoyle—an enormous buck toothed, diplostome-faced monster with eight oily, phthalo-green lance-like appendages baring the bulk of its weight.

The behemoth born of rodent and arachnid blocked the trackway inside the concourse. Mr. Black had no idea how it passed through the tunnel. Perhaps its bones were more cartilage than marrow. But no matter how that feat of wonder withstood one's ability to reason further, the fact remained. If that vhendo was allowed to hold its ground, the resulting crash would easily derail the assassin's plan for a speedy and unexpected assault of Wychstone from the interlinked passages beneath it.

The man in black focused harder, and the ring began to glow. Then he aimed his concentration at the skittering abomination roughly thirteen meters tall. The white-and-silver light burned hot in his fist. Unfortunately for the mother gargoyle, as Mr. Black could do nothing against the burn, this wasn't a spectrum of light she'd any fortitude against since it was supposed to make her angry.

It was like a flip was switched somewhere in the gargoyle's blood.

The ol' girl immediately adjusted her flaky wings and flew right at the massive vhendo's face.

Landing hard on the behemoth's chest, digging in her heels, the gargoyle bit and tore at the lumbering vhendo until she knocked it off the track.

The ponderous vhendo roared and turned on the

annoying, much smaller gargoyle, fighting her, pressing her, pushing her back to the cavern wall where it was hard to fly, thus creating more distance between its waxy carapace of grimy fur and the speeding maglev now three cars deep into the tunnel.

The mare moved carefully through every passenger coach. Mr. Black controlled her quick steps via bridle and bit, making sure she didn't lose her balance on the slick, sheet metal floor running the length of the aisles between each segmented compartment all the way to the lead engine car, which was previously the caboose engine.

Do not be too confident.

"Who's confident?" Mr. Black asked aloud to the empty shuttle.

Black's mind was a flurry of outcomes, body counts, monsters, and bloody metal, but something managed to remain outside his weary senses.

Caught in the rushing wind between two cars as the track beneath rattled by in a blur, an eerie sensation drifted over Mr. Black, and the mare bristled when she realized the trap they'd mindlessly walked into.

"Shit!" The damn thing with slimy, wormlike appendages nearly scooped the Horran right out of his saddle. The little suckers chewed at any bit they could suckle at. "Ahhh, damnit." It squeezed and slithered to regain its hold on Black's upper torso.

The gurgling sounds the unseen vhendo made as it struggled with Black caused the mare to almost buck between the racing cars.

Lucky for him, the cabin's old overhang jutted out from the side of the roof, forcing the vhendo to execute its ambush from above the ranger's left side. It never saw the pneumatic-powered blade on his forearm till it was buried deep in its chest. The small sleeve stinger on Black's right would've been far less effective.

Had time allowed, Mr. Black would've spit on the Beast from Beyond the Dark as it fell from the sailing maglev. Instead, he barely had time to witness the price of his escape as it played out for him through the next cabin's window.

The eldest children came swiftly and with great fury to their mother's cries, but their efforts were futile against the inevitable. The matron gargoyle, bloody and broken, was easily dispatched by the massive, hulking vhendo once her wings were crushed like so many old twigs and brittle leaves ready for the fire. Her corpse was tossed aside like a chunk of scrap hide to the lesser, smaller Beasts from the Dark to feed upon, which they did.

Always the mission.

"Always, Mel."

You know I hate that.

"I know." Mr. Black could still remember the first day she said that to him.

I am not a child anymore.

"No," he whispered, "you're a ghost."

Are you ready?

"Yes, of course, Melisande." He hated the name they'd given her.

When the last car of the maglev passed into total darkness, the tunnel fading away, occasional sparks still swirling out from the rear draft, Mr. Black surmised most of the gargoyle's brood would soon suffer the same fate as their loyal mother. That is, if they continued to try to rescue her now mutilated body, despite the swarming vhendo and other putrid subterranean vermin being summoned to banquet on the dead.

Another successful contingency.

Another red smear in the ledger.

13

"Steady," said Black.

The assassin stroked the mare's withers and removed the darū goggles from his eyes.

He'd need them in the deeper dark beneath Wychstone, but since he wasn't conditioned to them, if he wore them for too long, the alchemical lenses would affect him, starting with his eyes, which would twist his stomach and stifle his equilibrium, and that was no way to begin a fight.

Within the safety of the sealed-off subway tube rich with an early, now mostly forgotten version of the krypton gas still used in some Aership bladders, the maglev cruised along at an unimaginable clip.

As part of Mr. Black's elaborate plan, the sixteen-car subterranean maglev had entered the central airtight tube, switching off from metro's electrified track at the appropriate transition point with the remains of even older, more pedestrian modes of mass transit lost to time beneath them.

"Won't be long now," said Black.

The polarities and krypton gas reached complete molecular adhesion, creating a plasmatic energy field that coated the train's shell from one end to the other.

Now at max speed, the maglev would reach Wychstone Manor, some fifty or more miles away, in roughly eight to ten minutes. Eleven in total, if Mr. Black's internal clock included the unexpectedly slow departure from Mission Station due to the vhendo and the partial fault in one or both the linked diesel starter units, as well as another error message from one of the eight superconductors powering the ancient train.

The mare didn't like the tight, metallic dark, though. Even under Mr. Black's hypnosis, she seemed uneasy now. Perhaps waiting and snacking in the concourse wasn't enough to ready her for metro travel. He smirked at how her flat ears kept twitching, as if trying to locate some danger hidden among the various sounds within the compartments. His grin deepened as the horse scanned the windows, trying to see through the exterior blur. The speed made it even more difficult to penetrate because the maglev's emergency lights were all but nonexistent.

Really, had he a mind to, Mr. Black would've noticed there was enough juice in the batteries to power the lead coach's internal glow rods without seriously diminishing resources to the glitchy guidance system he'd pre-programed before the vhendo breached the tunnel. He knew better, though. Never get too comfortable. Like an old friend giving tough advice, fear was truly their greatest ally now.

Always hide in plain sight, thought Black, gazing into the undying pitch.

Quiet as a shooting star, cradled in a sea of pulsating quicksilver, the train flew through tubes of plaztacrete and Exalted alloys, the combinations molded into other various wonders and novelties about the subway lines, which alone remained to whisper, like broken tombstones, the multiple layers of desiccated histories and the empty worlds they burned in.

Minutes left, Mr. Black reexamined the operation: Wychstone Manor.

It was only slightly grander than the Two Sisters, if memory served him.

The lightly fortified exterior of the duke's country house couldn't be said to have genuine battlements. Though grand enough, the updates, added during the last gray skin flareup, including the watchtower in the northwest corner of the interior grounds and the gatehouse built into the perimeter wall, were only ever meant to be practical in their function. Essentially, their ability to keep out and intimidate the poor and tired citizens of the berg. But Mr. Black was no insufferable wretch come to beg for shillings while the duke was masquerading as though on holiday from affairs in Pehats Berg.

The double lattice gate outside the front door of the manor, separating the porch from the porte-cochère, with its wraparound fountain dividing the driveway before the overhang, was of equally little concern to the man in black.

The Agent of the Isles had no intention of going

that way. He smiled at the idea of strolling up the private gravel pathway, shadowed on either side by giant hedges, in the hopes of breaching the decorative barrier and presenting himself to the chasseur, who would then announce him in the parlor outside the duke's lavish drawing room as if he'd arrived for a mutually advantageous meeting.

Reloading the blasters, Mr. Black considered his actual approach, weighed his options.

The rye fields along the left side of Pike's Road, leading back in the direction of Krone, a hamlet just outside Pehats Berg, would be through the reaping now, leaving a clear view for many miles. The orchards would start bearing winter flowers soon, and the last grapes would be left to die on the vine, the soil made richer because of it next spring.

Contrary to the left side of Pike's Road, down the right side of the manor's main thoroughfare, the wild, sloping meadows skirting the edges of Bernwood Forest, which evened out and softened to tall grasses and gentle brush less than a thousand feet from the gatehouse of the estate, would be mired with various natural inconveniences this time of year.

Typical obstructions varied but always included two things: First were the deep pools of frosty mud created by gray bull toads. The ankle breaking burrows these little bastards left behind lay hidden beneath glossy layers of silt, mud, and camouflaged grasses for much of the cold season. The second most common obstruction this time of year was the countless beaver dams either quickly reconstructed or moved following the cyclical flooding

or freezing of nearby streams and rivers subterrane-
ously linked to Witcher Pond, which should've remained
Witcher Lake due to its size and depth, though Witcher
Pond seemed to have stuck since the turn of the century.

Consequently, the combination of these two natural occurrences, spread from the surrounding Bernwood
Forest to Sigien, the nearest hamlet east of Wychstone,
always seemed to trap the sexually confused bern trout.
The golden green winter fish loved to feed on bull toads,
hibernating or not though, often, their evolutionary
hunger separated them from their schools migrating
upriver to spawn at Lake Trifol.

This, of course, Mr. Black knew, meant local fish-
ers and illegal poachers on the duke's extensive property
would've likely already been working around the clock to
secretly cast and pull nets in order to quickly and quietly
haul away the winter bounty, including the beavers and
toads themselves if they were so inclined. As a reality, their mules, cows, horses, wagons, and hired hands
would've all since pulverized whatever easily travers-
able ground once existed between the mud and sludge,
between the fallen trees and thick grasses.

Therefore, Mr. Black was confident any advanc-
ing company of soldiers would be forced to travel by
road and not navigate local trails or hack new ones
cross-country as the crow flies from the east, through
the muck and thorns in and around Bernwood Forest.
Most importantly, their march would be slow at best
and cost nearly three times the effort to make up the
distance. That is, if the incursion involved any specific
timetable or if required any serious siege equipment as

they pushed farther west, past Pehats Berg.

"It could all be F.U.B.A.R., though," said Black to himself with a thin smile.

No, you were a great colonel once.

As Melisande faded, Mr. Black still had the walls of the estate to consider. Existing long before the manor itself and shielding nearly a third of the duke's entitled property, it was once said many of the stones predated Ellizium. This local myth suggested the wall might even be part of some ancient ruins. A relic from the world before, which could very well be true, at least to those with a mind like Mr. Black's.

For this entire realm of dirt and blood, over which the Scattered Kingdoms was reforged, was itself originally born of hallowed ground, predating the collapse of Gol and the League of Kings before that, because everything belonging to the descendants of Gol was once the center of a great Eyldeyryien Empire, a dynasty many ages old, now all but dead and forgotten by its conquerors.

So, whatever the case may be concerning the rumors kept alive by the occasional passing through of a Five C'Cervans tutor loosely contracted to teach only the berg's richest children, the facts remained the same.

The nearly twelve-foot-high walls would be fully supported by the duke's personal guard and tenant conscripts, as well as any knight, merc, or status-seeking peasant who might've heard the first alarm bells or were lucky enough to receive an emergency messenger pigeon from the duke's staff.

Mr. Black wagered the lot would number at least fifty swords.

If there's more, then Tarvarys knew Heimont was coming.

A chill blossomed around Black's tailbone as part of him wondered if the Sabbat was simply purging its weakest members from the fold. Why not? Wouldn't be the first time and always done right before...

The Horran set to dissecting the Enemy and the Sabbat's new leading man.

Lord Heimont Rohndolphn, though having sworn allegiance to Duke Tarvarys Talhgho before Wodan's Altar more than a decade ago, now apparently served their real masters with greater dedication and servitude, which is why he was going to betray the duke and take control of Pehats Berg himself.

The traitor wouldn't be alone in his bloody endeavor though.

The murder of Duke Talhgho wouldn't be a secret assassination, but a public, geopolitical execution, thus signaling just a taste of what the Sabbat and their Dark Father had yet to come for the fractured peoples of the Scattered Kingdoms.

Therefore, Rohndolphn would most likely be guarded by a squad or more of handpicked mutineers sympathetic to the cult, if not aspiring or already Black Thumbs themselves. And just as he'd shared with Deputy Emil Simkus before sending him back to the Two Sisters, each of Lord Rohndolphn's best would be in charge of a band of equally corrupted locals, wanderers, hired tough guys, and knifemen of the kind even Momma Bwulyaa wouldn't sully her reputation by consorting with.

Twice as many.

That raised the combined potential blades against

him to one hundred fifty.

Of course, if what he surmised about the seasonal terrain was wrong or if the invaders came fully prepared to roll over any challenge as they marched east to west across the country, then there'd be an additional forward scouting excursion party somewhere in the mix of killers added to the side of Rohndolphn's backstabbers and cutthroats, care of Prince/King Zahargan Marcus Urhal.

Finally, given the size and scope of the prince's broader intentions, since he stood to gain the most from blood yet spilled, saying nothing of other key figures across the realm likely to have their throats slit, food poisoned, or castle fired this very night.

"Damn it!" Mr. Black clenched his jaw. His head swam and ached with too many variables to consider what would happen after the prince captured Pehats Berg.

No vhendo at least, thought Black.

The man in black felt the ring softly vibrate on his finger, reminding him it was time for the final phase of the plan he'd worked so hard to synchronize with the speeding maglev. Because, of course, as always, Mr. Black set all of this into motion before touching a key on the H.U.B. before he even entrusted Mr. Halgin to Leeann and Ceann's wit and resourcefulness.

"…Riving at Vürsheim STA-tion."

The mare was naturally startled by the ghostlike voice that came in scratchy, broken waves from the walls of the coach outside the conductor's room. Yet, it was the second unexpected speaker who really caught her flatfooted. Mr. Black, too. So much so he almost drew his sword when the speaker repeated himself.

"This is an Areht facility. You are trespassing."

"Under whose authority?"

Mr. Black's eyes burned with fatigue as he struggled with the tethered com device.

"Who is this?" The speaker's voice was no longer scratchy. In fact, he sounded as if he was standing directly in front of the Horran's face.

"Who're you?" Mr. Black replied, buying time while he searched for his canteen.

"I am Shi'r to Majistor Razurmïesh—"

"Tell that spring goose…" said Mr. Black, between hearty gulps of Momma Bwulyaa's refreshing, graciously donated water.

"Say again?" the Areht asked.

Mr. Black returned the canteen to the pouch closest to the mare's saddle horn, again pressed the button on the corded mouthpiece, and replied, "Tell Raz, 'An old crow says hello.'"

The Horran then smashed the communication system and ripped the hand mic from the wall. He slammed the engine car's door behind himself and the mare. The smell of broken plaztaglas and fried wires lingered for some time after, which made sense since the compartment's air coolant system had failed over a millennia ago.

The maglev finally exited the safety of the metro's central tube system.

The depressurization made Mr. Black's ears pop. The mare's, too.

The maglev slowed, but only enough to exit the tube

and catch the single magnetic rail it would float over for the last few hundred meters. Then it would then dock at the long-forgotten metro platform beneath Witcher Pond.

Except, that's not what Mr. Black or the mare saw on approach. Instead, they saw a wall of rolling water, crashing and swirling toward them through the reddish-brown hazard lights shining down on the track from the sides of the route.

"We'll be fine," said Mr. Black.

The mare, nevertheless, backed away from the train's first exit door.

The Agent of the Isles was rather happy with his luck to this point. He was also kind of impressed with himself. Until now, he wasn't sure if the sealed construction hatch beneath the eastern tip of Witcher Pond was still functional. He'd no way of knowing if all the connections and components hadn't already failed due to entropy. It didn't help that this sector, one of the oldest still secretly linked to even larger subterranean systems across Uropà, seemed naturally opposed to Mr. Black's end goals, for it was one of the worst to read and adjust on the H.U.B.'s screens when Mr. Black had scrolled through window after window of information.

"Hold on," said Mr. Black.

The mare winced and neighed as the water rolled over the train.

With a great plunge, the maglev met the rushing whirl of darkness like a spear plunged through the guts of a bloated giant. Its sleek shape and piercing speed diverted the consuming, crushing volume. The industrial magnets did the rest to keep the deluge from crushing Mr. Black and the mare inside the coach or lifting and swinging the entire conveyance into the sides of the drowned subway line, similar to how a loose link of chain might be thrashed about when caught in a series of rapids.

When the last subterranean light flashing along the metro's safety zones finally failed, all the world outside the maglev became an oily mess of sloshing bile and darkness, slithering with glimpses of various aquatic life and flood debris. Twisted shapes and saturated dead things scratched and dented the hull as they passed through the murk and mud. The mare feared the sounds came from monsters in the liquid shadow, teasing their claws, rocking and roaring through the metal as they taunted the coaches.

"There," said Mr. Black, stroking her muzzle. "It's done."

Then there was nothing. No sound. No light.

Moments later, the maglev came to a stop. Ports opened as it dumped excess steam and heat.

"Thank YOU for ri-ding Fed-ERation Rail-s. Have A joyous day."

Thankfully, there was enough power in sections of the abandoned transit station's overhead grid to offer some semblance of guiding light, but what Mr. Black and his mare saw did nothing to ease their spirits.

Outside the train doors, all along the hull and as far Mr. Black could see across this much smaller and much older concourse linked to Wychstone, were heaping piles of mud. Millions upon millions of tons of it settling, bubbling into place beneath the sparse light flickering above the pedestrian transport junction.

"Admit it," said Mr. Black as he gazed across the still undulating, revolting mass of sludge highlighted in every glossy detail by the popping, sizzling lights above, "you didn't think it'd work."

No other voices in his head replied.

After goading the mare up the best slick pathway between the mountainous piles of muck, Mr. Black noticed hidden dangers lying in wait for the mare's knees and ankles. Not just giant furry leeches, armored eels, and snake ticks swirling among the putrid water, either. Huge rocks were unurthed as the mud further settled and the gray water receded, swallowed into holes unknown, as a dozen or more trees of equally impressive size and shape, with massive roots and boughs, were licked clean to the bone by the flood.

What is your backup?

Because of the sinkhole, the vacuum that pulled everything into the secret metro station with only a few of his earlier keystrokes, Mr. Black had no idea what remained of Witcher Pond or the portions of Bernwood Forest previously surrounding it above ground. Similarly, he'd no idea about the new and potentially inconvenient conditions he'd created across Vürsheim Station. Which tunnels had the deluge flooded with impassable shit? Which had collapsed entirely or were washed out? Were any of those passages the secret shortcut he'd planned on using to infiltrate Wychstone Manor?

"Not necessary, little sister."

Despite the mess, though, Mr. Black knew where many of the exits were. At least, where they were when long ago this relic of a bygone age had a curious amenity for its commuters, identified on the H.U.B.'s search screen as a *PARKING DECK*.

"Let's get this over with," said the assassin.

The mare climbed faster.

14

The front door of the Two Sisters swung outward.

"We're closed," came Daphnia's distant voice.

She wasn't lying. Not really.

Leann and Ceann could see the truth in Daphnia's face as they stood in the open doorway.

Honestly, Daphnia wasn't sure if she'd ever reopen. Not in the same way, at least.

Whatever Mr. Black had done, it brought the sheriff and his goons to her establishment earlier that evening, exactly what she'd worried about when Black first arrived in Pehats Berg. The sheriff and his men roughed up a few people, including her own, some worse than others, and made plenty of threats. Later, they departed the inn, but others eventually came to take their unwanted place, and this bunch, killers all, had words for her from Mr. Halgin. Political sayings and legal phrases she didn't like.

"More than an hour now," added Daphnia, now

muffled and more distant from the doorway.

Jezzy walked the length behind the bar, turning the corner to look and ask for something from the back of the house, but Daphnia slipped into the freezers beyond the kitchen. Jezzy could see the cool box through the glass in the two-way doors and, from the looks of it, there was no doubt Daphnia was pissed by the dismal hour she might finally get to sleep. Never mind the craziness of the evening already.

Jezzy returned her gaze to the front door.

"Harold?"

"Yes, ma'am," said the boy, who most resembled an unurthed ghost of his former self.

Waving to Jezzy, Harold Cross slowly walked ahead of Leeann, who remained behind by more than a few steps. She'd kept the left panel of the front door open as the stable boy continued down the runner dividing the Two Sisters' inner entranceway. Ceann, the younger sister, blew between both after finally releasing her side of the front door. She was eager for all of them to get inside the Inn.

"Girls?"

"Jez!"

Jezzy bounded over the bar, skin peeking through the rips in her partly undone leather-lined junker's jumpsuit.

The redhead's mane no longer flowed as it had when she first saw Mr. Black some hours ago. Now, it was tied back into bulky, messy knots and tucked beneath an old rag. Beyond its specific purpose, secret to everyone but Daphnia for the moment, the rag had a practical utility, to protect Jezzy's ears while she crouched and contorted herself for hours at a time between smoldering pipes and around searing oil.

"Margaret?" said Daphnia when she returned to the dining room.

In the corner of the nearly empty eating hall, past the first stairway leading up and back to the second and third floor rentals, about a dozen or more feet to the left of the now-covered piano and freshly swept musician's box, several rough-looking gents stood from the tables where Margaret had been tickling their knees and thighs, as well as more tender places in between, for some time now.

"Shit." Daphnia's eyes went wide. She quickly untied her apron.

For the past hour and a half or so, the only thing the aggressive loiterers had done was drive off regular business and consume themselves with the inn's girls and other pleasures. But now, one by one, the newly deputized brutes moved forward from their seats.

Margaret remained behind them. She was absolutely frozen.

It was clear now these ne'er-do-wells had been patiently waiting for such a band of parentless misfortunes to show up all bloody and dangerous-looking. Mr. Halgin couldn't have painted a better picture in the killer's heads before leaving them to ponder the night's atrocities over a few warm pints.

Of course, the fat man departed their company somewhere on the road outside the jailhouse, sometime after Leeann and Ceann escaped their own arrest and execution. Not including the vhendo. He didn't go off to attend to his own affairs alone, though. An equally leathery cohort of hired muscle remained at his side. Mr. Halgin had to look official. Important.

As acting sheriff, Mr. Halgin meant to intercept the approaching Urhal forces with all the grandeur and authority of his new commission. Because, if anyone was going to open Pehats Berg's gates, it was going to be him. A broken hand and pummeled ego had earned him that much, at least, for his years of sacrifice and loss. His time had come due.

And yet, after all that, there was really no cause for alarm.

Neither Leeann nor Ceann worried as the scum drew on them, some with weapons.

To be clear, though, the girls' confidence didn't come from the knowledge that both Cirilo and Emil merely took their time trailing them from the backstreets outside the inn, ready with their own bloody weapons in hand and supported by the largest of Momma Bwulyaa's dire-she-wolfhounds.

That would've been an easier, yet far more danger- ous way to resolve this issue.

Leeann had an idea. Unbeknownst to the knifemen, the real reason there was no alarm across Harold and the girls' faces was because they, too, were like Mr. Halgin. Special. Needing protection. A lot of protection.

That's why before the bastards ever got within arm's reach of Harold, who led the way in spite of his own fatigue and mental strain from the night's multiple horrors and deaths, Khalix dropped his camouflage. The massive moropod opened his muzzle, revealing big fangs and exhaling thick saliva and heat.

"Say hello, Khalix." Little Harold smiled sleepily at the inn's owners.

Khalix's lips curled, and his powerful jaws snapped in between deep grunts and barks.

After seeing the giant creature's teeth and hooked claws and hearing its booming roar, it wasn't long, maybe a few seconds, before all the brave would-be murderers scattered from the inn's public dining room in bewildered panic when they saw the real reason why Emil and Cirilo lagged behind, holding both doors wide for Harold Cross' new best friend to follow after him.

"Cowards," said the hāfu warrior.

As a further insult, Cirilo rubbed his open palm along the scarification across his skull. Then he shouldered his zhuge repeating crossbow. He would've shot them as they fled, but he didn't have any bolts left.

"Evening, Ms. Bruuner, Ms. Adilović," said Emil.

After hugging the girls, Jezzy replied for them both. "Evening, Deputy."

"You alright?" Daphnia now took her turn scooping up the girls.

Both Jezzy and Daphnia moved to properly greet and console little Harold, but he was more interested in lying down in one of their swell booths.

Cirilo filed back into the inn after Emil. He waited for their original furry partner to mount the inn's front stoop. Like Harold Cross, the dire-wolfhound was still rather nasty and bedraggled. She'd given everything in her earlier street fight with the vhendo, which Khalix later killed with a single blow, saving them all.

"Where is he?" Jezzy asked once they were all safely alone and inside.

"Who?" Cirilo signaled to Daphnia that he needed a shot.

Emil began, "He's—"

"He's dead," said Cirilo. He nodded to Daphnia and shot the creamy liqueur.

Without thinking, Jezzy launched forward and slapped Cirilo hard. Her hand hurt.

Tasting blood on his teeth, eyes tearing up, Cirilo caught her second swipe at his face.

"You knew what he was?" she yelled at him, struggling to free her hand.

"What he is?" Cirilo's eyes glistened with bitterness, jealousy. Years condensed to stillness.

"Yes," answered Jezzy.

"Then you know he's dead to you," said Cirilo, voice almost quivering.

"Shut up," she whispered.

Hardening his gaze, Cirilo added, "And if he's not dead yet, he's running toward it with every step he takes."

Jezzy deftly plucked a combination screwdriver and bottle-opener from her extra deep pocket and flashed it in Cirilo's face. "Shut up!"

Cirilo didn't shy away from her pointy, yet empty, threat.

"It's who he is," said Emil. "That's why we're all still alive."

Daphnia took Jezzy in her arms.

Jezzy quietly cried in frustration and anger before

regathering herself, wiping her face.

"Do you know something?" Daphnia asked, her sister's tears already fading from her collar.

"Ask her," replied Leeann, waggling a finger at Margaret.

Everyone looked. No one blinked. Then, like dominos, they each realized what they were seeing. It was true. It wasn't fear holding the professional teaser back, keeping her behind after all the others fled. It was guilt that rooted the Two Sisters' former best gal into place. Shame willed her to be still.

"Margaret?" asked Jezzy, licking a bit of snot and tears from her lips.

It was written all over her face. Whatever goodness she initially believed might've come from her little acts of quiet and discreet duplicities with Mr. Halgin's associates and men like them had, in fact, ended up being far worse. Far more complex. For the outcomes of Margaret's little betrayals, linked to events beyond her knowledge, boiled over into the streets, businesses, and homes across the berg.

She cried now because there was no stopping it. Not that such things could ever be undone, which is why the collective shock and shame of it now poisoned Margaret's gut, making her ill.

"I'm so sorry," said Margaret.

Leeann had been working it out in her head from the moment the coincidences and conveniences started piling up, all of it flowing back to the Two Sisters. Someone had known. Someone told. Someone was to blame.

"I didn't have a choice," pleaded Margaret. "I didn't."

Instinctively, Khalix and the wolfhound growled at the collaborator's excuses.

"You'll understand then," said Jezzy.

"Don't—"

Jezzy pushed her sister hard. Daphnia stumbled and fell back into the two remaining men.

Jezzy then articulated her left arm, detaching or allowing something connected to her forearm and wrist to dispense a second bit of wired hardware down into her left hand. Only one person saw this happen. Everyone else was focused on what came next due to their sequential perception of the simultaneous events.

"Stop!" shouted Daphnia.

It was too late. The service noid had already stepped out from behind the former waitress and bedroom brawler. Towering over Margaret, the mechanoid grabbed her by the throat and effortlessly crushed her neck with its pincer-like fingers.

There was no fight. No struggle.

Her eyes turned red. Her lips turned blue. Her life ended.

Margaret's body fell over sideways, and the unit returned to its cleaning duties.

"What did you do?" Emil asked, rushing to the lifeless woman's side.

From the moment she pointed out her suspicion, Leeann knew what was going to happen. She just didn't know who would kill Margaret. Nor did she know how. Part of her hoped she'd be the one to get the shot. Killing didn't seem so hard now. Pretty easy, in fact. Everything felt more visceral since she'd set the vhendo on fire.

It was like she alone could feel the world turning.

Which is why Leeann didn't become distracted by Cirilo's outburst when everyone learned more about Jezzy and Mr. Black's past relationship. Which is how she knew where to look. To see. To catch the backwater service unit entering the dining room, as it was always meant to, because it followed its daily preset programing to clear away all glasses and dishes as each table of customers emptied.

That's when Jezzy had secretly signaled it with her personal *clicking* tinker toy, which Leeann hadn't yet had a chance to even wonder about because Jezzy's quick hand concealed almost all of the device. Not to mention Jezzy's greaser suit, with its long, bulky sleeves that could've easily concealed other parts or equipment needed to summon the noid.

"You finished?"

Jezzy didn't answer Cirilo's selfish question. She simply walked away from her former lover. Daphnia followed.

"Leeann?" Ceann touched her sister's shoulder.

Whatever's in her hand made her head glow, thought Leeann.

It was beneath the rag above Jezzy's brow. She'd seen it.

15

Freezing rain moved in. The boughs swayed.

Mr. Black could see in the dark again. The trencher goggles Momma Bwulyaa had lent him worked just fine, thanks to the alchemical light from the no-burn flares she'd also parted with. And because he didn't need the earbuds, he could hear the creaks and groans of the wintery forest above him and the mare.

They raced west, following a specific series of identified subterranean passages and corridors beneath the long reach of Bernwood and the wild fields beyond the forest. Each intersection point, constructed of either plaztacrete, silica block, old red brick, or seemingly hewn from the urth generations ago by some unlucky servant's hands, was marked with a unique stripe of alchemical paint along the middle length of the junction.

Mr. Black noticed the special tracking and location method on previous visits to the catacombs beneath

Father Rai's Mission and, as far as he knew from the intel, there were at least a half-dozen other straphanger depots just like it spread across the Scattered Kingdoms. No telling how many smaller ones, perhaps even smaller than this one, existed across the Middle Realm. Mr. Black wasn't sure who made them or why, but he thanked them anyway.

The colored markings were extremely faded to the naked eye. On top of being damned hard to discern the paint by touch in some sections of the dilapidated halls and tunnels, which always ended at right angles.

The mare struggled not to slip in the tight and slick straight space as she carried Mr. Black, following the blueprint he'd seen on the H.U.B. earlier. After a few minutes, about the time it took for the echo of the mare's beating hooves to fade in the last area, a new sound emerged to fill the smooth stone passageways.

The thunderous combination of violence and valor, culminated in the muffled yet booming calls of armed men, living and dying, but it was also, Mr. Black presumed, a celebration for Rohndolphn's successful siege as the lord finally breached the great country house, with or without assistance from Prince Urhal.

The terrible mayhem in the not-too-high distance was carried down to Mr. Black and the mare through bloody vibrations spread out across the passageway. Their victory rattled in the walls, shaking pipes, echoing down deeper into places forgotten.

"Stay here," said Mr. Black after gathering his things from the mare's saddle and packs.

The mare neighed and snorted in protest. Her

sudden agitation reminded him that she couldn't see in the pitch darkness like he could, but only because the no-burn flares and darū trencher goggles enabled him to.

"What?

Trusting the Agent of the Isles to really and truly lead and push her through the metro, because their duties had flipped and he'd become her eyes instead of the other way around, was one thing, given their growing partnership. However, leaving her behind, abandoning the mare here in the spooky dark, considering everything she'd seen and gone through in the short time since Mr. Black first rested his bony ass on her saddle, was something different altogether.

Mr. Black flipped his goggles back up on his tricorne and broke the wrapping on one of his normal mining flares, then said, "Really, you thought I would leave you in the dark? I'm hurt."

The Horran playfully uncovered a brown apple hidden in the bottom of his bag, both donated by the gangster queen. The mare was most pleased. Then he looped the reins over a drainpipe and rigged the flare close enough to her flank without burning her tail.

"Be right back."

Mr. Black tipped his tricorn, then checked his favorite fighting knives. Leaving his bow and quiver behind with the mare because of the up-close-and-personal nature of the work he was about to get into, Mr. Black was confident he'd everything he needed.

With that first death, they have you for life...

Mr. Black stifled a bitter yawn. His tongue felt leathery, his teeth like scraped over bones.

The mare looked on with cautious support as the Horran, his last no-burn flare tucked into his weapon harness, ducked beneath a pair of fallen arches and climbed the hidden ladder at the dead-end.

The mare stomped her hooves nervously as Mr. Black drifted in and out of visibility.

According to the records he'd uncovered, this former escape route would take him up and out of the tunnels and sewers of the secret metro station beneath what'd recently become Witcher Pit.

Once up the ladder, the shortcut would land him in the dungeons beneath Wychstone Manor. As an odd side note, which Mr. Black briefly chuckled to himself about, this unique scenario wasn't entirely new to him, especially when he considered the whole breath of his service to the Arehthood.

Time to work.

Black grinned.

Melisande always had a private passion for killing traitors.

16

Mr. Black wasn't prepared for what lay on the other side of the duke's secret point of egress.

After exiting the hatch at the top of the ladder and returning the hidden manhole cover as quietly as he'd lifted it, Mr. Black paused as he caught the musty scent of old decadence floating in the still air beneath Wych-stone Manor.

It was a specific perfume first borne in the United Kingdom of Perryn, domain of Queen Gehddrin, Matrone Supreme of the Red Ladies. Exactly the last region of the world the assassin of the Silver Isles of El'shwn wished to find connected here in the dungeons beneath the duke's private estate, on the eve of his assassination at the hands of former Sabbat allies and servants to the world's first and only Enemy.

The unique fragrance had melded with a dozen or more spliced odors: copious sex, torture, body oils, incense, raven's wine and, finally, mind-numbing narcotics, the latter often left to burn till black in small decorative diffusers about the den.

The layered aroma caused Mr. Black's mind to race with new plots, theories, and phantoms.

The combined sexual funk circulating through the dungeon seeped into everything, from the vented hearth in the center of the room, to the ornate wood workings and the opulent fabrics draped about the dimly lit chamber. No longer exactly a tomb of damnation whispering final regards but, instead, it was a space of every indulgent, erotic confinement.

Of course, Mr. Black was thankful for the dungeon's transformation as he looked around through the darū trencher goggles, but he was also curious what dangers these new revelations might entail, what strains of intrigue might yet be transmuted into new and perhaps unseen obstructions, some with even deadlier outcomes.

Too bad he didn't have his sister's mind.

What's dead is dead, Black thought.

Unlike any other dungeon, whatever pain one might've felt here if, say, he or she were strapped to one of the various submissive devices about the confines, perhaps left to dangle from the ceiling, limbs restricted by plush leathers and soft furs or fine silks, the suffering would always be absolutely willing and consensual in nature.

The choice was part of the fun.

Such freedoms were always paramount, even if a safe word was required to survive a particularly intense rendezvous without prolonged injury, which could leave lingering markings a spouse or judge might see and later question.

A potentiality most people would wish to avoid.

However, as with all things swept into dark corners, there were always outlier participants of the Sovereign Rose and Thorn Club. Such individual practitioners of the Kamorri arts sought pleasure and wisdom through increasingly extreme means and methods.

Unlike their fellow liberators of common social norms, who otherwise coexisted undetected in regular peerage society, these mostly reclusive individuals hungered for something else, for a deeper knowledge that could only be attained, according to their evolved beliefs, through the oldest and purest eroticisms.

Their pleasures included all known sexual taboos, as well as other exciting, if not occasionally deadly, primal deviancies, many of a supernatural nature that could easily get one hung in most civil parts of the world. For such experiences were often said to be perverse or otherwise unnatural by the Faithful.

Mr. Black felt an ironic joy at seeing icons of the Ten repurposed across the den.

The spiritual annals were quite impressive and extensive.

Specified in great detail by those who bow and scrape for the Ten Pillars of Heaven, as first documented in a collection of eyewitness narrative texts, the oldest records identified some of the oldest Kamorri Doll and Blush Houses along the floating shores of Perryn's southern sprawl of islands, during the time of the Crusades.

They've always hated the flesh, thought Mr. Black.

After a few steps further, senses keen to the hallucinogens in the air, Mr. Black suspected these true sadists recently occasioned the duke's naughty hideaway and did so for one reason and one reason only: to carve out bloody illumination in the flesh of others.

Mr. Black knew this for sure because for this subgroup, pain and identity were simply broken mirrors of an even greater pathway to physical and mental enlightenment. Learning just how close they could be and still whisper in Uzamaza's mouth before he exhaled, and the world turned red—was the entire point of their every sensory endeavor.

At the height of such pleasures gifted by the ancient Perizian Death God, where life and death floated freely above the groping and groaning flesh, a master of the corrupted Kamorri ways, either the Fel Thorn or Fel Rose, would often persuade their victim to do the whispering in Uzamaza's mouth so they might then safely and engrossingly witness and catalog the victim's excruciatingly erotic agony.

Mr. Black shuddered to think about the possibilities. His fingers went numb. His back ached.

Could a Red Sister be one of the duke's secret allies in Rohndolphn's betrayal? Is that how Princess Patrycja Urhal returned from the grave? Was it possible that this long and sordid debauchery was the unforeseen prologue to tonight's red events? Was that the link to Lady Mina Genza, though she was never of the queen's court herself?

Fuck me, thought Mr. Black.

From the gently smoldering coals above the vented hearth in the center of the remolded pleasure dungeon,

Mr. Black grabbed a handful of ash and a tiny bellow. Ignoring the few abandoned cells, the Horran blew the fine smoky charcoal along the corners and edges of the main room.

In the dim light made hazy via the white ash from the hearth, the dungeon took on an amplified quality that further teased his exhausted senses and notions of reality.

"Where is it?" Mr. Black muttered.

It wasn't long before a secret draft pulled at the hovering will-o'-wisps caught in the soft gray cloud blown from the bellow, exposing the duke's private passage to and from this cave of masochism and mischief.

Once inside the shortcut to the first floor, Mr. Black began to climb.

17

The first floor of Wychstone Manor was ransacked, though at which point of its ransacking Mr. Black couldn't say exactly. He'd just discovered the first of many secret peepholes created by the duke or one of his predecessors.

With a second look to determine exactly where he was in the nearly blacked-out compound's dusty skeleton, the Horran noted a curiously dented kite shield lying abandoned near the manor's breached entrance.

Must've carried the ram with them, thought Mr. Black.

Assisted moments later by the sparse ambient light of a few wall sconces and the distant glow of torches somewhere just out of sight, Mr. Black spotted a few broken bolts that had pierced the escutcheon's painted metal-and-leather surface. One of the tips had blood on it.

By the looks of everything, thanks to Momma

Bwulyaa's trencher goggles, Duke Tarvarys Talhgho had apparently scraped together enough self-determination and fearlessness in time for his men and servants to sweep the various rooms, anterooms, cellars, and parlors before the outer wall of Wychstone was overwhelmed.

"He baited them?" Mr. Black whispered to the roaches and spiders crawling about.

Gathering anything that might hinder Lord Heimont Rohndolphn's siege, the duke's men took whatever might bar windows or reinforce doors, tossing away or destroying materials that would be used against them if the old estate were set ablaze, one of Lord Rohndolphn's favorite practices for removing derelict squatters behind on their taxes.

With so much of the pompous clutter and regal totems removed, leaving behind a film of ghostly white silhouettes and repainted mold spots in the cracked gypsum, it seemed to Mr. Black Wychstone was no longer a great country home at all.

Instead, the prevailing chaos without hope for retreat and no quarter for surrender, transformed the manor into something of a terrible nightmare: a great galleon, surrounded on all sides by a wintery muck and besieged by backstabbing mutineers.

They should've run but didn't, and when they needed to, they couldn't...

Ignoring the screams and clatter of swords echoing up and down the corridors, shattering the exterior glass, Mr. Black continued stealthily through the duke's crawl-space.

As he moved between the fighting, the walls occasionally rattled. Dust fell.

Blades and ballshot occasionally pierced the walls on either side of him as he scurried along.

After zigzagging for a bit to avoid being detected as he moved and shifted from one section of crawlspace to the next, Mr. Black finally made it to the back of the house. The narrow hallway he'd been following through the parallel crawlspace abruptly ended at a small midnight attendant's serving station. It'd been heavily rummaged through. A selective dry pantry loomed beside it. Behind the ruined wet bar lay a detachable panel.

Through another peephole, Mr. Black could see it'd been previously disguised to match the peeling wallpaper. Unfortunately, the interlopers had destroyed the tiny alcove's polite façades with their axes and swords while hunting for other means to the second floor—exactly what the pocket stairs, of the kind of which a housekeeper might be capable of climbing while assisted by the thinnest railing, was meant for.

You stung Heimont good, didn't you?

He'd already missed much of the action, but if it were any consolation, from Mr. Black's limited vantage point when he had, once free of the dungeons, climbed around in the wall nearest the kitchen's buttery and larder, he wouldn't have seen it anyway.

Even so, now the Horran was sure the duke had used most of his possessions to bar the grand split staircase in the center of the first floor, less than fifty feet from the entranceway at the heart of Wychstone.

Duke Talhgho wasn't ignorant. His ancestors had served in many historical battles.

Caught them right in the doorway.

The kite shield was likely the first to go down, or so that's how Mr. Black imagined it.

From such a high perch within a makeshift bunker of rolled rugs, stacked tables, and bureaus, the whole lot defended by a half-dozen people all armed with range weapons, the duke's men no doubt held the landing for far longer than the lord had expected.

It was a bit impressive really, how they'd fought off traitors stupid enough to attempt the stairway while volleys of quill, bolt, and ballshot rained down on their heads.

Mr. Black couldn't be sure, since he didn't see the slick carnage coating the rather exceptional split staircase after he'd exited the plush dungeon, but perhaps the duke's side had scored a few demoralizing deathblows beyond the enemy's rank and file provocateurs. That is, before one of them used their brains for something other than stopping projectiles and set about finding other means to the second and third floors of the duke's estate, as the damage behind the wet bar suggested they eventually did.

Mr. Black slowly climbed the pocket stairs, wondering if he was too late.

18

There you are, bastard.

Through the last peephole off the hallway outside the duke's purse room on the third floor, which doubled as a billiards when the duke was not counting coins or revising secret ledgers, Mr. Black now spied Lord Heimont Rohndolphn standing at the back of a large cluster of armored men. Most were still gasping and bleeding. Others came and went between the shadows and snapping torchlight.

They hauled the wounded and dead from the far end of the second floor, on the opposite side of the house, where the master and children's bedrooms lay, which is where Black guessed most of the final murders had happened before he left the dungeons. How exactly the duke's men ended up making their last stand in the other rooms, Mr. Black had no idea, except to think many panicked in the end.

Through the haze of burnt powder, sweat, doused torches and the din of moaning, gurgling death throughout the tight hallways, the Horran began to distinguish the newly drafted gravediggers from the traitor's men, who were also on cleanup duty. Few of the defeated still wore their domestic uniforms, and others willingly doffed Duke Talhgho's fighting colors, abandoning their defensive force regalia, and whatever armor or weapons they possessed upon surrender.

Mr. Black grinned, thinking how loyalty seemed to always fail at the tip of a blade or the threat of swinging ropes.

About the time Mr. Black drew parallel to the traitor in the hallway, mere inches separated by the defeated duke's crawlspace, he considered how the brutish viscount presented himself in both dress and manner exactly as one might imagine a corrupted lord of Pehats Berg should.

Rohndolphn was taller than most, lankier, too, almost scarecrow-like. The dark, muddy hair above his flat face was drawn back into a short, messy tail. Smudges of pale gray and frosty white, both once faded browns, shaded the wiry ends of his unkempt beard and bushy eyebrows, which were currently sprinkled with smears of fresh blood.

The truly striking thing about Rohndolphn as he surveyed the subsiding violence he'd created, ignoring the ichor-smeared dagger in his left hand or the bloodied fighting ax with hand shield in his right, was the unique birthmark beneath his right ear. Over the years, the nevus crept down his neck and curled across his throat the way an octopus' arm might if one were so inclined to let it strangle them.

Those old enough to remember the viscount in his youth once whispered frightful things about the blemish, which is why the patches dotted with moles and spiky hairs usually kept one's eyes from noticing what Mr. Black now considered to be the most interesting thing about the deceitful lord's visage.

A particular old, thick scar just beneath the viscount's chin, made permanent after repeated blisters, had peeled open beneath the latch of his tight chinstrap. The man in black had seen such scars many times before. That's why the Agent of the Isles now wondered if the Dark One's servant still viewed himself as a soldier of sorts. Was that his reason for turning against Duke Talhgho?

Is that—

Despite the right clothes and layers of cologne and cleansing powders needed to mask the numer-ous transgressions inherent to his rise in station, Lord Rohndolphn still exuded an otherworldly presence. A demeanor meant to soften, if not completely counteract, his otherwise oft-putting profile, specifically in the minds of those already subconsciously willing to let such dark deeds pass, if not join the ranks of his true master.

The scent lingered in the hallway, slipping through random ballshot and pike holes in the walls, where it wafted across Mr. Black's path as he pressed on through the crawlspace, nearing the duke's purse room.

You know what it is, brother?

Though the fighting was done, sweat still trick-led down Lord Rohndolphn's riding breeches and long sleeve tunic, dripped from his face and neck.

His single-breasted waistcoat was wet with gore beneath his new armor. The combination cuirass and leather skirt, commissioned in secret to celebrate his self-ish efforts and dark sacrifices, had protected him well from groin to neck against those he meant to murder this cold and wet September night.

Then you know what this means? Melisande asked.

True. The Horran was familiar with the eerie pher-omone: 6R1-7, otherwise known as the Whisperer's Rot, was a type of thaumaturgical consequence, kindled by subverting and modifying emotions, then reweaving and weaponizing them in the flesh of a host.

Once imbued, the alluring effect then grows natu-rally, building potency within the subject's body over an extended duration based on exposure to the source that initially teased them into darkness. It was not without its own side effects, though, many of which were uncondi-tional upon submission to the whisperer. An important detail usually overlooked by the Sabbat member once fully enthralled in the Enemy's warm embrace.

On the flip side, to anyone not already dancing somewhere along the Feld King's Crooked Spiral or otherwise commiserate with the Sabbat's goals and beliefs, Lord Rohndolphn's sweaty ass failed to exude anything remotely close enough to the number of pristine roses necessary to trick away one's wits and unconscious notions of self. Therefore, simply put, as far as Mr. Black was concerned, the savage looking viscount had every bit the aromatic grace and visual charm of a drowned rat freshly plucked from a vintage jar of pickled dog shit.

"Get it done, Dagny," said Rohndolphn's second as she approached.

The pounding on the purse room's iron door intensified.

Mr. Black wasn't sure how long they'd been at it, but from the irritation on Rohndolphn's face, he figured the traitor was yet considering the viability of using Duke Talhgho's M-noids, many of which were seriously damaged when they'd breached Wychstone's walls. Also, from the amount of debris beneath Mr. Black's boots in this final section of the crawlspace, it was clear enough to him something else was working against the killers, stalling their efforts to knock down the door. Would the noids be enough?

Mr. Black listened.

"You remember your part in this, Veucia," said Rohndolphn.

"I told you," replied the bearish woman. "He's a junker not a real Tinker."

"Then you better have a backup," said Rohndolphn.

Considering her own throat might still be slit, Veucia waved over an underling and told the injured man to run down and check on the M-noids nearest the perimeter. Certainly not all of them were destroyed in the fighting.

"My lord," said Dagny, "my acid will eat through the lock."

"You said that contraption wouldn't fail me, either?"

"On my life," replied Dagny, ignoring the heap of metal and liquid fuel once his prized Wells Light, which now lay trashed and leaking in the corner on its side.

"If it fails," said Rohndolphn to Sasha, third in command, "they drink it."

Because of the blood in his ear, Sasha inquired, "The acid?"

With a smug gesture, Rohndolphn turned and walked away in silence.

"Yes, my duke." Sasha grinned, blood dripping out beneath the scrap of torn bed sheet concealing his left eye.

19

"What's that racket now?"

Daphnia came up from the cellar hatch behind the bar.

Khalix looked up from where he and the semi-domesticated dire-wolfhound lay in a heap on a carpet nearest the warmest hearth in the inn. Their wounds were cleaned and bandaged, thanks to Jezzy and her assistants, Harold and Ceann.

The fact the inn's co-owner wasn't really fond of animals, especially ones who could eat her in two bites, gave the children something to giggle and tease her about while they worked to soothe their new friends. It also helped to keep Jezzy's mind on something other than the man in black.

Seconds later, Cirilo bounded down the stairs from his and Ceann's lookout spot on the roof, only accessible by a secret passage somewhere on the third floor. Daphnia had earlier shown him the way and lent him the key.

Only three men before him had ever held that specific keychain.

"Hey, Cirilo?" shouted Jezzy from the adjacent room.

Ignoring everyone, concerned only about whatever it was that'd summoned him from his deadly perch and insisted he make such a mad dash down three flights of stairs, Cirilo then threw open the Two Sisters' front door and saw Father Rai and Momma Bwulyaa standing on the porch.

"Get in! Get in!" He grimaced. The bandages over his stomach were slipping.

Father Rai and Momma Bwulyaa quickly filed in.

Half her pack of wolfhounds and a few dozen survivors from the mission followed them. Some were on crutches. Others were in wheelchairs or barrows. Everyone was loaded down with whatever they'd thought to grab.

"Bless you," said one man.

"Thank you. Thank you," said a young woman who, like the others, was one of the few able to flee the Mission on her own or with little assistance from the clergy.

"What happened?" Daphnia asked, wiping sweat and sleep from her face.

"It's gone." Father Rai stopped to help an old man find a place to sit.

"What's gone?"

"Everything," answered the priest.

Light Bringer Rai helped an old woman whose toes were bent and purple with bruises though the doorway and into the front hallway.

"What?" said Cirilo.

The Mission: it no longer straddled the middle heights of the Red Bern, just beyond the edge of Labor Ro's Junkyard. Once near, though not exactly in sight of Pehats Berg's East Gate, which was at the top of the ravine and far back from the edge—where Mr. Halgin and his band of killers were preparing for the arrival of the invading Urhal army.

Everyone took a moment to truly see and recognize how bloody and dirty the new arrivals were. How filthy and sweaty they were. The priest's cloak and greca were ruined. Muck was caked behind his ears, and his fingernails were coated in filth.

Father Rai and a few others were soaking wet. The worst looking of the bunch.

"How was the mission destroyed?" Cirilo asked.

"Vhendo," answered the priest.

"What?" said Daphnia.

He didn't repeat himself.

"Like the one from the barn?"

"Worse?" Jezzy asked as she returned to the open hall.

Cirilo glanced at her. They hadn't exactly had the time or right opportunity to spell it out. Not in detail. Other things needed doing. Saying. This was just another reason why Cirilo still regretted Emil's idea for them to wait behind for Momma to arrive, though the former deputy's plan also included the return of Mr. Black.

"How many?"

Momma Bwulyaa shook her head. "I don't know."

Hearing this, Leeann rose from what little sleep she'd gotten since helping Jezzy remove Margaret's body to the dumpster out behind the inn. After which, they'd spent a few moments together alone, outside, talking.

She blinked hard, then left the extra-comfy lounge chair she'd pushed to the edge of the fireplace near where the dire-wolfhound and Khalix now contemplated rising while Harold Cross, who was passed out in a booth, remained unconcerned. His snoring drowned out the world.

Too many, thought Leeann as she approached the women.

The rest of the pack circled the giant creature Khalix. A few of the wolfhounds seemed excited by the massive brute snuggled up beside the matriarch. The others were more apprehensive of the moropod. Truth be told, they feared his tail, which continued to twitch and slither about like a snake, taunting their natural instincts.

Quiet returned to the Two Sisters' common room. Awkwardness held it fast.

"So," said Leeann, "what happened?"

There wasn't much to say that anyone really wanted to hear or didn't already know or couldn't guess at, which is why they looked scared as Hel. Therefore, Father Rai skipped around in his telling.

The simple fact of it was, the type of death that clawed out through the tunnels and up into through the Mission, well, it was nothing they'd ever seen before. No way to prepare for that kinda evil. In their minds, the herd of monstrous, mutated, and malignant vhendo might as well have been a never-ending deluge of claws and fangs and fur and feathers and other things they dared not even imagine.

It's safe to say, if not for the few professional badasses paid regularly and well by Momma, in combination with half her pack of hounds, all their sacrifices thrown together to hold the area around the lift so the last stragglers might yet escape the vhendo surging toward the recovery ward at the heart of the hospital than—

"Poor bastards," said Cirilo.

Father Rai and Momma Bwulyaa alone knew how close they'd all come to dying. Many of the mission's patients would've simply been eaten alive by the vhendo, while others might've been lucky to be slaughtered outright. Death blows only. So lucky.

Meaning there were also the truly unlucky.

And if the stories were true which, in this case, Leeann assumed they were, the unfortunate souls left behind might've been captured, taken back to wherever the vhendo would later choose for a den beneath the Mission. They'd be kept alive. For hours. Days. Even weeks. Until their next feeding.

Never taken alive, thought Leeann.

"You're wet?" Leeann slipped a little on the puddled floor.

The other thing that saved them was a final safety net, care of Mr. Black.

By the time the last vhendo entered the Mission's sub-basement, about seven minutes after Father Rai exited the lift and bolted for the main recovery area, the syphoned water fired from Witcher Pond finally reached its long-awaited destination.

"I ran to tell everyone what was happening," said Father Rai.

But it'd already exploded from the Tunnel, just as Emil had earlier warned Momma Bwulyaa it would. She was ready.

He'd told her to prepare the sick and wounded for a wet descent down the mission's exterior stairway. The surrounding cage would suit them well in this circumstance by preventing anyone from falling over the sides of the railing. Leaving Momma Bwulyaa, Deputy Simkus then rode hard for Pehats Berg to carry out another piece of Black's business only a few hours ago.

The water rose quickly.

Faster than Father Rai could've possibly conceived.

The sloshing darkness overtook everything in its path, forcing itself into a surging wall that swallowed the various rooms of the mission's subbasement and basement. Finally, with nowhere else to go, physics encouraged the torrent up through the lift's shaft. Black foam spilled from the geyser, bubbling at such heights that it tore a hole in the roof.

Men and vhendo were swept up and drowned.

Churning with all kinds of dead and broken things gathered between the lift's shaft and the metro station some fifty-plus miles away beneath Wychstone Manor, the pungent water flooded the mission's central medical wing.

The combined flow, pressure, and debris broke through every window and door across the entire ward and rained down into the cavern, spewing into the Red Bern and along the ravine's rocky channel before it too vanished back beneath the urth.

They were halfway to the junkyard when the

supports gave out.

They watched as the mission collapsed into the river below.

"There will be more," said Father Rai, now that he'd finished explaining where the flood had flushed the first onslaught of vhendo that entered the mission during Momma Bwulyaa's organized retreat.

"*Vasha zdorhv'ye*," said Daphnia to the older woman on the stool before the bar.

Momma Bwulyaa swallowed the shot given to her by Daphnia and unfurled her fan.

"Where's Deputy Simkus?"

"You serious?" said Cirilo, answering his mother.

"That stupid, fucking do-well!" hollered the gangster queen.

"They're his kids," said Daphnia.

"Yes," replied Momma, "so what?"

Everyone gasped.

Her Iron Smile shined. "I had them sent for you fools. He knew that."

"Then why aren't they already here?" asked Leeann who, as always, remained impressed by Momma Bwulyaa's cleverness.

"I messaged Olyana to keep out of sight with the boys until it was light enough outside to come here without fear of those damn things sneaking up on them."

Obviously, no one questioned how the gangster queen knew where Emil's sister in-law lived. Momma always knew best where the lives and livelihoods of the berg's professional constabulary were concerned.

"So, where did he go?" Cirilo asked.

"His wife," said Jezzy, "she's still in the jail?"

Momma Bwulyaa shook her head, so sure was she that they'd need another body bag before the sun rose tomorrow. But Leeann wasn't so sure. She wondered what other pieces of Black's ever-changing puzzle the dependable officer was meant to ensure along the way while also recovering Gabija's body.

20

"She's waking, sire," said Medrick after setting aside the serving tray.

From the flickering glow provided by the short candlestick on his lord's counting desk, it was clear Medrick's nerves had settled into a fidgeting slosh of jelly and glass. The duke's sole surviving page still reeled from Lord Rohndolphn's assault on the manor, from which he'd miraculously escaped unharmed. At least, so far.

Duke Tarvarys Talhgho was in the middle of scratching out a series of new orders and fresh pledges on several sheets of signet parchment smeared with blood and sprinkled with crumbs of snuff spliced with cocaine so, of course, he spared but a glance from his work, though not for Medrick or the other two men lingering about the room. Instead, he looked over the singular beauty that embodied House Talhgho that lay unsheathed across his desk. The tailored shassock rapier combined aether technology and razor-sharp artistry.

Medrick again fumbled the hand scythe he'd taken up from one of Rohndolphn's dead. "Sire?"

Duke Talhgho turned from the customized weapon, ignoring the man who smelled of shit and fear and nodded to the older boy, Medrick. He swallowed an overflowing gush of licorice-colored brandy from his glass. And sighed as hot cinnamon, oak, and a hint of winter cherries reinvigorated his dry tongue, thinking himself better for not indulging the whelp whose boots were still heavy with cold piss.

Someone banged on the alchemically fortified metal door. They'd been at it for a while now.

"M'lord?" called Zelig, first of the duke's protectors now.

"We are safe," answered the duke without looking Zelig's way.

"Fer now," replied Zelig. He finished pacing the room, keeping away from the duke's third man who reeked of cowardice and filth.

"Unless they have a battering ram in their pockets," added the duke, in between another bursting gulp of brandy.

"Of course, m'lord."

"We are safe."

"Yes, m'lord," answered Zelig, his eyes focused for a moment on a wrecked bookcase.

Zelig turned away as the excess ran down his duke's mouth, spilling over the lord's graphite mustache and deflated chin, loosely braided with wispily threaded hair. The rich purple liquor continued to stain the duke's already ruined banyan frock, breeches, and pleated hose. In the end, it blended in rather nicely with other stains, evidence of the night's repeatedly bloody requirements. Such a mess.

With his throat now clear of the sweet libation, Duke Tarvarys Talhgho grimaced beneath his ruffled wig. From the armsman's studded gambeson vest and lacquered pteruges to his field boots, the duke wasn't sure how much of the vengeful splatter was his man's or that of his man's most recent victim. Either way, Zelig looked atrocious and as such, it reflected poorly on the duke's own splendid visage, no matter how he actually looked.

Duke Talhgho then scanned the purse room's nouveau riche decor.

Among the plush and frivolous space made visible only by the dainty light on his desk and another smaller lantern at the far end on a billiard table, one man lay dead from a bone-crushing heel kick to the sternum. He was the first to die. The *crunch* of his chest was so loud everyone in the room at the time heard it.

Another poor bastard bled out from his throat on the floor. The bandages weren't doing anything. While yet another man with a similar wound near his groin was, at least since setting aside his pole arm, now focused on draining a second bottle of the duke's quality. If he lived long enough to properly recover from the empty feeling rising from his feet, he swore to the Pillars he'd righteously set himself to praying and groveling his many remorseful thanks for the divine intervention that saved his pathetic life.

"I'm sorry," whispered he who reeked of hot ass and self-pity.

The duke absently considered what to do with this irrelevant, sick smelling weakling whose name he didn't know. Unlike Zelig, his usefulness had run dry and yet, oddly enough, the fool felt the worst of all three underlings still breathing.

Everything went to shit the moment the six sprang the witch's last-minute plan, a bottleneck trap of sorts to leverage the duke's position against Lord Rohndolphn. Even now, the fool was trying to contain his guilt. His shame and cowardice. His selfishness and fearful weakness. It wasn't his fault though, not really.

He was just a man, and she...

Also, the specially made chains were so damn heavy, yet slippery, and she was so damn fast and squirmy.

"I'm so sorry," he said again lowly, shamefully.

In truth, it was the fool's timidity, allowed to spread among the others, not including the witch, which pushed everything sideways shortly after they'd lured their secret prey into the duke's purse room. Doubt and fear led to the first man's death when an argument broke out, which Zelig would never forgive the fool for.

Finally, the duke turned his weary gaze upon his favorite and closest companion.

The freshly battered woman, wearing the remains of ruby-colored evening finery beneath an oil cloak, was stationed at the head of the room, standing directly in front of the alchemically hardened door. The duke's favorite goose-down recliner was behind her facing his desk. Her silhouette cast an attractive yet imposing shadow across the walls. She'd neither moved nor said a word, at least none they could understand, since her master had commanded her to bar the entrance against Lord Rohndolphn's cultish mercenaries.

The chained prisoner stirred again.

The duke turned his attention from the witch, his most adoring pet who, with all her senses targeting the lock failed to notice the loss of that she'd worked so long and hard for these many, many months: the duke's truly submissive and lovingly sympathetic interest for her wellbeing, down to her tiniest bruise or blemish.

Simultaneously, and with much more cause for concern, the red witch, because her Areté was so constrained by the enhanced lock's nuanced mechanisms, which were designed to foil even the most dedicated burglar, missed what no one else in the comfortable chamber could've perceived on their own.

Mr. Black was already inside, hiding in plain sight.

Unbeknownst to them, the Agent of the Isles had slipped through the cushioned slide-away panel, one of several decorative wall bumpers near where the twin billiard tables were outlined by the dim glow of a night lantern.

He'd made his move roughly about the time Medrick last refilled the duke's glass.

Wig adjusted now, Duke Talhgho returned to settling his paper affairs and ink futures.

Zelig signaled his liege to re-engage with the prisoner saying, "Her eyes are open."

When his mollycoddled stare finally detached from misplaced and dashed memories of privilege and splendor newly inked across the pages as best he could with shaky hands and hesitant fingers, Duke Talhgho nodded to the well-seasoned armsman.

"Get it then," said the duke.

Then Duke Talhgho stood from his counting desk, stepping around the unnamed sniveling fool and returned with goblet in hand to where he'd been earlier standing over the slack faced prisoner, prone in a chair.

"Patrycja?" whispered Duke Talhgho.

As instructed, Zelig returned from the duke's wall vault a few moments later, cradling a Sanguine Shard on a small, dark brown pillow embroidered in greens, golds, and black. The unified Urhal crest was greatly detailed despite being mostly obscured by the sinister token and the low light's limited reach.

Of those in the room, only one had ever clearly seen a version of the reincarnated silk sigil or the instrument on it. Mr. Black was thankful this combined variant wasn't clear enough for any of the ignorant onlookers to truly remember. Even so, his sense of it wasn't reassuring. With a quick look, the man in black was confident this most recent and wicked interpretation of the three Urhal's most regarded symbols and avatars would go far in its unified purpose, terrifying anyone who would stand against what was certainly a vhendoish image as well as its host bannermen in the wars to come.

Always more violence, thought Mr. Black.

"Wake up, Patrycja." Duke Talhgho signaled to his man.

"M'lord." Zelig set the ritual items aside, then slapped the princess across the face.

Following the insult to her person and station, the princess almost absently returned to a sullen posture. Her face cast down, drooping eyes glancing absently at Duke Talhgho's muddied spats and trim boots.

In reply to the princess' unintelligible moaning, muttering, and failing awareness, Duke Talhgho tipped the chalice in his hand just enough for a few fat drops to spill over the rim. Each berry burst sizzled across the links nearest the princess' innocent face and virgin neckline. She jostled and gritted her teeth so tight the duke could hear it.

"We do not have much time."

She howled again, and her gums wanted to burst under the strain.

"Dawn is upon us," said the duke, watching as her canines grew.

With another splash, more heat, her teeth extended into long fangs.

Eyes wide, Princess Patrycja Urhal better realized her dire situation.

She was no longer restrained in one of her host's less comfortable chairs by the sheer fighting strength of multiple large and sweaty abductors, each armed with several fiendish harnesses and pike poles fitted with roped ends and gagging bits. For most of those tools lay scattered and broken about the floor. No, that which completely immobilized the young woman now was something else. Something worse.

"I can't breathe…"

The silver-plated chains were more than three times her weight.

"What have you done to me?"

As further precaution, the industrial links once towed by the duke's riverboats and junk barges were outfitted with rusty makeshift bilboes with sharp burrs and unforgiving chinks. The cuffs were double looped around her wrists and ankles, attached to iron rings recessed into the floor below her, where an old rug had once lain in the back of the purse room, opposite the matching set of decanter stands intended to complement the billiard tables' cue rack in the adjacent corner.

"Where am I?" She sighed. Her lips trembled feverishly.

The duke watched with dispassionate curiosity as the prisoner whimpered and groaned under the toxic weight increasingly radiating across her body. He wondered if his inquisitiveness for such things came from his grandmother. She was sort of a fringe naturalist who claimed Arehthood ties, though that was during her teenage years.

"Release me!"

The duke replied, "Why did the king betray me?"

"It hurts!"

Most of her teenage flesh was shielded from the expensive allergen coating the chains, yet she was still too close for her immature condition. The pain was getting deeper.

"Why did Conquin side against me?"

The duke had known the Areht twenty years.

"What are they playing at?" asked the duke.

It was starting to come back to the princess now.

The accident. The secret. The midnight ceremony with her family. The dirt bath she awoke in. The blacked-out steam rail that carried her as a royal currier from her father's domain in the east. Her arranged room in the little backwater hamlet of Sigien before the duke formally wrote her, inviting her to stay in one of Wychstone's many guest rooms.

Flattered by the duke's invitation, and without Conquin to advise or chaperone her because he'd left on separate business of his own, a common grace afforded most Areht in the service of any respectable aristocrat, she accepted. Why not? It was nice being in the country. Alone. Unafraid. No one knew her but those who needed to. She felt free again. Certainly, no longer watched or whispered about as she'd been at home in her father's castle.

Everything changed, though, after her last supper in the duke's great dining hall, which was promptly served at sundown, whereas before, they'd been dining later in the evening.

Finished with her third helping of blutwurst, the princess mostly remembered returning to the guest room and finding her luggage opened and thoroughly rummaged. Several personal items were broken, clothes were torn, and something had been stolen from the secret drawer in the trunk her father's Areht advisor had built for this mission. His best men had sworn to protect it with their lives.

Of course, she went looking for answers and consequences as any angry princess would when so boldly insulted by a lesser noble sworn to her House. However, when she discovered the naked corpses of her father's most trusted men being rolled into wagons like slaughtered pigs on the way to market by Duke Talh-gho's M-noids no less, that's when her wants and needs suddenly strained her reason and royal honors.

The well-timed, sudden pull toward the purse room, shortly before the enemies of Wychstone neared Pike's Road, was too much for her to fight, so she quickly abandoned her hunt for answers from the duke.

If asked to describe what she felt while the people she'd come to know were then darting about the manor in preparation for the siege she was innocently unaware of, she might've said the feeling was instinctual, yet alien, an unknown carnal animalism swirling within an undying emptiness separate from herself, yet certain to overcome her.

Perhaps joining the two in ways she couldn't yet comprehend.

The spontaneous desire was stronger than any hunger or thirst she'd felt.

The unconscious compulsion made her mouth water and her head spin with ravenous cravings that would later frighten her when she finally learned the truth. In this state, she was no longer herself, but transfixed as a moth is to flame. So she ran. Faster than she'd ever run before. Her agility was that of an animal, each limb working together as instinct took over and reason faded away.

Even now she couldn't explain it.

Conquin had barely instructed her about her weakened condition since she'd awoken on a stone slab, her father and mother crying over her shrouded body sealed behind stained glass etched with unreadable markings.

Conquin! His absence was betrayal. It all made sense now.

This foreign Areht from the shores of the Silver Sea, implanted in her family the year she was away cementing her mostly forlorn engagement to Earl Fifus of Torm, was behind everything. *Everything!* It's why he grossly defended and vastly unprepared her for anything like this disloyalty. This craven grab for power.

"Whore!" shouted Patrycja when she was finally ambushed in the purse room.

As planned, the witch had summoned the princess to the farthest corner of the estate by harnessing a natural beacon of sorts. The evolutionary trigger was created from heart's blood, which the witch had syphoned from the princess' dead honor guard. Before their essence turned from inky purple to red fire, of course. Little did the witch know the new strength flowing through the girl's veins. But even if she did, it wouldn't have mattered much for what came next considering how newly damned the girl was.

That's when the duke's men sprang from behind the purse room's many pieces of furniture.

Violence, cursing, and darkness ensued. A bookcase was smashed in the process.

"Let me go!"

"No." The duke met her gaze. "Not until you tell me what I want to know."

"Release me, please."

Patrycja's body temperature reached a new phase now. She screamed. Her streamlined robe à l'anglaise, from her beige petticoat to her neat, swan-white engageantes, was gradually singeing in its most delicate spots.

The smell of burning soap and perfumes turned acrid in the air.

"I beg you. My father will—"

"He knows, princess. He knows."

Patrycja's heart broke, and her wailing deepened.

"There is only one way this ends," said the curmudgeonly miser.

The princess continued to sob and cringe against the burning silver.

"Have I not sacrificed?" Duke Talhgho threw his wine glass across the room.

Between the light from his desk candle that reached the witch guarding the heavy door, and the small lantern set near the billiard table, Duke Talhgho fumed and ranted his corrupted grievances aloud for all to hear: Years of bending over backwards and disposing of bodies and bloody coins. Years of kissing asses and cleaning messes, just as his father had done, and *his* father before him.

"Pehats Berg was supposed to be mine!"

At this point, the princess' cream-colored, close-body dress with woodland patterns decorating its edges, had begun to mottle with burning grays and deep tans. Not too dissimilar from a sheaf if laid too long beside a tenacious flame. Patrycja sweated profusely now, yet the running beads on her face and décolletage had a slight pinkish hue. Odder still, the moist mixture seemed to be congealing, as if it might soon become a paste, in the same way sugar water turns to syrup after evaporating in a boiling pot.

"Why was *he* chosen for this gift and not me?" In

truth, the idea terrified the duke.

She doesn't know, thought Mr. Black, drifting along the walls, out of sight.

The princess again lost consciousness.

Patrycja Domitia Marcus Urhal was yet another seduction deployed by the Sabbat, a seducer to tease and control those in their way. She was yet another innocent reforged into a tool for their violent ends.

Could she be Conquin's new Sanguine Childe?

Mr. Black now wondered what exact role her father, Prince Zahargan Marcus Urhal, must've played in orchestrating her sale to the yet unknown but clearly important servant of the Dark One, to whom this Conquin likely reported.

In fact, Mr. Black doubted she had any real notion of her new existence between worlds, assuming the princess at all understood her intended role in this ritual, considering how different the transition would be for Rohndolphn, compared to her own tragic experience with the Shadow's rapturous kiss.

For instance, the prelude to this particular strain of the necrotic affliction was made possible, in part, by the weaving of a Sanguine Shard. Such dilution alone would make it nothing like her experience, which was carried out in the old way: directly from the lips of an elder nekctu, but only after many nights and damnable choices were made for her by those who presumed to know best about the fate of her soul in the life thereafter.

From behind the billiard table, Mr. Black pondered to what lengths her family, entourage, servants, and attachés had gone to further this totally encompassing and permanent masquerade since her somewhat public death and funeral. What were they doing before now to normalize a life that would forever be haunted by the sun?

"Why Heimont?" begged the duke, almost hoarse from shouting at his prone captive.

As his bubbling frustration seemed to cancel everything out, silence briefly returned to the purse/billiard room. Then, as if spoken from the darkest corner of this night's bloody debts come due, a voice answered the flabbergasted duke, who was stunned by his own ignorance and shortcomings.

"Heimont would have only one master."

"Who said that?" Medrick asked without thinking.

"Whereas you, my lord, would still have two."

The duke looked about as though his eyes were playing tricks. They were alone, right?

"Who said that?"

"I did," answered Mr. Black.

21

Duke Tarvarys Talhgho snapped his fingers, signaling for Medrick to fetch him his unattended blade on the desk.

Mr. Black continued, "They can't have you bootlicking for anyone else now, can they?"

"Medrick?" Duke Talhgho snapped again before the page tossed him the modified shassock rapier. Then, once the sword was level with the darkness and tip first, he raised the small lantern from the billiard table.

"Sire?" The humiliated servant with soiled breeches pointed. "Look."

Half the silver chains had loosened and slackened about Patrycja's chest, slipping all the way off her shoulders seconds later. The metallic grading was slow and unsettling as he each link scraped the other.

The duke spun around to stab behind the still-standing bookcase. He found not assailant.

When enough of the heavy links had fallen from Patrycja's trim torso, the combined weight, then pulled most of the rest, including the portion looped through the rusty bilboes about her wrists and ankles, down about her shoes. The chains landed on the wooden floor with a heavy *thud*.

"What were you thinking?" Mr. Black asked.

"Zelig?" Duke Talhgho turned the disguised pin-hammer within the hilt of his rapier.

"I don' see anything?" answered the brute, trying to follow the jerky lantern light.

"Tempting the Rose Coast as your patronage while pretending to bend the knee to Prince Urhal and his thirst for conquest?" said Mr. Black.

"Fool," shouted Duke Talhgho. "Do something?"

"What did you hope to gain beyond a knife in the back?"

"What do we do, m'lord?" Medrick asked, eyes frantic in the candle's glow from the desk.

"The queen isn't what you think," said Mr. Black. "She's worse."

And her whores are everywhere, commented Melisande.

Ignoring the repugnant, shit-stained fool who again regressed into a limp fish floating in still water, the duke gestured for Zelig and Medrick to defend his mistress from this intrusive specter sneaking among the shadows.

"How did you think your true masters would respond?"

Statuesque before the smoldering and bubbling interior lock, the witch, much younger than her duke, was truly defenseless. Her nose, which had only just started to bleed, was quickly worsening, yet her focus remained enough to block out every other pain caused by her prolonged works.

Truly, she was the only thing keeping Dagny's trial-and-error tinkering from melting through the chamber's alchemically fortified barrier, the only thing keeping Rohndolphn's men from murdering them all once inside the duke's purse room.

"It's over, Tarvarys," said Mr. Black.

As only a vain duke could, he raged against such hostile informality while the man still stewing in his own incontinence and frailties finally fainted. Too bad he wasn't farther away from the billiard's table when he collapsed, for his face struck a corner of the slate. His head poured blood before he hit the floor.

Medrick called out, "Where is he?"

The walls! The walls! Duke Talhgho was furious with himself now that he realized what had caused his current predicament. He had forgotten to bar the hatches and servant passages throughout Wychstone, though he didn't think he'd underestimated the cleverness of his rival, who was ever the bull, never the owl.

"Come out you bastard!"

While attempting the bravado of a brawler, Medrick, the greener of the two remaining guards, was suddenly confronted by the strength of the man in black, who'd just grabbed his ranseur, which Medrick had only moments ago traded up for since the guard previously holding it lay cold on the floor, his throat black with blood.

"Zelig!" The duke again raised the hilt's basket guard.

"I see him!" Zelig, the toothless footman with the fuzzy dead growth on his bottom lip had already pulled his trusty skinning knife.

In a flash of synchronous actions, Medrick was back-handed at the edge of the flickering candle's light and disarmed of his pole arm. The page was then twisted, flipped, and thrown halfway across the room, shattering a barstool, and sending its broken legs spinning across the floor.

Mr. Black then extinguished the lavish room's only other flickering wick with his fingertips.

"Master," called the witch as the desk candle went dark, "the—"

"Stay where you are!" ordered the duke.

The Red Lady obeyed, slouching for a moment against the back of the duke's favorite chair.

"I got you now," growled Zelig.

Despite Zelig's best reaction time, though, which allowed him to get at Mr. Black's flank after he'd thrown down the boy, Zelig, like Medrick, was nonetheless immediately outmatched by the invisible specter in the chaotic light from his master's lantern.

"Son of a—"

The mangy old dog should've been more like the sprat and certainly less of a preening ass pretending to be a professional bodyguard. He should've stuck to what he knew, what he was good at. Namely, being hired muscle who occasionally did grifting highwayman's work for local authorities. Legal or otherwise.

At least Zelig wouldn't have ended up as he was now after only a few failed swipes and stabs in the air, desperately sucking wind and red air through a hole in his neck, before slumping over and dying behind the duke's favorite goose-down recliner.

He never saw Black nor blade, and the only thing he felt besides emptiness was the wind.

"Tarvarys Talhgho," said Mr. Black.

"Duke!"

"Not anymore." Mr. Black again dodged the targeting light of the small house lantern.

After a time, his eyes adjusting to the deeper darkness outside the reach of his lantern, Tarvarys became aware of the brazenly plainspoken and heavily armed silhouette wearing strange eyewear beneath a dusty tricorn.

"Who are you?"

Mr. Black spied the dispatches on the former duke's desk.

"Hard to keep track, so many trying to kill you?"

"You smell of the sewers."

Tarvarys angled the house lantern so its window would better strafe the somewhat insubstantial stalker.

"My apologies," said Mr. Black, memorizing the pages, "but it's your shit."

Tarvarys waited till the irritation passed, then said, "Hunting me for some time?"

"You could say that." Pieces of parchment vanished into Mr. Black's person.

"You have me at a disadvantage, sir."

"Do I?" Mr. Black paced the room, dropping each letter once he deemed it harmless.

As Mr. Black quietly scanned every scrap with scribblings, eyes keen for anything with Lady Genza's hand, Tarvarys loosened his cravats, exposing where one of his now dead attendants failed to powder his neck earlier that evening.

Mr. Black motioned for Tarvarys to close the window, diminishing the house lantern's glow. After appeasing the assassin's silent request for a darker chamber, Tarvarys picked away a bit of old, crusted snuff caught in his sweaty mustache.

Just then, as if to counteract the increasing mechanical hammering on the outside of the purse room's door, a small haze of swirling light emerged from some hidden place between the woman in red's articulated fingers.

Mr. Black paused to silently regard the witch.

Once combined and shaped, the witch's translucent cat's cradle offered its own eerie glow to the weakened light in the chamber.

After a moment, the duke asked, "If you are not Heimont's man, then what?"

His demeanor slowly teased the appearance of a numerical word-problem in his head. Seconds later, the solution seemed to settle beneath the obvious variables, becoming something the usurped duke simply wasn't expecting to solve.

Finished, Mr. Black dropped the last few pages of private correspondences on the floor and faced Tarvarys, who then noticed the last bits of fortitude eking through the man in black's intimidating persona. Mr. Black was beat.

The tells of this long night were in the assassin's now heavier steps and sluggish movements, and yet the otherwise methodical miser of Pehats Berg continued to overlook the most important thing that Mr. Black's skull-duggery about the purse room's lavish interior, a sort of walking prestidigitation, otherwise known in the trade as the Final Five Fingered Salute, was meant to distract him from.

"You're not here for me?" said Tarvarys, lowering the house lantern more.

"Not anymore," said Mr. Black, his thoughts circling back to the witch.

He didn't know if the glow from her art was part of whatever limited forces and/or elements she wielded or if it was something worse. That her esper, the invisible aura often displayed whenever an Areht strained to harness more of their Areté than normal, was turning on her, becoming something far more dangerous in an already hostile environment.

A ruptured anima burn could clear the field, thought Mr. Black.

"You do not look well," fawned Tarvarys.

The duke's elitist social embellishments were now rekindled as he cynically debated which of his fair prizes the man in black was sent to rescue or silence permanently. How could someone so blessed be so cursed?

"It's not me you should be worried about," said Mr. Black.

Still oblivious to what Mr. Black had already lifted, Tarvarys faced his pet.

"Cézann, my love?"

Tears streamed from the bruised woman in red as her hands continued to telekinetically knead the liquefied metal. However, many alchemical elements were beyond her ability to completely or even partially remake or otherwise supernaturally weld into something useful to save the barrier so, piece by piece, the cracks and fractures and weaknesses in the alchemical door endured. She couldn't make it whole anymore. The errors and remainders would soon be too many and there'd be nothing left to remake the door with.

She needs to be neutralized, said Melisande.

As Cézann pushed herself to the brink, the sizzling materials repeatedly made molten by powerful alchemical acids, were yet again, by her will, vertically backtracked up the drippings running down the door's inner panel. Her continuous efforts to hold the line and keep Rohndolphn out only slowed when she returned the messy chunks into the once finely tuned mechanical lock face to cool and harden.

Mr. Black interjected, "You ever seen a witch spontaneously combust?"

"What?" Tarvarys blinked.

"In thirty seconds," said Mr. Black, "she'll collapse."

"Cézann?" Tarvarys removed his less-than-perfect regal wig.

"AHHHH!" Medrick discreetly withdrew a paperknife from a drawer in the duke's desk. Then he leapt to his feet and lunged for the man in black's neck.

"No!" Mr. Black whirled, right hand raised.

The page cheered, "I'll save you, sire!"

Stupid boy, thought Melisande.

"Yes, kill him!" commanded Tarvarys.

Medrick stabbed Mr. Black in the hand, and the man

in black cursed in pain.

Medrick snarled and hit, fighting to remove the blade he'd buried in Mr. Black's metacarpals. How was he to know the man in black was going to close his own fist over the boy's, securing more than just the brass blade from doing further damage?

"Stupid, kid," grunted Black, fingers burning, elbow glossy wet with blood.

Flinching, panicking, shouting for glory as the much smaller Medrick flailed almost uselessly against the Horran's overpowering strength, Tarvarys Talhgho, with nothing left to lose, raised his father's pistolsword, aiming the barrel tip first at the one loose end he still had power over and pulled the trigger.

There was no pan powder burst. No external spark. No flame. No deafening bang, either, besides the sounds of Lord Rohndolphn's men continuing to beat and hammer the door of the purse room.

Tarvarys Talhgho's aether weapon let loose a single, teal-tinged static burst briefly igniting the darkness along the sword's blade nearest the modest barrel. That was it. That was all. And when the weapon's electrostatic discharge faded into the otherwise mostly consuming darkness of the purse room, only a trace smell of burnt gas remained.

22

"Don't be scared," said Ceann in a hushed voice.

She crawled out from beneath the comforting blankets and quilts Daphnia gave her and Cirilo while they kept an eye out from the Two Sisters' roof. Ceann didn't know where Cirilo had gone off too. She must've dozed off again.

"Come on, don't be shy," said Ceann.

She'd been at it for a while now. Off an on. Whatever the thing was, it wasn't a vhendo.

Of that, Ceann was sure, because it seemed terrified as it continued to cling to the outside of the building, getting tangled in the stringy beard moss growing up the side. Whatever it was, it couldn't have been bigger than a large house cat. Not by much anyway, based on Ceann's guess from the sounds it made while switching positions, creating new perches along the surface of the Two Sisters' siding and trim.

"I have food." Ceann smiled at the thought.

At least they'd been able to eat and rest a bit since they'd settled at the inn.

"You can have it," said Ceann, trying to reassure the poor thing.

Again, the skittering, clawing, brushing sounds shifted about.

"It's good." Ceann took a small bite of Jezzy's famous hedgehog stew.

Really, Jezzy had been a damn good cook once, which is why her line units, the M-noids, which regularly stepped in for human staff, continued to operate the kitchen exactly as she did, exactly as Jezzy's husband did when he was still alive.

"So, this is where you went?"

Ceann snapped round, the way Cirilo had gone earlier, her eyes low and wide. "Harold?"

"I'm sorry, Ceann."

Ceann controlled her surprise, swallowed the bit of terror that came up from her toes.

Harold smiled big. He stood still, paused between the third-floor ceiling and the roof, on the secret, drop-down ladder.

"I didn't mean to wake you," said Harold.

"What're you doing?" she snapped, looking down at the former stable boy from her crouched position in the assassin's cramped hidey hole.

Harold smiled as though she were playing games. "I've been following it, and now it's stopped."

"What's stopped?"

He looked square at her, as though waiting for a

trick, then quickly explained how he figured the winged creature would've already found its way inside the inn given how big it is. That is, if not for the Two Sisters having closed and locked all the building's heavy exterior shutters, many of which were simply decorated in wood with metal bones.

Harold Cross then appeared to zone out for a few seconds.

"Harold?" Ceann snapped her fingers.

"Ohhhhh," said Harold with a goofy laugh, his straying eyes returning to their proper orientation seconds later.

"What?"

"I get it now," he said.

Ceann looked around, not sure what she'd missed or overlooked.

"I'm sorry. Stupid of me." Again, he laughed and scoffed. "Good luck."

Ceann blinked.

Without another word, Harold scampered down the ladder, closing the hatch behind him.

"Harold?"

While Ceann wondered about what just happened, what little Harold Cross had been tracking around the darkened rooms and floors of the inn at this late hour without going outside the inn for fear of the obvious, something crawled over one of the roof's gables.

"Hello," said Ceann, turning back, facing the new arrival.

She'd expected a fat alley cat outwitted by a gutter rat or perhaps a large street rooster that'd somehow gotten confused or lost from its pen during the craziness of the evening. One could imagine her surprise when a tiny gargoyle dropped down over the arch and landed a few feet away from her.

The gargoyle was half her size at best, though more than two-thirds her weight, with splotchy blue and gray skin. She'd never seen rough and craggy shades like it before, so it was hard for Ceann to say for sure what exactly the muddled colors reminded her off.

"My name is Ceann," she said, offering the bowl of leftover stew.

The gargoyle fluttered its wings.

"It's all right. I won't hurt you."

After a moment, the gargoyle cautiously sniffed her extended hand.

Ceann smiled as it licked her fingers. Giggling, she noticed its tail was pitchforked near the tip and both segments wagged independently. "I have to have something to call you," she said with a secretive grin.

Uška soon ate the soup.

"You like it?" Ceann petted her new friend's horns.

Uška emptied the bowl quickly and tipped it over his head.

"More?" Ceann smiled.

23

Medrick gasped and gurgled as blood bubbled up from his throat.

Seconds before the ex-duke's pistolsword discharged its electrochemical powered load, Mr. Black's punchdagger sprang from the vambrace of his left forearm, and the wannabe hero, sick of cleaning chamber pots and other menial duties, suffered every inch of it as it sliced through his breast, wedging open his ribs and piercing his lung.

In the dissipating aether, the paterfamilias of House Talhgho thought he'd won. He then felt the assassin's quick-drawn counter shot, which the man in black squeezed off as the dead page landed with a *thud* on the floor of the purse room.

Tarvarys screamed, cursed, and stumbled back.

The barely aimed hipshot from Mr. Black's wheel-blaster, meant to disable Tarvarys' sword arm, had shredded the lord's shirt and biceps at the elbow. And because the ex-duke was counter-struck almost exactly while attempting to execute Princess Patrycja Urhal, Tarvarys' solid silver single-shot slug went wide of its mark.

Mr. Black flinched at his error in timing, for the expensive ammunition from the even more extortionate pistolsword still managed to blow off the right side of the prone princess' jaw and her right ear, flipping her backward, taking the chair and chains with her.

Tarvarys had meant to shoot her in the middle of the forehead, above her nose.

Being well within point-blank range, he'd hoped the slug would ricochet around inside the princess' skull a bit. No other way to really kill this type of nekctu, other than a rather messy beheading. That was his basic understanding of the damned's unnatural physiology anyway, which he'd only learned after paying considerable coin for genuine information on the controversial subject, of course.

Anger rising, Mr. Black advanced.

The next thing Tarvarys felt was Mr. Black's fist, then the floor.

Tarvarys coughed and gagged. His eyes were already swelling. When he sat up, his nose and left cheek poured blood down his face. He blinked back into coherence. He moaned as the foggy pain twisted the back of his eyeballs.

You were slow, said Melisande.

Mr. Black grumbled a quiet retort while eying the witch, Cézann, who'd yet to move.

Fifteen-seconds, thought Mr. Black. The pneumatic

punchdagger retracted.

"I'll pay you ten times your contract."

Mr. Black grunted to himself, tore a strip from a billiards towel, and bound his bleeding hand. Then he dropped the bloody paperknife on the floor beside the fallen pistolsword and stomped out the house lantern the duke had dropped during the commotion.

"Did you hear me?"

Mr. Black didn't. In his lucid haze of pain and tiredness and anger and never-ending violence that forever taunted the ghosts of his past, the Horran absently rested his bloodied hand over the pommel of his sword. His fingertips, free of the binding about his burning knuckles, peppered blood all over the hilt and scabbard.

The purse room door bowed slightly at the hinges.

Cézann's knees were visibly shaking now from the strain.

That's no junker's tool, thought Black.

Nor alchemy, said Melisande.

Tarvarys struggled to stand. "I'll honor any arrangement—"

Honor? Tarvarys Talhgho's funds and title were forfeit to the realm. His estate was overrun and burning. His wife and children, if they still lived, had already abandoned him though, surely, he abandoned them first. Lastly, his allies and servants were dead or betrayed while his enemies continued without rest or mercy, to say nothing of Lady Genza's hunters, the Beasts from Beyond the Black likely stalking the woods outside Wychstone's walls that very moment.

"She lied to you," said Mr. Black.

The sword in his scabbard fed on the droplets of his blood.

Neither a Mistress of the Veyl nor a full-fledged Matron of the Queen's Red Order, Mr. Black could now see and roughly identify the young *witch's* place in all this mess, which Tarvarys had created, for she'd been purposefully inserted into this political war-zone, a conflict that, by now had, in so many ways, quietly split the western half of Uropà, essentially the Middle Realm at large, in two.

Because, of course, the mere existence of this red pretender here, on this night, only further complicated the realigning of the Scattered Kingdoms' power structure.

"She used you." Mr. Black readjusted the binding on his hand till it stopped bleeding.

Tarvarys looked to Cézann.

"You were her target."

Heat-stress marks began appearing around what remained of the alchemically reinforced door's enhanced lock. The metal turned white, powdery.

Rohndolphn has an ace up his sleeve?

"So do I," said Mr. Black.

"Varys?" moaned Cézann.

Tarvarys Talhgho—not the duke, not the husband or father, not even the Sabbat's influencer, but the man— ran and caught his dedicated servant now drained to the point she could no longer stand.

Cézann crumpled into Tarvarys, as though made of knotted char cloth, and he cradled her in his arms. Not the way one would think, the way an addict fawns over a refilled narcotic pouch several weeks past due.

Cézann smiled at her lord and passed out in his arms.

Tarvarys' eyes filled with suicidal tears and a lifetime of regret.

Rohndolphn would burst through the door any second now. They all knew it.

"She's a Kamorri Iconate," said Mr. Black.

A Frankish lowborn raised in one of the island's Blush Dens, sensitive to the Tuch on a sliding-empathic scale, employed and empowered through various means but always to specific ends as determined by her betters, the elites and nobility of Perryn, to whom this caste of potential lunatics often owed their livelihoods, considering the many afflictions associated with their psionic condition if left unchecked or uneducated.

However, the Red Isles' peerage usually only deployed such subtle proxies and influencers against their own social, political or business rivals—their own version of the time-honored game of Swords and Crowns.

Tarvarys rubbed Cézann's forehead and cheeks in disbelief.

"You were a means to an end, Tarvarys." Mr. Black's hilt was now clean of blood.

"Stop it," said Tarvarys, pleading.

"She was after something," said Mr. Black.

"You're wrong," snapped Tarvarys.

"Something only you had access to."

But only after Lord Nadezhda died stealing it for him, of course, which then sent his grieving widow, the Lady Nadezhda, into the arms of her lover, Countess Kseniya Rohndolphn. Both of whom were then murdered either by Rohndolphn himself or by one of his men, likely Sheriff Kozlov. But Mr. Black couldn't be sure after this bloody night. His head swam, and his bones felt old.

Barely mindful, Tarvarys continued to soothe the motionless woman laying across his lap.

"She's not who you think she is."

As an Iconate in the pocket of the Red Ladies, Cézann's Tuch-based empathic abilities made her a versatile mole and, as a Kamorri, she was probably a sexual placater by trade, at least since her first bleeding. If she'd been a Kamorri man, a similar initiation would've been equally true, but the man in black had no time to explain this combination of perizian dangers long aimed at Tarvarys' weakness for such indiscretions, especially since he'd been under Cézann's influence for so long he was unlikely to accept whatever Mr. Black had to say.

Tears streamed down Tarvarys' chin.

Cézann probably hailed from somewhere along the most southern shores of the United Kingdom of Perryn. Mr. Black discerned this from her coastal complexion, mannerisms, and the distinctive beauty marks at the edge of her mouth and right eye.

Some of Cézann's other inviting features further informed the rogue her Junoesque bloodline wasn't indigenous to the islands of her Queen and Matron Supreme. She was special. A curiously blended favorite perhaps, much like the queen's mixed son, Prince Merovech, who'd been a source of many societal complications and dramatic whisperings since his birth, a series of uniquely historical event for reasons beyond those obvious to the citizens of the United Kingdom of Perryn.

What did all this mean to the Horran?

What game were the Red Ladies playing against the Sabbat? Or with them?

Mr. Black's mind raced with intrigue, anger, sadness, and blood.

Think, said Melisande.

Someone, with or without the Court of Queen Gehddrin's knowledge and permission, had learned of the duke's nefarious dealings in the neutral zone of Pehats Berg. This person or group had also attained a certain degree of pedigree knowledge causing further turmoil between a handful of the Scattered Kingdoms' rulers and lesser nobility.

This person or persons then arranged an introduction between Cézann and Tarvarys.

Sometime after that, according to Mr. Black's loose theorizing, between seconds of mental static and physical discomfort, the same person(s) then financed resources and safe travel for Cézann's long-term embedment at the duke's side.

A journey by ship and carriage, which took the witch from the islands of the U.K.P., some three thousand miles south by southwest and deposited her here in this unremarkable plot of foreign urth outside Pehats Berg's neutral zone, called Wychstone Manor, where the no-longer secret armies of the Enemy, the vhendo, and the amassed Urhal forces, led by their newly declared king, Zahargan Marcus Urhal, would continue Father Midnight's conquest across the western half of the Scattered Kingdoms.

Such a joint military excursion of this kind might not have been seen by human eyes since the First Age, when the last vhendo still roamed in small herds, a time when mighty behemoths hunted along the Vahast, the Borderlands, and the Lands of Nor in the icy north. A time when the first Crimson Blooded separated themselves from the lesser Sabbat members and Black Thumbs to destroy the Ark by sinking the Isles of Blue Mist beneath the bronze waves of the Hammer Sea.

Nothing is Coincidence or Convenience, said Melisande.

Urhal horns sounded in the far distance. Somewhere beyond Pike's Road.

"I'll tell you everything," swore Tarvarys.

Wheelblaster re-slung, Mr. Black scowled beneath his tricorn and trencher goggles.

"Just save us!" pleaded Tarvarys.

A second Urhal horn answered the first. The scout's reply came from the marshes, somewhere in sight of the estate or perhaps even closer.

"Too late for that," said Mr. Black.

Ceasing his sniveling, Tarvarys sensed a new edge in the man in black's tone. Not only that, but Mr. Black fell back, retreating into the shadows. The ex-duke had a terrifying thought: since Zelig's death, no one had been watching, much less guarding, the Sanguine Shard.

"It's safe with me," said Mr. Black, now that Tarvarys finally caught on.

"Varys," said Cézann, "where's the shard?" She sensed new, eminent danger.

"They'll kill you for it," said Tarvarys.

After a moment, Mr. Black replied, "She'll kill you first."

Glassy tears broke behind Tarvarys' eyes. He smiled and looked down at his weakened pet, confident she'd never betray him or otherwise harm him. But, instead of finding love, he saw only her horror reflecting back.

Cézann tried to speak, to warn him, but it was too late. *Some potent blood*, thought Mr. Black.

As quiet as a midnight arrow sailing through a black sky, Princess Patrycja Urhal reappeared behind Tarvarys and Cézann.

"You did this to me!" Blood ran from the princess' reddened eyes.

"It's impossible!" screamed Tarvarys.

Blood spilled from her lips. "You killed me!"

Tarvarys couldn't look away, no matter how much he wished to.

Parts of the princess' face and head were still a violent mess of exposed bone and torn flesh from the silver slug he'd blown off her jaw and ear with, but she was regenerating. Quickly. The pain was already a distant memory.

Tarvarys mumbled more pathetic apologies and promises.

"You tried…" An insane grin slowly curled the princess' crimson lips.

Ignoring the red-faced witch, whom she planned to deal with next, though much more slowly, Patrycja instead focused on the first and only thing, the craziest thing now dominating her swirling, bloodthirsty mind.

She needed to feed, and she wasn't hungry for just

any food. No. This time, she knew exactly what she wanted, what she was going to have, how it alone could satisfy her. It all made perfect sense now as she sniffed the air, in the same way it made perfect sense for a baby predator to attempt its first kill, alone. It was instinct, and it was glorious.

Tarvarys looked rapidly about the room, but Mr. Black was nowhere to be seen.

"Bastard! You've killed us!"

In a blur, Patrycja wrapped her hands, now free of rusty bilboes and toxic silver weight, around Tarvarys' buzzard-like neck. Then, so excited by this newfound strength compelling her to tease and torture the blood bag, she simply lifted the former lord from the couple's cuddle till they were eye to eye.

"Cézann, I…gah…ahh guhghg—"

The princess bit directly into his throat, cutting off his final confession.

Tarvarys Talhgho grunted and choked and squirmed as he struggled to free himself but, in the end, all he could do was wait to die. And the only sounds he heard, life fading from his eyes, were Patrycja's gulping and slurping as she learned to swallow as much of his salty blood as she could as fast as she could.

Fearing for her life now that she'd failed to secure the Sanguine Shard against its falling into the wrong hands, Cézann stayed low and struggled to crawl away from the neonate bloodsucker feasting on the worthless duke, who, at that very moment because of Patrycja's ravenous feasting, appeared several days past dead.

The Kamorri Iconate made it halfway to the panel

along the wall with the cushioned bumpers behind the billiard tables, through which she assumed Mr. Black had only moments ago escaped, but she'd never make it all the way and not because of her wounds or how near totally depleted she felt. No, it was over because, right then, Rohndolphn's efforts to break down the purse room's alchemically fortified door, paid off.

Sure, it took Dagny's constant pounding and a salvaged M-noid to finally knock the damn thing down, and this only after Cézann stopped fighting their every inch of progress for the past hour or so. Nevertheless, Rohndolphn was successful. The Sabbat was right to trust him. His men were through, led by Sasha and Veucia, his two best. It was over, finally, and the new duke of Pehats Berg was ready for his eternal prize.

The only problem was Cézann had orders not to let that happen.

No matter what.

"Patrycja?" said Rohndolphn, now kneeling before the princess.

The young nekctu stood with her back to him, feeding on a second victim now.

This was strange to Rohndolphn. Not that Patrycja was surrounded by dead bodies or the fact she seemed to have already sucked Tarvarys Talhgho dry. No, what was strange to the new duke was the witch wasn't struggling in the princess' embrace. Really, their union, their hugging, didn't seem violent at all.

Instead, it appeared quite passionate and mutually exhilarating. This was nothing like how Rohndolphn imagined or fantasized it would be once the power was his. On the other hand, perhaps there were many perks he simply wasn't aware of yet. And what did it matter? Such tantalizing possibilities were now his to behold.

"For my sisters," moaned Cézann, just loud enough for Duke Rohndolphn to hear.

The princess couldn't stop eating. Nor would she be stopped, so said her glaring eyes.

Duke Rohndolphn pointed, "Kill the witch!"

Cézann smiled, knowing her blood was too rich. Too sweet.

Sasha and Veucia, barely had enough time to think, let alone react to the death and bloodshed littered about the billiard room, before Cézann's esper, in a final act of self-defense, triggered by blood loss, caused an immediate anima burn, which then ruptured, because the overflow was intrinsically connected to the beating of her own heart.

"For my queen," said Cézann. Her eyes closed as rich blood spilled over her lips.

The auspicious shroud swimming between worlds, invisible to the naked eye, then ignited Cézann's body in pure radiant energy loosened from unknown depths of her Areté. The resulting expulsion of pure Tas, a shockwave of heat and light and other fantastic forces beyond their visibility or understanding, then destroyed the purse room and much of Wychstone Manor's third floor on that side of the captured estate.

24

"See?" said Mr. Black, ducking low beneath an old drainage pipe.

The mare whickered and softly brayed in reply to her returning rider's sarcasm.

He grinned, testing his bloody palm. "Now, don't you owe me an apology?"

The mare turned and nipped at Mr. Black's boot once he was seated in the saddle. Then snorted and continued up the ramp leading back down one of many long forgotten and abandoned corridors toward the metro beneath Witcher Pit.

"Okay, fine," Mr. Black admitted in the darkness. "The flare burnt out. Happy?"

Keeping her pace, the horse accepted his token apology. He plucked a bug of some kind from his beard, then wiped a trail of sweat and blood from beneath his tricorn. He sighed and stretched. How he wanted to sleep.

"Really, though," Mr. Black added, "I wasn't gone very long."

The mare snorted again. She was simply content to be leaving the otherwise pitch-black tunnels, junctions, and sewer passages beneath Wychstone Manor. Her time alone in the dark hadn't exactly been pleasant, since it reminded her of the first few dingy corners she was stowed in after she was sold off as a foal, though that now seemed a lifetime ago.

When they arrived back at the sunken metro, Mr. Black offered a final, "I'm sorry."

He was, but for something new now. Something again unexpected as the metro came into view. He slowed the mare's lazy trotting to a walk, then screwed closed the no-flare, and returned it to the harness.

His borrowed darū trencher goggles could now pick up the first hints of open, natural sunlight. The rays, many still gray and weak and cool, reached down through the darkness like transparent fingers splayed wide by some ghostly forest spirit. The confusion of moisture and shadow then thinned, and the whitening yellow grays pushed back the predawn shroud concealing the open throat and mouth of Witcher Pit.

Mr. Black whispered, "Shhh." They crept forward.

High above him, outside the pit's mouth, once considered a lake by some, Mr. Black could see the tips of horses' ears. From the angle leading out, he guessed they were tied off just around the new edge surrounding the giant washed-out hole in the ground.

A moment later, and the assassin spotted two Urhal

soldiers. He halted the mare and their concealed position to the soldiers' right, he watched the two cautiously as they descended the main stairway that once led down into the metro, though it was now a massive hill of congealed mud, rock, and mangled vegetation.

The Agent of the Isles wasn't sure if they were alone or just the first squad through the hazardous marshes that blanketed the right side of Pike's Road as it snaked its way back through Bernwood Forest.

Either way, if they continued in the same direction once they reached the bottom of the cavernous pit, they'd still intercept the station's concourse and maglev before he did. That wouldn't do. That was Mr. Black's quickest way back to Pehats Berg, though certainly not through the same tunnels beneath the mission, since he hoped his plan had worked despite the resulting devastation to the lower ward of Labor's Ro.

However, all was not immediately lost, for instead of the two encroaching soldiers stumbling into his plans for extraction and possible redeployment, Mr. Black watched as something worse happened. Seven more soldiers clambered out of a small cave mouth, waved the other two over, and thereby fucked up his plans for escape. They just didn't know it yet.

"I'm always so lucky," he muttered.

Melisande said nothing, though Mr. Black *felt* her cutting thoughts.

Mr. Black drew his wheelblaster and rested it on his lap.

The two Urhal soldiers joined the larger group as they continued to entertain themselves during their long patrol by torturing and killing whatever happened to cross their path, including, in this case, an unlucky nursery pod of snapping, warted, diapsid reptilian beasts, commonly referred to as bog trolls or pond hags. Really, they weren't as liminal as their distant cousins, who were Grendel's true blood.

Between knee and thigh-high to the well-armored men from the Scattered Kingdoms' east, the ill-fated pups carelessly scampered about as though they were children at play and not creatures surrounded by mocking predators. The troliks threw rocks and debris in every direction, showing little to no fear of the men's axes or swords, nor even to their torches, really, as they were chased all around the burrows and deeper holds that made up the long-abandoned metro station.

Mr. Black watched as one man, likely the detachment's leader, began reloading his muzzle.

At the same time, the largest of the gangly pond scum, the one with horns, covered in bloated scales, dripping in pine algae and pond weed, had just violently strong-armed a shortsword away from one of the commander's greenest recruits.

Fuck me, thought Mr. Black.

No doubt the young man was shitting himself as the foolish trolik's demeanor became a bloody terror while it flaunted the two feet of good steel just inches from the man's face. And with good reason, for he would've likely been stabbed to death if not for the commander's first reaction shot, which blew off the trolik's tail. The other soldiers laughed when another man in the unit joined his commander with his longbow and broadhead tips and shot at the now clearly enraged and frantic troliks.

To avoid the shots, the pod centered upon a single, humongous mound of sludge and rock.

What the foreign soldiers failed to realize though— either because of natural ignorance or the bloody fever-ishness inspired by such collective and cooperative acts of barbarism inflicted on the weak and defenseless—was not similarly lost on Mr. Black.

For even with his diminished awareness, teased by sleep and annoyed by pain, the assassin knowingly watched it all play out just over thirty meters from the base of the two largest hills of combined sludge and mud, one of which led out of Witcher Pit.

He was so close to true sunlight, yet there was no stopping what was about to happen.

A large man shouted a warning at him in a heavy scattered dialect.

"Take it easy, friend." Mr. Black wasn't sure the pike-man understood him.

The other men turned, weapons at the ready, torches raised high.

"Füdest, dh ez Klabin, ik ben tülorhen?"

The archer loosed an arrow. He missed and re-nocked.

Mr. Black had barely raised his wheelblaster against the alerted soldiers now coming toward him when, suddenly, a male bog troll began to unurth itself beneath the soldiers' feet.

Huge eyes blinked through the mounds of crust-ed-over sludge, where the sink hole had earlier dragged it down, leaving it for dead, separated from its young, beaten, and buried alive.

Nothing is coincidence or connivence, thought Melisande.

"Let's go!" Mr. Black spurred the mare to gallop up the hill.

When Mr. Black and the mare were a third of the way up the muddy slope, the bog troll extended its long neck and croaked like the King of All Swamps and Marshlands. The reverberating ribbits echoed in every direction. Seconds later, it crawled clear of the heavy stones, clawing away broken trees and thick pools of wet filth, to finally stand at its full measure. It was massive and finned, and yet serpentine, in-spite of its bulky torso and segmented shell.

The Urhal soldiers didn't know what to do. Everyone shouted.

"Peryekä!" cried the Urhals' commander.

With a single bite from its robust beak, reinforced by an inner row of densely packed molars, the bog troll chomped through the slowest soldier hiding behind his metal shield. The poor wretch's hips and legs fell away like useless meat as the bloody rest was swallowed whole by the bog troll in a single gulp.

With orders shouted, panic contained, the remaining soldiers split into two groups.

Eight of them turned on the giant beast, while their commander returned his sights to the man in black, who was almost free of the pit.

Crack!

The mare's right hind knee exploded. Mr. Black shouted. The commander had aimed for her thigh. He got lucky.

Biting his tongue, Mr. Black attempted to holster the wheelblaster but failed as he struggled with the reins. He dropped it, cursing as the mare slid again, spreading her legs wide in an attempt to recover and shift her strength in the pooled muck, but it was no use. They were too heavy, going too fast.

Rider and mount tumbled back down the hill, landing hard at the bottom in a wet heap of curses.

Satisfied the man in black wasn't going anywhere now, the lead scout dropped his powder rifle, choosing instead the two-handed broadsword at his hip. The roughly four feet of layered steel would do better against the bog troll now that his men had it surrounded and fearful of their numbers.

"Get, up," the man in black told his mare. He coughed up pond water first, then blood.

Why did his ankle hurt now? No, it was his lower calf. Mr. Black looked down and saw a gaping arrow wound in his upper ankle, though the Urhal archer was likely trying to lame the horse seconds before his commander succeeded.

The mare was just putting its hooves beneath them when the bog troll exhaled a powerful, pained roar, which his pups soon mimicked. The mare whinnied, squealed, and bucked in reaction as the terrible cacophony reverberated through the subterranean complex. Mr. Black covered his ears as best he could and fought to stay in the saddle.

The Urhal commander gave a satisfying shout. His sword was now halfway through the bog troll's hip. His heart pounded. His bravery and resolve appeared to have paid off, which is when he erred, as most men do when captured by bloodlust.

If he'd left the sword in place, retreating or side-stepping so his men, two armed with bladed poles, might exploit the bog troll's moment of true weakness and pain, then the commander might've survived the encounter. Perhaps his cohorts then would've even won the day, but that didn't happen.

Instead, in the precious moments it took the commander to retrieve his honor from the beast's sticky, bulbous flesh, the towering monster answered the puny man's irritating metal stick with a mighty back paw, which drove the man's limp body some twenty feet away, through a cluster of stone and debris and mud.

When the bog troll finished pressing its dominance, the man's entire body was oddly indistinguishable from the rest of the ruined landscape, save for all the bright red outlined by brown and gray and black.

Now without a leader, the soldiers panicked. Each man's orders confused the others.

Move! You have got to move!

The bog troll caught two more soldiers beneath its swishing bulk and crushed them.

Mr. Black's eyes burned behind the trenchers. His skull thumped, and his limbs felt loose and numb. Thus, he failed to notice the bog troll raced toward him, which was a problem for more than just the obvious reasons.

Namely, the Agent of the Silver Isles had assumed the Urhal soldiers would've put up a better fight. The lives of seasoned men should've bought him more than enough time to escape from the hole, but he was wrong.

Everything was broken and failing, and he still had such a long way to go. The Sanguine Shard still had to be taken to...

"Fas—"

When the bog troll hit the mare, everything stopped.

It was like she had galloped straight into an invisible, reinforced barricade, half as tall as one of her legs that struck her between the soft gap in her neck and sternum. Bones were immediately broken. Exposed tissue detached from her muscles, causing an unnatural wrinkling effect across much of her body.

The bog troll followed its epic haymaker with an equally impressive face shove.

Lifted off the ground, the lifeless mare toppled headlong down the heap, neck over tail until, finally one of her hoofs snagged near the bottom of the ragged pit, where putrid water still pooled from when it was first flushed into the station by Mr. Black.

The bog troll roared in triumph.

When Mr. Black awoke, the world was red. He gritted his teeth. Something was broken.

The bog troll was some distance behind him now. How'd it get there?

You were thrown.

Mr. Black shook his head. It hurt. Blood ran down his nose. He shouldn't have done that.

We survive, brother.

Melisande could feel his confusion and weakness as he struggled to remember events before the collision and his momentary blackout.

When the blur parted enough, Mr. Black remembered his training. How he'd instinctually freed his boots from the saddle's stirrups before drawing the grapple gun from his shoulder harness and squeezing the trigger in some random direction above his head, not really aiming for any particular rafter or overhead support, mere seconds before the bog troll—

"We always survive." Mr. Black groaned, ignored his guilt, then rolled over onto his back.

Staying away from the warming rays of sunlight, the troliks feasted on their father's freshly provided bounty of arrogant Urhals and horse flesh. Some amused themselves with the soldiers' helmets, tokens, cards, and trinkets, playing with the reflecting and refracting light, almost teasing one another with it.

Their father wasn't so content. He picked at the corpses, ignoring his own wounds, perhaps wondering how he was going to return his remaining family to the forest above. Or perhaps he feared where they would now live since the pond was no more.

Mr. Black panicked then. Every drop of his blood and sweat turned to ice.

Shit!

Down the hill of mud, strewn with heaps of moss and torn grasses, but at an angle halfway between the mare's corpse and the rest of the pod of hungry, playful troliks, one little semi-green gangler stood apart from the rest. She was alone, holding something shiny she didn't want to share with the other pups.

Where is it? Melisande thought.

The crystal caught the sunlight, sparkled ruby red.

"Of course," groaned Mr. Black.

He stood up as best he could and winced. Spat more blood and filth from his teeth.

Such a display of fortitude only further incited the bog troll's naturally hostile attitude toward humans. Worse, the Horran didn't flee when clearly spotted, something of an indirect challenge. Even if he'd wanted to, though, the ranger wouldn't have made it free of the pit before being overtaken.

"The mission," said Mr. Black as he dropped the broken darū goggles on the wet rocks.

Always, intoned Melisande in a similar, mental whisper.

Mr. Black then partially unsheathed the ancient sword at his hip.

"Nowhere to hide now."

The troliks whined and cried and scattered from the frightful weapon.

No retreat. No surrender.

Melisande was fully aware of the consequences now that the corrupted blade was exposed.

Paternal instincts multiplying its rage, the bog troll charged at Mr. Black a second time.

Whispering to himself, Mr. Black spread his feet, and drew his two-handed Still Sword.

The bog troll didn't slow.

Mr. Black didn't yield.

The world turned.

Epilogue

"Shh," said Cirilo, "go back to sleep."

Ceann frowned against the sun as he lifted her into his arms.

"Ani, Uška?" she sighed.

Cirilo looked at the petrified gargoyle curled beneath the blankets.

"Yes," said Cirilo, "he's coming, too."

He simply couldn't carry both. Little Harold Cross hinted as much when he explained Ceann's new situation and friend earlier that morning, after breakfast, of course. He had been the first to wake after Khalix.

As always though, the Tuched youth, who might've been considered dimwitted and slow by some, was used to being ignored, conditioned to it, you could say. That's what made it really great and new that Cirilo winked at him when he had returned from the roof's hidey-hole with only the small girl in his arms, signifying his own arrogance and ignorance.

A few minutes later, Ceann was snuggling again with Uška, opposite the brothers Mose and Valter, in the back of one of the two large wagons they had gathered and outfitted outside the Two Sisters, the first of which Leeann presently assisted Olyana in covering the top of. Once looped and tied off, the caravan's oiled tarp allowed the children to quickly and quietly fall back asleep in the cooler darkness.

All morning, Olyana and Emil had shared their intentions of someday returning the borrowed wagons to the Two Sisters. The goods, wares, and contraband, however, borrowed from the inn's soon-to-be-trashed storerooms, including Jezzy's secret stores, which Momma Bwulyaa had always kept freshly stocked, were really only enough to get some of them halfway where they were going.

Their new destination was a last resort, which Mr. Black had demanded Momma Bwulyaa swear to beneath the Mission before she led its frantic evacuation. The potentiality of which she wasn't to reveal to anyone before its time, not even to the girls, unless they should come to said knowledge on their own, something she'd suggested, given her former life as one who was entrusted with Mr. Black's silver coins.

"You sure you won't change your mind?" asked Emil.

"Nah," said Daphnia. "We'll be fine."

Emil looked up at the roof of the inn, at the corner where Jezzy stood, wrapped in a quilt, her gaze reaching long into the east. She held something soft and small to her face. It almost seemed to Emil that she was smelling it or kissing it or both as she slowly scanned the horizon.

"It's a nice spot," said Daphnia after Emil finished describing where on the road west he planned to stop the wagons so they could bury Gabija.

The former deputy lovingly patted the cloth concealing her shrouded body beneath the heavy wagon that creaked under Khalix's bulk.

Emil would rather not have used the jail's bedsheets, but there was no other option, and he had limited time to recover his wife, as well as the bodies of Maria and Benzan, whose sacrifices demanded an equally proper burial.

"From there?" asked Daphnia.

Emil shook his head. "Momma said we'd talk afterward."

Together, they watched as one of Jezzy's service automations gently lifted Maria's shrouded corpse and carried her into the inn. From there, her and Benzan's bodies would be taken and buried together near the fields and meadows they'd played in as children. It's what Leeann said they'd want.

From the passenger seat, Father Rai advised, "We must be going now."

The Lightbringer of Saint Ingmar was thankful for the Two Sisters' hospitality and Pillar charity for those who needed or wished to remain behind. They'd promised to care and shelter them, no matter what happened, though Daphnia was confident this storm, too, would pass, like all the others the Scattered Kingdoms had suffered through.

Cirilo climbed into the driver seat of the first wagon.

From there, he could keep an eye on his rotosha tied up behind it, along with everything else they'd commandeered or outright stolen for this new journey.

"Ani?" said Leeann as she climbed in behind Harold and Khalix.

Cirilo grinned, then yawned. "Yes, Imōto?

It was nothing. She just wanted to give him a quick hug to say thanks.

Cirilo hugged her back.

Momma Bwulyaa groaned as Leeann settled into the back of the wagon beside Khalix and Harold. She wasn't confident it had ever carried an unconscious longhorn before, and now the wagon was loaded to the brim. And so, if the axle broke, they'd know for sure Khalix weighed more than a male bull.

Emil looked over the wagons to make sure they'd left nothing behind.

Bells rang in the distance, their notes as faint as smoke in daylight.

"That's my order." In all Father Rai's years, he'd never heard the bells ring. Except during times of emergency, for this wasn't the tiny bell the leaders of his order were sometimes allowed to ring during seasonal celebrations, or the many holy days throughout the Pillar's calendar year.

"They're here," said Leeann.

Everyone awake or not busy with the journey ahead turned toward East Gate.

"I'm excited," whispered Harold.

"About what?" asked Emil as he took his own seat, teasing the braided reins in his hands.

"Sad you're not coming with us, though."

Emil leaned closer. "What are you talking about?"

Harold's eyes got big then, as big as his grin. He whispered. "To Jarren!"

"What?" Emil pulled the young boy close.

Momma Bwulyaa distracted Leeann with her Iron Smile and tattoos so she wouldn't overhear them.

"Or maybe the Vaha—"

With his fingers now tight over Harold's mischievous lips, Emil looked around and pulled the young man halfway out and around from beneath the canvas.

Only Olyana, Emil's sister-in-law, had seen their quick exchange from the second wagon. She'd been saying her goodbyes to Mose and Valter, who slept at the time, before leaving them and heading back to her own family.

Of course, Emil had advised against it, but Olyana couldn't really bring herself to listen to him because of her pain for Gabija. She'd eventually heed his words, though, but they wouldn't go west. Her husband had family in the far north. That was their bet.

"It doesn't matter," Emil explained, "even if you're right—"

He shook his head, and his exhausted thoughts trailed off. He didn't want to know or think about anything. Too many surprises for one day. For one lifetime.

The wagons began to roll.

"Don't say another word," said Emil over the bouncing and creaking of the wagon.

Harold smiled to himself, fingers fidgeting with his

new clothes.

"Mr. Black's orders. You understand?" Emil couldn't wait to tell Momma about what Little Harold had just said about Jarren and the Vahast.

"Okay," said Harold. His smile became a sleepy frown.

The wagons rolled faster. The streets of Pehats Berg flew by.

"Oh well," little Harold added, "this is better. She'll be happy."

"Who?" asked Emil, looking over his shoulder.

"She's singing," said Harold. He yawned and laid back down next to Khalix.

Daphnia waved to them a final time as the wagons vanished beyond the Two Sisters.

In less than an hour, they'd be out of sight of Pehats Berg.

In roughly an hour, the Scattered Kingdoms would be at war.

About the Author

Wade Garret lives in Atlanta, GA with his wife, daughters, and a convict of a dog. When not reading or writing, he can usually be found nestled in a chair at his favorite tattoo shop.

Stay in the Loop

Subscribe to the Epic Publishing mailing list to stay up to date on new releases, author interviews, giveaways, and more. Go to www.epic-publishing.com/subscribe to get started.

CPSIA information can be obtained
at www.ICGtesting.com
Printed in the USA
BVHW070144240922
647915BV00013B/266